Y0-BDI-599

SEEING DOUBLE

Book II of the Elizabeth Reinhardt Series
Book I of the Olive Branch Series

Nancy J. Alexander

Copyright © 2015 Nancy J. Alexander

All rights reserved.

ISBN: **1512160296**
ISBN-13: **978-1512160291**

DISCLAIMER

This is a work of fiction. Names, characters, groups, businesses, places, events and incidents are either the products of the author's imagination or used in a fictitious manner. Any resemblance to actual persons, living or dead, or actual events is purely coincidental.

CONTENTS

AUTHOR'S COMMENTS

The context for <u>Seeing Double</u> is the compelling situation in the Middle East, a place whose conflicts and controversies remind us daily how polarizing religious and ethnic differences can be and how continual is their struggle. It reminds us that extremism is nourished by generations of deprivation, frustration and alienation; by generations of indoctrination and isolation from other viewpoints and belief systems. The situation reminds us that sadly in spite of mankind's great intellectual prowess, achievements and vast cultural accomplishments a regressive pull toward that which is most primitive within us remains. My heart goes out to those whose lives have been ruined or cut short by extremist fundamentalism and to those embedded in the irresolvable battle for the supremacy of truth. I am always aware of the reciprocal power that hatred will have on generations of children as yet unborn in that part of the world where never-ending violence swirls through the sweltering sands.

ACKNOWLEDGEMENTS

I would like to thank cousins Pam and Cindy, sister Carol and brother-in-law 'Bus' and niece Lauren; and Kay and Susan for their efforts reading and reviewing the book and providing valuable feedback on characters and content. Their efforts have enriched <u>Seeing Double</u> and hopefully empowered it to address the issues broiling in the Middle East from a more human though fictional perspective.

As always many thanks to my production director and valued advisor Tiffany Wrightson, to my energetic marketing director Ashley Taylor, to my pitch perfect audio-engineer Julian Comanda without them NJA Productions would not exist. And of course, thanks to all of you who have read or listened to my work; who follow me online, read and comment on my blogs and constitute the core of my enthusiastic readers.

NANCY J. ALEXANDER

1 FIRST ENCOUNTER

His voice was soft, cultured, and he spoke with a Middle Eastern accent, possibly Israeli. "How do you do, Ma'am," he said with a polite bow. Extending his hand, the young man said, "I am Ari Ben-Aviv, ma'am and I am most pleased to be making your acquaintance."

He was striking with tousled black hair and skin that was the color of toasted almonds. He had perfectly sculpted features and an enchanting smile. More beautiful than handsome, he was flawlessly dressed in a tailored navy suit and open collared lilac shirt. His smoke grey eyes were magnetizing, conveying sincerity with a hint of desperation. She indicated a cozy seating area, antique furniture embraced by brocade draperies and tall potted palms. Dutifully he moved toward an over-stuffed chair and perched on its edge, eyes scanning the room from corner to corner. She remained standing, curious, observing him.

"How can I help you Mr. Ben- Aviv?" she asked beginning to move toward her chair.

"Would you be so kind, Ma'am as to lock the door to this office, please? I know the request is a strange one, but I would feel more comfortable if you did so."

"Of course, if it makes you feel more comfortable," the woman replied crossing the room.

The door to her office locked automatically, but she went through the motions to reassure him. It was a curious request, but in her line of work she was accustomed to unusual requests. "Is there anything else before we get started?" she asked not expecting anything.

"Well, actually, if you would not mind, would you please to close also the curtains?"

Surprised, she looked at the young man and then glanced at her half drawn brocade draperies. Things were not adding up. This was not the way meetings of this sort usually began. She was about to sit down and ask him to explain his requests, but she changed her mind. Something told her she was dealing with something altogether different. The woman crossed to the window and studied the street below. Three men wearing fitted prayer caps, knee length cotton tunics and baggy pants, were arguing with each other gesturing and casting glances at her building. They were here for this man, this Ari Ben-Aviv. She knew it. Without taking her eyes off the men she asked, "Exactly why are you here, Mr. Ben-Aviv?"

On the faded oriental carpet his black Zelli loafers moved restlessly. "I'm afraid I'm being followed," he said in a hushed tone, "May I speak freely?"

"Of course, it's perfectly safe here," she assured him.

"How do you know?" he pressed, "Have you had your office checked for listening devices?"

That got her attention; she turned slightly, "No, I haven't. Why would I do that?"

"Because I'm in danger," he said quietly.

Processing the irrational thought took milliseconds. If he was in danger, why should she search for listening devices? She'd only just met him. Was he suggesting she knew about him in advance; she should have been prepared for him? Was he paranoid or was this something else? She had received a call from him days before asking for this appointment. He sounded urgent, but declined to discuss his predicament over the phone. The call had come up as 'caller unknown' on her caller ID. So prior to this meeting she had no information about him. She still had none.

Elisabeth Reinhardt, a clinical psychologist, frowned slightly. Standing at the window, she now inclined her head toward him, observed his restless shoes, his hands folded calmly on his lap and his eyes scanning her face intently. Inconsistent non-verbals, interesting...

"I'm in danger," he repeated.

"Danger from...?" she asked watching the men pacing on the sidewalk.

"People are following me," he whispered, "lots of people. I'm not crazy, I know they are there. You see them there, do you not?" his head motioned toward the window, "They are out there watching, waiting. Is that not correct?" She moved her eyes to his. Silent affirmation.

"They follow me," he added. "Like a chameleon I disappear before their eyes. They say I transform myself and disappear. One minute I am green the next minute I am blue. They want very much to catch me. To get me before I disappear again."

"Why come to me?" she asked again, "Why not go to the police?"

The young man raised his eyes to look at her, in a voice deep with innuendo, he said, "Because I know the truth."

A chill ran up her spine triggering an alarm that spread through her system. Her eyes studied him as his eyes studied her. In the recesses of her mind, a fragment of memory tingled. A tiny blip from long ago. An image spiraled then it vanished. There was something about this young man, this Ari Ben Aviv. There was something about him that she couldn't pinpoint.

"You have been highly recommended to me," he had said on the phone. Who had made that recommendation? Why hadn't she asked him that? Who knew about her and how did that person know this young man? Moreover, why had they recommended her to him? Her mind raced through the possibilities, but there was no time to think. On the street, she saw a polished black Mercedes pull up to the curb and one of the pacing men slipped into the back. The other two stood guard, continuing to glower at her building; their hostility barely contained.

"The truth?" she slowly responded to his statement.

"That is correct, Ma'am, yes the truth. It is all important."

Then she was certain. He was playing the role of a psychiatric patient. But it was an act, a cover story. Two things were certain: He was not here for therapy and he was in mortal danger. So perhaps was she. She was nearly certain about a third thing, too, but pushed that thought aside for the moment.

"Do you not agree that the truth is all important?" he continued to ramble.

"Of course," she said making a decision as the door to the Mercedes swung open and a white-haired, long bearded man got out. He wore a wrapped muslin turban, and a tan long-sleeved, floor-length djellaba; he was treated deferentially by the three younger men, who grew increasingly animated as they gestured toward her building. "Truth is important to all of us," she replied absently.

"The problem is that there are many truths," he said. "There is the truth of one group of people versus another group. Say the Arabs and the Israelis. There is the truth of one *G-d* versus another *G-d*, one holy book versus another holy book. On and on it goes. Those are all different truths, are they not?" he asked.

"And, what truth are *you* most concerned about?" she was on auto-pilot now, barely keeping up her end of the conversation. She wanted to keep him talking until she figured out what to do. In the event that they were being overheard she wanted to keep up appearances.

"Your truth and mine concern me most," he replied vaguely.

So she said, "Tell me about yourself, Mr. Ben-Aviv tell me about your truth...." Her beckoning fingers invited a soliloquy. The young man turned in his chair, intent on her as she watched the street. He knew now that she knew. They were in this together.

"My father was born in Lebanon," he began, "His father's father had an olive grove near Houla. They traveled throughout the area....in my grandfather's time...."

As she stood under the palms, she saw the older man get back into the car and the three younger men prepare to cross the street. Putting her finger to her lips she crossed the room...

"...traveled back and forth across the border between Israel and Lebanon selling olives and olive oil...they had many camels and many servants. They traveled across the desert...."

She moved toward her carved mahogany desk and the heavy mahogany bookcases that lined the back of the office.

"…my mother was from Israel…" He watched with rapt attention as she reached up to the neckline of her beige silk blouse and extracted a long antique gold chain from which a small key dangled.

He rambled on, "…my mother's family worked on the fish farms not far from the border, she was 13 ….."

Opening a narrow desk drawer, Elisabeth Reinhardt slid back a narrow piece of molding and unlocked a concealed panel…

"…born a… a sabra… I was raised in my mother's land …."

Barely listening she waited as the bookcase glided open revealing a narrow staircase. She pointed to his feet and pantomimed an instruction. He did as she directed then rose to follow her…

"I lived you see as a citizen of two worlds…"

She touched a number on her cell, texted 'urgent, pick-up in 5' and pressed 'SEND.' As they descended, the office wall closed silently behind them.

NANCY J. ALEXANDER

2 ON THE JOB

He slumped behind the steering wheel of his old maroon Camry, partly hidden behind a UPS truck busy with deliveries. He was heavyset and could hardly fit behind the steering wheel. A former policeman, in his mid-40's, he had been reduced to occasional PI work for a small downtown firm specializing in surveillance. He had not been told the reason for this job. He was told very little these days, just enough to know what to look for. He was tired and bored. After ten hours, it was hard to keep his eyes open. The driver in a brown uniform returned to his truck and drove off. The man felt exposed and wished another truck would come and park in front of him. He pulled his Chicago CUBS cap, blue with a little red bear, over his eyes and slouched down. Reaching into the plastic bag on the seat beside him, he pulled out a package of gummy bears and tore through the cellophane.

He wondered for the thousandth time what she could be doing up there for so long. He wondered if he had time to run to MacDonald's down the street. He really had to go. He couldn't decide whether to walk the few blocks down Stony Island Avenue or whether to drive down there and risk losing his parking space. It was a perfect space. His hand was on the door handle when he saw her. He cursed softly, piss poor timing, he thought, grinning at his play on words. She wore knee high boots, jeans and a loose fitting jacket, a scarf, red and gold in a geometric pattern was wrapped around her shoulders. She walked under the overhang toward the small parking lot near her building, her wavy black hair hung nearly to her waist. In her twenties, she had good posture and a brisk energetic walk. She slipped into her tan Honda Civic and headed into traffic.

The man followed at a discrete distance afraid she might recognize his car from yesterday. He wished he'd thought to switch cars that morning so he wouldn't have to worry about being made. He hoped she wouldn't take too long to get where she was going because he really had to pee. *Suck it up*, he told himself as he made a sharp left and shadowed the Civic along Chicago's Dwight D Eisenhower Expressway toward Lake Michigan. He was right behind her as she zipped into the parking lot on Museum Campus Drive and hurried toward the delivery entrance of The Field Museum. He drew a short grey wig on over his limp brown hair, stuck on a pair of sunglasses and hurried after her.

From his place behind a dumpster, he spotted a 3 inch black boot heel as she ducked through a small metal door with a sign that read NO ADMISSION EMPLOYEES ONLY. Her voice musical and lilting floated past him in the breeze. She was calling to someone. What is she up to? Ten minutes passed when he decided to follow her inside. In fits and stops, he crept up to the loading bay. Huge metal doors gapped open, two 16 wheelers sat side by side while uniformed men driving forklifts unloaded crates. Duck-walking beside a forklift, he crept into an enormous concrete space filled with gigantic crates, shelving units and work stations equipped with computers and clipboards of paperwork. There was no sign of her.

Weaving through the space he found his way to a hallway, mounted cameras swiveled back and forth and beside each metal door was a square metal keypad. Extracting his iPhone, he snapped off several shots until he heard footsteps approaching. Her scarf wrapped as a hijab, she entered with a distinguished-looking man; grey haired with a thin moustache, he wore black rimmed glasses and a well-tailored suit. He spoke with a clipped German accent. The woman seemed relaxed, smiling as she reached out to accept the Field Museum Gift Shop bag he held out to her. Peeking out the top of the bag was an oblong cardboard box. He could just make out a few letters 'D...NG...R' scrolled across the top.

3 PASTA PUTTANESCA

She parked on S. Oakley and carried her Field Museum Gift Shop bag into one of several homey Italian restaurants oozing mouth-watering aromas into the air. He followed her into the restaurant intending to use the facilities and return to his car, but his timing was off by 10 seconds. He ran smack into her exiting the Ladies Room as he was entering the corridor to the Men's Room. The both muttered 'excuse me.' He looked quickly away and she looked directly into his face. She didn't recognize him, but etched his features into her mind. She'd recognize him the next time she saw him. She had an eidetic memory. He knew he'd been made and his usefulness on this case was no doubt over. He'd just lost his job all because he had to pee. Miserably, he purchased 2 slices of pizza and returned to his car to wait.

She was ravenous. It seemed days since she'd eaten and the smells emanating from the kitchen started her stomach growling. She ordered her favorite pasta, a house salad and a glass of Chianti, slightly chilled. Seated at a table for two by the window, she studied the mid-afternoon traffic. She was intensely beautiful with delicate features and a chestnut complexion.

While she waited, she enjoyed her wine and some freshly baked bread. It had been nearly a week since she heard from him and she was on pins and needles until she got his text this morning, proposing this meeting. At this hour, the restaurant was nearly empty, so after a quick check of the wait staff and a table of three businessmen enjoying coffee and cannelloni, she turned her attention to the street. She watched as the man she'd bumped into bit into his second piece of pizza and stared off into space. Not far from him, sat a dark van with tinted windows. The window on the passenger side was open a tad and a tiny curl of smoke drifted out. She watched the passing traffic, noticed an old blue SUV pass her window for

9

the second time in the last few minutes. There were parking spaces available, but the SUV passed each one of them.

Warning signals were going off in her head. Still she waited for him. Her loosened hijab slid loosely to her shoulders. Nearly 7 minutes had passed and still Camry man sat there. She didn't like it. It was odd and in her line of work odd meant trouble. People were generally predictable and transparent. They bought their pizza, they ate it and they drove away. They didn't sit aimlessly in their car doing nothing. This man was doing nothing. He wasn't reading or talking on his phone or even napping. Something was definitely off. The black van still sat, more cigarette smoke curling out the crack in the window. She made mental notes of the license plate numbers and car details, like the small dent on the left front fender and rust around the van's wheel well. The SUV was no longer in sight. That was curious.

She was pondering this, dipping bread in seasoned olive oil when a large, broad man with a face like a bulldog pulled out a chair and sat down opposite her. "Hello, Darling," he said with a smile, leaning forward and blowing her a kiss.

"Sweetheart," she breathed, staring at the stranger, "it is so wonderful to see you again." She leaned forward blowing a kiss in return and said, "The pasta puttanesca is excellent here you should try it..." As the waiter took his order, she extracted a .38 special Smith and Wesson from her purse and tucked it under her napkin.

"I'll have what she's having," the stranger told the waiter then nodding toward the napkin said, "That won't be necessary Samira, Ari sent me."

Instantly, the woman's stunning green eyes turned predatory, "Who are you?" she whispered harshly, "How do you know my name?"

"Your brother sent me, my name is Gil McCray. Let's have a nice quiet lunch and I'll fill you in on everything I know. Okay?"

"Why didn't he come himself?" she hissed. "What have you done to him?"

"Nothing. Really, I'm one of the good guys," he said with a grin.

"Why I should believe you," she hissed again, "anyone could say he is good guy!"

"Let me show you," he said. "Do you see that guy across the street in the maroon Camry? Well he's been tailing you."

I know that," she snapped, "I nearly knocked him over coming out of the ladies' rest room."

"Okay, well do you know who he's working for?" he asked with one raised eyebrow.

That got her interest. She eyed him like a hawk zeroing in on its prey.

"And," he continued, "Do you know he was outside your apartment this morning, and he followed you to the museum?"

She gawked at him, "And how do you know such a thing?"

"And," he continued, ignoring her question, "do you know that there's someone else tailing you"

He flicked his eyes toward a parking space on the other side of the intersection, where the black van sat.

"Also I saw these people. And do you know who in the hell are they?" she spat...

"They, my dear, are the CIA," the man replied, smiling as the waiter sat his drink on the table.

"How do I know you are not with them?" she challenged, "You could think I'm some dumb woman who knows nothing at all."

"I could, my dear, but I don't," Gil said handing over a small folded note. It was written in Hebrew and said '...*dearest sister, trust me and trust him... soon our paths will cross.*' She read the note twice. Nodding briskly, she slipped the note along with her gun into her handbag. She breathed deeply allowing the tension to leave her body, but her eyes remained frozen in a hostile squint.

"Relax, my dear" said the man, "un-squint those beautiful eyes and have some wine, I'm a friend you haven't gotten to know yet."

"What if I do not want a friend," she said lips pursed.

"Oh, I think you'll change your mind soon enough, dear," he said pleasantly, nodding in the direction of the waiter approaching the table with a large tray on which sat two pasta bowls filled to over-flowing.

Just wait till you taste this, Darling," she smiled demurely glancing at the waiter, "It is, how you say, delicious."

4 SNAKE CHARMERS

Heat emanated from the colored tin roofs as tanners spread freshly dyed hides out to dry. Irregular rooftops were outlined against the early morning skyline. Scattered palm trees emerged as the sun rose and in the distance a caravan of camels loaded with merchandise appeared trudging across the sand. Marrakesh the jewel of the desert was the trading place where people from all over the country gathered to buy and sell. Stepping out of the shadows, the young man was bombarded by countless sights and sounds and smells of this ancient place. Hundreds of brightly colored handmade carpets hung side by side; tents displayed everything from traditional djellabas and gandoras to long ropes of dried figs, stands held racks of hand-made sandals and baskets overflowing with spices.

Under faded umbrellas, women covered by their long clothing sat selling colorful scarves, stacks of hats, pretty woven baskets or brightly painted bowls. Children scampered about begging tourists for money while men unloaded their donkeys or sat smoking and talking together. The air was dusty, hot and heavy with the mingled smells of cooking meats, human sweat, exotic spices, frying bread and animal dung. The combined sounds of hundreds of people milling about displaying their wares, bartering, arguing, laughing or chatting was deafening within the narrow tented alleys of the marketplace.

Although he'd been here before, Rafi was overwhelmed. Slender, yet muscular, he was broad shouldered with a thick shock of black wavy hair and a café au lait complexion. Strikingly handsome, he looked the part of a native, but he didn't feel like one. He wanted to be anywhere but here. He was worried about many things, but the fear of dust getting under his tinted contact lenses, was high on the list. That would be a deal breaker. He walked slowly along in his long tan djellaba, his tarboush on his head, hands quiet at his sides. "Rafi, check in," the voice tinny and clear sounded in his ear. He was glad the team was with him. He was nervous and was glad for their support. Moshe, the team leader, had been his best friend since they joined Mossad three years ago. Using the pre-arranged signal Rafi raised his right hand to his neck and scratched an imaginary itch.

"Mosquitoes are bad this time of year," teased the voice. Rafi scratched again, teasing back. *Laugh now, fella,* he thought to himself, *you may not be laughing later.* On reflex, he checked to make sure his weapons were securely in place. As he wandered toward the tiled courtyard, he saw a large group of people, old and young Moroccans and tourists in a circle watching three men sitting on a rug. The men wore loose fitting djellabas with long sleeves and a hood. On their heads they each wore a colorful tarbauch; they were seated in front of several round flat baskets. One of the men was playing a crude wooden flute while another man lifted the basket lid exposing the lean head of a cobra snaking its way up, skin flaps swelling. The man played as the serpent danced slowly in front of his face, seemingly entranced by the music of the flute. Another man holding a snake in his hands walked around the circle displaying it. The snake could be seen moving through the man's hands, the awed watchers backed away as he approached them. Caught in the rapture of the moment, Rafi was unaware that four men, similarly dressed in belted caftans and fez hats encircled him. "Come with us," one of the men said, poking Rafi in the back with a hard object. Wordlessly, Rafi turned and walked off with them. The sound of the crowd clapping and the flute playing faded behind him.

The car ride seemed eternal. Sitting blindfolded between two bulky guards, Rafi used his skills to help orient himself. He had gone willingly, yet they blindfolded him, so they didn't want him to be able to retrace his steps. That meant there was something permanent about this location. The guards had not been rough with him, so they weren't under orders to harm or intimidate him. That was good news. And yet, they were not talking to him or offering him any water. So he was more like a prisoner than an invited guest. Two men were in the front, one was the boss and two guards were in the back with him. The man on his right had a bad cough. The man on his left smelled bad. The boss had a harsh voice and spoke with a Tunisian accent. The driver was silent; Rafi sensed that he was afraid. Four men had come to pick him up. It was interesting that so many had been sent. Had they been expecting a fight? He had agreed to meet and had come willingly, so why the muscle? Sending a message about their power?

The men spoke rarely, only to each other and only in Darija, the Moroccan

Arabic dialect commonly used throughout the country. No one spoke to him and he spoke to no one. It was a quiet trip. He heard no traffic on the road and hoped that his 'friends' had been able to keep up with him. He wore two GPS transmitters one in his sandal and one had been sewn into his underwear. He listened carefully, but could hear no other cars on the road. He concluded they were driving through the desert and that his friends were staying far out of sight so as not to arouse suspicion. At one point, the car stopped amid some bleating and he decided that a herd of sheep were crossing the road. Ten minutes ticked by, during which he heard what sounded like a helicopter hovering close by. The men in the car seemed to hear it, too, because after a flurry of words they picked up speed. They stopped briefly once to refresh themselves.

It was dark when they arrived. The guards led him into a tent lit only by a small fire around which a dozen men sat. All were covered from head to toe except for their eyes and hands. No one spoke. Rafi was shoved down into a spot in the circle, his blindfold was removed and he was handed a cup of water. Still no one spoke. The air smelled of camels, hashish and unwashed bodies. Wind whistled outside, picking up speed, breezes wafted through the tent. Someone waved a hand and the tent flaps were closed and lashed tightly together. Inside the tent there was silence as Rafi drank his water and the men puffed on their pipes.

"Thank you for coming, my young friend," the leader finally said.

Rafi raised his head and returned the greeting in Arabic, "I am honored to be of service, my revered leader."

"First we will eat, then, we will talk," the leader announced as servants arrived with trays of food and a large brass samovar filled with mint tea.

They arranged the trays in the center of the circle and left. As the men began to eat, several musicians carrying ghitas and lotars, entered the tent and began to play. In his ear Rafi, heard Moshe's voice muttering, "At least you get to eat!" Rafi smiled and reached for the baba ghanoush.

NANCY J. ALEXANDER

5 MENARA

She stared at the computer screen watching images moving on the maps in front of her. Her eyes were weary and her anxiety mounting, but she had no recourse. It had been days since a report had come through and all she could do was watch and pray. Over and over again, she chanted prayers, praying to the only G-d she believed in, in the only language she truly felt was hers. From her window, she could see the Houla Valley and beyond it the lush mountains of Lebanon. This had been her home since 1945, just 2 years after the kibbutz was founded. She had been a child when they moved to Menara, full of hope and enthusiasm for the land and its people. She was older now and wiser. Hope and enthusiasm had been replaced by reality and determination. When she looked out the window, she no longer marveled at the progress her people had made cultivating this once barren desert. Neatly planted rows and rectangles that supplied her country with freshly grown food stretched out before her. People worked in those fields, worked and sweated and grew old in those fields, and for what? The simple satisfaction of doing G-d's work? All that energy spent on survival knowing that in a moment's notice it could be obliterated. Their crops grew yes, but so did their enemies.

Their enemies, *Yes*, she thought. It was all muddled after a while. Enemies, friends, lovers…. She knew how those lines could blur, she knew better than most. She rubbed her eyes and looked again at the screen. There was movement now. She thought she could track them. Hands on the keyboard she began to type. In seconds, words appeared and she typed her response. Then picking up her cell phone, she spoke a few words, "One hour from now, get everything ready…. as we discussed. I'll meet you there." She rose turned off her equipment and walked down the steps onto the driveway, pushing buttons and setting alarm systems as she went. She was excited now, but not in a good way. They had been planning this day for years and it was almost here, an important day in more ways than one. Climbing into her jeep, she checked her rearview mirror catching her reflection for a moment. She was a handsome woman, grey-green eyes with a chestnut complexion and strong features. Her long dark hair, streaked with grey, was tied loosely at her neck creating a reckless look that belied her true nature. Hadara Eiliat was not reckless. She was highly organized, having worked for Mossad as a covert operative along the Lebanese border for more than a decade, she was focused and intelligent.

Recently appointed division chief, she was a born leader. But she was stepping out of her comfort zone on this op and she had more than just success or failure riding on it, much more. As her jeep bumped along dry rutted roads, she listened to the lines of chatter streaming across her com unit. There were four distinct conversations going on in different languages, but Hadara was able to keep track of each one. She would be ready with her report when the time came. She hoped everyone would be on time. Time was of the essence in an op like this. Time and a little help from above! She whispered a prayer in her native tongue begging *G-d* for help and mercy in this most urgent time of need. She prayed that they would all be safe.

The winding road climbed high into the mountains. The view was fabulous, a panorama of the lush Houla Valley. Below a flock of cranes took flight just as a helicopter approached from the south. On landing, a three man formation rushed forward, weapons pointed, followed by other men carrying equipment. Two officials, flanked by bodyguards, climbed out wearing starched tan uniforms. The old stone building was ensconced in vines and surrounded by trees. It was rectangular, 2 stories high with a flat walled roof and arched doors and windows. Three stone steps led to a carved wooden door which is where Hadara joined them. Without speaking they entered a large stucco room simply decorated with a long cedar table surrounded by 16 armchairs. Plywood was nailed to the inside window frames so the only light in the room was artificial coming from large, bronze chandeliers hanging over the table and flashing computer screens that lined the back wall. The floor was tiled; a long hallway led to the back of the building and mixed aromas of coffee and cooking drifted outward. Four men stood guard around the room, rifles at the ready and two men sat at a bank of computer terminals staring at the screens.

The meeting began with a short prayer as a simple meal was served. Pushing her plate aside, Hadara began, "Gentlemen, we have inserted an asset in the "Sword" camp with a strong cover story that should appeal to its leader. A three man team is assigned as backup. So far the asset's cover is intact."

General Kfir asked, "Have you gotten any solid information yet?"

"Not yet, General" Hadara said, "Our communication works only one way, it's too dangerous otherwise. The asset is under constant surveillance."

What she did not include in her report was the identity of this undercover asset and just how worried she was about this mission. She sent the agent best suited to the job based on all that was known about the target, but she regretted the decision.

"Well, Hadara," the man said sensing her conflict, "I gather something about this is bothering you, but this mission is of utmost importance. We cannot underestimate the damage this 'nut-job' can do. He's new but already he's got a shit load of followers trekking across the desert after him. This guy is one dangerous SOB plus he's a lunatic. He's convincing, I'll give him that, but still a lunatic."

"I understand General," Hadara said, waiting to go on.

"Alright," said General Mizrahi interrupting, "What's happening in the U.S.? You've got a bunch of folks over there right?"

"Yes, Sir," Hadara answered, "We have a cross division task force involving several agents and their handlers over there tracking down a nuclear arms network."

"Making any progress in finding anything?" Kfir asked.

"Yes, Sir," said Hadara, "We have firm leads in several cities and some very talented undercover work is going on over there. We should know more within the week."

General Kfir studied her face, "Do you feel alright about this American group Hadara? You seem a bit edgy about them. In fact you seem a bit edgy altogether tonight. Is anything else bothering you about these missions? Anything you haven't mentioned yet?" He'd worked with Hadara for fifteen years and knew her well. He sensed there was something going on she hadn't yet disclosed.

It took her several minutes before she answered, "No, Sir, just the usual mission worries."

An hour later, after discussing the matter exhaustively, General Mizrahi changed the subject, "There's a rumor out there about a turncoat in Beirut. A big muckety muck. Know anything about that?"

"Just rumors at this point, Sir, nothing definitive," Hadara replied. "I have some ears on the ground and I'm following their posts. If there's something there it will come out eventually."

General Mizrahi retorted, "If there's something there we need to know sooner rather than later. And that means big problems for their PM and he's a pretty tough guy himself. A high up guy with lots of clout could destabilize their whole regime. We can't afford to have that happen. You have some personal contacts over there don't you?"

"Yes, Sir, I have lots of contacts," Hadara said somewhat evasively.

"I see," the General replied with a hint of irritation, "Well, you best light a fire under your contacts' behinds because that shit could be a game changer."

The meeting went on until midnight ending with speculation about how these problems might all be related.

"These rumors of a turncoat in Beirut, this new group forming under the egis of a strange 'nut-job', these unknown contacts of yours, all seemed connected somehow," General Mizrahi said to Hadara. He was a seasoned military man and he knew when there was a bigger issue even though he could not yet see it.

Turning to face her he said, "I trust you'll have more information for us the next time we meet. Can I trust that, Hadara?"

"Of course, sir," Hadara agreed hastily.

Driving away amidst the sound and dust of whirling blades, Hadara Eiliat reflected on her decision to withhold information from two of the most powerful Generals in Israel. She had never broken protocol this way, but she felt certain it was the right decision. After all, she didn't have the whole story yet, she rationalized. For now *"The Chameleon"* in all its manifestations would remain her secret. It seemed only fair, she thought wryly; after all she was where it all began.

6 THE TRACKERS

They crossed the street with the determination of hunting dogs focused on a scent. Bodies tense, they walked in tandem, hard eyes surveying everything in their path. They had been on this trail for nearly a year and were now within striking distance. They had orders from their revered leader and they would follow those orders to the death if necessary. Nothing would stand in their way. This was their mission. They pushed through the double glass doors of the Northern Trust Bank Building in downtown Chicago, strode into the elevator and pressed 3. They were nearly there. They could almost taste their victory. At the end of a quiet hallway, they found the door. The name-plate read: *Elisabeth A. Reinhardt, PhD*. They pushed into the empty waiting room and kicked in the inner office door, tumbling forward as the door gave way. Guns up, they confronted an empty room.

Confused, they scurried about making certain their quarry wasn't hiding somewhere. Nothing remained but a pair of black Zelli loafers poised in front of an over-stuffed chair. Muttering in their native tongue, the leader picked up the shoes and examined their soles. They were still warm and the transmitters were intact. How had he known? Angry the leader directed one of his men to start searching the building floor by floor starting with the Men's Room. He directed the other man to search outside in case they had escaped the building. The leader remained in the room a few more minutes. He was puzzled. His mind raced through a hundred possibilities. There was only one door in and out of the room and they had not passed them in the hallway. They had been here minutes ago and now had disappeared. He had to be here somewhere.

It was a lovely room, comfortable with Oriental carpets, bookcases and plants, but the leader did not see beauty. He saw defeat. Looking out the window he saw the Mercedes idling at the curb. With a sickening feeling in the pit of his stomach, he prepared to report this failure to his revered leader. Before leaving, he stepped over to the desk. The appointment book was open to today's date with appointment times listed. On several lines there were initials in capital letters written in a woman's hand. On the line for this hour were the letters ABA. Those letters meant nothing to him. There were no phone numbers or other notations and all the desk drawers were locked. That told him nothing. Nothing! They knew this man only as 'The Chameleon.' He wore many faces, assumed many identities and moved quickly he seemed to be in two places at the same time. They had followed him all over the world and thought they had cornered him in this office but poof he disappeared again. Vanished into thin air! Swearing, the leader turned and stomped out of the room.

~~~~~~

Pablo Ruiz had pulled into the alley behind the office building in less than 5 minutes. He slowed down just long enough for them to jump into the backseat and flop down before pulling away. Pablo was one of two employees working for Protect and Serve, a private security agency headed by Gil McCray, a former Chicago Police Department detective. McCray passed the detective exam after only 4 years on the force; his record for clearing cases was outstanding, but he sometimes found the 'rules and regs' a bit too restricting. After fifteen years and a number of conflicts with administration later, Gil McCray and the CPD had parted ways. A highly moral man, he fought for the underdog and earned the reputation of superhero in the city law enforcement community. So when he left the force to open Protect and Serve he had lots of referrals from his brothers in blue and soon expanded his organization to include two other top law enforcement professionals, one of whom was driving this get-away car currently transporting two stowaways Ari Ben Aviv and Elisabeth Reinhardt.

"Where to?" Ruiz asked Elisabeth, who had risen to a seated position and was checking her cell phone for information from her team. Elisabeth Reinhardt was not just a psychologist specializing in trauma recovery in her private psychotherapy practice in Chicago. She was also the head of the Chicago branch of Chevra Hatzollah, an international organization formed by survivors of the Nazi Holocaust whose mission was to help innocent people who had no one else to help them. Translated from Hebrew, the name means 'group of rescuers'. Although it was founded as a Jewish organization, religious affiliation was not a condition of membership, nor did it influence decisions about whom to rescue. The sole criterion for receiving help was that individuals be in desperate, life threatening circumstances as a result of political persecution, abuse, cruelty or some other type of victimization and have no other help available to them. Many unofficial ties had been established with law enforcement agencies, but their firmest alliance was with Protect and Serve.

"We're cleared for S-1," Elisabeth said, reading her messages. She reviewed pictures taken from cameras installed in her office building and saw three men, guns drawn, barge into her office. She reviewed police reports that had been forwarded to her which described the incident and indicated police were giving chase to the men and the cleric. She frowned. This was wholly unexpected. There had been no warning from their networks, which were at this moment being alerted about this situation. "Gil will meet us there in 90," she said puzzling over their information lapse.

"You got it," Ruiz responded as he turned onto Rte. 294 heading north.

"I can sit up now yes, Ma'am?"

"I think it's best to wait a bit, just wait till we're sure," Elisabeth told him. "Are you comfortable enough?"

"Yes, Ma'am, I am fine and very grateful to you and your driver friend here," the passenger said and was silent. After a few minutes he said, "This afternoon, an appointment was happening, I was to meet with …a … person at a certain time. It is quite important that a message can be gotten to her."

"What time is your meeting?" Elisabeth asked.

"At 2 o'clock this afternoon, I am expected to be there at a certain location," said the young man worriedly.

"We have time," Elisabeth said checking her watch, "We'll take care of it; give me some time, Okay?"

"Yes, of course, I will remain silent now, thank you for your help."

Elisabeth nodded at him and sat back reflecting on the events of the last hour. She thought about the silent passenger curled up on the floor on the SUV. She realized several things didn't make sense. First of all, there was his presentation as a rather fragile young man. He must be important enough in the tangle of Middle Eastern conflicts to be chased down this way. But in what way was he important? Could he be an operative? That didn't make sense given his behavior and attitude. But perhaps all that had been an act.

And what of the men chasing him, they seemed organized enough, yet they risked being identified and captured, at least on camera, racing about in downtown Chicago, breaking into professional offices in a bank building with guns pulled. That didn't make sense. They were taking huge risks unless they knew they had someplace safe to hide. What place could be safe enough to hide from the authorities? If they were tracking this young man, why hadn't they waited until he was in a more accessible, less public location? Even the cleric got out of his car and talked openly with these young men who were about to commit a felony or many felonies. He stood in the open where cameras could capture his image and car's license plates. That meant this young man was a high value target for them. But that didn't make sense.

This young man, this Ari Ben Aviv, didn't make sense. He seemed innocent and frightened. He was so compliant, following her instructions, depending on her to save him. Why would that be? If he was a trained operative, he'd be inclined to give orders, not follow them. To assume the initiative not depend on some unknown woman to rescue him. Nothing in this situation was making sense and Elisabeth Reinhardt was a person who needed things to make sense. Was he really a tough, well-trained operative? If he was then why act like he wasn't? Why take all these risks and create this scenario in this way? Why not just contact her and talk with her directly about whatever he needed?

Who was this man who presented himself as frightened and needy? If he knew he was being followed, which he apparently did, then why had he led those men to her office? Didn't he realize he'd be cornered? Did he really think a locked office door would keep 3 ruthless pursuers out? What kind of trained agent would walk right into an office and get cornered with no plan of escape? Or did he know that she would get him out? Could he possibly have known that she could get him out? If that was the case, he knew more about her than he should have known, more than he had any right to know and if that was the case, then this drama had been more about her than she realized. The number of people, outside of her established network, who knew about her hidden back door, could be counted on one hand. And that thought brought to mind another thought. If today's events were about Chevra Hatzollah what was the endgame? Perhaps it had been his plan to force her to reveal herself in this way so she had no choice but to run with him and bring him into the inner circle of Chevra Hatzollah? If that was the case, then she and her whole organization might be in danger.

She signaled to Pablo to drive past the highway exit. She needed time to think. She did not want to bring this young man into the bosom of her organization without being sure about him. She texted her brother, Manny, their internet researcher, and explained some of her concerns, then returned to her thoughts. She didn't think she was in danger from the quiet young man on the floor, if he meant to harm her he would have done that already.

No, if he had bad intentions, they were being directed toward something else, something more devious, more complex. The shoes were another mystery. They didn't make sense either. If he knew he was being followed why hadn't he figured out how he was being tracked? Why hadn't he realized they had placed tracking devices in his shoes? He had apparently evaded these men for a long time, so he had to have cultivated some skills in avoiding capture. And if they had been close enough to place trackers in his shoes, then why had they not captured or killed him then, wherever and whenever that had been? Where does one leave one's empty shoes long enough for someone to put tracking devices in them? A hotel or a gym? If someone was close enough to access his shoes, why hadn't they just accessed him as well? Could they have somehow accessed his shoes before he bought them, a store perhaps? If that had happened, he must have ordered those shoes in advance and if that was the case, then a much larger plot was afoot.

Perhaps he ordered the shoes online and they had accessed his computer, checked out his order and interceded somewhere between the factory and his doorstep. But if that was the case wouldn't they have an address where the shoes were being delivered? Why not capture him there? Perhaps their goal had been to follow him somewhere not just capture or kill him. If that was the case where were they expecting him to go and what were they expecting him to do there? Had he been important to them because of where he was going and who he was going to see? There again, it led back to the question of her, her office and her role in Chevra Hatzollah.

She texted Pablo, who was negotiating a traffic snarl, to make sure they weren't being followed. He signaled the 'all clear' and she texted him to pull off the road and find someplace where they could talk to their passenger. Pablo pulled off the highway and after about 10 minutes pulled to a stop behind an abandoned gas station. The rear parking lot was filled with dust and aging vehicles, it backed onto heavily weeded stubble of trees. Without a word, Pablo got out of the car leaving Elisabeth looking at Ari Ben Aviv.

The young man raised his head as the car stopped and got onto the seat next to her. "Are we here now?" he asked.

"No, we are not, Ari, may I call you Ari?"

"Yes, of course do call me Ari," he smiled at her, "Why is it that we are now stopping the car?"

"I need to talk to you," she said.

The rear door opened and Pablo Ruiz said, "Come with me" reaching for Ben Aviv's arm. With only moderate, alarm the young man complied and walked with Ruiz into the back of the abandoned gas station. Handing him a JC Penny bag, he said, "Put on these things and put everything you have in the bag."

In the meantime, Ruiz examined the young man's wallet carefully running his fingertips over the seams. He found several hundred dollars, American, and another 25 bills of various denominations that appeared to be Israeli shekels and Lebanese lira. He had an Israeli driver's license that bore his picture, a Lebanese driver's license that bore his picture, several foreign credit cards and a MasterCard issued by the Bank of America. There were no photographs, notes or any other personal items. Forth-five minutes later, they were driving down a two lane road, through a quiet residential area, having disposed of Ari's clothing. The area was thickly treed with large comfortable homes set back from the street. A 6 foot high brick wall surrounded the property located at the dead end of a sparsely populated street. The wrought iron gate slid open as they approached and closed as they passed through heading toward a large red brick home built in the late 1970's. The surrounding lawn and garden was attractive, but not ostentatious and the curved driveway led to a two car garage with open doors that slid closed as the car pulled in.

"We're here," Elisabeth said as Ari Ben Aviv rose to look at his rescuers.

"I am most grateful to you both for getting me out of that trouble," he said extending his hand to Elisabeth and Ruiz.

"You know, Ari," Elisabeth said in a business-like manner, "that is exactly the issue I want to explore with you. Come inside with me."

7 MIDNIGHT MEETINGS

The air was surprisingly cold and strong winds blew around them as Rafi and his escorts walked past closed tents of sleepers. The camels lay quietly together in small groupings, chewing their cuds, long eyelashes lowered against the swirling sand. Faint rustling could be heard around the campsite, vague and indistinct sounds of people and animals, of tents flaps twisting in the wind. The sounds of the desert, the scents in the air; specks of light broke through as moonlight peeked past scattered clouds. It felt otherworldly. Although he had lived in this world off and on throughout his life, it felt odd to be so far into this world, a world he knew, but didn't belong to. As his escorts walked with him to his assigned tent, he tried to absorb every aspect of his surroundings. He needed to know as much as he could about this place, these people. He needed to incorporate them into his mind and his spirit. He needed to belong here, if only for a little while. Everything depended on it.

His tent was small. There was a rug for sleeping at the far side of the tent. Next to it stood a small table on which a brass samovar, an empty cup and a copy of the Koran had been placed. Next to the table a carefully folded sajjada lay ready for morning's prayers. A dim oil lamp sat on a basket near the entrance. The guards watched as he crossed to where the holy book sat, kissed his fingers then touched them to the book, murmuring prayers of devotion with a bowed head. Then they bade him goodnight and backed out to take up positions on either side of the tent flap.

Breathing a sigh of relief, Rafi settled down on the carpet and closed his eyes. A tinny voice in his ear asked, "Down for the night?" To which Rafi said nothing. His communication system didn't work both ways. If they could see him, then he could signal to them. If not, it was one-way or no way at all. Rafi was just drifting off to sleep when he felt something touch his back. A hand reached in from beneath the tent. Startled he jerked away until he felt a slip of paper touch his palm. The coded message read: *Al Queda sending messenger to question you. Authorized to kill. Prepare for emergency evac. Watch for signal.*

Rafi signaled his understanding by scrunching up the note and replacing it firmly in Moshe's hand. He would present himself as his father's son, believer in the true way. He could do this. He had been doing it most of his life, one way or the other. He had always lived in two worlds. How he functioned like the *Chameleon* he was. He could do this. He would be fine. He would wake at first light and begin his prayers. That was the most important thing he needed to do. Begin his prayers. With that thought in mind, he fell asleep.

Elsewhere, Hadara Eiliat paced on her balcony. As the clock struck midnight, she stared at the moonbeams poking through the clouds and thought about all the things that could go wrong. She was just about to go inside and try to sleep when she heard a sound. A soft whistling sound… She wasn't sure if it was a night bird, an insect or perhaps a signal. She held her breath and waited, listening with her whole body. Again she heard the sound; closer now, coming from somewhere near her balcony. Hand on the butt of her revolver, she waited. Slowly she extracted her gun and reached for the flashlight clipped to her belt. Backing up she crouched behind a chair and waited. The whistlers could be assassins whistling to one another, it could be someone calling to her, she was taking no chances. She heard it again, this time a few feet below her balcony. Slowly the whistle changed. It became a snippet of a children's tune. She recognized it as a song about a goat that had been bought for 2 zuzim. Smiling, Hadara holstered her weapon, re-clipped her flashlight and walked to the railing. "So Yosef, you forgot how to ring the bell, maybe? Come in the front," she said hearing him chuckle. Unlocking the latch she walked into the kitchen to fill the kettle.

Yosef came in smiling. "Gotcha rattled, yes? I still got it in me," he said with a grin.

"Sit," she pointed at a chair, her eyes smiled at him, "you bring me word?"

"Yes, things are alright for now," he assured her and began to fill her in on the news. He had many sources throughout the Middle East. A face and attitude that could blend in anywhere, Yosef was a traveler. He looked ancient with long scraggly hair, a wrinkled face, a messy beard and a brown belted robe. With only slight changes in appearance and accent he could blend in with every group in the region. Yosef Yadin was Hadara's oldest friend and confident. Having been born a few weeks apart, they were raised together on the kibbutz and had become inseparable.

It was the philosophy of their community to instill a work ethic and the spirit of cooperation in their children at an early age. Thus Yosef and Hadara, along with several other children their age, worked in the fields picking fruit and vegetables starting at the age of 5. The children enjoyed their work, laughing and singing and making a game of their efforts. Over time, as the two of them gathered crops, they encountered some children doing similar work on the Lebanese side of the border and as children do they formed friendships. Every day Yosef and Hadara would wander over to their favorite spot bearing gifts of figs or oranges and visit with their friends Jamila, Hakim and Abdullah Faysal.

In that part of the world, the name Faysal was synonymous with olives. For generations, the Faysal family labored in their olive groves, planting and harvesting olives and pressing olive oil. Caravans of camels laden with olives and olive oil carried their wares throughout the Middle East. As they grew older, the children shared more with each other about their way of life. They knew that their countries didn't get along and that the outlook for peace was bleak. But as children, they didn't understand such divisions, they were friends. Over time, the children learned many things about each other: language, customs and beliefs. As they approached adolescence, Hadara, Yosef, Jamila, Hakim and Abdullah formed a secret 'pact.' They called themselves *The Olive Branch*. They decided to devote their lives to creating peace between their countries. Injustices and cruelty surrounded them and they were determined to change that for future generations.

Knowing it would be met with disapproval, the children never spoke to anyone about their developing friendships. The five children spent every possible moment together and soon their little group became the most important part of their lives. They were the best of friends, sharing ideas and feelings and plans for the future. When during their adolescence Hadara and Hakim found they were attracted to one another, it seemed a natural part of their lives together; it became just another secret to be kept. Only Yosef, Jamila and Abdulla knew about the young lovers and their silence was guaranteed. The five teenagers became inseparable, talking endlessly about their countries, developing secret plans about who they would become and how they would help the peace process. Over time they developed unique ways of communicating with each other. There were some made-up words with special meanings and assorted signals.

When just before his 17th birthday Hakim announced his intention to marry Hadara it was no surprise to the others. The five children had known all along of the love Hadara and Hakim shared. There were, however, some major obstacles to their plan, namely that such a marriage would be forbidden by their families and there was no place where such a marriage could exist openly, not to mention they lacked the resources to arrange for such a marriage. Flooded with emotions of sadness and frustration, they vowed to continue their relationship in secret until they could live in the open. In the meantime, they would do the best they could until they could figure out how and where to marry.

As members of *The Olive Branch* moved off to follow their individual plans some things changed. On their 18th birthdays Hadara and Yosef joined Mossad and Hakim and Abdulla joined the Lebanese Army. Jamila as per her parents' wishes left to obtain a business degree in the United States, so she could take charge of the family business. Jamila became the group's default post office. She was responsible for getting, holding and passing coded messages between the lovers and arranging for meetings with the friends on the rare occasions when they could congregate.

Hadara and Yosef excelled in the Mossad. Because they were intelligent, talented young people, it was decided that they would attend university and study subjects that would be helpful in their future roles within the organization. Thus in their 19th year, Hadara and Yosef traveled to the United States where they attended college and graduate school specializing in world history, political science and computer technology. In addition, they learned a number of languages including Russian and French; they had already mastered English and several Arabic dialects. As a subscript, they were to learn the ways of the Western world so that they would understand the culture, its values and its psychology.

Upon returning, they took up different positions in Mossad. Yosef was to infiltrate as many groups, cultures and organizations as possible working as a covert operative. Fluent in all Middle Eastern languages and dialects, he was also exquisitely familiar with religious dogma and political nuances that characterized their part of the world, while Hadara was to remain on the kibbutz and work her way up the ranks assuming increasing responsibility for operations along the Lebanese border. This was a perfect solution for her as it met some of her more personal needs. Now, she smiled at her friend as she reached across her kitchen table, poured Yosef a cup of tea and settled down to hear what he had learned.

A world away, Ari Ben Aviv and his sister Samira sat side by side on a sofa in a big brick house in a Chicago suburb. It was nearing midnight and the core group of Chevra Hatzollah was continuing to collect information about the situation. They had no formal relationship with Mossad, but had worked with some of their agents from time to time over the years. At this point, the issues were unclear, but what was clear was that members of a Middle Eastern rebel group were determined to kill Ari Ben Aviv. Manny's searches on the 'dark net' uncovered rumors that Ari had some mysterious nickname and was important in the world of Middle East espionage. Samira said she was here as his handler. They were working to establish a back channel to an underground weapons network operating out of several US museums.

Since arriving at the safe house Elisabeth had been able to learn little about Ari's request for an appointment, his knowledge about tracking devices in his shoes, and his general skill as a covert operative. His answers seemed vague and oddly circular. It seemed he was waiting for something before he could answer her.

Elisabeth had been able to confirm that Ari had known the three men in the street were following him but did not think they would break into a public building. In the event that they did he believed his hand to hand combat skills would enable him to protect himself. He claimed not to know about her hidden exit but he did know about her connection with a secret organization and was hoping that she would lead him to it.

They later learned that the men had indeed broken into her office, destroying her doors and terrorizing other building occupants. The police declared the building a crime scene and closed it to the public pending a police investigation. She had been told the police were seeking her as 'a person of interest' in their investigation. The men reportedly had fled the scene; they were last seen turning onto a street where several Arab Consulates were located. Manny and Gil were monitoring that situation and said Dr. Reinhardt would make a full statement to the police as soon as her safety was assured.

But Elisabeth was focused on Ari and had yet to determine why he had contacted her in the first place. Ari said he had been referred by a friend, but she had no idea who that friend might be. She needed to discuss this with him because nothing was making sense. As for Samira, her work was unclear as well. What she was doing with a bag from a museum gift shop filled with bomb making materials remained unclear. Once everyone arrived, Elisabeth introduced her siblings: Reina, Stella, Emanuel, Samuel and Simon and the three members of Protect and Serve.

Stella and Reina were both lawyers. Stella Reinhardt Krieger established a small firm specializing in criminal defense cases and Reina Reinhardt Alpert was now a Judge on the US District Court, for Northern Illinois. Her brothers, Simon and Samuel, were identical twins and co-owned S & S Shoes operating under the tagline 'Special Shoes for Special Feet' they specialized in orthopedic shoes, which were distributed internationally. Emanuel (Manny) owned and operated a computer business called 'BE WISE Data Storage', which specialized in internet security. Elisabeth had married a man named Martin Schreiber when she was 23, but he contracted leukemia and died when their daughter was five. She never remarried and resumed use of her maiden name by which she was known professionally.

The Reinhardt children lived productive lives. All were devoted to humanitarian pursuits either in their professional or volunteer lives. They were charitable and generous with their time. They served the community in many different ways. They knew they were the lucky ones, they all agreed on that. They would never forget those who were less fortunate. They would never forget those lost in the concentration camps or those who had been so damaged, that their experiences at the hands of the Nazi's would live forever in their tormented minds. Not one day passed when the Reinhardt children did not give their thanks to G-d for their good fortune and pray for the health and well-being of their people. If they knew one thing for certain, it was that they would fight injustice and abuse of power, of any type, every chance they could, to do otherwise would be a betrayal of their people, their religion, and their belief system. They knew that injustice and abuse of power took many forms and felt that it was their personal and collective responsibility to stand up and fight for what was right. If their fight meant personal risk or jeopardy, well they would just have to take that risk. The Reinhardts fully embraced the Jewish concept of *Tikkun olam* which means "repairing the world" (or "healing the world"). This suggests it is humanity's shared responsibility to heal, repair and transform the world. The Reinhardts' commitment to *Tikkun olam* led them into worlds far beyond the norm.

Ari and his sister greeted each member of the Reinhardt family with warmth and familiarity. They said it was as if they had always known each other. There was something entirely different about this meeting; all the members of Chevra Hatzollah felt it. It was like a reunion. Elisabeth then introduced 'Protect and Serve' led by Gil McCray, whom Samira already knew. The one-time Chicago detective introduced his two associates. Pablo Ruiz, (large and Hispanic, a former DEA agent, worked for years patrolling the Texas-Mexican border until his wife and daughter had been inadvertent victims in a shootout with the Los Primo Cartel. He was heartbroken for years until he ran into Gil. His work here with these people had given him a new lease on life, a purpose he had all but lost. Pablo was a 'people person' his magnetic personality pulled people toward him.

The third group member was a man called 'T-Max.' Bald, black and tattooed, he was an intimidating presence. Standing 6'3' and weighing 280 he could scare a person to death just by frowning at them. 'T-Max' was an enigma. Although he looked like a brainless thug, he had graduated with a Masters in Computer Science from MIT. He'd worked the NYP's Gang Unit for 8 years before joining forces with Gil and Pablo. 'T-Max,' aka Thomas Minister, had gotten his moniker working undercover with teenage gangs. Along with Manny and Sammy he helped construct Chevra Hatzollah's complex computer network, installing most of the connections in the field.

They decided to interview the siblings individually. Elisabeth and her brother Sammy started the interview with Samira while Gil and Stella motioned Ari into another room. As coffee cups were filled and refilled, the meetings dragged on till the early morning hours when the Chicago suburbs slowly sprang to action and the interviews gradually wound down.

8 EAVESDROP

It had quickly become a matter of great importance – at first it was a hint, a whisper, a rumor. Nothing substantive. Nothing specific. People, who appeared to have nothing in common were congregating, people glanced meaningfully at one another then turned away. Something was happening. He could see it in the crowd; he could feel it in the air. He needed to learn what was going on. Yosef crouched with a group of men selling handmade clothing, hats and robes to tourists in a small marketplace between Tiberius and Hoshaya, when a phrase floating by made his heart nearly stop. It was rapidly spoken, urgent and hushed "…push them into the ocean…" Two men were whispering, their body language conveying purpose, intensity, their manner familiar as they huddled behind a hemp line on which several handmade carpets were hung. Yosef peered silently through a tiny space between two carpets. The men hadn't noticed him. They wore traditional tan thoubs with gutrahs covering their heads. One of the men was older with a greying beard, while the other, in his twenties, sported a dark, thick beard. The cacophony of the marketplace faded as Yosef focused on the two voices and funneled energy into memorizing the words he heard.

From their dialect, he determined they were Lebanese. "…huge explosion...when the *great man* comes...," said one man.

"... Be a shock ….entire world... Jews…spies like grains of sand…know nothing!" said the other excitedly.

"… a war unlike any they have known.….." said first man.

"will be ready," said the second man, "not like …when the infidels… lashed out... we will push them into the sea…our land…our …"

Yosef feigned sleep as the men hurried past. Panic surged, as he watched them from under drooping eyelids. A plan was forming and his people knew nothing about it. He needed to follow these men and learn what they knew and he needed help. He needed to get help without losing his quarry. Before the sun set this night, he would know all he needed to know.

As he passed a raggedy young man selling oranges from a weathered cart, Yosef stumbled, nearly fell and released a string of invectives about his bad luck and wretched feet. That was the signal. The young man, Mikhail, sprang into action and within a few minutes a ragtag trio joined him weaving inconspicuously through the marketplace. A simple surveillance plan was devised. An urgent message was sent to Hadara, who contacted Mossad; a team was dispatched to rendezvous with Yosef. They needed to see who these men were meeting and where they were going before capturing them.

Unrelenting heat beat down as they followed the pair along a narrow cobblestone path toward the outskirts of the tiny village. Here amid clumps of random vegetation, a few trees provided shade for children who ran about playing. It was less populated here, so the team pulled back and watched as the two men approached an open air café. Tables with faded cloth umbrellas were scattered about; men crowded around them scooping hummus with pita bread and drinking sweet mint tea. Succulent aromas rose from smoky outdoor grills as the two men greeted a third man in the traditional Arab manner. The third man was short, heavy set, swarthy and similarly dressed. He was accompanied by two muscular men with stony expressions and the demeanor of warriors. They crossed their arms and positioned themselves at the entrance to the café. Yosef frowned. This was significant. This third man must be important, very important to have two guards protecting him in this simple village. Finding out this man's identity was crucial. They needed to break with their usual low profile protocol. They would need to go inside and find out more about this third man, this meeting.

Inside, the three men walked to a back room reserved for private meetings. Across the street the team debated. Was it more important to avoid detection or was it more important to find out what these three were saying. They could always follow and capture them to find out the plan. They agreed on a compromise. Mikhail quickly rearranged his garments and entered the café on the pretense of using the restroom. As luck would have it, the restroom was adjacent to the room where the three men were sitting apparently engrossed in some kind of negotiation. Mikhail affixed a microphone to the rickety wall and retreated before another patron arrived.

They heard enough to confirm the urgency of this mission and relay information in bits and pieces up the chain of command. It was not long before aid arrived in the form of an undercover assault team. The team totaling six men sat on the ground opposite the café smoking and playing a dice game as the listened through their earwigs. They learned that the original two men were indeed Lebanese. They were called Muhammad and Imad and they were uncle and nephew. The third man was a Syrian named Boulos. They were negotiating a weapons sale. Boulos had ties to a new extremist organization that had been growing since the demise of Osama Bin Laden. Calling itself *The Sword of Justice* it was spreading like wildfire with pockets of activity in Syria, Saudi Arabia, Lebanon, Iraq and Jordan. The two Lebanese men were acting as middle men for an unknown weapons dealer and Boulos was offering to buy a large amount of explosives from them for an as yet undiscovered colossal assault plan.

Yosef and his band sat under the trees across from the little café for over two hours until the three men departed. It appeared their talks had not gone according to everyone's satisfaction, as they broke off at the entrance wordlessly walking in different directions. The negotiations had hit a snag. Muhammad and Imad walked south toward Tiberius with half the follow team in pursuit. They walked slowly and stopped several times to talk with people along the way. Each contact was photographed for follow up. Boulos and his guards walked north toward where their Jeep Wrangler was parked. They were followed by trackers who alternated positions and vehicles as they made their way across the demilitarized zone into Syria. Yosef rode with this team.

By late afternoon after illegally crossing the Syrian border they watched as the men got out, walked briskly toward a small house. It was a simple one story structure made of stone and mud with a weathered door and small square windows spaced evenly around the building. Outside the door, loosely stacked cinderblocks enclosed a small garden of limp, dying plants; rough-hewn logs covered the roof on which a satellite dish about 4 feet in diameter stood erect. As the men entered the house they abruptly pulled off the road bumping along a narrow path into a scraggly grove of cedars snapping photos and looking for a place to hide and wait.

9 THE HOSTAGE

The child could hear swirling sand pounding against the parched hide as she lay curled against it, the thin carpet barely buffering her small frame. She was cold and frightened. By her count, this was her third night here in this tent with these strangers. She had not seen their faces; they had kept her bound and blindfolded, but she recognized several of them by voice. Three men and one woman were with her, she clearly heard other voices, people talking outside the tent, their voices urgent and hushed. She thought they were talking about her. The woman who cared for her was kind and helped her eat and relieve herself, but would not answer her questions and did not comfort her when she cried. The men moved around her busily, but they had not touched her, only the woman. She thought the men were guarding her, but she couldn't figure out who they were guarding her from or why she had been taken in the first place. Saroyah did not understand any of this. One minute she was enjoying her kittens and the next she was gagged and thrown in a trunk. It was unreal, like a dream. She was scared and confused and more than anything she wanted to go home. She knew her mother would be terrified and searching for her. All of them would be searching for her, she was sure of that. What she was not sure of was whether they would find her.

Perfectly still and hardly breathing, she listened for sounds that could help her learn where they had taken her. Camel, donkey and horse sounds could be heard off in the distance as could the sound of automobile motors and car doors slamming. People were up and busy even at this late hour of the night. Based on the time of her dinner and the quietness around her, she thought it was around the middle of the night. She had decided she was in a camp of some sort. She'd been in camps before, they were familiar to her, but this one felt different. She didn't hear children's voices or anything that seemed like family life going on in the camp. No women talking and laughing as they cooked or did the washing or carried their babies about. No, there was something very different about this place of mostly men who talked little between themselves and seemed somehow formal with one another. Like an army maybe? Just 11 years old, Saroyah was mature for her age, the youngest of 4 children born to Jamila Faysal and her husband Gamil Ajram, she had lived in the Faysal Family Olive Grove her whole life.

Just over the border from Israel, she had learned a great deal about the Arab-Israeli conflict and understood that her family had connections, involvements in this long-standing conflict that made them important. Her uncle Abdullah had an important role in the Lebanese Army, her uncle Hakim also worked for their government, but his wife Hadara lived in Israel and was sometimes spoken of in whispers. Often there were raised eyebrows and subtle head shakes when Saroyah would come upon adults speaking of them. She never understood about that, but she knew it was important and she wondered if that had anything to do with those men she'd overheard meeting at the Olive Grove. Maybe that was why she was here now, tied up, blindfolded and frightened.

10 RECOLLECTIONS

Elisabeth Reinhardt sat perfectly still watching cardinals, black capped chickadees and gold finches dart about the garden, lighting on their feeders, pecking for seeds in the freshly mulched garden. It was a beautiful garden, newly emerging sprouts and awakening blossoms. The morning sun was just rising in the east amid bird song and the early morning sounds of a community preparing for the day. Her eyes burned with lack of sleep and her mind struggled to recall a fleeting piece of information, an image from years ago, a word a gesture. She closed her eyes and concentrated on the image, tracked back from the moment it flitted through her mind. Samira had ended an elaborate tale of events when with a toss of her glossy black hair she had uttered, "es beshert," meaning 'it was meant to be.' In that instance a memory flashed through Elizabeth's mind. She rose left the room where she and her brother Sammy had been interviewing Samira and secluded herself in the enclosed patio overlooking the garden. There she sat trying to localize the memory. Something about that small phrase, that feminine gesture, that expression tugged at the back of her mind.

"Es beshert, es beshert," she repeated closing her eyes and breathing rhythmically. That was familiar. Someone from years ago, someone she knew well, someone she had worked with. Who was it? She focused on the story that Ari Ben-Aviv had told her in her office. She had been barely listening, worrying about their escape, worrying about the men in the street who looked menacingly at her office building searching the windows for clues as to his whereabouts. What had he said, this handsome young man who now sat in their Chicago safe house talking with Gil and Stella? Who was he, really? Reviewing his words and concentrating on their content. She had thought he was making it up as he rambled on. She had thought it was a story for the listeners, whoever they might be, but now she thought

41

differently. What he said was fitting into a picture slowly forming in her mind.

She had been a young psychologist, just finishing her Doctorate, working at the Student Counseling Center at the University of Chicago. Her daughter had just turned five and she was working part-time so that she could spend more time at home with her. Her husband Martin had just been diagnosed with leukemia and was undergoing treatment, the prognosis was not good. Elisabeth remembered herself at that time; young, just beginning her professional life, a wonderful child to love and raise and a sick possibly, no probably, dying husband.

She remembered herself at that time, how she looked and felt. She remembered the treatment room she used at the University's Student Counseling Center, a space she shared with three other clinicians. She used that room on Wednesday and Friday mornings from eight to noon. She had loved those times, those students. They were fresh, idealistic and sometimes troubled. In her mind she saw a young woman who reminded her of Samira. She looked like Samira, sounded a lot like her, too. Neither Ari nor Samira had fully disclosed the reasons for their time in Chicago, how and why Ari had called her and come to see her. For a young man seeking her help, he had been oddly uncommunicative, evasive even. Samira had been no better. The Chicago branch of Chevra Hatzollah was more than a little confused and just a tad irritated. Here they were reaching out to these two who apparently needed their help and wanted their help and they were being stonewalled. The answer lay in her memory, she was sure of it. The key to unlocking their mouths lay in the recesses of her mind.

She thought back to the Student Counseling Center and reconstructed her therapy space. Breathing deeply she moved into a trance, clearing her mind of everything present and allowing herself to float into the past. She envisioned the small square room in the basement of the Humanities building. The cold linoleum tiled floor was brown and green; the desks were blocky school teacher desks. The chairs were metal with slender padding covered in green plastic. A tall black filing cabinet sat in the corner containing one drawer where each of the psych fellows could deposit clinical notes. Elisabeth brought the files into view. In her mind, she stood at her open drawer examining the pale tan folders, staring at the tabs on each where she had written names in her characteristic bold square print. Last name followed by the first name and then the middle initial. After the name there was a 5 digit number. In her mind she reached out her hand and extracted a file. The name on the tab read *"Eiliat, Hadara A   74319."*

11 IN THE OLIVE GROVE

Jamila paced back and forth in the hallway weeping and waiting for an answer. In one hand, she held an iPhone which she stared at as she wept. In her other hand she clutched a small stuffed bear Saroyah loved. How could this happen? Who were these monsters that would steal a child from her home, her little girl, an innocent little child who knew nothing of the world? Jamila wanted to scream! She wanted to throw something! She wanted to kill someone! Whoever had taken her little Saroyah would pay, and they would pay with their lives. Jamila had never before been so angry, so terrified, so determined in all her life. She had resources. She had connections and she was determined to use them. She would do anything to save her child.

Gamil looked devastated as he entered with her brother Hakim. He rushed forward and embraced his wife and they wept together bemoaning their child's fate and expressing their mutual fear for her safety. Hakim came forward and embraced his sister and her husband as they wept, whispering assurances that they would find out where the child was being held and she would be safely returned. Jamila looked up at her older brother, her red eyes begging him for the truth and asked, "Is Hadara helping? Does she know who did this?"

Hakim nodded solemnly, "of course she is helping," he said but offered no additional information. The less said the better. At this time, they all understood that.

Amal and Hala Faysal sat silently on the sofa watching and listening. Never before had such a thing happened to their family. Now in their 70's, they had turned over the operation of the Olive Grove and family matters to their daughter and her husband. Now Jamila turned to her parents and said "Abbi, Ummi, I do not wish to upset you but I felt that you needed to know what happened here." Her parents reached for her and she knelt before them. "We are a family, my child," her mother said, "Your pain is our pain. Do what you think is best and we will be with you as ever you need us."

"And for advice, my daughter," her father said with his characteristic slight sarcasm, "We are not without a modicum of wisdom, you know, so come to us as you wish."

Turning to his son, Amal said "Hakim are you doing all you can to help your sister in her troubled times?" Hakim came to the older man and took his hand, "Of course Abbi, Hadara and I both are going full force on this. It is complete madness."

Amal Faysal took his son's face in his hands and looked directly into his eyes, "This has to be more important than anything else in your life. You will use your contacts to the fullest extent possible to help resolve this, do you understand me Hakim?" Lowering his voice to a whisper he said, "I know that you have many contacts that others do not know about. There are those who can help. Now is the time to take risks. Do what is necessary to save Saroyah."

"Of course, Abbi," Hakim replied trying to move out of the older man's grip, but his father held fast. "Hakim," he whispered again his expression deepening, "your role in this may be more critical than you realize. Whatever needs to be done you must to do it and quickly."

Hakim was not certain what his father meant but he nodded his assent and with a slight bow, extricated himself from his father's clutches. Hakim had some facts about his father's history with hidden matters of state but through the years there had been hints that Amal had not been a stranger to covert activities. Now he wondered exactly information his father had about his activities and how he had come by this information.

Turning to his sister Hakim asked, "Have there been any communications from the kidnappers?" Gamil watching these exchanges gave Hakim a curious look before turning back to his wife. She shook her head and turned away. Gamil did not know what his father-in-law had said to Hakim but it was secretive and intense and it worried him. He didn't think there had been any contact from the kidnappers and wondered why Hakim was asking Jamila the question and not him. Men were to talk to each other about such matters not to the women and yet Hakim was treating Jamila as an equal. Gamil was being excluded, his role was being minimized. He sensed that something oddly out of order had just occurred. He wondered what was going on. Did they know something he didn't want them to know?

Jamila's outburst interrupted his thoughts as she shouted "I am stuck in this house doing nothing while thugs have stolen my child! And none of you are doing anything to get her back. SHE IS MY CHILD!! I cannot stand it," she screamed, "I simply cannot stand it. I will find them and kill them myself with my own two hands, I swear I will!"

"I know this is horrible my beloved" Gamil said, stepping forward into the space between Hakim and his hysterical wife. Hugging her he said "but right now your place is to stay here. Our children need you. They are worried and frightened and they need their mother to take care of them." he insisted trying to redirect her attention to her older children.

She was having none of it "Do not tell me who I should be taking care of," she shouted. "These children are not young. They are able to take care of themselves." Jamila said "It's Saroyah who needs me. I must find her since no one else is doing anything. I'll offer a reward. I'll go to the newspapers!" She was becoming more agitated as the men escorted her into the sitting room, where servants had a tea set waiting on a large brass tray. "Let's sit down, have some tea and I'll tell you what I know," Hakim suggested.

The room was elegant, befitting a Lebanese family of longtime fortune. High round ceilings displayed original hand-painted scenes rivaling the Sistine Chapel. The walls displayed pastoral oil paintings and intricate woven carpets covered dark polished floors. The colorful tasseled pillows arranged on satin sofas all attested to the family's distinguished social position. This room, like the rest of the house, was impeccable. But at the moment, the room and all that it conveyed meant nothing to Jamila. She could be standing in a filthy shed for all she cared. Turning to her brother she said, "Tell me everything you know."

Down the hallway and around the corner to the kitchen, a silent cluster huddled, in the doorway listening. Three Ajram children and four elderly servants crowded together to hear what was happening. Kalina, Lutfi and Layla, ages 13, 15 and 17, had been given very little information about their missing sister. The children were close. They spent all their time together and were rarely apart. Having been raised on what was essentially a family compound; they had little association with other children their age, rarely left the compound and never on their own. They were home schooled by specially selected tutors. For one of them to be missing, even for an hour, was an unheard of event, surrounded as they were by servants, tutors, workers and guards. The children felt sick to their stomachs. It had now been 2 nights since she had gone missing and they could not get a straight answer from anyone.

The servants clung to each other as they enfolded the children. They had spent their entire working lives in this complex; they and their parents before them. They were as identified with the Faysal-Ajram family as anyone could be, but in the back of their minds they fretted. Would the family turn against them? Would they begin to suspect that one of them had taken Saroyah? They, of course, would never think of doing such a thing, never. This family meant everything to them. But they knew when people get desperate, they turn against each other. Would the time come when their safe, secure lives would be torn apart by these people who took Saroyah? Would they, too, become victims of the nameless, faceless criminals who kidnapped the little girl?

Their fearful, wet eyes met across the bowed heads of the Ajram children and together they uttered silent prayers to *Allah* to save them and bring the child safely home.

12 IN THE PRESENCE OF MY ENEMY

Rafi woke at first light and began *Salat al-Fajr,* morning prayers starting with the washing ritual called *wudzu* in which certain body parts are washed in a certain manner and order, starting with the hands and ending with the feet. Then kneeling on his prayer rug, he bowed, first touching his forehead on the rug then rising up Rafi repeated "*Allahu Akbar, Allahu Akbar, Allahu Akbar, Allahu Akbar.*" (*Allah* is the Greatest") four times. He did this in the privacy of his own tent, but knew that he was being carefully observed for any irregularities that might occur. Muslim prayers are very specific and ritualized, so strict adherence was essential. Rafi was not concerned about this though, having spent much of his childhood among his Lebanese brethren, these customs were as familiar to him as Jewish ones. He could move with ease between the two religious ceremonials and felt something meaningful during each one. He considered himself to be devoutly religious, but for him, the two cultures/religions co-existed as one interlocking belief set. He saw the meaning and beauty in each and deeply respected, actually believed in, the tenants set forth by each faith. In his mind, they weren't all that different when you pared away linguistics and rituals. The essential messages were the same. Have faith, believe in an all-powerful deity, be reverent and respectful, practice acts of kindness in your daily life, avoid certain forbidden actions and behaviors and live your life according to the essential principles of the faith.

Rafi was folding his prayer rug when he heard a commotion outside of his tent. Moving toward the doorway he saw three men dragging another who was struggling against his captors. He was instantly seized with fear that Moshe or another team member had been captured, but as he looked he saw that the man was older and heavy-set. He was relieved, but also fearful for the man. Instinctively, he wanted to rush forward and help him but knew he could not take that risk. Stepping forward, he asked one of his guards what had happened. Glancing at him with cold reserve the guard answered that it was none of his concern. Pursing the matter with an innocent demeanor he asked, "Has something bad happened? Are we in danger?" Staring at the struggling foursome the man answered, over the sound of the prisoner's cries, "Not anymore," with a slight sneer. A chill ran down Rafi's spine. *"Ma'assalama,"* he said politely as he bowed his head and moved away from the guard toward the main tent where he would join *The Great One* and his cadre who would be finishing morning prayers and getting ready for breakfast.

~~~~~~

Somewhere in Syria, Yosef and his team watched and waited for the man identified as Duquq Boulos to leave the little house in the desert. It had turned dark and in the rusted van they were debating whether or not to venture closer to the house so they could hear the conversation inside. Hours had passed. The darkness was nearly total. There was no sign of activity, no sound at all. A few flickering glimmers of candles could be seen as Elias crept forward on his belly, a tiny microphone hidden in the folds of his shirt. Elias Talmi was the youngest among them; small and slender he was well suited for creeping about in the middle of the night. Still, Yosef held his breath and prayed earnestly that the young man would safely accomplish his mission. Sol Abramson, a member of Kidon, Mossad's most celebrated anti-terrorism unit, had arrived to head the mission. He sat stoically staring through his infrared night vision binoculars, watching Elias inch toward the target house. Sol watched as Elias approached the window closest to their location, affix the tiny microphone to the underside of the wooden sill and slowly reverse direction.

Faint metallic voices could be heard, accented Syrian, Lebanese, and Iranian men's voices talking in hushed tones. Turning the volume up a bit and checking to make sure that the tape recorder was working Sol listened carefully as the man they knew as Boulos outlined a complex plan that a new Jihadist group was about to begin which would culminate in the collapse of nations. He spoke of the plan as originating elsewhere, so it was clear the plan was not his.

Events were designed to set off a rolling domino effect that would change the entire world. A quick glance between Yosef and Sol affirmed the team's orders; everyone snapped into action. They would invade the little house and overpower the men inside. They would capture them before they alerted anyone to their predicament. The plan was dangerous. They were on enemy soil and were about to invade a dwelling filled with armed combatants, capture them in complete silence and flee across the DMZ through miles of hostile territory. Getting caught would set off an international incident and lead incontrovertibly to death.

In places near and far, the men and women of Mossad were working overtime to assure that didn't happen. Leaders at the highest level of government were at their command centers. International calls had been made. Communication equipment buzzed, keyboards clicked, agents listened to recording devices, teams of soldiers and agents waited silently in the desert for the 'Go' signal; plans were rapidly unfolding, dangerous plans.

13 NEPTUNE'S HAND

"AS FROM THE DEPTH OF THE SEA,

A MEMORY STRETCHED FORTH

REACHING THROUGH THE WAVES

LIKE A BREACHING BLUE WHALE…"

It had been a death-defying act even back then when she was just beginning her quest, just beginning to understand her true mission on this earth was to travel beyond socially sanctioned behavioral definitions. Social sanctions were for the faint of heart, conservatives oriented toward convention and approval. These terms did not describe Elisabeth Reinhardt. She was that rare human being for whom safety and self-gratification were not paramount. No, her priority was social justice. Her priority was fighting wrong-doing and abuses of power wherever and whenever they occurred. As the birds squabbled over seeds and feeder footing in the backyard of the Chicago safe house, her mind traveled back to the day she first met her.

Hadara Eiliat entered the office rather shyly. She sat beside the door, on the hard metal chair with its thin padding and pulled her thin ochre shawl around her shoulders; raising her expressive grey-green eyes she had said, "I am honored to meet you. It is right that I should have found you. It is 'beshert.'"

Naturally authentic, Elisabeth grinned and gently replied, "Whether it is 'beshert' or not remains to be seen… Then she said, "I gather it is not your anxiety that brings you here today."

Hadara smiled broadly and nodded agreement, "You are of course correct in both your statements. Allow me to further explain myself."

Those explanations took more than the allotted treatment hour and, in fact, went on for several sessions during which time a plan was outlined and bond was forged, a bond that had endured until this moment in time.

The appointment slip, filled out by the secretary at the Student Counseling Center had listed the woman's name, the date of call and described her presenting problem as 'anxiety and difficulty adjusting to the college.' Exactly how she was assigned to work with Elisabeth Reinhardt and not one of the other dozen therapists working at the Center was never known. It turned out that Hadara Eiliat had not come for help with anxiety or academic adjustment, but she was seeking help and psychotherapy for a more hidden problem. Hadara had hopes and dreams that were in conflict with her heritage and the customs of her family. She had fallen in love with a young Lebanese man whom she had known since childhood.

The story was identical to the one that Ari Ben Aviv had related to her during his rambling discourse in her office when she had been so distracted by the murderous men about to burst through her door that she barely took note of the content. She now remembered his words and how they dovetailed with the words that Hadara had spoken decades before. Those conflicts had been aired, issues, needs and confusions discussed and eventually decisions had been made. By the time Hadara was ready to return to her native Israel, she was prepared to deal with her dilemmas in an unusual, and not completely satisfying way. When their therapeutic work had been completed, more covert aspects of their relationship began. Memories of that time flashed by in milliseconds. She was squatting in a storage locker aboard a Mediterranean cruise ship, transporting foreign intelligence through customs, meeting with foreign operatives under her parents' noses.

It was her parents' fiftieth wedding anniversary and the Reinhardt family had traveled to Israel to celebrate. Their holiday which began in Jerusalem ended with an extended Mediterranean cruise. The ship was large and lovely filled with all the modern conveniences and activities of the day. The family met every night in the main dining hall to enjoy a scrumptious meal, seated around several tables elaborately appointed with Venetian Damask tablecloths, shining silver and beautiful floral arrangements, they chatted happily. It had been 4 years since Elisabeth had last seen Hadara. Since that time Elisabeth had received a few brief personal updates saying she was doing well. Two waitresses approached the Reinhardt's tables and began to distribute aromatic platters. Glancing up Elisabeth recognized a familiar face as the waitress placed a steaming plate of Sole Meuniere in front of her smiling father. An instant head shake was enough to signal Elisabeth into silence. On high alert she waited until Hadara positioned salmon with a lemon-caper yogurt sauce in front of her. A corner square of paper peeked from under the edge of her plate. Casually she extracted the paper, slipped it under her napkin then onto her lap. The note was written in Hadara's scrawling handwriting: "Need help. Meet 11PM, storage room 172A, lower level aft. Urgent! H"

What happened next was, as they say, history.

At precisely 11PM Elisabeth and her brother Manny slipped into the aft storage room armed with nothing but a flashlight and a Swiss Army knife. Hadara moved through the shadows like a cat. The cold war had just ended with the collapse of the Soviet Union, the US and Russia were at odds in the Middle East, with Russia supporting the Arab countries and the US supporting Israel. At that time the KGB was active in global 'spy games' vying with the CIA, MI 5 and the Mossad.

Hadara motioned them to follow her to a dark corner of the room and said "I am being watched. There are Russian agents onboard attempting to discredit U.S. Middle East policy by connecting the crisis in Kuwait to the Arab-Israeli conflict. We do not want this. US emissaries have been meeting with Saddam Hussein trying to bargain him into withdrawing from Kuwait. I have obtained documents that establish certain Russian officials undermining these efforts. It is urgent that you carry these documents to safety. The fate of the free world is in your hands." Glancing hurriedly around the darkened space, Hadara handed Elisabeth a small beaded evening bag, covered with green and gold sequins on a black tapestry background. The design on front was in the shape of a dragonfly and the straps were of braided beads. "It is sewn into the lining" she whispered as Elisabeth slipped it over her shoulder, "someone will contact you when you get home. Please be safe." With that she was gone.

Sipping her coffee, Elisabeth watched birds flit around the feeder in the Chicago safe house and reflected on how that moment had influenced her life choices. Less than a month after the cruise, Elisabeth and her siblings established their branch of Chevra Hatzollah which led to the connections that now presented themselves, connections she was only just beginning to realize. What she knew was that the two young people sitting in her interview rooms had long roots traceable to the young woman she had known, treated and spied for so many years ago. These two were, she knew, that woman's children. Why they were here and why the deceit?

With a deep sigh, she rose, turned from the beatific scene in the yard and returned to the house determined to unscramble the mysteries of the two new strangers and further the mystery of the men who had broken into and damaged her office.

14 HIDING IN PLAIN SIGHT

Saroyah listened carefully for the sound of movement, fabric rustling; footfalls soft in the desert sand. She sniffed the air for the scent of food. She sniffed the air for the scent of heat rising off the desert sand. It calmed her to know what time it was. Helped her feel like she knew what was going to happen. Feelings of panic had peaked and flooded so many times she thought she was getting used to them; feeling less and less each time as she felt further and further away from herself. Sometimes it felt like she was floating or maybe dreaming. Sometimes she thought she could hear singing; the songs that the servants in the kitchen would sing as they did their work. She wasn't sure if she really heard them or not. Maybe people here were singing those songs. Maybe it was just the wind. She was homesick. She loved to go and sit in the kitchen and talk with the staff, listen to the stories they told about the old days before the hatred grew so big. Sometimes she helped fix the food; she loved shelling the nuts for the baklava and chopping up cucumbers for salads.

She thought of her sisters and brother. She knew they would be worried about her. She thought they must miss her. Then she worried that they would be mad at her. Then she had another worry. She remembered the time they had played 'hide and seek' and Kalina had been gone for about 2 hours hiding in a shed. What if they thought she was just hiding somewhere and wasn't missing at all? What if they weren't looking for her? No, she told herself. She had been gone a long time; longer than a few hours, it was no longer a game. She counted the times the woman who fed her had come, it had been 8 times. That must mean that she'd been gone about 3 days. Her family would be worried by now and they would look for her.

She thought back to her last hours at home. She remembered playing with

Assi, her Abyssinian cat who only a day before had been pregnant, her belly large and bulging. But that day Saroyah saw that she looked emaciated and that must mean she had had her kittens. Excited she petted the cat as she ate her breakfast outside the kitchen where the cats were fed. She couldn't wait to see the newborn kittens. Happily she trailed after the cat as she raced to a remote part of the Olive Grove where the large animals were housed. There were barrels of grain and behind them tucked in a discarded sack a litter of newborn kittens were curled, pink and tiny. Saroyah, small for her age, wiggled into the spot and lay admiring them listening to her cat purr while her kittens nursed. So focused was she on the kittens she was unaware of the men gathered outside the animal pen just a few feet away. But as their voices grew more distinct she began to listen and in listening became increasingly alarmed. The men were not simply workers; they were not simply talking about work or their families. No, these men spoke with a fury. They were planning something and the thing they were planning was horrible. She heard them talk about bombings and killing people.

Peeking through a crack in the wooden wall she saw five men. One was familiar; he was a grandson of a servant. One man was well dressed with a trimmed beard and a fancy men's suit. Another man, older with a long grey beard was referred to as *The Great One*. That seemed odd to her. He didn't seem so 'great' to her. He must be some kind of an Ayatollah, she decided. Two other men looked like they were guards. They stood very straight and didn't talk or sit down. She wondered who they were and why they were here on her property? She wondered how they had gotten through the locked gates and who the well-dressed man in the fancy suit might be. She saw the guards carried many weapons. Frightened she decided she must run for help, she must tell her mother and father. This meeting was a terrible secret, a secret too big for her to carry all by herself.

She wiggled out of her hiding spot and that's when it happened. She bumped into a crate, spilling some feed. The guards heard her, saw her running and knew instantly she witnessed their meeting. They caught her within minutes. That was the last thing she remembered before waking up in this tent with these strangers.

Now lying bound and blindfolded, she feared she might never return home. In her fear-induced thoughts, she sometimes thought she heard her mother's voice calling to her; *"Saroyah Sagheerah"* she'd call, 'Saroyah, my little one' and then she'd imagine her mother hugging her close and telling her that she loved her. *Yes, Umm will come for me, Umm and Abba will come for me, I know that they will*, the child told herself over and over again. "They'll figure out where I am and rescue me. *Kahli* Hakim and *Khala* Hadara, they have some special powers. I have heard it whispered. They know many people and will find a way to save me. If these people want money, my parents will give it to them. We have many camels and many olive trees. *Allah* has blessed us with much wealth. I will pray that Umm and Abba find me soon. I trust in *Allah* to help my family to save me. Soon I'll be home again. Soon I'll be freed from here. Soon... Soon... Soon...," the child whispered to herself, as tears escaped her blindfolded eyes and crept down her cheeks.

Rafi listened in respectful silence as was appropriate for his age and status. Being an outsider, he was unfamiliar with the specific expectations that this group would have for him. He listened carefully observing every gesture, sound and movement. He watched those around him, trying to determine the unspoken rules that are present in every group. He needed to know these people and know them fast, who were trusted, who had *The Great One*'s ear; he watched those around him compete for the man's attention, noticed who was aligned with whom and who appeared distrustful or alienated from whom. His life and the success of this mission hinged on his knowing these things. Rafi had outstanding intuition and he needed to use all his powers of observation and sensitivity to deal with these people surrounding him. The people gathered here were from many different places including countries currently at war with each other. *The Sword of Justice* touted as the solution to the Middle East Crisis spanned political divides and geographical jurisdictions.

It seemed his handlers worked a miracle to get Rafi included in such a group. He was curious about what *The Great One* had been told that made him willing to open his tent to a stranger, one so young had no power or authority. Those assembled here were seasoned officials or government representatives. They were familiar with one another and with the ways of the group. He felt uneasy being here; and was convinced another agent should have been chosen for this assignment. His *handlers* had given him the assignment of collecting information about the group and its members. They needed to learn about *The Sword of Justice*, its principles and agenda, purpose, power and strength. They had hinted that *The Great One* would be responsive to him. Rafi wondered why they said that. He was told to present himself as an eager student. That, he was told would work. Listening in silence, he decided, was his best plan. He would seek out the *Great One* as his mentor. Every powerful man wants disciples who will worship and learn from him. He would present himself as a devoted follower of the Koran who was passionate about the needs of the Arab world. He would attach himself to the *Great One* as a devoted disciple and given that he had none of the complex alliances the other members did, he would speak with a fresh unencumbered voice. He would become his assistant, his helper, and his confidant. Rafi was not sure exactly how to accomplish this, but he was absolutely certain this was to become his role. He would carve out a relationship with *The Great One* that would guarantee him safety from the jackals who glowered around him. He would rely on his intuitive people skills and his oratorical skills. He had always had a way with words and could be an impassioned, persuasive speaker when motivated. His knowledge of the Arab world, its politics, language, customs and religion was excellent, thus he reassured himself. Relieved, he breathed deeply and relaxed taking in all that was being said and done, secure in the knowledge that he could play this role well and it would enable him to deliver what his handlers needed. Assuming of course that this actually was his assignment, he was prepared to provide it.

Ari and Samira were blurry and exhausted. Their conversations with their hosts had stretched into the early morning hours. The sun had come up and the neighborhood was coming to life as people drove off to work or school with a clatter of trash cans, slamming car doors and barking dogs. Samira was spooning sugar in hot coffee when Elizabeth entered the kitchen and sat down. Sammy, Stella and Gil looked over at her expectantly as she asked, "So how is your mother these days? It's been years since I last heard from her."

Ari and Samira smiled wryly surprised Elisabeth had figured it out so easily. "What gave us away?" Samira asked with a toss of her hair. "You did," Elisabeth said, "just like that," she indicated the swinging hair. "That, plus 'es beshert!' I remember how often your mother used to say that." Stella, Sammy and Gil exchanged glances and Samira explained "Mother knew Elisabeth years ago," and to Elisabeth, "She's well, thank you, she sends you her warmest regards."

"It seems," said Elisabeth, "that she has sent me her children as well. Tell me why didn't you just come out and tell us your mother was Hadara Eiliat to begin with? Why this charade?" Simon, listening from Chevra Hatzollah's base began a name search. "It would have taken no time, at all, and would have saved us hours of unnecessary consternation."

"We regret the deception," Samira responded, "it was necessary that we buy some time until we could be sure we could trust you." It was a half- truth but she thought she'd start there.

"What makes you think you can trust us now?" Gil asked calmly.

"We are not tied up," Ari said with a slight smile, "and you haven't shot us yet."

"It takes that little to earn your trust?" Stella shot back annoyed at the deception.

"In our world," Ari said "those are not small favors, plus," he nodded toward Elisabeth, "your sister did save my life earlier today."

"Right," Elisabeth responded, "about that, who were those thugs who wrecked my office and would have killed us both? And exactly why were they after you, and more importantly, why didn't you warn me outright that we are about to be attacked?"

"You must believe me," Ari looked into Elisabeth's eyes beseechingly, "I did not think these men would make a breach into your office, I assumed they would wait outside for my return. I did not think even thugs would break into the office of an American psychologist in the broad of daylight. I knew that I would be in danger when I left, but forgive me, I did not know they would come into the building chasing after me and endanger you. It was an error in my judgment, I regret to say. I am so very sorry, dear Doctor Reinhardt. I thought you would perhaps hide me somewhere. I was hoping for at least that much help. I did not know how effective your hiding would be. That big escape was a big surprise to me I did not expect."

Elisabeth recalled the young man's anxiety and demeanor as he sat in her office. She nodded and moved on, but she did have a lingering doubt. The only reason she could think of for that kind of set up was to force her to reveal her hidden exit. But how could he have known about that? And even if he did know it existed why would he want to find it? What would make her hidden exit important to this young Israeli spy? She tabled these questions and moved on.

"Ari, who were those men and why were they after you? They had a compelling reason because, you are right they wouldn't have taken such a huge risk otherwise."

With a sidewise glance at his sister, Ari began his tale. "As you may recall, my mother, she is with the Mossad. Samira and I are also with the Mossad."

Elizabeth nodded, "We figured as much" she said.

"Of course," Ari nodded "It is as you say, in our blood," another wry smile. "We," here he shrugged toward his sister, "are one of 5 two-people teams who are here in your country to locate people who are selling and transporting certain elements that are needed to make nuclear bombs. Weapons grade Uranium and Plutonium is being shipped along with certain antiquities through several museums here in the United States - one of them is in Chicago. Packaged inside of huge crates containing rare artifacts, these materials are being sent to museum warehouses; later they are repacked and shipped off as gifts from the gift shops or as museum items going abroad. Samira and I are tracing that pipeline. We located one of the, what you call 'men of the middle'."

Samira smiled and corrected "Middlemen."

Ari nodded and continued, "An employee at the Field museum, he is called Friedrich Müeller is one of them we think. Mr. Müeller works in the East European Rare Documents division of the museum. The men following me want the weapons for themselves.

Samira took over saying, "Müeller gave me a sample of these materials just yesterday. I told him I was a buyer working with a big deal Syrian weapons dealer, who is trying to access these materials to sell to an emerging terrorist organization operating across the Middle East. This big deal dealer has many contacts in the weapons trade including the Russian Mafia. My luncheon companion, Mr. Gil has the gift shop bag Müeller gave to me. He took it from me at the restaurant, isn't that right Mr. Gil?" She grinned at Gil.

On the other side of the table, Gil grinned back, "You are quite right, I gave it to Sammy to check out." Samira joined in, "The people following me outside the restaurant were your CIA, in the black van and I think the same group of what you called 'thugs' who were following Ari also were out there in the blue SUV. They are from Al Queda in Iraq. But we think there is a bigger worry. There is a new terrorist organization called *The Sword of Justice*. They are a newly formed violent group who are intent on world destruction. They are collecting weapons and military grade nuclear components from across the globe. They purport to be a religious group seeking justice in the name of *Allah*. We are not certain about their exact mission but know they are willing to demolish entire cities, if not countries, in the name of *Allah* and they will stop at nothing to destroy Israel."

Gil nodded then asked, "And the Camry? Who do you think was following you in that?"

"Now, that I do not know," Samira said shrugging. "He was clumsy, that is all I know. And *not* very good at his job, either. I nearly knocked him over in that restaurant, so he is not good at avoiding detection," she said with a dismissive shrug.

"And what, pray tell, do you plan to do with the material Mr. Müeller gave to you?" Elisabeth asked looking at Samira.

"I am going to test it," Ari answered, "I am a scientist, you see. My specialty is nuclear bombs, how to make them and how to destroy them. The latter would of course be my intent here. We have a lab set up and I'll test the materials there, it's not far from here in…."

Next to him, Samira stiffened slightly in her seat, signaling that Ari was saying way too much. Compliant, Ari shrugged, smiled his slightly crooked smile and bent his head over his coffee adding sugar as he stirred.

NANCY J. ALEXANDER

15 THE DOMINO EFFECT

Sol Abramson studied his laptop plugged into a 1500 watt transformer in the back of the van. Although the sun had been gone for hours, he was sweating from the heat. *What a G-d forsaken land this is*, he thought for the hundredth time and wished more than anything that he was sailing on the Mediterranean enjoying the cool breezes and the beautiful blue water. He loved the sea, the peaceful movement of his boat gently lulled by the blue waves; only sailing could calm him so completely. In front of him, the screen flashed urgently, yellow highlighted messages marched from side to side announcing that reinforcements would be arriving momentarily. Helicopters would be landing. The sleeping terrorists would be awakened within moments. The assault had to be instantaneous with no warning time for guns or instant messages to others of their group. They would be captured and flown to an air strip miles from here. There, they would be interrogated and their plan would be learned. These were dangerous people. Dangerous to his people.

A philosopher at heart, Sol Abramson appreciated the irony here. He knew that these people he viewed as dangerous terrorists saw him the same way that he saw them. Each group firmly believed it was right and had truth and justice on its side. Ironic and sad beyond all sadness, he reflected that perhaps there was no true truth, no truth above all truths. Truth was relative; relative to where one stood on the continuum of truths. Truth related to geography. Truth relative to one's relatives! Yes it all related to where one had been born, the family each person had been born into, the language they spoke, the bible they read, the G-d they worshipped. It boiled down to the relativity of relativity he thought. It all boiled down to this unsolvable puzzle, this international, cross-denominational rubix cube!

Breaking into his concentration Yosef whispered, "They're here." Sol, Yosef and Elias checked their weapons and crept toward the rendezvous spot. Five men heavily armed, dressed in flak jackets and night vision goggles were waiting. "It's a go in 3, 2, 1…Go, Go, Go…"

The assault on the little house was launched. Six minutes later the area was vacated. The opponents had been overpowered, the house thoroughly checked, all equipment packed and loaded. Five of the eight man team lifted off, their captives bound and drugged on the floor of the chopper. The confiscated computers and electronic devices were stowed in the rusty van with the rest of the team that crept toward the Israeli border. Riding in silence with guns at the ready, they watched for an ambush. Daylight would soon arrive and with it came new danger.

~~~~~~

Jamila sat face in her hands, the folds of her hijab falling loosely around her shoulders; her distress evident as she listened to her husband and her brothers strategizing. Hakim put his arm around her shoulders and said "Hadara phoned ten minutes ago and told us the Israeli's located the camp where Saroyah is being held. According to Mossad, she is safe and being well cared for. Hadara said she cannot make direct contact with her because she might inadvertently alert her captures."

What Hakim did not say was how anxious that conversation had made him. Something was wrong. Hadara's voice was unnaturally tense, her words guarded. He looked at his brother-in-law as he said "Hadara says Mossad has an undercover operative in place, one of their agents is embedded in the camp." Hadara didn't tell her husband that the embedded agent was Rafi and that rescuing Saroyah would place him at risk. Only she knew how precarious this situation was. Two lives hung in the balance; two families were perched on the brink of disaster. Hadara hung up the phone, her face pale, her hands frozen with fear she clicked out the words on her keyboard. 'Mission's a Go! Get child out!'

Tears flowed as Jamila pondered her child's fate. She could not understand a world in which children were hurt, used as leverage or bait. Why had they taken her child? She could not understand this. Why *her* child? Who was she that this had happened? What made her child important in this crazy world of hatred and death? The child had done nothing. She knew nothing, of that she was sure. She was convinced that the child was taken because of someone else, as leverage or punishment of some kind. She looked at her husband pacing nervously in front of the window. Gamil Ajram was a kind man, a good Muslim man, who worshipped as *Allah* had decreed. He had been a good husband to her and a good father to their children. All their years together he had done nothing to attract attention, nothing to bring them and their family into the center of world events. Now their child was a pawn, no, a domino in this complex series of events. It couldn't be the child's fault, that made no sense. People did this kind of thing for some reason. What connected her child to a group of villains? With fresh suspicion Jamila looked over at her husband. There was something different about him. She couldn't put her finger on it though. Something was off. He was upset, of course they all were, but there was something else. Something was making him jumpy, evasive even. He was avoiding her eyes. He was moving away from her. Something else was going on with him.

For the life of her she could not comprehend how this had happened. Her mind traveled back to her childhood, how the 'pact of five' had vowed to help solve the problems between their two countries. They were idealistic, filled with hope and passion. Their friend Yosef, her brother Hakim and his wife Hadara had indeed gone on to solve many of these international problems; her brother Abdullah too had traveled a righteous but different path. She was the only one of them who had not gone on to help solve world problems but all five of them still proclaimed loyalty to *The Olive Branch*. None had forgotten or betrayed their commitment. Through the years they had been working together in secret toward the betterment of their world and now this had happened.

Could it be an accident? A coincidence? No, she didn't believe it was a coincidence. No they were targeted for some reason. Something had happened that had pointed the finger of fate toward her, her child, her family. Jamila was a traditional Lebanese woman. She lived by the *Koran* and the principles of her people. She lived in her parents' home, cared for them as they aged, helped run the family business and raise her children all according to the scriptures and the rule of *Allah*. Jamila, along with her brothers, had been educated at the best schools both here and abroad. An avid reader, she kept informed about world politics, economics and governmental policies. She followed the news about her own government closely.

Lebanon is a democracy with both a Prime Minister who heads the Council of Ministers which holds Executive Power in the government and a President, who is elected by the Parliament. For the past 12 years, her brother Hakim, held an important governmental job and had served as 'public policy advisor' to three Prime Ministers. His job often involved clandestine travel to attend top-secret meetings across the globe on behalf of the Prime Minister.

Frowning, she looked across at her brother and wondered if this could be laid at his feet. He was important. He was in the spotlight, not her and not her little Saroyah. She wondered if he had done something to enrage the Prime Minister so much he would order this kidnapping? And this was no ordinary kidnapping. There had been no ransom demand, no contact. If the kidnappers didn't want money but wanted something else they didn't seem to want it from her and Gamil or did they? Her eyes wandered over to her restless husband. She frowned. He too worked for the government. He hobnobbed with important people every day. He worked with important secrets involving money and deals. How could she be sure he wasn't involved in this somehow? Would he tell her if he were? She stared at him through tear weary eyes and felt sick.

A betrayal loomed somewhere and it had to be connected to this family, who else would even know about her little girl? As she listened to the discussion in the background, Jamila was overrun with feelings she had never before experienced; anger, paranoia, suspiciousness, even vindictiveness. She didn't know who to trust. She didn't know who had betrayed her, but as she looked around her living room, she felt certain it was someone close by. Jamila had always been a peaceful woman, never raising a hand in anger, rarely raising her voice above a conversational tone, but now she felt a murderous rage. She could kill whoever had caused harm to her child. She didn't know who that was, but when she found out, nothing would stop her from seeking revenge.

The Great One listened carefully as the plan was outlined. Part of him, the *Holy Man*, was grieved at the use of a child in this complex manipulation they were about to launch. That part of him abhorred the plan but there was another part of *The Great One* that was pragmatic and militant, a strategist, a master manipulator of organizations and countries. He had insisted that the child not be harmed, but also realized that this child had it in her power to bring down their newly founded organization. While no one knew exactly what she had heard, it was clear she had in her power to reveal enough of their plan to lead the authorities to their doorstep. He was assured repeatedly that the child was being well cared for and that she would not be harmed at least until he ordered them to kill her. Yet he could see that alive she provided the needed leverage. Her family and some of her relatives had considerable power and influence in their countries not to mention money. Money and power were crucial to a movement such as his. Money permitted them to complete their mission, *Allah's* mission, to achieve world dominance. In his mind he saw that the future of his grand scheme could boil down to one little girl.

How ironic that a child could be the key to success or failure. It was portentous that the one time he broke his own rule never to hold meetings outside of his own campsite this happened. It must be a message from *Allah,* he thought. He had ignored the advice of his advisors and broken with his established principles.

He wondered momentarily if he had been betrayed and the child had been planted to spy on him but he dismissed these thoughts as ludicrous and extreme. That did not make sense... a little girl as a pawn in some international intrigue? It had been some horrible accident and now he was responsible for the distress of a child. More than that he was responsible for her life and perhaps, he reflected she was responsible for his!

The Great One believed he was a moral man, fighting a Holy War against infidels and sinners and here a young Lebanese child, innocent by all measures, had been caught up in his secret web. Yes it distressed him. It put him in conflict with his values. He tried to say 'things happened for a reason' and that 'one had to concentrate on the greater good' but still his heart was heavy. He was distressed by these developments and as if that weren't enough, there had been rumors that there was an infiltrator in his camp. They were just whispers but they worried him. He reasoned it was a risk one took if multitudes of followers were to be allowed to join the movement. Inevitably there would be infiltrators from other camps and groups.

Many new people had come to join *The Sword of Justice.* They were the rank and file members living in communities throughout the Arab world. They did the daily work of spreading the word, gathering information, attending rallies, committing acts of terror against the enemy. They carried out the daily work of the organization, they were the worker bees. There were those who did the daily or menial work in the camp, providing the necessities, clothing, food and safety and lastly there was the 'special circle.' The important advisors, who thought, decided and led the group. They were the ones who gathered around him now sipping mint tea and talking to each other as he listened. Sitting in a meditative position, head bowed, eyes closed he concentrated on their words and his thoughts. He prided himself on being an excellent judge of character. He believed he could tell a man's character by the tone of his voice, his breathing and his eyes. Since the meeting started he concentrated on those things, especially on those things he could hear. He listened to their conversation as an eavesdropper, not taking part, not weighing the value or meaning of their words, but listening to the heartbeat behind their words.

There were men from across the Arab world chosen for many different reasons, sent by governments to find out about this new group, and then there were the former followers of Osama Bin Laden, perhaps looking for new leadership now that their leader was dead. He knew these men had many allegiances and were not completely loyal to him or his goals. He listened to them and put them into categories; those he could trust, those he could not trust and those he was unsure about. Two of the men now sitting in his inner circle would be put to death, he was sure of that, one would be sent away because was not trustworthy enough. But one had captured his interest. He was drawn to this one, a new follower, a young one. Him, he liked. The young man seemed eager and honest. He was smart with fresh, open ideas. He sensed no fear in him, this Rafi Tahan. He was...*The Great One* thought, the perfect apprentice. He was the prize. He would choose this young one and teach him everything. He would hold him close and groom him to become the next leader of *The Sword of Justice*; Rafi Tahan was charismatic with a voice of billowing silk. His newest disciple would become *The Chosen*.

16 LANDINGS HAPPY AND OTHERWISE

Blinding sun shone through the windows as El Al's Boeing 747 taxied along the tarmac toward the Tel Aviv terminal, engines droned loudly. Upon hearing the pilot's voice asking passengers "to remain seated with their seatbelts safely fastened until the airplane had come to a complete stop," there was rustling of excitement as people readied for departure. The long line inched through the terminal toward Customs where one by one weary travelers presented passports and answered questions. Entering a small booth, she offered the guard her passport and official papers indicating that she was a consultant with the STARNET Program in Chicago and had traveled to Israel in order to evaluate children who sought admission to their program. The security guard, who spoke fluent English, had many questions, among which was where she intended to stay and for how long? He was also interested in whether she knew anyone currently living in Israel and if she intended to visit with them during this trip. She told him she had reservations at the Shalom Hotel in Tel Aviv and hoped to stay about 10 days. With a small smile said she had no friends in Israel, but hoped to make some. The guard smiled back and returned her paperwork welcomed her to Israel and gestured her to move forward.

Loudspeakers cycled through announcements in Hebrew, English, Arabic, Spanish, and French as people retrieved their luggage, greeted their recipients and departed Ben Gurion Airport in various vehicles headed into the sweltering heat. She had just settled into her luxurious room when a sharp knock heralded the arrival of a large bouquet of flowers and a basket of fruit. The greeting card said "Welcome to the Promised Land." The card was unsigned. After typing a brief text message in her smartphone, Elisabeth Reinhardt settled down to wait.

The CH 47 whop whopped through the pitch-black desert sky heading toward the US Naval Air Station in Souda Bay, Crete. Known for its reconnaissance missions and air refueling support for Operations Desert Shield, Desert Storm and Iraqi Freedom, Souda Bay was the perfect destination for their undercover mission. It was a safe distance from heavily infiltrated terrorist locations, not that any place was completely safe, but here they would be able to get the supplies and support they needed to complete their tasks. Sol Abramson checked his watch for the fifth time and spoke into his headset to the pilots. He muttered acknowledgment of their response and leaned against the chopper wall to wait.

Duqaq Boulos and four other men lay tied and gagged on the vibrating metal floor surrounded by their Israeli captors, guns trained on their sleeping heads. They had been given enough drugs to keep them sedated for several hours, at least until the chopper landed and the men were confined to their cells. The Israelis were feeling good about their mission. They had been able to invade the little 'safe house' in Syria and capture the men without a single shot being fired. Every move had been pre-planned and well executed. They owed their success in large part to Mossad's Emergency Readiness Division. Division teams were trained to launch capture or rescue missions at a moment's notice. The Division was split into 6 units and each unit had three teams. Each team had 10 members with distinct jobs. They manned computers and made all necessary arrangements with foreign and domestic government agencies, managed equipment like helicopters and firearms while still others managed the flow of information, internal communications and allocated or relocated people as needed, and then there were those who went into the field, risking life and limb to do the Division's work. This team had been lucky enough to have two of their top agents involved. Yosef Yadin, legendary under-cover man who'd worked with Mossad his whole adult life had been responsible for locating and identifying Duqaq Boulos. He urged Sol Abramson, one of the Unit leaders, who only went into the field if the project warranted it, to personally participate in this extraction.

They had little hard data on Duqaq Boulos, but this mission was urgently important. Mossad researchers were burning the midnight oil trying to learn as much about him as possible. He appeared well connected with the newly forming *Sword of Justice*, about which they had precious little information. They knew, however, from what they observed at the small café near Arbel Cliffs and from overheard conversation at the little Syrian house, that this man was connected to a large looming plot against the state of Israel and the United States of America. Of that there was no doubt. Sol ran through his various options for obtaining information from these captives. He was inclined to take it slow however there were other pressures in the field that made speed a priority. But Sol Abramson was a man of principles. He'd make sure the prisoners were not harmed, that they were given food and water. He would approach them in a reasonable manner and wait until his researchers provided him with information about these men before he began to interrogate them. His preference was to approach his prisoners in a cooperative manner and hope they would reciprocate. There were ways if they didn't.

~~~~~~

Lying flat on their stomachs at the base of the Mount Lebanon mountain range, Abdullah and his assistant Shamir stared through their long range binoculars scanning the expanse before them. They had been camped in the dry semi-desert of the northern Beqaa Valley since they received the report three days ago. The report had come from an undercover Mossad group who had followed two men from a small marketplace near the Arbel Cliffs. Abdullah wondered if Yosef had been involved in this mission. His old friend was one of the best undercover guys Mossad had and if Yosef was involved, his brother Hakim's wife Hadara could not be far behind. Those two were peas in a pod! Surprising, he thought for the 100th time that they had not been the ones to marry. He thought back to those days when his brother Hakim would sneak off with Hadara and not come back for hours. Those two were so much in love. Abdullah was pleased to think how their little pack of five was still working together if only in this removed coincidental way.

The man who had been captured was named Muhammad Chehab. He had traveled with his nephew Imad to meet with a third man, a Syrian named Boulos who was trying to buy weapons grade uranium from them. A deal had apparently not been reached and the three split up. These two had been followed to Tiberius where the Israeli's captured them and they revealed that a shipment of high quality uranium was expected to be flown in and dropped in the Beqaa Valley. It was expected to arrive at any moment now. Packed in UNICEF bags containing food and medical supplies the nuclear material would parachute to earth. Because the Israeli's could not retrieve the materials without breaching agreements with Lebanon, the Lebanese Army's special Intelligence unit had been notified through covert channels and a secret mission had been planned. They immediately agreed to meet the shipment because they didn't want rogue weapons dealers dragging nuclear materials around their country.

It was rumored that a mercenary group out of Russia and Azerbaijan was supplying weapons to the Middle East and had arranged for a small fixed-wing aircraft to deliver it parcels to this isolated place and when it arrived Abdullah would be waiting. He would stop this nuclear poison from getting into the hands of a militant extremist group. He would thwart this Russian-Azerbaijani group from further destroying the Middle East. Abdullah was a patient man with good vision. He understood the implications of nuclear weapons in the Middle East and he understood how it could play out. He had lived here his whole life, listening to his father converse sometimes in secret, about such matters. He more than his siblings understood the role his father had played working to create peace in his beloved Lebanon. As a child Abdullah talked with the other members of *The Olive Branch pact* about the worries of their country and throughout his career in Lebanese Army Intelligence he carried out his father's commitments to peace in the Middle East. Abdullah did not fully understand the reasons that their little group formed such a strong bond and had remained committed to each other for so long, but he knew that they had. He was as fully committed to bringing peace to the Middle East as he had been when he was a child. Now as he lay here on the desert floor he knew that he was doing the right thing for his country and for the 'pact.'

As he waited he worried about his young niece. He wondered where she was and why she had been taken. He wondered what had happened since he had last spoken with his sister. Deep cover prohibited use of cell phones but he felt guilty for being out of touch when his sister needed him so much. But orders were orders. He did not know where the enemy was hiding. He didn't know who else was here, waiting, hidden amidst the shadows and rocks, crouched near the thin soil with its low-lying shrubs? He and Shamir saw no one and heard nothing. Not the sound of a match being struck, not the sound of boot scraping against rock. Lebanon has a complex geography ranging from its lush Mediterranean coastline to its snow-covered mountainous slopes. Some of its areas are densely populated, but this part of the country is sparse in plant and animal life.

The mere fact that this site was chosen was enough to convince Abdullah that the plan was devised by someone who knew his country well. Here there were no hungry people rushing to collect parachuted food or UNICEF medical supplies. Here there were snakes, lizards and invisible men. In all the country, this was the best place for hiding. People could move in and out of this area virtually undetected. Those who would be here to meet the plane would be able to move in, grab the stuff, and move out with no one the wiser. They would be focused and move with intent. That's what Abdullah was counting on. He expected them to be so focused they would not notice two men with guns creeping up behind them. They would want only one thing from the sacks and boxes that would be falling to earth. But they would not take time to sort through packages. They would grab everything and stuff it into some vehicle or load it onto camels and be off as fast as possible. Those waiting to pay them were impatient to make their bombs. Somewhere in this great expanse were terrorists, enemies to his people and enemies to the world waiting to take the next step in their war. They could not be allowed to take that step. They had to be stopped.

17 PAST TO PRESENT

They were learning more about Herr Friedrich Müeller of the Chicago Field Museum. Manny Reinhardt, their computer maven, easily determined that Herr Müeller had initially worked for the Gutenberg Museum in Mainz, Germany for 12 years; from there he went to the Museum of Fine Arts in Lyon, France before coming to the Field Museum in Chicago 4 years ago. His area of expertise was "Rare Documents from the late 18th and 19th centuries…" Locating personal information about Herr Müeller, however, was proving a bit difficult. The Müeller family had owned a small vineyard in the Rhine Valley where young Friedrich, surrounded by ancient castles rising out of the mists, became engrossed in the history of his country, which led him to an interest in historical documents. Aside from late life professional development, his early story was more elusive. It appeared that young Friedrich participated in the HJ, or the Hitler-Jugend, the second oldest paramilitary organization of the Nazi Party, developed for male youths from age 14 – 18. The HJ were viewed as future Aryan Supermen and were programmed to hate all other peoples as having impure bloodlines. The group emphasized physical and military achievements over academic studies but loyalty to the Third Reich was overarching.

Manny speculated that Friedrich's interest in historic documents grew in value as Hitler grew in power. Ancient documents were used and misused by the Third Reich to reinforce propaganda and public indoctrination. So over time, Friedrich's position within the government grew in importance. It was known that Herr Müeller's father, Heinz served in the German army, but his rank and branch of the service remained a mystery. The absence of information about the family rang an alarm bell for Manny. Having lived through Hitler's Germany the Reinhardt family suffered untold traumas and losses at the hand of that regime, they were sensitized to the cloud of secrecy surrounding the Nazis and those involved with their activities. Were it, he reasoned, to be the case that the Müellers were Nazi sympathizers or active members of the Nazi party; it would make sense that Herr Friedrich Müeller's lifetime hatred of the Jews would influence both political beliefs and subversive activities.

Six months before, Mossad learned that museums across the globe were being used to smuggle components to be used for weapons of mass destruction. Several such middlemen had been identified and those researching museum personnel compiled a list of likely suspects. Ari and Samira had come to America as part of the team organized to track down these terrorist supporters. Presenting herself as Samira Tariq, a Syrian working with others seeking to purchase weapons grade Uranium, she contacted Müeller subsequently obtaining a sample of the product for testing. Ari, a scientist by training, was to test the sample packed in the gift shop bag Samira was given in the warehouse.

Today, she planned to meet the Field Museum's *Rare Document Specialist* at a French café where she would wine and dine him ostensibly to continue discussing the terms of the sale, giving the team time to do their work. T-Max needed ample time to break into Müeller's office and search for information. Pablo and Ari dressed as drivers for the TRANSWORLD SHIPPING COMPANY maneuvered their 16-wheeler, bearing crates containing AFRICAN ARTIFACTS, into the warehouse loading dock. Carefully, unloaded their precious cargo loaned to the Museum by the Isidor Kahane Collection housed in Zurich. This exceptional collection of culturally significant art was to be put on display for the first time in the United States. As this was an extremely rare collection, those delivering it required ample time to carefully unload and relocate their crates. Under the guise of situating their cargo they searched for weapons grade materials.

Since Müeller was an important link to other brokers in this terrorist network, it was essential that he be fully investigated. Samira intent on keeping her guest occupied, noted that he seemed increasingly ill at ease. She wondered what accounted for his attitude change from the robust, confident man she met just a few days ago. This man was nervous, his eyes roamed the room checking out every diner; his voice squeaked with tension. Something had spooked this guy and she didn't know what. Worried he would bolt, she ramped up the charm, engaging him in a meandering discussion that touched on various topics; she kept her eye on a pulsing vein in the corner of his forehead. When she talked about menu options the vein was nearly still, when she mentioned Lebanon, that vein started to pulse more rapidly. She wondered if news of the desert drop or Boulos' capture had reached him. She dropped the word 'Mossad' into the conversation as a passing comment about world security and the man's vein started to throb. Herr Müeller was definitely not enjoying this elegant French cuisine. He nearly jumped out of his seat every time the door opened. Intuitively she shifted her strategy to a more primitive one. Smiling coquettishly, she inquired about whether there might be a Frau Müeller or perhaps a girlfriend. She hinted that perhaps she would be interested in the position. Flirting shamelessly, she distracted him from his open-door obsession, re-directing his attention instead to her unbuttoned blouse as she murmured sweet nothings and plied him with steaming mouthfuls of bouillabaisse.

Pablo and Ari slowly unloaded their crates of African statues and masks and using pocket-sized detection gear wandered around the lower floor of the Museum until they were able to locate 3 containers with uranium and plutonium. Within forty minutes, those containers, replaced with look-alikes labeled AFRICAN ARTIFACTS, were fastened securely in the back of the truck which slowly pulled away from the warehouse.

With surveillance equipment installed, hard drives duplicated, contacts identified and warehouse inventories copied, T-Max strolled out of the Museum texting an innocuous message from 'Verizon Wireless' that said "Your bill is now available online..."

18 SHOP TILL YOU DROP

The advertisement read 'Visit Adina Textiles, near the entrance to Tel Aviv's famous Merkaz'. Adina's prided itself on having the finest exotic textiles in Israel and was located right next door to The Treasure, a delightful café featuring "mouthwatering Middle Eastern specialties at very reasonable prices." Wisps of artfully highlighted hair escaped her wide brimmed hat as Elisabeth Reinhardt strolled along the neat paving stones of Nahalat Biryamin. With her cloth shoulder bag slung over her shoulder and dark sunglasses blocking out more than the Mediterranean sun, she inspected colorful merchandise displayed on slanted tables or hanging in store fronts. Bicycles, motor scooters and motorcycles wove through the sidewalks and streets. A meandering crowd of mixed ethnicities carried packages and backpacks, pushed strollers or walked arm in arm; some of the men wore yarmulkes or traditional Orthodox black coats, some women wore headscarves, still others wore traditional Middle Eastern garb. It was a bustling commercial area, jam-packed and noisy. Cars, mostly compacts, crowded the streets; trucks blocked traffic as they unloaded their wares or collected trash. Horns honked, people talked, music blared from buildings or balconies.

Casually Elisabeth selected various items; a teal shawl glimmering with sequins, two hand-painted silk scarves, a paisley backpack and a pair of sparkly gold sandals; an ordinary tourist shopping in an open marketplace, as natural as can be. She could almost forget what she was doing in this marketplace as she shopped surrounded by exotic sights, sounds and smells. She could almost enjoy it. As she approached the outdoor section of the café, she heard laughter coming from a table next to the building. Turning she saw three faces, two she knew well, one she had not seen in years; it was older yes, but it was the same face; a strong featured face striking even in this moment of dress-down spontaneity. Hadara Eiliat sat with Elisabeth's twin brothers sharing platters of hummus and pita chatting like the old friends they weren't. She was delighted to see Hadara looking so healthy and confident. She and Hadara had shared a strong therapeutic bond during those early years and Elisabeth hoped that the work they'd done had served her well. She was about to approach their table when she saw Sammy's head shake and his hand jerk up in a cautionary signal. Following his gaze she saw someone kneeling on the sidewalk, as she turned to walk away the air exploded. Noise, smoke and chaos filled the marketplace as panicked people ran for shelter. Screams filled the air. Elisabeth felt strong hands propelling her forward. Dizzy, she felt something warm running down her face and allowed herself to be moved through space. Minutes expanded into timelessness, her eyes stopped focusing, her ears stopped working and all she heard was a deathly silence as her ears stopped transmitting. She knew the man was talking to her, she could feel his lips close to her ear, but she heard nothing and didn't care. By the time she was tossed into the back of a car she had lost track of time and place. The only thing she knew as she floated into unconsciousness was that she was in the backseat of a car and she was not alone.

~~~~~~

Hadara Eiliat lay quietly on the floor. She sensed men moving around her, but they did not approach her. Unmoving she listened hoping to find out more about her situation before they realized she was conscious. She didn't know who they were and didn't know if she was safe or being held captive. She thought back to just before the explosion. She was sitting with Elisabeth's twin brothers. They had come to her Menara home and filled her in on the details to date. They had traveled to the marketplace where they planned to meet with others of their group. She had seen Elisabeth. It was wonderful to catch a glimpse of her, the woman who had helped her so long ago was the one to whom she had sent Ari. ... she hoped Elisabeth was alright, unharmed by the bombing.

She remembered how the world turned upside down; booming sounds of a bomb going off, sirens blaring, buildings crumbling, glass shattering, walls collapsing, people screaming and running. She and Sammy had run toward the street; Simon had run somewhere else. Hadara had tripped over a bicycle, fallen. Sammy pulled her up and off they ran through the screaming crowd. She didn't know if she had been the target of the attack or if it had been random, one of those bomb-in-vest terrorists obeying the Jihadist directive to die so that others might die. Was this Al Qaeda or Hamas? Somehow it felt personal, not random, and if it was personal she may have been the target. She hoped that her friends had not been hurt in the attack.

She hoped that she was not now in terrorist hands. If she were, it would take all her strength of body and mind to survive it. Surreptitiously, she checked to see if her wristwatch was in place. It contained a GPS locator and if she still had it on that meant Mossad could locate her. Her head was facing away so she couldn't see her wrist. Slowly she rotated her hand slightly lowering her wrist to the floor until she could feel the clasp against the wooden floorboard. It was there, she was relieved. Remaining motionless, she concentrated on listening to the different voices and accents. It seemed most of them were in an adjoining room but sensed one person, perhaps her guard, remained nearby. From a distance she heard Hebrew, English, and Lebanese accents. At first the voices were a blur fading into each other. As she listened, she felt a rising sense of alarm. Something did not make sense. One of the voices should not be here, it did not belong in this scene.

She felt her guard moving, he was sitting behind her. A rookie mistake. She risked opening her eyes a fraction, a small window was across the room. She gazed through the dirt streaked glass. She saw only darkness, a beautiful starry sky stretched into forever; no lights, no buildings, nothing, just expansive darkness and a lovely sky. Seeing no landmarks, she reasoned she had been taken out into the desert far from civilization. The cinderblock room was large and empty. From the angle of the window and the smell of gasoline, she concluded she was on the second floor of a warehouse or a garage. Fully conscious now, her mind raced through possibilities. The bombing in the marketplace was the beginning of a larger plan that involved her and her children and, her little niece and her husband and his family, perhaps even the Reinhardts. She didn't know why she had been captured or by whom. Snippets of phrases drifted in and out. "...up to you..." "How ... expect me to...?" "...she knows you... she trusts you..." "... what will happen ..." "there isn't much time..." "...her life..." "please, I beg..." "...not an option..." "...get it from her..." They were arguing, several men with different accents. She thought they were talking about her. What bothered her most was that voice, the one that did not belong; something was terribly wrong.

19 WITH THE DAYLIGHT COMES THE DAWN

Saroyah opened her eyes when she heard rustling around her. Still blindfolded, she had become accustomed to the different sounds of the times of day. She heard men starting their morning prayers, she heard the women preparing the food for the day and she heard the camels beginning to stir. She was aware of her own body rhythms now, her need for food, her need to use what passed as a bathroom in this desert camp. She knew that if she called out someone would come to help her, but she wanted to wait a bit longer to see if she could learn more, perhaps she would hear something revealing when they thought she was still sleeping. She recalled the man from last night, the one with the educated voice. He sounded like a teacher. He acted polite but there was a frightening seriousness about him. His accent sounded Syrian but not the ordinary kind. It was different, sort of fancy. The man asked her lots of questions about what she had overheard at the Olive Grove. He wanted to know what she remembered, if she had seen any of the men, could describe what they looked like. She had not known what to say. She was always taught to tell the truth but she was frightened. She knew that she knew too much and if she told him what she remembered she knew it would be bad for her. The truth was, she remembered everything, their words, their names, their faces. The truth would get her killed, but lying was a sin. No, she decided there were no safe answers, so she curled up and remained silent.

Musnah's grandson Imad had been to her home many times through the years but this time he was different. He acted mean and talked about bombs and attacking people. Someone called *The Great One* was there and someone else whom they treated as if he was very important. Two important men had been there meeting at the Olive Grove. Over and over again the man with the 'teacher's voice' asked her questions and over and over again she said "I don't know. I was just petting my cat, she had kittens." She worried they would hurt her if she didn't answer their questions, but then she reasoned that she was a child and her family was important so perhaps they would not hurt her. Perhaps they would ask her family for money and then she could go free.

Saroyah no longer cried. She had adjusted to her life as a blindfolded prisoner. She had stopped thinking about her family and how much she missed them. She focused instead on the present. The sounds around her, the questions she was being asked. These things were important. For the moment, she did not fear death. She believed they would take care of her, feed her and not harm her, at least for the moment. She knew she was there because of the men she saw. She knew the grandson but she could describe the others and she understood that seeing them was a problem. They had not wanted to be seen. Ever! By anyone! That meeting was to have been a secret. She expected them to kill her but they hadn't done that. When that hadn't happened she realized that for some reason she was important to them, as long as she was important to them they would not hurt her.

As she lay in silence, she felt rather than heard a presence. She inclined her head in the direction of the presence and waited. She wanted to call out, but she didn't want to call the guards in case this was a helper of some kind. She sniffed and caught a different scent; something like fresh air and camels. She sniffed again and it moved closer to her. It whispered something to her, something in Hebrew. Her captors didn't know she spoke Hebrew. She was Lebanese after all and lived her whole live as a Lebanese child. She had relatives, however, who were from Israel and when they were together both languages were spoken, so Saroyah became fluent in Hebrew. She instantly knew that the person in the tent was here to free her. In the barest of whispers she asked, "Higata l'azor li?" (have you come to help me?) The whispered answer… "Cain."

~~~~~~

Duqaq Boulos felt the chill from the concrete floor seep into his bound body as he lay in the bare prison cell. He heard faint noises, metal against metal, boots tramping, men's voices; foul odors permeated the space around him, but he could see nothing. The space around him was pitch black. He moved his face against the surface, no blindfold, blinking his eyes several times he thought he could see the barest hint of light across the room opposite where he lay. That relieved him; for a horrible moment he feared for his eyes, but now he thought he saw some light. He had no memory of what happened in that little house near the Syrian DMZ. One minute he was sleeping on a small cot with his guards nearby and the next moment he was here, wherever *here* was. He tried to remember more details, but there were none. He had been captured somehow, safe in his homeland, safe in a small 'safe house' and now he was here. There was no doubt in his mind that this was the Israelis doing and, perhaps, the Americans as well.

Working as an arms dealer had its risks. For himself, he had no stake in this fight, he was a mercenary. Yes, he was a Syrian and yes, he loved *Allah*, or thought he did, but, that wasn't his primary motivation. His primary motivation was money. The blood and the gore, well that was an added bonus. This new organization *The Sword of Justice* was desperate to act on its hatred. It was new and had to prove itself to its hopeful followers fast or it would lose them. In the Middle East there were many extremist groups. Some presented more extreme religious rhetoric while others presented more geo-political positions - all used terrorist tactics - preaching violence in the name of *Allah*. Groups like Al-Qaeda, Hezbollah and Hamas and now this new group. These movements were large and well-funded; there was a multitude of fringe groups working together or separately in every Arab nation and every group was eager to buy what he had to sell. And he, Boulos, had lots to sell. It was interesting, he thought, that they had so much money to spend on their wars and no money for the impoverished ragged people they claim to be fighting for. It made no sense to him. Why not take that money and use it for the people, for food and housing, for schools and factories? He wondered such things, but laughed at himself. Who was he to question it? It was better for him, after all, if they wanted to spend all their money on guns and bombs. That was his business, wasn't it? He never found out who was funding these death-oriented movements but concluded those who funded the movements were pretty rich. The *Sword of Justice* had offered him $500,000 American just to locate some weapons grade materials. He was to get another $500,000 when he delivered it. That was a lot of money and Duquq Boulos thought he was just the man for the job.

He had been working with a group of mercenaries operating around the Caspian Sea when he got wind of this newly formed group and decided to approach them. He thought he had been very clever when he left his old partners. He knew they would be brutal if they ever found him. The Russians and Azerbaijanis were no joke! He felt a sudden pang of anxiety as he worried that perhaps they were his captors. That thought was terrifying. He preferred to think it was the Israeli's or the Americans, their torture techniques would be more humane. As he prepared himself for what was about to happen, he wondered how he should 'play' it, should he present himself as an innocent in a bad circumstance or perhaps as a follower of the holy man or as the mercenary he was. In the end, he reasoned it might not matter. The end was, after all, the end.

~~~~~~

Ari Ben Aviv woke up face down on a metal laboratory table staring into a clear glass beaker refracting the sun's rays into a splendid sprawling rainbow. He had been testing the sample Friedrich Müeller gave to Samira, when he'd dozed off. Ari, who received a degree in Chemical and Nuclear Engineering from the Imperial College of London, found his skills were in high demand with Aman- Israeli military intelligence, Shin Bet- Israeli internal security and with Mossad- responsible for worldwide intelligence and counterterrorism. He was glad to serve his country in any way that he could. Raised as he was with discussions of political intrigue, undercover work, religion and international problems, Ari was well versed in all aspects of The Middle East. He knew the governments, cultures and languages of every country throughout the region and during his years with Mossad had, along with his siblings, worked undercover in most of the world's hot spots. He and his twin had great fun during those missions because they could do what no one else could do. They could telecommunicate. In many ways, they shared the same mind. As identical twins, they created a unique language understood only by the two of them. They could share thoughts and ideas without uttering a single sound. In time, they learned to master this skill and even at a distance could communicate. He smiled to himself as he remembered some of their adventures, which is how he thought of them now. Pausing he let his mind drift to connect with his twin far away and undercover.

In his mind, he saw Rafi sitting with a group of men discussing the philosophy of their organization. He felt Rafi's anxiety and knew he was in danger from those around him. The men listening to Rafi seemed awe-struck. Rafi had always had a gift for words, expressing himself with eloquence and passion. He had 'right side' brain power, intuitive and emotional, while Ari was master of the 'left side' being analytical and objective. He knew the pressure his twin was under to complete the mission but the fear of being discovered was torturous. Concentrating intently he sent his brother a message… it was one only he could send. "Tell me your worries and I will give you the answer." Within minutes he felt Rafi relax … and Ari went to work.

Several hours later, Ari looked across the room at Samira asleep on pillows scattered on the floor. Her black hair strewn around her in a mass of tangles, she looked like a fairy-tale princess. Pale sunlight was poking through the metal shutters of Bio-Tech which had been closed for repairs for the past 3 months. Ari and Samira had taken up occupancy of one small wing. They and the others assigned to this mission learned that several arms dealers had connections with American museums. One such connection was with a man called Muhammad Chehab and his nephew Imad. Recently captured they revealed that an arms shipment was to be air-dropped into the Beqaa Valley. The other connection was as yet unidentified dealer who had ties with a new terrorist group calling itself *The Sword of Justice*, a fast growing group with a radical message of violence and a policy of 'non-negotiation' whose goal was to erase Israel off the face of the earth along with the entire industrialized world.

Woven through this network of arms dealers a rumor floated that a well-placed Lebanese official was behind these operations. While that official had not been identified, the rumor mongers hinted that he was not a member of this new group but was manipulating its funds for political gain. Reportedly this man, high up in Lebanese government, privately scoffed at the tenants of this new group which was committed to the idea that only Arab nations should occupy the earth.

Ari knew that shutting down this nuclear supply line was critical to the fate of the entire Western world. He also knew that his twin was smack dab in the middle of that powder keg.

NANCY J. ALEXANDER

20 LOCATION, LOCATION, LOCATION

They heard it long before they saw it; a low droning sound beyond the cirrus clouds, humming like a gigantic mosquito. Squinting they watched it appear, a tiny speck growing larger and louder. They moved slowly keeping pace with the image, squatting low as they inched forward, watching for other watchers, watching for an ambush. The two had worked together for many years they moved in sync, one looking right the other left. One moving forwards the other waiting, rifle at the ready. They were heavily armed, with long and short guns, knives and hand grenades, they were prepared for anything. In the early daylight, they could see the cliffs around them see the flat desert floor stretching in all directions. Nothing moved. They stopped. This was not right. There should be others waiting for the shipment. They knew from the captured uncle and nephew that others were to retrieve these packages way too important to be left lying around the desert waiting for some wandering Bedouins to stumble across them. They saw no one. They would need to wait until the crates were dropped. Wait to see who ran forward to pick them up and cart them away. Being first was too dangerous. They would stay put, flat against the desert floor, camouflaged and motionless like a blunt-nosed viper.

Shamir saw them first inching forward on their stomachs, just the merest flash of sunlight on metal. There were four of them clustered in an outcropping of the mountain range to their left. With the slightest gesture, he alerted Abdullah to their presence. Slowly they scooted sideways so they were facing their enemy. The small plane was nearly over head now; they could see the cargo hold opening, someone was near the opening. Within minutes parachutes carrying shrink-wrapped crates would tumble out of the plane. Abdullah pressed a few buttons on his phone sending pictures of the plane and its clearly visible tail number to headquarters. The plane would be tracked until it landed wherever it was going. The pilot would be arrested and questioned. Whatever else happened today, their efforts would not be in vain. Finding the locus of control was the main goal. They had to find out who loaded that plane and who hired the pilot. They had to stop them before the entire world became a nuclear wasteland.

~~~~~~

Elisabeth woke to find herself in her hotel room. All was as she had left it and she was alone. Puzzled, she rose scanning the space. She had a blinding headache. Reaching up, she felt her head had been bandaged and the side of her face was scraped and bruised. Random memories clattered across her mind like balls on a pool table. She stood, aching and unsteady and crossed the room to look for her phone. There was a text message from Gil, "For your complimentary coffee, call room service." Smiling wanly, she did. Within minutes there was a knock on the door. Wearing a bell boy's uniform, Gil entered with a loaded tray which he placed on the table near the window. Pulling out a chair for her, he grinned and poured her a steaming cup. "I was wondering when you'd grace us with your presence," he said.

"I see you finally found a job worthy of your skills!" Elisabeth retorted eying his outfit. He chuckled as she accepted the cup and sat down. "Any aspirin?" she asked. "On the tray, mi 'lady," he bowed gallantly and she reached for the pills. "Tell me what happened. Where is everybody?" she asked "I can't remember anything."

"There was a bomb in the marketplace. We think Hadara was the object, but we're not positive."

"Is she okay?" Elisabeth asked in alarm. "What about the twins?"

Gil sighed and shook his head slightly, "We don't know exactly. "No one is reported killed but several were injured. Simon and Sammy were with Hadara..." he said putting his hand up to stop her further alarm, "They are fine and will be here momentarily," he continued to nod as Elisabeth relaxed slightly, "At this point we think she was kidnapped by a small terrorist cell."

Elisabeth gasped, "How are we going to get her out of there?"

But Gil interrupted, "Hang on a minute, I got a coded message this morning from Yosef according to him, Mossad is tracking her. For the moment, we're waiting to get word on what's going on there."

"Do they know where she's being kept?" Elisabeth asked.

"Mossad has a good idea; they have eyes on the ground. We're waiting to hear more."

Two quick knocks on the door indicated that the twins had arrived. Simon and Sammy, slightly battered and bruised, entered the room to hugs and back slaps. "You haven't lived until you survived your first *Hamas* bombing," Sammy quipped.

"Not funny, Sam," Elisabeth frowned, "People were hurt and buildings destroyed and businesses ruined…"

"I know, Sis, just trying to keep it light," Sammy defended himself.

They all sat around the table, shared an informal breakfast and reviewed their experiences. "You signaled to me at that café Sammy, what did you see?" Elisabeth asked.

"There was a man behind you, he had been pacing back and forth and casting glances at our table. He looked distraught and when he began to kneel I knew we were in trouble. I got Hadara as far as I could, she tripped over a bike and then we were running toward the street outside the marketplace when three men surrounded us, grabbed her and hit me over the head. The last thing I remember is running feet kept tripping over me until finally someone dragged me to the side of the road where I stayed until I could get up."

Elisabeth sighed and patted his hand and said, "Oh my *G-d* so it's really the Middle East…" turning to Simon she asked, "And what about you?"

Simon said, "I was right there with you, sis, in the backseat of the car this mad man was driving."

"So you got us both out of there?" Elisabeth said turning to Gil.

"That's why I get the big bucks, right? I'm your go-to guy!" Gil said with a flourish.

"Okay, so we're all good and funny. Mossad is working on getting Hadara back. What do you hear from home?" Elisabeth asked.

"Manny checked in a few hours ago. They are busy tracing and tracking. Everyone is safe, except perhaps our new German friend. He has a few surprises waiting for him," Sammy said.

"Yosef told us there would be no rescue attempt for Hadara at this point but they had the situation under control. We are charged with responsibility of making a plan to get Saroyah and her family out of the country. Mossad thinks the child was kidnapped by *The Sword of Justice* to pressure someone close to the Faysal family. They know of no other reason why a child would be taken but if that's the case why have there been no demands? Why else would a terrorist group kidnap a kid?" Gil asked. "There's something fishy about the kidnapping cause it doesn't add up."

"Let me think about that," Elisabeth said.

"While you're thinking, we need to find out more about what we're dealing with. I've been researching the main groups we might be dealing with" Simon said as he clicked away on his laptop and pulled up reports on the main fundamental Islamic groups.

Let's start with *Hamas,* he said:

"Hamas believes in the absolute authority of Islam in all aspects of life, and that resisting the "enemy" (i.e. Israel) is a religious duty required of all Muslims. Hamas' charter states that their goal is to "raise the banner of *Allah* over every inch of Palestine." Hamas does not recognize Israel, and believes that all of Israel, including the West Bank and Gaza Strip, rightfully belongs to the Palestinian people. While Hamas has offered that it will "settle" for the West Bank and Gaza in exchange for peace with Israel, many Israelis are skeptical that any true peace can be achieved with Hamas. In fact, Hamas never talks of "peace," but only of a "hudna"—a temporary truce—leading many in Israel to believe that should their government accept such an offer, it would only be a matter of time before Hamas set out to realize its original goal and occupy all of Israel.

"Hamas believes based on religious writings, that the land of Israel belongs to them, and as the rightful occupiers, they are legitimate in their attacks on the Israeli "occupiers." They believe the land is non-negotiable, and Hamas' charter calls loudly and clearly for the destruction of the Israeli state and an establishment of an Islamist government in its place. Hamas has claimed over and over that there can be no peaceful negotiations with Israel, only jihad ("holy war"). Hamas has said that their beliefs are not anti-Semitic (anti-Jewish), just anti-Zionist, but a number of their statements, such as denial of the Holocaust, smacks of the contrary."

Elisabeth asked, "Does it seem like Hamas could be behind the bombing in the marketplace and Hadara's kidnapping?"

"Not sure," Simon answered as he continued to type. "Okay, listen up you guys, here's the scoop on Al-Qaeda:

"Al-Qaeda is a global militant Islamist organization founded by Osama bin Laden; it is both a multinational, stateless army and a radical Sunni Muslim movement calling for global Jihad and a strict interpretation of sharia law. Characteristic techniques employed by al-Qaeda include suicide attacks and simultaneous bombings of different targets. Activities ascribed to it may involve members of the movement, who have taken a pledge of loyalty to Osama bin Laden, or the much more numerous "al-Qaeda-linked" individuals who have undergone training in one of its camps in Afghanistan, Pakistan, Iraq or Sudan, but who have not taken any pledge. Al-Qaeda ideologues envision a complete break from all foreign influences in Muslim countries. Among the beliefs ascribed to Al-Qaeda members is the conviction that a Christian–Jewish alliance is conspiring to destroy Islam. Jihadists believe that the killing of civilians is religiously sanctioned, and also opposes man-made laws, and wants to replace them with a strict form of sharia law. Al-Qaeda has fragmented since bin Laden's death into a variety of regional movements that have little connection with one another."

"What about Hezbollah?" Sammy asked, "Where are they in all of this? We need to differentiate these groups so we can understand more about how *The Sword of Justice* fits in.

"Hezbollah whose name means "The Party of God" derives its ideological inspiration from Iran and gets moral and financial assistance from both Iran and Syria. Formed in 1982 in response to Israel's occupation of southern Lebanon, its stated objectives include the establishment of a Shiite theocracy in Lebanon, the destruction of Israel, and the elimination of Western influences from the Middle East. It has professionalized its military capabilities and also joined Lebanon's political process and enmeshed itself into the social fabric of Lebanese society. Its base is in Lebanon's Shiite-dominated areas, including parts of Beirut, southern Lebanon and the Beqaa Valley, where it ran training camps that instructed members of Hezbollah and other terrorist organizations how to conduct assassinations, kidnappings, suicide bombings, and guerilla warfare. Hezbollah operates in Europe, North and South America, East Asia, and other parts of the

Middle East, and it is believed to be responsible for a number of other high profile terrorist attacks."

"Sounds like Hezbollah might be involved in this," Gil commented, "They are a political party in Lebanon. If there's a hidden high level government official involved in funding nuclear arms, maybe they are part of the kidnapping as well."

"Hadara didn't seem to think so," Sammy answered.

Simon picking up from his twin added, "She is convinced that this *Sword of Justice* did the kidnapping."

"Well Hezbollah is rooted in Lebanese society, do we know if there is a connection between the two groups? It seems they are competing for the same followers," Gil answered.

"Hadara seemed cautious about something," Sammy continued, "there was something odd about what she said, I thought," turning to Simon he added, "did you pick up on that too?"

"Yep," Simon nodded, "I didn't think it was about Saroyah, but there was some other personal reaction to that group, something she didn't want to talk about."

"Yes! Exactly!" Sammy exclaimed, "I was about to ask her about it but the bomb went off and all hell broke loose!"

Elisabeth nodded, "There's more going on here than we know. This is not a random or even a usual kidnapping, there are several possible terrorist groups that could be involved or contributing to the confusion and there are issues with the family we've remained in the dark about. I'd think there would have to be some insiders involved. The Olive Grove is a walled compound people can't just stroll in and out of there."

Gil, silent up to that point, said, "Let's concentrate on what we can do to get the mother and kids out of the country after Saroyah is out of wherever she is. That's what we're doing here after all, right?" Gil wanted to get organized. "Let's get clear about what we'll need. 1. We'll need passports and airline tickets, 2. We'll need cover and cover stories that make sense. 3. We need to get Jamila and her children out of Lebanon and into Israel so we all can leave together. 4. We'll need a plan to get all of them through the country and the airport if they are being chased. 5. Starnet will have to be onboard with all this and we'll need the paperwork to back it up." Turning to Elisabeth he asked, "Does Jamila know you or has Hadara told her about you?"

"I'm not sure," Elisabeth said turning to her brothers, "do either of you know if Jamila is aware of us being here to help?"

"Yes," Simon said, "I had a brief phone conversation with her when we first met Hadara. She was too distraught to talk much, but I think she'll know who I am if I call her."

"Good," Gil said, "let's make a list of what she'll need to do and give her a call. We are at a bit of a disadvantage, strangers in a strange land with two kidnap victims to worry about, one of whom is our main contact…"

"Right," Elisabeth interrupted, "I'll get with the family and get the facts we'll need for forged passports and the Chicago team can take it from there."

"Okay, back to Middle East facts" Simon said reading from his screen, *"The Sword of Justice* shares some views with the other groups, but is more extreme. They don't concern themselves with Palestine or specifics about property lines or land allocation, their focus is global and it involves the annihilation of every country that is not specifically populated by Arabs. World destruction is their goal.

"Their 'final solution' is nuclear! Because they are *Allah's* chosen people, they believe this nuclear war will not affect them, their people or their land. They believe that *Allah* will create an *invisible shield* like an enormous tent and will hold it over his chosen people and they will be protected from the nuclear fallout that will blacken the earth obliterating all life, plant and animal. They proclaim thirty days after their nuclear holocaust, *Allah* will produce a great wind which will cause the earth to spin on its axis faster than the speed of light; as the earth spins all nuclear debris will fly off the surface of the planet into outer space where it will dissolve into millions of tiny harmless particles.

"They believe that everything will disappear: buildings, highways, all remains of human, plant and animal life. All evidence of Western civilization will be obliterated, all technology eliminated, every aspect of present life and culture will evaporate and disappear spinning off into the infinite blackness. Only oceans, rivers, streams, mountains, forests and flatlands will remain. The earth will be cleared and as fresh as the day it was first created. They believe then *Allah's* people will migrate across the earth, grow and multiply and create a whole new world in *Allah's* name devoted to his teachings."

The group was silent absorbing the sobering sentiments. "So, you see" Simon continued "it's not just the promise of a blissful afterlife that impels the followers of *The Sword of Justice* it's annihilation of the world as we know it and the creation of a whole new world."

Sammy ashen-faced added, "All human races and religions will be destroyed. Every aspect of global culture will be destroyed. Arabs alone will survive the nuclear holocaust! *Allah* will be the only *G-d*! Islam the only religion! All enemies destroyed. Nothing left to fight about! Middle East problem solved!"

21 WHAT HANGS IN THE BALANCE?

Rafi smiled and nodded at the men around him. When he spoke, words glided off his tongue. He spoke with conviction and intensity. He spoke of the destruction of Israel, world destruction and world peace. Of the Arab people being supreme and finding themselves free with a whole new world to build and explore. He spoke of *Allah* and his supreme power protecting his chosen ones and of the beauty to come when Islam rules the world. As he spoke, his voice took on a hypnotic quality mesmerizing those around him. *The Leader* was transfixed; all the more convinced that Rafi Tahan was sent to him by *Allah*. His youth and religious fervor would bring more converts into his organization than any other single effort. Rafi Tahan would become the voice of *The Sword of Justice*. He would become the face of *The Sword of Justice!* Even he, *The Great One*, was not so eloquent; with all his ideas he could not turn heads the way this young man did. *Yes*, he smiled to himself as he put the hookah to his lips and inhaled the filtered smoke deeply, *this young man is Allah's gift to me*, he leaned back with satisfaction and closed his eyes.

Rafi's stomach churned with anxiety, but he smiled and charmed the listeners with his velvet voice and his youthful enthusiasm. He knew his cover was good for now, but worried that any minute something would come unraveled. He raised his hands to his eyes, worried as always that his contact lenses would slip and his grey-green eyes would be revealed. What a nightmare that would be! He pushed the thought away as the group talked on. Bowing his head, he entered a meditative state and in the clearing found Ari's spirit. The twins always knew when the other was in trouble. Now Rafi felt Ari's support. Ari sensed what was happening here, he knew that the situation was precarious. Rafi and Ari were like two sides of the same coin, linked inexplicably to one another mentally and emotionally. He remembered how as small boys they could beat anyone at any game. Their telepathy was extraordinary. Without words or gestures they knew what the other knew, thought what the other one thought and felt what the other one felt. They knew what cards were in their twin's hand, which way the twin was going to hit a ball, move a chess piece or feint while fencing.

He wished more than anything that this mission was over and short of that wished that Ari was here with him, helping him. These people were truly frightening. They were ruthless and absolutely convinced of their absolute rightness.

He wished that his little cousin Saroyah had not been brought into this. That complicated things for him. He wanted her out of this camp not just because of her own safety but also because she compromised his safety. What if she somehow came in contact with him and recognized him? How could he expect a frightened child to remain silent? To act as if they were strangers?! Wouldn't it be more likely that she'd run to him? Call out to him? And what if he saw her? Could he remain unemotional? What if they harmed her in his presence? He could never remain silent and expressionless then, that would be impossible and would certainly mean instant death to both of them. Moshe had gotten a message to him during the night that he was being redeployed to get the child out of the camp. That left Rafi without back up. Rafi didn't like it but feeling Ari's psychic presence helped.

More relaxed now, he thought about what he needed to do next. He wanted to look around the camp, get more familiar with the layout. He didn't know the protocol for these *Sword* meetings. They had prayed, they had eaten, they had talked, they had listened and they had partaken of the *hookah* and now *The Leader* appeared to be asleep and the others seemed to want Rafi to talk more with them. He didn't know what else to talk about. He decided it was respectful and safer to be a listener so he returned to the role of junior member and inquired as to the ideas and opinions of his elders, hoping it would buy him time to figure out what to do next. He listened politely as the men droned on and wondered if it would be rude or impertinent to leave. Perhaps a bathroom break would be permissible. As the noon hour approached and the sun grew hotter, Rafi grew tired, restless and uncomfortable. Quietly, he excused himself and went in search of a bathroom, or whatever passed for one in a desert encampment. He hoped he could learn something of strategic importance about the layout of the camp like where his cousin was being held and what happened to the poor man he had seen being dragged off earlier. He hated to think of what had happened to that man during these past hours. As anxiety flooded his body, he fervently wished this mission were over, but he knew he couldn't leave yet. He had a mission to fulfill and could not leave until he learned what *The Sword of Justice* was planning.

～～～～～～～～～～～～～～～～～～～～～～～～～～～～～～～～～～

They stood looking down at her talking to each other. She was awake and she thought they knew it, but they had not touched her or spoken to her. They had made no effort to interrogate her, if indeed that was what they planned to do. Their purpose was unclear. Who they represented was unclear. Why they were holding her was unclear. They moved away speaking in hushed tones. She was pondering possibilities when she heard it again, faintly from across the other room, 'the voice' speaking in low tones. It was him, she knew it was. The man was urging something, asking for something. His tone stopped just short of pleading. She knew what they wanted had something to do with her but she didn't know how whatever they wanted involved him.

Gamil Ajram knelt down next to her and touched her shoulder. "Hadara?" he asked "Can you hear me? Are you alright?"

Slowly she roused, turned toward him, blinked and answered drowsily, "Yes, husband of my husband's sister, I am alright. What happened? Why have you brought me here? Who are all these people?"

"I have not brought you here," he said, "these men say they found you. I came to help identify you. They tell me they are going to help us get Saroyah back. Can you sit up now?" he asked, helping Hadara sit up. He handed her a cup of water and asked again, "Are you alright? Were you hurt in the explosion?"

Hadara shook her head, but was puzzled by his question. If indeed they meant to help her from the explosion why had they not laid her on a cot or covered her with a blanket? They hadn't examined her, given her medical care, tended to her wounds, offered her water or food. *So no!* thought Hadara, *Something was not right here; something did not make sense. His explanation did not make sense. Why bring him here to identify her when others could do that? And how did he know that they could help with Saroyah?*

"Who are all these people Gamil?" She said again, "Please, help me up and introduce me to your friends," she said. What she didn't say, but what she was thinking was, *What exactly are YOU doing here Gamil? You work for the Lebanese Department of Agriculture not some underground spy service? How did you get connected with these people?*

Gamil helped her to her feet and together they moved to a rough wooden table. She sat stiffly on a bench, drank the water they offered and looked at the odd collection of men gathered around her. "Let me introduce myself Ma'am," said a tall blond man in his 40's wearing a starched tan uniform. Extending his hand, he said "I am Lt. Walter Ross, US Navy." Taking his hand, she introduced herself. The next man to speak was young, with a few days growth on his cheeks; he wore wrinkled desert khakis and badly needed a bath.

He extended his hand, "Mikhail Gendel, ma'am, I'm a freelancer working undercover for Interpol," he said, but his twinkling eyes conveyed a secret message.

As Hadara took his hand she saw a tiny Hebrew letter inked on the loose skin between his thumb and forefinger. It was Yosef's sign. Calmer now, her eyes indicated 'message received.' The third man was older, an Arab possibly Moroccan. He spoke softly, kept his hands folded in his dark green Djellaba. He did not offer his hand, (a devout Muslim would not shake hands with an unrelated woman) but his voice was cultured and very polite.

"How do you do, ma'am, I am called Husain Hatolla," he said with a small bow "I am here to represent a certain committee of the United Nations. It is called the 'Middle East Resolutions Committee.' The committee is working to stop incidents which could spark a series of events ending in global destruction. My nation does not wish to have great segments of the earth destroyed, so we wish to stop this particular organization which is called by the name *The Sword of Justice*. For that reason," he paused and gestured to those around the room, "we have come together. We are as you see an uncommon group but we believe that we share a common goal and you, Ma'am are part of that goal, I believe."

Uncommon group indeed, Hadara thought, and wondered for the hundreth time what was going on.

22 CONNECTING THE DOTS

The HP LaserJet shot out page after page, reports from the Mass Spectrometer that had finally completed its analysis of the samples Ari Ben Aviv processed most of the night. It was as he feared. Every sample tested proved positive for weapons grade Uranium 233, Uranium 235 or Plutonium 239. Deuterium and Tritium also present. Standing at the printer, Ari read through the reports, face ashen. Samira rose and walked over to him, putting an arm around his shoulder she read along with him. Together they uttered a brief prayer in Hebrew "Dear *G-d* please keep us safe and guide our footsteps through the dark days ahead."

"Come, let us sit for a moment and gather our thoughts," Samira said ushering her brother to the makeshift seating arrangement across the room.

T-Max and Pablo entered the room as they were consolidating their information; seeing their expressions T-Max said, "Okay, so it's bad, right? What's the plan?"

"Communication is first on our list." Samira said, "We need to contact Mossad and the other four agent groups in the US who are also exploring this angle and let them know what we found. They have not progressed as far as we have yet, so we'll take the lead on pipeline tracing from our end."

"Do we need to have some personal conversations with our dear friend Herr Friedrich Müeller?" T-Max asked, with a devilish grin.

"I believe that is wise to do, yes" Ari answered, "and let us be doing that as soon as it is possible." He glanced at his sister who nodded her assent.

"Shall I bring him back here or take him to our country home?" Pablo asked.

"Oh, I think some fresh country air might do our German friend some good, he's been looking a bit haggard." Samira drawled in her imitation Southern accent, "We'll finish up here and meet you there this afternoon."

"You want me to do the catch and escort by myself?" T-Max grinned "or should I take this slacker along with me for company?" He bumped Pablo playfully.

"Can't do a little grab and drag by yourself?" Pablo shot back as they walked out of the room together, "Need me to show you how it's done, is that it?"

Samira grinned at Ari, "quite a pair those two," she commented.

Ari nodded checking his cell phone. "Our brother Mr. Manny has done some analysis of the information that was removed from Herr Müeller's museum office. He says that the flash drive has much information on it. That is most good to hear, do you not agree Samira?" Ari asked. "He also told to me that sisters Stella and Reina are working on the extraction plan. Processing passports and developing cover stories and making arrangements for them once they get here. That information will be forwarded to Jerusalem by courier tomorrow, taken to the US Embassy. Gil and the good doctor Elisabeth are making arrangements for the pick-up and delivery.

"Alright let us complete our list first and then we'll divide up our tasks," Samira suggested. They spent the next 40 minutes writing down all the things that needed to be done that morning then divided up the tasks. Aside from contacting the other 4 museum teams who were making sure the nuclear materials would never reach their destinations and identifying the chains of command in this pipeline, there were other pressing issues: rescuing their mother and little cousin. Samira had gotten word earlier that Mossad had agents in place at both locations, but so far it was presumed they were both still captive. Rafi's situation was unverified, but Ari assured her he was alright and gave her a little run-down of his impressions. And then there was the issue of their missing father! It seems no one had received a message from or about their father for days. His job, working as a Lebanese attaché representing the Prime Minister, seemed to take him everywhere and no one was quite sure what he did, but Hakim Faysal made it a daily habit to contact each of them. They sighed and exchanged a few worried comments, both of them feeling conflicted. Too many things were happening with too many members of their family all of them of critical, life-threatening importance and they felt powerless to help. They were continents away…. worlds apart.

~~~~~~

Duqaq Boulos opened his bloodshot eyes at the sound of heavy boots approaching. Through the night he had heard the sounds of his guards screaming and protesting their innocence, saying they knew nothing about any operation. This morning, however, the sounds had changed. Now, there was conversation. The screams had ended. Now, they would be given food and water, there would be comfort. The men had broken. He was not surprised, not really. He knew they were not committed to the cause. They were low level mercenaries and he knew they did not know much. They would tell what they knew, but what help could a few pieces of a huge puzzle be? No, he knew that the pressure would be on him. He was the lynchpin. He had been the one the Russians contacted. He had been brokering their nuclear arms deals in the Middle East for years. He knew about the deep pockets in countries like Syria and Iran. That's where the 'big bucks' were. Hell those guys had as many 'bucks' as gallons of oil!

He knew his captors would want to hear all about the Russians and their Azerbaijani friends who had a corner of the market in the field of weapons production and export. Duqaq Boulos had been in on this action with them for years. Only recently had he gone off on his own little independent venture and struck a deal with *The Sword of Justice* people. That's where he planned to earn <u>his</u> 'big bucks' as the Americans would say. This was going to be his last big deal, his retirement package!

He listened to the boots outside his cell and knew they would be expecting more from him than from the others. Soon, he knew it would be his turn. He had been alone since being captured, ignored. No one had come to speak to him or ask him anything. This meant one thing and one thing only. They were collecting information from the others, who seeing nothing to gain from silence, had talked. When they approached him they would know he was the head of this operation, he was the boss and they would come after him with all the force and tricks they had. They would cause him pain; make him feel helpless. They were ruthless barbarians, that he knew to be true, but perhaps he thought, I don't need to suffer. Why not just tell these *G-d-less* sinners what they want to know. Why should I suffer for *The Sword of Justice*? Why should I suffer for those mercenary Russians and Azerbaijanis? I am not one of them after all I am just a business man and business men make deals, right?

Then he thought:

Perhaps if I tell them everything I know they will let me go. I can cut some kind of deal: information for freedom. Yes, that's it. I will go free, perhaps I can promise to forgo my weapons-trade business. I was going to do that anyway but I can let them think I'm doing it for them, as part of my deal with them.

Boulos relaxed momentarily comforted by the thought that he could go free then he thought, *No, I am being a fool. They'll never let me go. They'll never free me from this hellhole. They'll send me to Gitmo or whatever they call that place across the ocean where they hold the faithful followers of Islam.*

He wrestled irritably with his thoughts. *I have one main decision to make. Will I make them kill me or will I kill myself. I will not allow myself to be tortured. I will die before I tell them one single word about my work or my employers. I owe silence to those who paid me. Hell, no I don't. I owe them nothing, they are using me to do their dirty work. I can make a deal with these fools and they'll set me free.*

His thoughts went on in this vein until the door opened and Sol Abramson walked in.

Abramson was older, grey-haired and muscular, and he moved with the stance of a military officer and the grace of a dancer. In his dark eyes were untold stories of horror and a deep wisdom. This was a man to be reckoned with, a serious soldier, a leader, a man whom others trusted, this was readily apparent from the way the men around him treated him, with respect and loyalty. Sol Abramson was a curious culmination of many influences. A Rhodes Scholar, having attained a Doctorate in Philosophy and Theology from Oxford University; he graduated from Tel Aviv's most prestigious Yeshiva having studied Torah and Talmud there from the age of four. During his lifetime, he became an ordained Rabbi, served in the IDF (Israeli army) attained the rank of Lt First Class and then joined Mossad and became a member of the *Kidon*. He stayed with Mossad rising through the ranks.

Now, he stood looking down at his prisoner saying nothing. He stood there staring for a long time as Duqaq stared up at him. Then he turned on heel and walked toward the door. On his way out the door, he issued two commands: "Untie him. Give him food and water."

Moshe Aaron was crouched down in the supply tent hiding behind burlap sacks of dry goods. He could smell the mint and figs in small baskets near him. He was nearly faint from hunger and thirst, but moving risked detection, so he stayed where he was and waited. He had made contact with the child. She now knew that people were here to help her and would be less panicky. He hoped that her change in attitude would not be detected by her captors. He assumed that they would assume she felt safer because she had not been hurt. No doubt they had seen similar changes in attitude with other prisoners. Through his ear piece he heard his teammates as they spread out around the periphery of the camp. They had a skimpy plan that involved grabbing the girl in the middle of the night and running off with her into the dry, dark desert. It was kind of reckless. Plain and unsophisticated, but that was the best they had come up with. No guns, no revolt, no bloodshed. They would cut a hole in the back of her tent, grab the kid and run. What they would do if someone saw them, they weren't yet sure. What they would do if someone shot at them? Well they weren't sure about that, either. Yep, Moshe had to admit. It was a hellava plan!

They agreed to do nothing with Rafi, just leave him in place and 'please *G-d*' he would be safe until Moshe could reconnect with him the following day, assuming he lived through the night. Once the girl was safe, they would continue their original mission, *G-d* willing.

23 GOOD LUCK, BAD LUCK

"So," Hadara said, "exactly who are you people? I'm getting a funny feeling that there is more here than meets the eye, or in this case, the ear." She smiled at her little wordplay. Looking around the room at her 'captors/allies' she asked, "Who here wants to tell me the truth? Two gold stars to the first person who raises his hand!" She was feeling stronger now, more like her old self, a no nonsense leader in one of the best covert organizations in the world. The men exchanged glances and remained silent. "Okay, guys, that's enough fun and games, tell me what's really going on. Gamil? Mr. Lieutenant Sir? Mikhail, whose working for who knows who, Mr. United Nations representative? Anyone?" A hunched old man in dirty coveralls entered with a tray of food and some bottles of water. Everyone sat down at the table and helped themselves.

Walter Ross was the first to answer, "Some of us were unsure of you, ma'am, of your loyalties. It was rumored that Hezbollah was about to grab you. Then it was rumored that you were working with them and you had set off that bomb in the marketplace yesterday and so we brought you here."

Hadara thought, *that explains why they treated me like a prisoner but didn't hurt me. They didn't know what to make of me. Okay, she thought, that makes some sense.*

"We found your brother-in-law and brought him here to identify you. He vouched for you. We also ran your fingerprints and determined you are who you claim to be, but we were unsure of, well, who you are working for."

Hadara nodded as if this made sense. *They 'found' my brother-in-law? 'Found' him?? Really? Exactly how had that happened? He just happened to be strolling down the street and they happened to ask if he was my brother-in-law then commandeered his help with my identification? That's a non-starter Lt Ross!*

This was not the first time she had been questioned. It was not the first time her loyalties had been brought into question. She had, after all, lived most of her life under a cloud of mystery. *Who could blame them for their questions? That part seems reasonable, sort of, I'll hear them out,* she thought. "Okay, let's say I'm with you so far," she said, "Let's move on … who are you guys supposed to be exactly and who are you working for? The U.S.? The UN? Hamas? Lebanon? Who?"

"Well, probably, between us you've got everything covered," the Lieutenant smiled coolly. We're sort of a joint task force, informal, of course, but you get the idea."

"No, I don't actually." Hadara said, "Who exactly pulled this informal task force together? Who are you really working for? Interpol? Terrorists? Whose lame brained idea was it to capture and hold me here?" She defied them to answer.

"Mine," said a familiar voice, as Yosef walked through the doorway. As he walked forward, Hadara rose and they hugged. "Are you okay?" he asked briefly examining the cut on her forehead.

"I'm fine, just trying to get some answers from these guys, they are surprisingly evasive."

"What they told you was essentially right," Yosef said with an emphasis on 'essentially.' There was a question about who bombed that marketplace and since you're high profile there were some who thought you were the target and some who thought you were in cahoots with the bomber. And you, my friend are much too valuable a commodity to let go of! I wanted you safely out of the way so I sent in Mikhail to watch over you and support this group's efforts to get you and hold you till I got here. Mikhail pulled Gamil into it so he could keep an eye on *him* too!" Yosef said with an 'I'm just kidding' wink to Gamil.

Some freelance Moroccans were working the gig and suspected you were a bad guy, that's sort of how Mr. Hatolla got here," at this the Arab gave a slight bow and added "Once they realized who they had captured, they contacted me, I contacted the UN and they asked me to stay and make sure you came to no harm."

"Well, for a covert operative it seems a lot of people know who I am!" Hadara commented wryly.

"Well, Ma'am" Husain Hatolla interrupted, "with all due respect, your capture was not just about you, as important as you may be it is also about Middle East peace. My country, Morocco and I would add the United Nations advocates finding a peaceful resolution to our mutual problems." he added with an edge.

"Of course," Hadara replied seriously. She then looked at her brother-in-law and asked, "What about you Gamil? How exactly was it you got involved with all this. And please don't insult my intelligence by saying they found you so you could identify me? That makes no sense. How do you even know these people?"

Gamil looked uncomfortable, "I contacted Yosef to see about leads to Saroyah's kidnapping. I figure someone knows more than they are saying and thought if I hung around with people coming to this from different angles I'd pick something up."

"What?" Hadara nearly exploded. "You or someone thinks a bombing in an Israeli marketplace is connecting with Saroyah's kidnapping in Lebanon? Who is the 'we' who thinks 'all this is linked?' What kind of Kool-Aid are you people drinking? Gamil, are you actually suggesting I had something to do with her kidnapping? Me?!" Hadara was outraged.

"Hadara, you must not take it personally, Jamila is frantic; we had to check out every lead. We have no idea why she was taken, but she is a child. It is us, the adults around her who have connections, who are important. She is only a tool, a way to maneuver somebody. Those who took our child took her because of us, one of us. It has to be that! Doesn't it?" he exclaimed. "People don't kidnap a little girl because of the child herself! What would make her valuable to them? We didn't think you kidnapped her, but rather those who did take her may have done so to manipulate you!"

"And what... you were following me... you and your 'merry band of men'?" Hadara shot back at him.

"Hadara yes, we were following you, just to see if some others were following you, going to approach you about Saroyah." Gamil answered.

"Who, Gamil? Who was following me?" Hadara's days as an interrogator were coming in handy.

"Some of the men from the Olive Grove," Gamil said adding reluctantly, "And we saw you with two strange men. And there were other people following you as well. One a very tough looking American, that's why we called in the U.S. Navy to liaison with us."

"You make it sound like the whole operation was your idea. How was it you got in charge of this operation? This is way out of your skill set I might add. Plus it doesn't in the slightest explain your connection to our UN Select Committee Member here. You guys seriously need to get your story straight. I could drive an armored tank through the holes in it." Hadara hissed.

"Please Hadara, do not be angry with me," Gamil pleaded, "I was desperate."

Hadara sighed. It was clear she was not getting the truth and was not about to get it any time soon. He spoke about emotion but not fact.

Changing the subject she asked, "Okay Gamil, say you're worried and upset, I give you that but how could you plan something like this? You had to have help. Who was helping you? And, by the way where is my husband in all of this? Is he involved in this marketplace tailing, bombing, kidnapping deal?" Hadara demanded. She was becoming more emotional than she expected. It surprised her. Perhaps she was getting too old for this work. *Perhaps*, she thought that *hit on my head messed up more than my good looks.*

"Hakim is upset and worried," Gamil continued, "he is angry with us for all of this," Gamil said gesturing to the roomful of people. "He wanted to be here, but was unable to come. He proclaimed your innocence more than once. He had been waiting for you at the 'Grove.'"

She frowned at him for a moment, wondering why he lied. She *knew* her husband was not at the Grove. His last text said he was headed to Azerbaijan plus Jamila told her yesterday she'd had not seen either of her brothers for two days. She knew a pack of lies when she saw it not to mention a pack of liars. However, some specific phrases stuck with her. The phrase about Saroyah not seeing anything had a poignant ring to it. Without another word she stood and she headed for the door, "Okay, I'm done here. I assume I am free to go. Your little task force can be disbanded now. Thanks for your hospitality."

With Yosef by her side she left saying, "I want a full briefing, now, starting with what's going on with my children and Saroyah. And by the way why didn't you come 'identify me' yourself instead of sending Gamil or whoever else you sent! Where the hell have *you* been?"

"Calm yourself, my friend," Yosef said putting his arm around her shoulder, "I will tell you everything."

~~~~~~

His crisp wingtips clicked as he walked along the tiled corridor at a quick clip; he was rounding the corner to his office when he heard a sound behind him. Whirling around, he was shocked to see a large black man, bald with a diamond stud in his pierced ear approach him quickly. The man called out "Friedrich…wait up my friend!" His arms encircled Herr Müeller in a comrade-like hug as he stuck a needle in the German's neck. Lifting the unconscious body he carried Herr Müeller into the *Rare Document Specialist's* office, deposited him in a chair and texted "It's time!" then began to unbutton his shirt. Within minutes an ambulance pulled up and a uniformed medic walked briskly into the building pushing a stretcher; moments later two paramedics sped away, their sleeping passenger strapped down, blissfully unaware of the siren screaming around him. As the ambulance headed toward the highway, T-Max turned off the siren, slowed his pace and smiled at Pablo. It had been an effortless catch and grab. Their guest was unharmed and their ETA was 75 minutes.

Tucked away in a dilapidated grey farmhouse in the Illinois countryside, members of Chevra Hatzollah were preparing for the upcoming interrogation. Stella clicked away on a keyboard organizing their information about Friedrich Müeller. They needed every piece of information about him they could find before interrogating him. Manny and Stella had combed through the data stolen from his office; it was a virtual gold mine. Müeller, arrogant and confident, had done nothing to hide or disguise any of his covert data so his hard drive included a completely accessible list of contacts including names/places/roles of everyone involved in selling or shipping weapons grade nuclear materials. Outlined on the screen was the complete pipeline of sellers and buyers from the bottom right up to the top. The decision had been made to contact the officials immediately after they had interviewed him and gotten what they needed. They would pass custody of Herr Müeller along with all his information, to the FBI, Homeland Security, the CIA, Interpol, Mossad and whatever other national and international agencies would need the information. After they were done with him the government could decide what to do with him. This data was crucial to fighting *The War on Terror* and they certainly wanted that information in the right official hands.

A room was being prepared with the necessary equipment. This man, this Nazi sympathizer, aka Islamic extremist sympathizer, was going to help unravel and destroy *The Sword of Justice* before it could implement its plan for world destruction. It seemed unreal even to say it, but the Reinhardt family knew better than to dismiss the possibility, no matter how farfetched it seemed. Having lived through the horrors of WWII, they knew how far a charismatic leader could go and how many lives could be destroyed at a whim. They knew that the masses were gullible and could be converted to mindless followers swept away by such a leader, who could persuade through garbled promises mixed with intimidation. They knew if people heard twisted logic and self-justifying phrases long enough they would stop thinking for themselves. The masses would let self-preservation assuage their consciences and denial cloud their thinking; soon right and wrong would intertwine like a distorted caduceus enabling the most horrific plans to be implemented without moral considerations.

Reina and Manny Reinhardt were ready. They stood and looked around the room they had set up; it was constructed of concrete blocks and it was windowless and empty, save one metal table and 3 chairs. An ensemble of spot lights hung from the ceiling and a narrow table displaying an intimidating array of medical equipment sat by the doorway. Pleased with the results of their efforts they waited for the others to arrive.

~~~~~~

Abdullah and Shamir crouched under a cluster of scrub trees squinting into the sun as the plane dropped its precious bundles to earth. They watched as two men hiding near an outcropping rushed forward and hoisted the crates into a camouflaged SUV; no sooner had the men loaded the crates, 3 rugged-looking Bedouins galloped up on horseback. "They've got Kalashnikovs!" Shamir said as the shooting began. Two of Bedouins climbed into the SUV while the third man thundered away with the rider-less horses. "We need one alive." Abdullah said raising his rifle. When the SUV was nearly parallel they rose out of the sand, shot the driver, wounded the other man, climbed into the vehicle and drove off, with their prisoner bound and gagged.

Knowing that others could be watching, Abdullah decided they needed to leave the valley as soon as possible and head toward their compound hidden in a populated area where they could blend in on the congested streets. Zahlé, the third largest city in Lebanon was the shortest distance away. They pulled through green wooden gates into a rectangular complex topped by a faded red tiled roof.

"Three sturdy men in working clothes took the prisoner away and carried the confiscated materials up a flight of stairs to a large room equipped with long wooden tables, a few desks and some office equipment. Hakim sat at a large desk. "How did you do, brother?" he asked as Abdullah and Shamir entered the room. "Fine, I don't think we were followed, but keep the guards posted. I need a few minutes to clean myself and then I will tell you everything. See if you can get us something to eat in the meantime will you, Shamir and I are parched and starving." Of course, my brother," Hakim said. He was an unofficial member of this little group. Having been charged by the Prime Minister with looking into illegal arms moving through their country, Hakim had a dual purpose for being there: fact finding for the Prime Minister and supporting his brother in his mission. They both thought that in some strange way this was related to Saroyah's kidnapping.

The Prime Minister had asked Hakim to look into whether there was a leak in the upper echelons of the Lebanese government. He suspected that someone in his inner circle was involved in illegal arms dealings with a specific terrorist group. Hakim was there to determine if there were covert ties between his government and terrorist organizations and/or Russian/Azerbaijani arms exporters.

Frowning, he texted a message to the guards posted on the roof of the building "Stay alert, stay on guard until further notice." He texted a second message to the men who were tracking the plane from the Beqaa Valley. The plane had been traced to a small airport in northern Syria where the pilot and was being followed. Their men on the ground were shadowing, photographing and awaiting instructions. "Report status ASAP!" Hakim was especially interested in this pilot's information because it could yield important information. A third text was sent to the kitchen staff requesting refreshments and a fourth text went to Hadara, inquiring into her welfare and apologizing for not being with her. He explained that he had been called away unexpectedly and was sitting in the Istanbul Airport about to board a flight to Narimanov, Azerbaijan. He did not know when he would be able to return home. Oh, the burdens of his job as an attaché! The text closed with "I love you my dearest, you and only you my beloved Hadara. I cannot wait until I return and hold you in my arms again. I remain your adoring husband…"

24 THE SANDS OF TIME

The air was cold. Sparking stars studded the deep blue sky as far as the eye could see millions and billions of them glimmered everywhere. The constellations were so clearly outlined it looked like they had been stenciled. All was quiet in the camp, only the guards roamed about, rifles slung over their shoulders, alert Belgian Malinois at their sides. There were 8 pairs walking in an easily timed pattern from point to point. Moshe and two newly arrived agents lay flat among the camels who had settled down on the cool sand for the night quietly chewing their cuds, long lashed eyes closed. It was approaching 2:45 when they moved. One at a time, creeping from point to point, they ran hunched over for a few feet then stopped and waited for another break. Two guards nearest them had stopped for a chat and a smoke. Their voices carried on the silent night air were clearly heard. "...first thing in the morning," said one guard.

"What happened..." asked the other one.

"...report from a courier and from that man we caught the other day..." said the first.

"So where are we going to go?" asked the second man. "It's not yet been decided, *The Great One* will inform us after morning prayers. He says he'll get his message directly from *Allah*."

"Ah yes," said the other man nodding agreement "it's only right that it be that way, *Subhan'Allah.*"

Amidst the warm air, Moshe felt a chill right down to his bones. They were breaking up camp. In a few hours they would fold the tents, load up the camels and move to another location. That endangered their whole operation. It meant that Rafi would need to have his tracking team back with him and fully attending to him during such a move. It meant that the child needed to be rescued tonight. There was no pushing back the schedule, it had to be now. Prayers would start at the crack of dawn and once that happened there would be no chance of getting her out or getting Rafi's team up and ready. *It's now or never*, he thought as the team crept forward to the child's tent.

Jamila could not sleep. She was upset. Her stomach churned, her mind raced. How could she sleep when her daughter was gone? She paced through the gardens, smelling the floral scent around her and looking up at the magnificent starry sky. She saw little. She had not heard from the rescuers; she didn't know where her husband or brothers were. She knew that Hadara would be angry with her, thinking she had accused her of the kidnapping. She had said no such thing and told her so. She had no idea who would have told her such a thing. It was a blatant lie, but she couldn't care about that now. Hadara had come and gone, upset that Hakim was missing. Why she expected him to be there she did not know. She said she thought he'd be here waiting for her, but he had not been here for days. Jamila told her that and Hadara seemed confused. Jamila didn't pay much attention to what Hadara had said; she couldn't care about that now. She had her daughter to worry about. Hadara told her she had a plan and that Jamila and her children should be ready to leave the country. Jamila had just stared at her. Nothing made any sense. She was going nowhere until her daughter was safe.

She asked Hadara if the men were going to help with this family evacuation. Hadara had shrugged and reminded her about the people, her friends from America who would be helping. Jamila said she remembered and would be ready but she didn't mean it. She pleaded with Hadara to just please save her baby. Hadara left soon after that discussion realizing that Jamila had no idea where any of the men were. According to her, Abdullah was gone. Off somewhere doing G-d knows what. Hakim was not where Gamil said he would be and she could not determine if Hakim was where said that he was. She still had not heard from him and that was most unusual. Gamil had not shown up at the Olive Grove since she left him at that warehouse, even though he had indicated his intent to return home. It was strange that all three of the men were missing. As Hadara and Yosef drove away she decided not to focus on what she did not know but instead to focus on what she did know. A plan was in place and she would focus on its completion.

Jamila continued to pace. She had stopped trying to figure the men out, their schedules were ridiculous and who knew if any of it was true. These men were so full of secrets and lies. When they were children with their big plans and hopes for building a safe new world for their people, the secrets had been part of the fun. No longer was that true for her. It was not that they were bad men; she never thought that. Her two brothers and her husband were good men, busy on secret missions and secret missions meant secret lives. Who knew what they were really up to? She never knew and had stopped asking. Jamila gave them the benefit of the doubt, she assumed what they did was justified even if it needed to be kept secret. If it weren't for the fact that her child was mixed up in all this, she wouldn't be asking now.

Wandering through their gardens she realized she didn't know who to trust. She had long suspected that one of her household staff was behind this. Who else would know where Saroyah was and when she would be there? She wasn't snatched from her school or from a marketplace; she was snatched from here, from her home. Jamila could not imagine that it had anything to do with the child herself. Not really. That made no sense. How could it? It had to be about one of the adults or perhaps the whole lot of them; powerful and rich as they were. Perhaps it was a plot against the Lebanese aristocracy and her little girl was the pawn.

No, the more she thought about it, this thing had to involve an insider. Perhaps more than one...after it would not be all that easy to steal an 11 year old. And the kidnapper had to get in the gate. They had guards posted all over the place. No one from the outside could just come in and wander around grabbing little girls. How did they get in here in the first place? The Olive Grove was well guarded. It was a big business now, not like when she was a child. Large concrete walls had been built with turrets and gun posts. At the front gate a guardhouse stood with an automatic gate, guns and guard dogs. The Faysal Family Olive Grove had become a huge sprawling complex with many workers and many trucks. They were a wealthy family with a successful business. They had much while others around them had little. Jamila could understand how people would be tempted to commit crimes. Money was essential and there were those who would do anything for money. Perhaps it had been one of their guards. The kidnapper got past the guards somehow. Not once, but twice! Coming in and getting out! And how in the world had they gotten Saroyah out past those guards anyway? In a sack? On a camel? In a car trunk? How had they done it? And who had helped them?

Jamila decided someone in her household could not be trusted. The men were all away doing something she didn't know about, so that left finding her daughter up to her! "Okay," she said to herself, "I'll have to do this myself. I'll find out who in this house has betrayed me and I'll find it out today!"

~~~~~~

"So the solution to the Middle East problem is world destruction?" Elisabeth asked as they completed their crash course in Islamic Extremist philosophies.

"That's about the size of it," Sammy said reaching for the carafe of coffee.

"It's time to coordinate our efforts," Gil said as he tapped his cell phone and walked over to the door. "Your friends are here," Gil said as he opened the hotel room door to Hadara and Yosef.

"Elisabeth," said Hadara warmly as they embraced, "It's been too long."

"It has indeed," Elisabeth said smiling at Hadara, "and you must be Yosef," she turned extending her hand. "I've heard so much about you please come sit down both of you." Introductions were made, coffee was poured, and reports were given.

"How did you get away from whoever had you?" Elisabeth asked Hadara.

"It's a long story…" Hadara began…

"Let me explain," Yosef interrupted and briefed the group on the whole fiasco. As Gil and Elisabeth listened they realized that most of the story was being omitted, especially those parts that related to the identity of the group holding her. That done, they moved to the Saroyah issue. "It's been determined that she was taken by *The Sword of Justice*. Mossad has people in place on site," Yosef explained and they were to move in and get the girl before morning prayers today but so far there had been no word. We have another operative in place at the camp," Hadara tensed up at this point, "and we have no word from him either."

The group was silent sensing her tension. "Is that Rafi?" Elisabeth asked her directly. Moving her eyes in Elisabeth's direction, Hadara sighed and nodded slightly.

There was a moment of stillness around the table as all present empathized with her *mother's* fears. With a nod, Yosef asked Gil for an update. The two men had been in communication for several days and a trust had developed between them. Gil picked up with the Chicago story. "...the information we've gotten from Müeller's office is good and solid; it takes us up to the top of the terror cell. Ari verified the chemicals are top grade so that's worrisome, but it fits the scenario. Our group will continue to work on him and as much as possible before handing him over to the US authorities. You'll be getting full reports from Ari and Samira with everything that Mossad needs to know about the situation so I won't take up time now filling you in on all those specifics."

"There is at least one more piece that we're unclear about," Hadara said slowly, "regarding an undercover action in Lebanon, something about a fixed wing aircraft dropping nuclear material into the Beqaa Valley and heading back toward Syria. I have reason to believe that will become significant. Mossad heard about it and picked up the trace of a small plane landing on an airstrip near the Syrian border. We started tracking the pilot of the plane on the ground only to find that we are not the only ones following him. There are at least two other parties tracking him. We have to make sure we pick him up first. Hadara looked at Yosef who nodded and rose to leave the room when a beep from his cell phone stopped him. After a moment he handed her his cell phone. We've intercepted some of the mobile calls coming from that area and....." Yosef explained watching Hadara's face. A frozen expression came over her face as Yosef continued saying "...we have localized some of the numbers and who they are calling; we are cross checking to find out who all is involved in this thing." He ended and the group fell silent, something of major import was palpable in the air; they all felt it. Glancing at Hadara, they knew to leave it alone.

"Look," Sammy offered, re-focusing the group "We're just here to help you guys, we don't have a dog in this fight," he grinned as he quoted an old *Hop-along Cassidy* show, "So you don't need to tell us anything we don't need to know."

"Exactly," Simon piped up, "just tell us what you want us to do and we'll do it!"

"Thank you my friends," Hadara said smiling weakly at them. "We should be hearing from the team on Saroyah any minute now. Then we'll know what direction to take."

25 ROUNDUP

Her legs felt wobbly, but the adrenaline coursing through her body helped as they raced through the moonlight to the waiting truck. Hoisting her into the back, the men threw themselves face down on the sand as the truck sped away. Faint cries were heard from the campsite signaling her absence had been detected. Saroyah crawled into the false bottom of a basket filled with dried lentils aided by a bearded agent wearing the baggy clothes of a poor farmer. She could hear several vehicles in the distance as the search for her began and the unmistakable ring of gun fire sounded. Around her bushel baskets of cotton, wheat and barley swayed slightly with the movement of the ancient flatbed. She heard the 'farmer' warning her to be quiet and still if they were stopped. She didn't need to be told twice. She was young, but she knew the stakes. She knew all too well what would happen if she were found. Terrified, she remained silent, barely breathing as the truck bumped along through the darkened desert.

~~~~~~

It was not yet dawn but inside the musky tent, the forces gathered; the servers stood around the periphery; the advisors sat in a circle, silent witnesses while Galed Rachid stood stiffly facing *The Great One*. His eyes were downcast in shame as he bore the onslaught of angry words. "How did this happen? How did a small child manage to escape? I do not understand how this happened! It is inconceivable! You must find her immediately! I do not care what it costs, do you understand me? It is essential! She can identify us, she has relatives who hold much power; they can reach into the heart of several governments and mobilize great forces against us! Do you not understand how important this is? You must re-capture her or if that is not possible, eliminate her!" Galed Rachid felt his ears grow hot; he felt his throat grow dry. To be called out this way was humiliating, having his troops witness such a tongue lashing was an insult to his authority, his esteemed role in the organization. He could not believe that *The Great One* would speak to him this way, with such disdain and disrespect!

Heads would roll when he learned which of his people had let down their guard. He would blame this on someone and do so in a most public manner. The thought of that mollified him somewhat. He wished that *The Great One* would stop talking; they were losing valuable minutes with this useless lecture. Quickly, he began to nod and make affirmative noises...agreeing that this was a horrible situation, that the child must be re-captured and as soon as possible. He begged to be allowed to leave so that he could do his work in serving *The Sword of Justice* by capturing the child.

Upon leaving the main tent, Galed issued several instructions: find out how the child escaped, find out who helped her, find her and re-capture or kill her. Divided into groupings, his army scattered through the camp and into the desert. One group returned to the tent where the child had been held captive and began interrogating and searching for evidence; another group traced a barely visible track that led from a slit in the back of her tent into the dessert; another group headed toward the child's home to see if she returned there; yet another group headed toward Israel to see if they could hear word of her from the streets and marketplaces where supporters of their movement might be located.

Climbing into the lead jeep, Galed Rachid moved into the desert following the faint track of what appeared to come from a farm truck. Rachid had been with *The Sword of Justice* for just over a year now, having been sent as emissary from the Iraqi government to establish a relationship with this emerging Islamic extremist group, he soon was chosen as First Deputy for *The Great One*'s personal army. He had been impressed with the leader's ideas and communicated as much to his superiors in the Iraqi cabinet. Over time it had become his job to serve two masters, he was devoted to *The Great One*, but also obligated to report back to his superiors in the Council of Ministers in Bagdad. Although Iraq is a democratic, federal parliamentary republic that elects its officials, it also has an elaborate underground network of paybacks and a complex system of checks and balances with barbaric consequences for failure or betrayal. Galed Rachid was familiar with the system of justice that actually ran his country. He had not only seen the exacting punishments netted out, but had handed out a few of those punishments himself. He wanted nothing more than to manage his dual alliance without being killed. He was under no illusions about the situation in which he now found himself. If he failed to find or kill this little girl, this Saroyah Ajram, he would meet his maker at the hands of *The Great One* or at the hands of his own government. If he brought shame on his country that would be the end of him, it was a national point of honor.

~~~~~~

Hadara burst through the door her face aflame. Pulling Yosef toward her she hissed "Tell me what in the hell is going on here? That is impossible. I have never been so angry in all my life!" They raced toward the exit and hurried down the rear stairway toward the parking lot. "Don't jump to conclusions, my friend," Yosef hastened to reassured her and calm her down. "You don't know why he's where he said he isn't or isn't where he said he was, whichever." "He lied to me! He flat out lied to my face! I will wring his lying neck," she whisper-screeched. "How dare he tell me he is in Istanbul and be in the desert with his brother? What kind of BS is this?" "Hadara," Yosef said placing a hand on her shoulder, "these are difficult times. There are many things going on that you and I are not aware of. Perhaps he's on a secret mission. Perhaps he is protecting you in some way. You cannot condemn the man without even knowing what is going on. Please be patient and calm down. We have a mission to carry out. For all we know Hakim has one too so you must not let him know that you know he lied about his whereabouts. That could put him in danger. You do not know who might be monitoring his phone and text messages. You must act normally to him until this is over." Hadara tried to steady her voice before speaking. "I will calm down, Yosef, of course you are correct. The mission comes first. We will do what we need to do, save Saroyah, save the world and then I will wring his lying neck!"

~~~~~~

She had a plan. She was not sure it was a good one, but it was a plan nonetheless. She crept into her parents' room while the elderly couple slept and eased herself into a closet. In order for my plan to work, she thought, I cannot look like myself. In the dim light she found one of her mother's old black dresses. One of the more conservative ones that she wore before the 'modern' times began. Over her head she draped a dark shawl wrapped so that it covered her head and most of her face. Slipping her feet into a pair of worn sandals, she retreated to the hallway breathing a sigh of relief that the first part of her plan had worked. Hunching her shoulders, she snuck down the rear stairway used only by the servants and entered the kitchen. She paused listening for any sound of movement in the room; hearing nothing, she scurried across the room and tucked into a cupboard used only when they had large parties.

She was nodding off when she heard voices. They were preparing for the day as they always did, chatting about the usual things and beginning their usual tasks. She listened as Baha asked if there had been word of Saroyah? Fawz answered that she had heard nothing. Durrah said she was so worried about her and talked about what a terrible thing this was and what a wonderful child Saroyah was. Musnah remained silent. Her silence was unnoticed by her chattering companions, but in the cupboard, Jamila felt her pulse quicken. This was the clue she had been waiting for. She waited and listened as the women inquired about one another's families, Musnah, again, offered nothing. At length, Baha asked her if there had been word of her grandson Imad? Musnah mumbled something unintelligible. Fawz followed up with more questions, all equally evaded. She wondered why Musnah was being so evasive. She had heard nothing about Musnah's grandson. Twenty minutes of kitchen clatter and jumbled conversations continued when she heard Durrah ask, "Do you know who's holding him?" A shock wave jettisoned through her when she heard Musnah answer, "The Jews, I think, we are not sure." Jamila reacted instantly. She burst out of hiding, strode across her kitchen, screaming for the guards to come as she confronted the terrified cook. "What have you done Musnah? How could you betray me? Betray this family? Have you betrayed my Saroyah to save your Imad! Did you not think to come to me? To come to Gamil? Now they are both missing. You are the link!"

~~~~~~

Hakim, Abdullah and Shamir sat together at one end of a long table laden with crates from the recent desert run, scooping fresh Baba Ghanoush with chunks of pita and drinking mint tea. They were trying to determine the identity of the other groups who had been in the Beqaa Valley waiting for that plane. Their wounded captive had been treated for his injuries, but was still unconscious. The photos Shamir had taken of the groups had been forwarded to their experts so while they waited, they turned their attention to the men carefully unpacking the crates. Having photographed the crates from every angle, the men proceeded slowly, noting every marking and stamp carefully, examining all the wrappings and labels. They needed to track the route of the nuclear materials contained in the crates; not just their last stop before being air dropped into the valley, but every stopping place along the way. They needed to know where the materials had been manufactured and who handled them along the way. They determined that some of the materials had been manufactured in Russia, some in North Korea. So far they had identified several way stations for shipments of nuclear materials. One was located in Turkey, another in Belarus and four others in major U.S. cities. In each instance, museums were used to pack and transport materials disguised as meticulously wrapped *Old World* artifacts or manuscripts.

Every now and then Hakim glanced at his cell phone. He was nervous. Hadara knew him well. If there was a word out of step, one single aspect of his meticulously worded text message that was off, she'd know it and she was not a woman who countenanced deception. This had happened only one time before in their long painstakingly crafted marriage and it had not been pretty. It had nearly cost him their relationship. Wiping sweat from his face he looked up to see Abdullah staring at him. "Come, let's take a walk," he said to his brother. Once outside he said, "You are constantly checking your phone, my brother, what lie did you tell her this time?"

Hakim looked down at the ground as they walked and shook his head, "I didn't want her to know about my being here with you today. We do not know what we will do with the information we will obtain and I did not want to raise questions with her that I am not in a position to answer. We do not know how all of this will play out. I do not know how my family may figure into all of this. My children are away somewhere. I have no idea if they are a part of this somehow. Hadara knows where they are, but as is our agreement, I am not told of such matters. These are Mossad secrets. As much as I love her and she me, there are things we do not share with one another. This time I made up a story, so she would not suspect that I am involved with this. For all I know, they are involved in it too, in different perhaps opposing ways. It's been hard to have a family such as ours, filled with love and secrets. We have great love for one another, but on occasion our familial loyalties are undercut by loyalties to our countries."

Abdullah sighed and patted his brother's shoulder, "We always knew these things would happen. We knew it when we made our little childhood pact so many years ago. We knew it when you and Hadara fell in love and planned to marry in spite of everything. We agreed to work for peace within and between our countries, but we always knew that there would be times when conflicts would arise. We agreed to trust that one another's intentions were pure even if specific actions seemed to contradict our pact."

Hakim nodded and they walked on in silence. Then he said, "I hope that this time will be no different. I hope that what you and I are working on will be compatible enough with her goals - that it will override her reaction to my dishonesty."

"Be calm, my brother," Abdullah said with a slight grin, "It's not like you have taken a mistress, right?"

Hakim grinned back and said, "My brother that would be so much more forgivable! Hadara is a most understanding woman when it comes to matters of nature." The men were laughing at that when they heard Shamir running toward them shouting.

26 NORTH-SOUTH-EAST-WEST

The plan involved several switches; they would travel 50 minutes to a narrow valley where another vehicle would be waiting and that one would travel 20 minutes to another vehicle there another switch would occur, and on it went until 2 hours later they were to arrive at a tiny speck of a village where a helicopter would be waiting to carry her home. Saroyah did not know what the plan was, but with every passing minute she grew a bit more hopeful that she might survive this trip. Silently, she prayed to *Allah* to carry her home to her family. She could not wait to feel her mother's arms around her, to be surrounded by all that was warm and familiar, to tell her story of what had happened to her. Even now, stories sped through her mind; the screams of the captured man, the jolt of fear every time someone entered the tent. These days had been terrifying, never knowing if she would live or die, never knowing if they would make her scream like that man who was captured. She had heard everything. Her tent was just feet away from the place she thought of as the 'torture tent.' The man spoke to his captors in Hebrew and they spoke to him in Arabic, several different dialects, but all Arabic. Over and over they asked the same questions. He had proclaimed his innocence till his final moments. It was horrible. She could do nothing to help him. No one came to save him. If her time came to be in the 'torture tent,' she thought, no one would come to save her either.

She did not understand why *Allah* had not come to help that man. *Allah* or the man's Hebrew *G-d*, whatever *he* was called had both left him to die. Why did the *G-ds* not help when people called upon them? Wasn't that what they were supposed to do? Wasn't that why people prayed to them? She wondered how all this had gotten started way back in time when religion was first invented. Perhaps *Allah* or the Hebrew G-d had been younger then, had more energy; maybe back then they were more willing to help people. Perhaps now they were older, she thought, like my *ajdaadi* (grandparents), and perhaps they could no longer move so easily. Perhaps they slept more, like my *ajdaadi* (her grandparents) do. Perhaps even *G-ds* got old and hard of hearing. '*Allah*' she screamed it as loud in her mind as she could, trying to get the sleeping or perhaps the hard of hearing *G-d's* attention. "Please," she shouted in her mind, "please hear me, *Allah*, please help me." Tears rolling down her cheeks, Saroyah silently shouted her prayers hoping that her beloved *Allah*, who must be old and tired after all his years of being a *G-d*, would have the energy to save just one more person, just one more time.

~~~~~~

They straightened when the alert sounded. It was shrill and high pitched. It sounded like Morse code. Two long beeps followed by a short one. Cameras installed in trees along the narrow winding road were programmed to signal when a vehicle arrived. They watched as a white LIFELINE ambulance with its striking blue crisscross logo, its lights and sirens off, pulled up in front of the old barn door. A rusty grey van pulled up behind them. Over the intercom they heard T-Max say, "We're home, Mama. Ready for some of your fresh baked cornbread and fried okra," in his throaty southern drawl. Manny pressed a button raising the tattered barn door, steel reinforced on the inside and muttered 'Ain't no cornbread here, old man, you'll have to settle for some stale bagels!' as the tiny caravan drove forward.

Within minutes the team was assembled. Herr Müeller, bound and blindfolded, sat upright in a straight-back chair while the others took their places at the one-way mirror. "Do you have the questions ready?" Samira asked Reina. "I think so, you can take a look at them, they're up on the computer over there," she gestured to her workstation as Ari and Samira walked in that direction. "Add or change anything you want," Reina added, "We have plenty of time to chat with our guest and are in no hurry to start talking to him." "Well," Ari said, "in some ways, Ma'am, that may be the truth, but in other ways we may have, I worry, less time than we think. We have been unable to reach our compatriots in New York City. I do not know if this is a problem or if it is not. If it is a problem and our compatriots are in trouble, we may not have so much time."

~~~~~~

The phone rang as the briefing ended, Hadara, immediately transformed into an experienced Mossad officer quickly said "*Cain...cain*, ... How is she? ... You have seen her? *cain*...wonderful... exactly... uh huh...And the other matter? Good… uh huh … alright… that is good. They are all in place, yes? He is covered? And the other matter? *Cain*…. Do you have an update? Uh huh. Do you know where that will be? …. Alright we will meet you there," she ended the call looking relieved. "Saroyah is rescued. Rafi's team is in place. They are all safe." Hadara paused collecting her thoughts then she spoke pointedly to Yosef, "This phase is done, we have to move and move quickly." Gil leaning against a doorway checked his iPhone and glanced at Elisabeth inquiringly. Perceiving a slight nod he turned his attention back to his phone. The second phase of the project was about to begin. One at a time, Yosef and Hadara left the room walking in different directions. They were followed two minutes later by Gil. Following circuitous routes, Hadara and Gil met at a helicopter launching pad while Yosef drove two other agents in a battered jeep to the tiny village where the extraction team was waiting.

In the back of a small Hasidic Synagogue, two disguised Mossad agents huddled with a little girl. They had been waiting for just under an hour when they heard the whirring blades of an approaching helicopter; they were about to leave the building when they got an urgent text. "*Bet kaf raish pay vav lamed…* " it warned 'armed men with rifles would be arriving within minutes.' Frantically, they searched the synagogue for something to shield themselves with so they could run to the chopper. Uttering prayers of forgiveness they gently removed the holy *Torahs* from their sanctified arc and lifting the arc above their heads, they tucked their bodies inside as best they could and raced toward the helicopter whipping up a dust storm nearby. Amid a barrage of gunfire they lifted Saroyah toward the open door. Bullets pinged off the surface of the chopper; the child cried out in pain as a bullet slammed into her leg. Arterial blood squirted wildly as she was dragged into the rising chopper. "I hit her," Galed Rachid whooped triumphantly to his men who continued shooting as the chopper rose into the air. Hadara bound the wound to staunch the blood flow. Leaning out the open door Gil fired on the enemy while Yosef and the other agents joined in a counter-assault. Three of the terrorists were mortally wounded, but two managed to escape.

On the chopper, make-shift tourniquets were applied to Saroyah's leg where her femoral artery spewed. Above the din of the whirling blades and the child's cries, Hadara issued the pilot an order: "Find the nearest hospital, the child is losing a lot of blood and her situation is urgent." Both Hadara and Gil had basic paramedic training and worked to stabilize and comfort the child as best they could. Another bullet had grazed her right side not far from her kidney and immediate treatment was required. Coded messages were relayed to all concerned through Mossad's restricted network as they flew toward Yitshak Ben Zvi Hospital in Beersheba.

Sitting in the Emergency Room waiting area, tears flowed as Jamila held her three children and prayed to *Allah* to save her youngest daughter. After they received word that the child was out of surgery and her condition was stable, Jamila pulled Hadara aside. Emotion glistened in her eyes as she asked, "Have you talked to them?"

"No, Not a word," Hadara answered her lips tight in anger, "I've called all of them many times but there has been no answer."

"Where can my husband be? Where could any of them be?" Jamila asked Hadara. "He should be here with his daughter. They should all be here with us, Gamil, Abdullah and Hakim. They should all be here! So where are they?" she cried in frustration.

"I do not know. I'm as upset about this as you are!" Hadara exclaimed. "I vacillate between worry and anger. If they aren't here, where are they and why aren't they answering us. I've called and called. Supposedly Hakim is in Azerbaijan of all places. What in the world he's doing there is anyone's guess!" Where the others are is a mystery to me. She didn't tell Jamila that her husband Gamil had been present at her capture site. She did not say that his being there was another mystery. She also did not tell her that Gamil had lied about Hakim's whereabouts. Although she was convinced that Gamil was mixed up in something nefarious, she could not bring herself to burden Jamila further.

"Well," Jamila said with a strength she didn't feel, "we'll just have to do this without them. They are of no use to us now! We have to get out of here; out of the Middle East. It's up to us, Hadara, just you and I! The men have failed us. We are not safe here and we must leave." Breaking into tears she confided, "I found out who was spying for our enemies. It was our old trusted cook Musnah. I am heartbroken to say it, but that's who did it. She put my child's life in danger. She did it!"

Hadara reached out to her sister-in-law, comforting her. Yosef had mentioned this and she knew this was just a tiny piece instead she said, "I know that Musnah has been with your family since you were Saroyah's age. We all loved her. She was everyone's favorite." Hadara remembered when they were young Musnah would sneak treats to them in a little covered basket, so the children could picnic together in the olive grove. Musnah had known about the 5 friends. She alone knew that they met regularly, the two Israeli children and the three Faysal children. She had known and she had kept their secret!

Jamila said she thought Musnah's grandson was involved in something big. She thought he had somehow been coerced into stealing Saroyah for ransom money. Hadara told her the rest. It seemed Saroyah had witnessed a meeting of some kind. The child had been captured to keep her quiet. Jamila gasped. She had not realized that her child actually had a direct involvement with the men who kidnapped her. If that were the case, Jamila now realized, the men shooting at her in the little village had been trying to kill not just re-capture her. She was a witness to something secret and important. Then an alarming thought sprang into her mind. With so many places where men could have secret meetings what brought them to the Olive Grove? How did they even know about that side gate? About that remote spot where the seed was stored?

It was rumored the grandson was involved in the illegal weapons trade, working with some underground Russian illegal weapons cartel but something about that didn't make sense. Could so young a man, a boy really, have that much sway over men of great power? Could he be the brains behind this whole scheme? The more she thought about it, the more confused she became. It didn't make sense that they were at the Grove because of Musnah and her grandson. Someone else had drawn them to her home. This mess was bigger than an old cook and her grandson. It made no sense.

Hadara interrupted her thoughts, "We need to find out everything Musnah knows. Give me a minute I have an idea," she said, and crossed to where Elisabeth and Yosef were talking.

27 WHERE THERE'S A WILL

The ragtag caravan had made its way slowly across the desert. Heavily loaded camels and donkeys swayed and brayed trudging after one another. The vehicles formed a parallel caravan. First two guard vehicles, guns pointed out every window, then limousines carrying the prestigious guests, then a limousine carrying *The Great One* and his immediate entourage, then more guard cars. The line seemed endless as it wove across the hardened sand. The heat of the day had faded to evening when they stopped. The servants began setting up a temporary camp for the night. Food was prepared in large pots suspended over stick fires and *The Leader* and his chief advisor, Zuhair Bayan were discussing location options for the next campsite. Three alternate sites had been selected. One was along the Syrian-Jordanian border, one was in central Iraq and the last one was in Turkey near the border shared with Azerbaijan. Each site had risks and advantages. The location needed to be remote with limited access so it could be guarded and defended but they needed to be close enough to supporters in order to spread the word. If opposition forces were to discover the camp, the support of the local people would be critical. There was, they admitted, a downside to that, as well: the populace could not always be trusted. These were poor people and that meant they were vulnerable to bribery and threats. The men agreed the most remote location would be preferable and had sent scouting parties out to investigate the potential sites.

〰〰〰〰〰〰〰〰〰〰〰〰〰〰〰〰〰〰〰〰〰〰〰〰〰〰〰〰〰〰〰〰

Zuhair Bayan sighed loudly; it was too bad such a seemingly small decision had to be so complicated. In his experience small decisions such as this were made by others. He had served as an official in the Syrian government for many years. He owed them much. The government had paid for his housing and education for years with the understanding that they would benefit from his learning. He studied at the London School of Economics but in addition had obtained a degree from the Southampton Medical School and was licensed to practice medicine in several countries. The Syrian government had sent Bayan to join this group ostensibly to support them but also to evaluate its leader. Bayan's continued loyalty to his own government was unquestioned and inviolate. He reported to them regularly. He had been ordered to embed himself in the new terrorist group and make himself indispensable. Bayan had been able to use his medical degree and his degree in economics to his advantage soon gaining *The Leader's* trust.

Bayan was an arrogant man. He was used to being in charge, to having many people report to him. They did 'the leg work.' They were paid and paid well, he thought, to do his bidding. They researched and studied many options available for each decision and reported the summaries to him so that he could decide based on their information. Zuhair was a strong, healthy man. For a man of fifty he was rather attractive, he thought. People noticed him as he passed. He thought it was because he was handsome but it was also because of his birthmark. Zuhair Bayan had been born with an unusual mark on his right cheekbone. It was purplish-red in color and curved like a sickle. Port-wine stains are not harmful, so it had never been removed. He had come to believe it resembled the Russian Hammer and Sickle symbol. It was his personal sign of power!

He was pouring over maps when he heard a sound near the opening of his tent. "Perhaps I can be of some small assistance, to you, revered one," a handsome young man poked his head around the flap of the tent. "*The Great One*, hallowed be his name, suggested I might offer my services to you. I have studied for many years at university and know many things about geography and governments. If you would allow me the honor of entering your tent, I would like to offer you some small assistance." Bayan gave the young man a hard stare and with a small sneer he asked, "What is it you think you know that I do not already know?"

"No doubt, honored sir, I know nothing that you do not know, but perhaps if I listen as you speak your learned thoughts aloud, I might reflect your thoughts back to you in such a way that you could hear your own ideas more clearly than if you simply think your thoughts without speaking them." The Chief Advisor was taken aback. He fully expected the belligerence of a youth who was full of pride and arrogance, but here was the exact opposite. This young man appeared to be intelligent, but not overly prideful, interested, but not pushy. He seemed polite and genuine. And, what he said made sense. Bayan thought hearing my own thoughts aloud might be a good idea. He was just beginning to understand why people in the camp were talking about this young man and why *The Great One* was so taken with him. I should find out more about this young man, he thought. Pausing for just a minute, he nodded to the young man and said, "Come in. By what name I shall call you…" "I am called Rafi," said the young man, bowing slightly he stepped into the tent.

~~~~~~

Shamir rounded the building at the speed of light. His hair blew wildly in the wind and he was waving a paper in his hand and screaming "Abdullah, Abdullah…."

Hakim and Abdullah turned and rushed toward him, "What is wrong, Shamir?" they both asked at once.

"The ingredients, some of them are pre-mixed. I think they are about to blow up!"

"How can that be?" Abdullah asked, "No one would be tossing a live bomb out of a plane!"

"No one would be that crazy?" Hakim asked.

"We can take no chances, sir, we must leave immediately!" Shamir was nearly hysterical.

"That cannot be," Abdullah argued again, but Hakim shook his head.

"It is better to be safe than sorry, Brother, we can always return," he said and picked up his cell phone. "Evacuate the compound immediately" he texted all those present, "grab as much evidence as you can and take the prisoner with you. Get out now!"

They rushed forward piled into their vehicles and sped out of the gates heading into the desert. They had traveled a mere 5 miles when the earth beneath them shook like an earthquake measuring 6 on the Richter scale as behind them their compound exploded into a million fiery pieces.

~~~~~~

Musnah wept softly in the corner of the kitchen where she sat on a small wooden stool. Two stern guards, assigned to the house, looked down on her with pity and confusion. She was indispensable in the Faysal kitchen; warm and generous she baked the staff special desserts on holidays and always carried out leftover dinner portions to everyone on duty. It seemed unreal to them that they would now be guarding her! They were under orders not to let her out of their sight and they were not about to ignore their orders, but this didn't seem right. These were tense, frightening times at the Olive Grove. Fawz, head of the kitchen staff for nearly twenty years came over and asked if she could speak to Musnah, but they turned her away. They were under orders that no one would speak with her except Jamila or her husband. And speaking of Gamil, where was he these days? With a huge family crisis, he was nowhere to be seen. This was highly unusual, the guards thought as they exchanged quizzical looks with each other. Something was definitely going on here and Musnah was the least of it; that's what they thought.

When they thought back to the time when the child was taken, they remembered some strange goings on in the area near the animal pens. Now they were unsure about whether or not to report what they had seen. Perhaps they would be in trouble for not reporting it sooner. And perhaps if they didn't tell now what they knew they would be in worse trouble! They sighed and moved closer to each other so they could whisper back and forth. At length they decided it would be best to tell what they saw because it might, after all, be helpful. Either way, they thought they would be in trouble, they just didn't know how much.

28 NEXT STOP

Boulos was enjoying *Lubee* (green beans and lamb) when Sol Abramson opened the door. He sat down and calmly looked across at his prisoner. "Are you enjoying your meal?" he asked calmly.

Boulos looked at him curiously. He had been prepared for torture and probable death but hospitality, now that was a surprise. "What do you want of me?" he asked.

"Just a little business transaction," Sol answered with a shrug. "We are two businessmen negotiating. I want to buy and you want to sell. It is simple, right?"

"Well," Boulos answered, "it all depends on what you want and if I have it, right? Supply and demand is part of any business dealing, is that not correct?"

"Yes, of course," Sol nodded. "So, I will tell you what I want to buy and you can decide if you want to sell it, and, if so, for how much."

Boulos was startled. This was unlike any enemy interrogation he had ever experienced. He decided to play along. "I am listening," he said, feeling more confident, "But I want to start by having you tell me who you are. One cannot do business with a stranger, is that not correct?"

"Of course," Sol agreed easily, "My name is Sol Abramson and I am a unit leader with the Emergency Readiness Division of Mossad," he said directly. "We are seeking information about *The Sword of Justice* and want to know everything you know about them."

"Ahhh," Boulos responded after a moment, "that might be much information. For that information, I would be receiving how much dollars?"

"Good question," Sol nodded. "For one thing, you would be given your life. For another thing, you would be given your freedom. For another, transport and relocation to any place in the world you want to go and for a fourth thing, you would be given enough money to live comfortably for the rest of your life."

Boulos was silent for a long while staring at his captor. He took a large gulp of tea before responding, "It seems that this is a very generous offer. You must very much want to find these *Sword of Justice*, people. I am inclined to accept your generous offer, but one thing, I confess, confuses me. What guarantee have I that you will, shall we say, play it straight with me? Let us say that I tell you much about these people. I tell you all that I know down to the last drop of tea, shall we say..." Boulos grinned as he turned his empty cup upside down, "and what if after you get your information, you decide to give me nothing, or worse, you kill me?"

"Those are reasonable questions," Sol nodded seriously, "but it does cut both ways. What guarantee do I have that your information will be adequate and accurate? That you will truthfully tell us everything you know. Perhaps you will tell only a small amount or leave out the most important facts?" Sol parried. Boulos pursed his lips and nodded. The two men sat silently looking at one another for a while. Then Sol suddenly clapped his hands on his knees, "How about this: We transport you now to another location, not a prison, and once we are there we have a few long conversations. Perhaps a prison cell does not convey the proper attitude for a negotiation such as ours."

"Ah that sounds encouraging. But answer me this, what guarantee do I have that you will not shoot me when we leave here?"

"So," said Sol, "you are asking me more questions about guarantees... how about this: We hire you. You go to work for us. You become an undercover agent for the Mossad. We keep you on our payroll even after you give us this information we need right now. In the future, you could be useful to us with your many contacts throughout the world. Think of it as a career change. Instead of selling weapons and ammunitions you can sell information to us. We will be your only customer. You will be 'on our payroll'. Does that put your mind at ease? We have no reason to kill you if you are working for us, right? Even after *The Sword of Justice* has been eliminated you may be able to provide us with information about other matters. If you want to quit or we no longer need you, we shake hands and you walk away with your freedom and your Swiss bank accounts." Sol opened his hands in a 'what could be more reasonable' gesture.

Boulos nodded. He was stumped. Never in his life would he have expected this kind of treatment, this kind of deal. He thought this man this Sol Abramson must be crazy. Yet here he was in a prison and many worse things could be happening to him. He thanked *Allah* for his good fortune and knew that this was the best deal he would ever get, certainly not the kind of treatment he would have gotten from the Russians!

"I'll bring in some paperwork for you to sign bringing you on board as a confidential informant for the Mossad and we'll take off," Sol said moving toward the door.

"You must keep this a secret from the others," Boulos hissed to the closing door, "if word gets out that I am alive and working with you they will kill me for sure."

"That would do neither of us any good, would it," Sol replied turning. "We will make sure you are reported to have died while being interrogated. The others will not be getting out, but as you say word seems to travel." He stood and offered his hand to his now confidential informant and asked, "How good of an actor are you? Start screaming and after a while we'll fire some bullets and put an end to this charade."

～～

Theirs was a true romance. The kind of story Nora Roberts writes. For Jamila and Gamil it was love at first sight. They met while studying at Duke University in North Carolina and fell madly and passionately in love. Their families were delighted that their children had found one another and arranged an elegant formal wedding, which most of the country's upper class attended.

The Ajram family was wealthy and well-respected. They lived in the outskirts of Beirut where Gamil's parents were practicing physicians and his grandfathers had both served as cabinet ministers. The Ajrams were known for their generosity, having built a museum dedicated to Lebanese antiquities. For the first 3 years of their marriage Jamila and Gamil lived in Raleigh while Gamil completed his Doctorate in Agricultural Economics and Jamila completed her Master's in Business Administration. After graduation, Gamil was offered a position as Financial Advisor to the Minister of Agriculture.

Upon return to Lebanon they settled at the Olive Grove so their children could be raised in a safe contained rural environment and Jamila could gradually assume responsibility for the family business. Gamil and Jamila had a strong foundation rooted in the Muslim faith and cultural traditions; there were strong gender role definitions, good family supports and most of all, there was love. The couple rarely went for more than a few hours without communicating by phone, email or text messages. Major decisions were discussed and mutually agreed upon. That is until now. This was the first time in their nearly 20 year marriage that Jamila was not able to depend on her husband. Not depend on him was an understatement; she couldn't even get in touch with him!

As she completed her packing, Jamila slipped behind her beautiful floor length gowns and knelt on the closet floor. In the dim light, she rotated a small dial until she heard a metallic click. Her fingers searched the darkness for the large billfold that held their 'rainy day' money. It was gone! The billfold and all the money it contained were gone! In a panic she leaned forward and yanked everything out of the square iron box. Birth certificates, marriage license and wills were there but the money was gone. Urgently she shuffled through the passports finding only five. Gamil's passport was missing! Jamila stared in disbelief at her hands as it dawned on her that this was a far greater problem than an aging cook crying in the kitchen. Not answering text messages was one thing. Taking their money and his passport was quite another! Her mind swirled through the possibilities. She didn't know what was going on but she knew something wasn't right.

〰〰〰〰〰〰〰〰〰〰〰〰〰〰〰〰〰〰〰〰〰〰〰〰〰〰〰〰

Herr Müeller felt his stomach turn. His eyes scanned the square nearly empty room, stopping at the table by the door. On it were tools and unfamiliar things. He felt a fear he never experienced before. In the distance, he heard voices but he could not make out their words. Any minute he expected them to barge through the door and his torture would begin. *I have been foolish,* he thought, *foolish and arrogant. I thought they'd never find me. I thought I had them outsmarted and when I sent those Syrian thugs after that boy I thought that would be the end of things. I had to get rid of him; handsome boy, but always sneaking around, looking through my trash. I knew he was a spy, probably a Jew but a handsome one. I thought once those Syrians got rid of the boy my worries would be over. That beautiful woman, Samira must have been part of this mess somehow. I trusted her. She came with such good credentials and she is so beautiful that she distracted me.*

Müeller ran through various scenarios trying to think what to do. *Maybe I can talk them into letting me go,* he thought. *I'll convince them it's some kind of big mistake. I'll say I was an innocent bystander. Someone else at the museum could be to blame. I'll say I was set-up. Yes, that's a good one. Americans always like to say someone set them up. They are such cowards, those Americans. I'll say I had no idea what was in those packages, someone asked me to watch over them, that's all.* Then he realized they could have collected information against him by now. *If they have evidence against me and I lie to them it will make it worse for me. What if the arms network has been compromised? What if they know everything already? What if they got into my office and my computer? Dummkopf! I should have protected that computer. Dummkopf what a stupid idiot you are,* he said to himself. *Even my in house, they will probably find things, but they will not be clever enough to find the important things. Those things are hidden forever!* He sneered reassuringly, *when I get out of here I'll take care of these oversights. I'll hide things better.*

The idea of strangers going through his precious possessions tormented him. His home had always been his sanctuary. He never married and rarely had visitors so there was no reason to hide things. Housekeepers were always closely supervised. Things were kept the way he liked them so he could appreciate them.

Watching through the one-way mirror, the members of Chevra Hatzollah were dividing tasks. Samira, Pablo and Stella would concentrate on their prisoner while T-Max, Ari and Reina would go inspect the curator's home. Manny would devote himself to making extraction arrangements for the group in Israel and there was a never-ending flow of information to be monitored… Manny had a lot to do before the away team could return.

As his fingers sped across the keyboard, the interrogation team entered the small square room lit by a blazing spotlight and T-Max drove toward Müeller's elegant, manicured home in the suburbs.

~~~~~~

Rafi was awake. He could not sleep with the movement of the truck as it swayed and bumped along the desert floor. He had not been told where they were going and had pretended not to care. As long as he was with *The Great One* …the one who's judgment reigned supreme, that was all that mattered. The details of the trip were not shared with the loyal followers who seemed unconcerned with such mundane details as the destination. They slept near him, huddled on their rugs snoring peacefully. Rafi was glad that he seemed to have been accepted by the others. He could learn more this way. It did have a downside though; he no longer had time alone to communicate with his team. Being surrounded by others meant he was being watched 24/7, and a single, out of the ordinary act could lead to detection. Sliding his fingers along the leather binding of his small Koran, he assured himself that the tracking device was still in place. Tucking the book inside his robe he concentrated on blending in.

Earlier that day, after their mid-day prayer *The Great One* had called him aside for a private meeting. With great solemnity and ceremony he told Rafi he had been selected as his personal apprentice. Rafi greeted the announcement with the proper amount of awe and gratitude. But inside his heart thumped rapidly and he could hardly catch his breath. Sometimes his skin crawled as panic surged through his body. *The Leader's* affection for him grew with every passing day and Rafi felt himself growing attached in return. His kindness and obvious warmth elicited a fondness for the man. He did not see him as a *G-d* or a Messiah or even a wise leader but as a lonely, fragile man who really needed an emotional connection with someone. Rafi felt that within the labyrinth of piety and politics he had created, the man had not one person to whom he could turn for warmth or caring. Beneath *The Leader's* rhetoric, beyond his strong inspirational presentation, was a man emotionally dependent on the shallow adoration of others. Rafi felt his stomach twist with guilt knowing how deeply his inevitable betrayal would wound the man. He had never been in this position. He didn't think he could go through with it. He had never experienced such divided loyalties. He kept reminding himself that this was the same man who advocated, in fact developed a plan for, the total destruction of the known universe. This is the man who would murder his family and everyone he had ever known. No matter how kind *The Great One* was to him, Rafi could never lose sight of the truth. Rafi could never lose sight of *The Great* One's true mission in life or for that matter his own mission.

He had realized since he'd accepted this mission how easy it would be for someone with a fragile grip on reality to be swept away by a leader such as this. The man was convincing and engendered respect even though he espoused cruelty and destruction. Rafi had studied sociology in college and learned about brainwashing in cults. *Now*, he thought, *I am experiencing what that is like first hand.*

Moshe's voice in his ear interrupted his thoughts. "Rafi, check your sound." Rafi breathed a sigh of relief. The voice grounded him and he was grateful for that. He checked his listening device. Glad Moshe had eyes on him and could see his slight nod. Then there was Ari. The closeness they had shared throughout their lives was a rare gift in this world of danger and uncertainty. Ari and Rafi shared a unique connection, rare even among identical twins. As toddlers, they not only had their own language, they communicated complex ideas without language. Eye contact, the slightest curl of a smile, a simple shrug conveyed paragraphs of information. As they grew older, their telepathy expanded. By the time they were 5, they no longer had to be in the same city in order to communicate with each other.

Hadara instantly perceived the value their gifts could have to Mossad and the free world but she also worried that it would put her sons' lives in danger. She knew there was a direct correlation between value and danger. Concerned that others would exploit their talents, she insisted that only Hakim and Samira know the extent of Rafi and Ari's abilities. Most people had some idea about their special connection, but assumed it was a simple 'twin thing.' By first grade the twins were fully telepathic.

Each twin could signal the need to communicate. Initially it was more experiential, simple feelings of fear, anxiety, anger, and excitement were most easily conveyed. Later other communications developed. Those occurred through the transmission of ideas and images. Soon archives of data could be transmitted from one another. What one of them knew, felt, thought or saw could be instantly transferred to the other. All without a single memory stick or computer keystroke.

But the marvel of their relationship went beyond their telepathy. The marvel was that each twin maintained his own unique personality, preferences and friendships. Though they knew and felt one another's thoughts and feelings they remained distinct individuals. Rafi was fun-loving and outgoing, great with words and people, charismatic, dramatic and emotional; while Ari was shy, serious, didactic and fact-based. He loved science and higher mathematics. Both twins valued their interdependence above all else. Once in Mossad, they carried out many successful missions, which had only been successful because of their unique relationship.

As Rafi bumped along through the desert to destinations unknown, he fervently wished that Ari were part of this mission. Lying there, he felt rather than heard Ari's voice. It was calm and reassuring "I've got your back...." The voice said. Rafi smiled slightly and fell asleep.

29 LONG DAYS NIGHT

The fifty-six foot Sea Ray glided across the Mediterranean toward the Aegean Sea and the beautiful Greek Island Serifos. Red-roofed, white stucco houses, trimmed in blue, jutted out of mountain sides like a living travelogue. Five men stood aft looking out at the unparalleled blue water waiting to land. The arrangements had been made; monies had been transferred to a special account in Sol Abramson's name. The funds were dispensable and untraceable. Boulos stood next to Sol seeming calm and unafraid. He was sure that his information was good and that he would end up having made a good deal. For reasons that made little sense to him, he trusted this man next to him. He seemed to be a solid and reasonable man and more than that, he seemed to have a deep spiritual sense about him. Sol Abramson almost seemed like a religious leader, not that Boulos considered himself to be an expert on such subjects, but it turned out, he was right! Duqaq Boulos had discerned the former Rabbi in Abramson; it gave him a sense of comfort. He believed that he could trust this man, Then he warned himself to be cautious. Abramson may be kind but he was still his captor.

"We're almost there," one of the crew called from the bridge and Sol glanced again at his watch and texted something into his cell phone. He felt good about his agreement with Boulos. He knew that the man was just a mercenary and hardly deserving of respectful treatment, but Abramson approached everything in an above-board manner and preferred persuasion to violence - he found persuasion to be more beneficial in the long run and less stressful in the short run. Boulos didn't know it, but Sol had struck similar bargains with the other men, who were at this moment being followed by other teams. None of the men had been tortured or killed though he made it appear that way. He had a unique, respectful way of approaching 'the enemy.' It was congruent with his moral values and it got results. Not that Sol couldn't kill or even torture if he had no other choice, it just wasn't his preferred method of operating. The men had given over their information and he had paid them for their help. He saw them as mercenaries not terrorists. It was a narrow distinction but a distinction nonetheless. If prisoners were determined to be terrorists they were turned over to the Americans, as part of the agreement between their two countries. What happened to them after that was not Sol Abramson's concern. He assumed many of his former prisoners permanently resided at Guantanamo Bay.

Docking the yacht took a matter of minutes, during which time Boulos found himself surrounded by men with guns hidden under their jackets. He was escorted to a waiting van, which lurched up narrow, winding roads to a remote villa perched on top of a picturesque mountaintop exploding with color. Vibrant tropical plants thrived; pink and red bougainvillea vines blossomed, white stucco buildings gleamed and their brilliant blue trim reflected the extraordinary sapphire sea. Everything was enhanced by the sparkling sunshine reflecting off every surface.

Once inside, the guards spread out checking doors and windows while Sol and Boulos entered a quiet meeting room with a long polished table and cushioned arm chairs. The air mingled the scents of lemon furniture polish and sea air. The draperies were opened to a panoramic view of beaches below and the lolling sea. This estate belonging to Mossad was used for private meetings of the highest caliber. While they waited for the meeting to begin, recording devices and video cameras were set up. This was to be a well-attended multi-national summit with representatives from America, Canada, Great Britain, Australia and Israel. While he waited for the meeting to begin, Boulos stretched out on a floral upholstered sofa and dozed off.

~~~~~~

Hakim was a nervous wreck. He checked his cell phone about fifty times, seeing message after message from his beloved wife, each message sounding less worried and more angry. He could feel her coldness stretching across the miles that separated them. He wanted more than anything to return to her, to make up and have things return to the way they had been before. He knew he was in big trouble. He recalled this coldness in her tone only one time before. It was a time when she had single-handedly tracked down a Mossad mole. This was the tone of voice he heard from her just before the mole was dispatched. He now sympathized with that mole. He felt more and more like his life was at an end. That perhaps the divided life they shared, living in separate worlds, having secrets they could not share had run out of time. On some level, he always felt they were living on borrowed time.

His role as special attaché to the Prime Minister was at the center of his current problems. At times, he was an official representative of the Prime Minister, representing him at the United Nations and black tie occasions. But sometimes his role was investigative, leading Hakim to the world of squalid back alleys, smoky cafés, and lavish baccarat games. He had connections and informants across the globe, always ready with wad of cash and an easy smile. Hakim Faysal was a charming man, handsome with a friendly glib style. Everyone, from people living on the streets to people living in regal embassies, liked him. No one, not even his wife ever suspected...

∿∿

Well established in the area west of Al Qubayyat, the Shaloub family had flourished in the textile industry. When their business expanded to include global markets, they grew wealthy and powerful. They prided themselves on their business acumen and praised *Allah* daily for their successes. Devout Muslims, they believed in sharing their wealth. They rebuilt their aged mosque and hired many unfortunates to work in their factories. Their textile business became the most successful in the Middle East. When time for expansion came, subsidiary companies were opened in France and Italy. Several Shaloubs had served in Parliament and one served on the Judicial Tribunal. The family had been educated abroad and married well within Lebanon's narrow upper class which networked across the country linking all the major industries: paper, jewelry, chemicals and olive oil. In the fifth generation of Shaloubs, five sons and three daughters survived to adulthood. The youngest of the sons was called Arman. Arman was a serious child, tending toward introversion; he was interested in learning and thinking. When at age four he was told that his name meant *whole, immense, universal* he felt proud and began to assimilate those characteristics into his personality. "I will be a great man one day," he told himself. One day he asked his mother if his name meant he was supposed to be an important person, a person who could save the world.

His mother hugged him and answered "Of course, my Arman, you can be anything you choose."

With a name like mine, I can be a G-d. I can save the world, he thought. However unlike most childhood beliefs that wax and wane over time, this belief expanded. By adolescence, Arman was convinced he had been born to save the world.

His mother knew Arman was different from other children. She worried about his oddities, his isolation and his strange ideas. She worried that he had little interest in playing with other children, or taking part in family activities, even refusing family meals. He would disappear for hours wandering around the compound muttering to himself and writing page after page of notes in perfect Arabic script. As a solution, she sent him to a boarding school in England known for its strict management of problem students, thinking if he had more structure he would snap out of his dream-world and start acting normally. The opposite proved true. In a foreign setting, Arman grew more withdrawn, increasingly immune to criticisms and punishments. The world he lived in had as little meaning to him as the people around him. The only thing of importance was his message. He called it his *Cataclysmic Regeneration Plan* and he shared it with no one. *The day has not come for my true plan to be revealed*, he thought. *The people are not ready*. And so he studied and wrote and waited for the time when he could unveil his manifesto.

30 WINDING PATHS

It was rather small for a tutor, but beautifully landscaped and in perfect condition. Much like the man himself, attention to detail was evident. One could not be a rare documents expert in a huge national museum without being more than a little obsessive! The home was furnished in old world style with huge oil paintings on dark paneled walls with heavy brocade furniture perfectly arranged. It was picture- perfect like a model room in a museum, not a single personal item anywhere in sight. Not a photograph, not a scrap of paper. It took them all of twenty minutes to go through the house from top to bottom and find nothing of meaning. Still they wandered around looking at the place where this man had lived since coming to Chicago, there had to be something someplace, they reasoned, and so they tapped on walls and removed objects from their frames and pedestals. After a 2 hour search two secret locations were found: one in a bathroom linen closet, the back of which opened to a small room filled with computers, communication equipment, and world maps bearing stick pins and a set of two-way radios. The team photographed and investigated the sight thoroughly but learned little about the underground network. The second hideaway was in the basement, behind a recently installed gas furnace. The space was about 40 feet long, lined with glass fronted cabinets behind which dozens of different types of guns were labeled and displayed. Many of them were ancient, old pistols from World War I and II, musket guns from the revolutionary war. A Civil War cannon sat in the center of the room, round black balls stacked nearby.

Across the room weapons of mass destruction were on display. Near each category a colorful poster hung, detailing the cabinet's contents. Nuclear weapons were displayed with framed photographs, labels and descriptions. Biological weapons were displayed in vacuum sealed containers, agents such as anthrax, botulinum toxin, ricin, and smallpox sat ready to assault populated areas at a moments' notice and lastly chemical weapons, like sarin, chlorine and cyanide were displayed along with hundreds of others. There was a special section with graphs and pictures devoted to the Nazi concentration camps and the gasses used to annihilate millions of people.

In another area, every naturally occurring poison known to man ranging from poison arrow frogs, rear-fanged snakes and lion fish to plants like oleander, belladonna and English Yew were stored. All items were perfectly labeled, its poison detailed and displayed with museum quality precision. Also displayed were raw materials needed for making bombs, different styles of pre-assembled car bombs accompanied by eight by ten photographs of successful bombings by the IRA and Al-Qaeda along with handwritten instructions for assembling and deploying bombs. As they were leaving the room T-Max noticed Ari transfixed in front of the exhibit. "What's up, Bro?" He asked coming up behind him and placing a hand on his back.

Jolted from his reverie, Ari stammered, "I was immersed into my thoughts, you might say."

"Okay," said T-Max turning to leave the exhibits, "We've got to move on now."

"I shall come in one moment," Ari replied as he pried open the lock and slipped a tiny brass vial, its label unmistakable, into his pocket.

Photographs along with detailed text messages were sent to Manny, with instructions to notify the FBI, the CDC, Homeland Security, the Chicago Police Department and anyone else that Manny could think of. This situation was well beyond the scope any of them expected and it was definitely time to bring in the 'big guns.' The away team planned to split up in order to reduce complications with the Feds. T-Max remained behind to escort a group of tense-looking government officials through the picture perfect Tudor home owned by one Herr Friedrich Müeller, a soon-to-be-former employee of the Field Museum.

~~~~~~

Galed Rachid, First Deputy of *The Sword of Justice's* protection squad, stared at the Yitshak Ben Zvi Hospital in Beersheba through his Bushnell Elite binoculars. He was agitated and aggravated. Not only had they failed to capture the child, they had not killed her. He was certain he had wounded her and seriously, there was so much blood squirting from the helicopter's open door, she had to be hit. But she had been alive when they took off, he heard her screaming. She could have died in the meantime but he had to be sure. Now here he was crouching in the brush near a hospital parking lot waiting to find out what happened to the child. To make matters worse, he lost three men in an impromptu gun battle. Where these attackers had come from he had no idea. Who in the world were these gunmen? Now he was down three men and it could take hours to bring in replacements. He might have to bring in men who were untrained, a risky move on his part. His men needed to be top-notch, trained, and ready to do battle.

Galed Rashid sighed and thought, *This whole situation is becoming a nightmare.* He saw himself as a warrior, fighting for the truth of his master, Shukri al-Sierawan, *The Great One*. He already had been humiliated by his master, for a mistake he didn't make and now he could expect nothing less than more of the same, all because of some little girl. The whole idea was ludicrous! He was a soldier not a babysitter! What in the name of *Allah* was a child doing in the middle of this great movement anyway?

Staring through the blazing sunlight, he barked out instructions to his diminishing band of soldiers ordering two of them to enter the hospital and get a status report on the child, find out her medical condition and where she was being treated. They needed to eliminate her, but could not afford to get caught so for now the instructions were 'observe and report.' Two of his men ripped and dirtied their clothing so it looked as if they'd been in a car accident and limped into the Emergency Room looking for Saroyah Ajram.

NANCY J. ALEXANDER

31 HI HO SILVER, AWAY

Sammy saw it first and pointed it out to Elisabeth. It was a light blue head scarf with pink flowers on it. They had several in stock. The two of them had been trekking through shop after shop in downtown Tel Aviv; picking up items that were on their shopping list. The plan had been devised while they were waiting at the hospital for Saroyah to come out of surgery. Their long list of necessary supplies were divvied up, Simon was combing through medical supply houses looking for the things they needed to make their plan come together. It was a high risk plan, involving many people, disparate locations and several check points. Yosef was coordinating with Manny, both hard at work making plans with youth organizations and paying their way through a maze of bureaucrats to obtain the needed documents.

A serious talk with Musnah was needed. It was decided that Elisabeth would travel to the Olive Grove and interview the cook. Layla, Jamila's oldest daughter was assigned to act as translator. It promised to be a difficult discussion, but the tearful cook had essential information.

~~~~~~

Assuming the posture of a grieving husband Gil, traditionally dressed positioned himself on the floor across the hall from the curtained area where Saroyah lay. Head down and eyes averted, he watched the crowd around him, seeking out those who meant harm to the child. He did not expect them to try and kill her here in the hospital, but he couldn't count on that. These were desperate circumstances and desperate men. He watched as two men in tattered clothing limped past the child's bed, peeking behind the curtain as often as they could. Gil kept an eye on them. Their clothing was dirty, but the dirt appeared to be spread on the clothes with even strokes. There was no blood on the clothes and their limping was inconsistent. No, Gil thought, these men had been sent in here to complete a mission. To watch or kill he wasn't sure, but he knew they were enemies.

With his cell phone buried in his sleeve, Gil texted Hadara who sat behind the skimpy curtain, patting her niece with one hand and pointing her gun toward the curtain with the other. They had agreed that a gunfight in the hospital was to be avoided if at all possible and believed that the two limping men would avoid one here too. Another attack on the child was to be expected but would occur later, after she left the protection of the ER. The *Sword of Justice* could not afford to be caught in an investigation about a gun battle in an Israeli hospital. That would stir up ill will. Besides, Hadara thought, it served their plan perfectly if the soldiers followed them. In fact, their magnificent plan would not work if they didn't.

~~~~~~

He sensed rather than heard the voice. Like a whisper, it roused him from a troubled sleep, frowning he tried to recapture it, but it was gone. He tried to remember what he had heard. Was it Moshe? Was it Ari? He couldn't be sure it was either of them. He waited in silence and soon heard it again. Two men in the front of the truck whispered softly. "...before daybreak...must be done ...a traitor...ordered it..." His hair pricked at the back of his neck as fear shot through his body. He strained to make out more words, but it was impossible.

He was convinced they were talking about him. He had to notify Moshe, but how could he do that? The ear com worked in only one direction and the pea-sized mike sewn into his collar would not pick up his thoughts. Then he pictured Ari. Ari would know what to do. If the whispers were about him things would rapidly deteriorate.

Breathing deeply he went into a deep meditative state. Oceans away, Ari was logged onto a wine-tasting chat group used by Mossad for covert conversations, when he was jarred by a flash. He signed off and turned his attention inward. Within seconds, he knew his twin was in trouble.

Rafi's anxiety came through in jagged waves. 'I'll take care of it' was Ari's response to his brother. Using more conventional means of contact, Ari tracked Moshe down and texted him 'Rafi may be in trouble prepare for emergency extraction.' Reading the text Moshe was momentarily puzzled about Ari's information then he figured it out. Within minutes Rafi heard "Got your message..." Grinning in spite of himself, Rafi felt like a kid again. Faster than the speed of light! He and Ari were up to their old tricks and *Baruch Hashem*, they still worked. Rafi settled in with the movement of the truck and fell asleep.

32 BY THE SEA

To the uninformed observer it looked like any other business meeting taking place this large comfortable room. The sea was magnificent, a rich blue dotted with white yachts floating past. With men sitting around the table tapping on their laptops it seemed like an ordinary meeting until you noticed four muscular men with bulges under their jackets positioned attentively around the room. Two stood stoically at the windows gazing out intently, another stood with his back to the door facing inward and a fourth stared fixedly at the prisoner. Duqaq Boulos, slouched in his chair, appeared carefree as he sipped his tea with a self-satisfied expression on his face. To him, this was the greatest outcome possible. Gathered around him were representatives of some of the most powerful nations in the world. He was amazed, impressed with himself. He'd always liked an audience and this was the most exclusive one ever.

Seated around the table were representatives from several countries including Lt Walter Ross of the US Navy, Gerald Magnum Harris, Assistant Secretary of Defense, CIA station chiefs from the Beirut, Damascus, Baghdad and Eudora Winders, representing the English Prime Minister and Sol Abramson.

Sol began the meeting "Mr. Boulos," he began "As you can see there are many people who are interested in what you have to say. The agreement that we reached before still stands and your agreement is between you and Mossad. Everyone here knows about our agreement" he said passing out copies to all present. "Even though your agreement is with Mossad these people are interested in this terrorist organization you seem to know so much about so they have been invited here to talk with you, as well. You can feel free to answer their questions, no harm will come to you from me or any of them no matter what you know or don't know. Is that clear?"

Boulos nodded his head and grunted assent. "I will be happy to tell you what you want to know. Ask away," he invited with a crooked smile.

Abramson: "Now Mr. Boulos, since this is an official debriefing, we are going to use a more formal question and answer format, do you understand?"

Boulos: "Sure, whatever..."

Abramson: "Mr. Boulos, you were hired to do some work for a group called *The Sword of Justice*, is that correct?"

Boulos: "Yea.. uh huh..."

Abramson: "Mr. Boulos, do you know the real name of the person referred to as *The Great One*?"

Boulos: "I have heard several names for him so I'm not sure. He goes by Shukri al-Sierawan, but I have heard him called Arman. I think that is his real first name but I never heard his real last name so I don't know if that helps or not." He shrugged.

Abramson: "Do you know where he is from or where he lived as a child?"

Boulos: "Somewhere in the north part of Lebanon near the Syrian border, I don't know for sure, I never went there, ya know."

Abramson: "Why do you think that is where he was from?"

Boulos: "I heard him say his soldiers were never to go near that area. I assumed it was because he has family there.

Abramson: Do you think he is protecting them or perhaps is estranged from them?

Boulos: How can I know such things? Never in my presence did he speak of family. It is just that of all the places he refuses to go, this area he most avoids. He is an odd one, do you know? He rarely talks and when he looks at you has this strange distant look in his eyes."

Abramson: "Do you think his strange look is due to drugs that he uses?"

Boulos: "Of course he uses hashish… he is always with the hookah many times a day, but I do not think that is the reason for his look. It's something else, more different than the drugs."

Abramson: "Does he make sense when he talks or does he seem confused, off point?"

Boulos: "He makes sense, but if a person thinks of the things he says they do not make sense. He is not hard to understand but the things he believes cannot be real."

Abramson: "Like what things?"

Boulos: "There are many crazy things like invisible tents to be forming over the Arab world. Things such as this…" Boulos drifted off. "I am not certain but the things are not real. I pick up ideas, you know from the people around there."

Abramson: "Okay, do you know if he went away to school, like to a university somewhere in the US or England?"

Boulos: "No. I do not know of this, but he speaks English clearly and I have heard him speak about England many times, so I think it is there that he attended school. He is very smart. Perhaps he is smarter than anyone I have ever known. Intelligent, but strange, you know? Like they say about geniuses, they are smart, but crazy. Do you know?"

Abramson: "When he speaks does he speak with any kind of accent?"

Boulos: "Of course yes, he speaks Arabic with a Lebanese accent, but there is also a touch of English to some of his words, so that may be why I think he was in England. Is it not true that you have to be someplace for many years before you speak with the accents of that place?"

Abramson: "So your best guess would be that he was in England for a while?"

Boulos: "Yea, he says a few English words that are only from that place you know like 'righto'… stuff like that… little words."

Aaronson: "What about his religious practices?"

Boulos: "He is a devout Muslim and demands the same from all of his followers. Everyone must come to pray five times a day and there are no exceptions. Even those preparing the food and serving it must come and pray."

Abramson: "So there is nothing unusual or different about his Muslim devotion?"

Boulos: "No, only he says that he needs to think after prayers and asks those around him to speak to one another so he can listen. It is how you say, weird. He goes into a sleeping state, closing his eyes and sighing. He refuses to speak or be spoken to. I think he does this after every prayer. I think it is some kind of religious thing but I guess it could be a kind of spying. So he can hear what the people are saying about him."

Abramson: "How long does that dream state last?"

Boulos: "Oh it could be an hour or more. He just sits there with his eyes closed and listens or sleeps or whatever he does."

Abramson: "You said there were women there. Is he ever with any of them in a more personal way?"

Boulos: "If you mean the way I think you mean, it is an absolute no! He doesn't even look at them. I do not hear him say he has a wife or children. He speaks nothing at all about personal things. Perhaps he is one of those holy men who made the promise to be without women... You know?"

Abramson: "You mean he's taken a vow of celibacy?"

Boulos: "Yea that is it. Perhaps it is that but I do not think it bothers him. You know like it would a normal man."

Abramson: "So he doesn't act like a 'normal' man?"

Boulos: "Not at all in those ways, like you mean. He doesn't like people really. They are not real to him and especially women. He shuns them, shuts them out. There are none who he speaks to or lets be near to him."

Abramson: "Do you know if he has ever worked or had a job?"

Boulos: "No, I do not think he ever works. He is a thinker. He talks and listens. He does nothing. He is served by others. He thinks he is a leader.

What kind of work could one like that do?"

Abramson: "So he never talks about working or past things he may have done?"

Boulos: "His hands are soft like a baby and his skin is pale and smooth. Never is he in the sun or working in the fields. His voice is soft like a girl's. I think he is rich all his life, taken care of, not working not doing anything before this. You know?"

Abramson: "Do you think he is from a wealthy family?"

Boulos: "Most assuredly it is yes. He is not a man of the people. He does not know how to do many things. He is spoiled rich. He sits and thinks and pats his beard. Always he is running his hands down his beard, like this," Boulos demonstrates

Abramson: "How old do you think he is?"

Boulos: "I think maybe fifty, but he looks many years older, not because of wrinkles but because of a weak tired look, bent back, grey hair. It seems he never exercised much, never worked hard."

Abramson: "So what do you think he has been doing all of these years?"

Boulos: "I do not know. Perhaps he just sits around and thinks. That's what he does now mostly. Thinks and watches people. Oh I forget ... he also writes. He keeps many notebooks and writes with long pens dipped in ink. Always he is writing and there is one whose job it is to carry his notebooks. Always that servant is near him with a big basket with woven handles. That man carries his books for him. Everywhere the man carries that basket and follows him from tent to tent. It is his only job. His name is Abdul-Jalal which means Servant of the Great. I do not know if he was given this job because of his name or it he was given this name because of his job. One does not know these things. Perhaps the servant was chosen first and that is how he decided to call himself 'The Great One'!" Boulos chuckled at his little joke. He was enjoying his time in the spotlight. He did love an audience.

Abramson: frowning at the man's frivolity asked "What does he do with these books, does he read from them to others or just write in them?"

Boulos: "He mostly writes in them. And he keeps them close by. There are times when he reads from them to groups of people. They are in a stack beside him all the time. When he leaves the tent Abdul-Jalal gathers them up and follows him. ”

Abramson: “What does he want from his followers?”

Boulos: “He is looking for people who can spread the word for him. Spread his message to the people so he has many followers. He wants many followers, but you see he is shy and is not so good a speaker. Unless he is facing many, many people, then he can be more like a leader, one who others want to hear. You know? He needs a few select followers who are good speakers and can speak for him.”

Abramson nodding slowly: “Where do you think his many followers have come from?”

Boulos: “Everywhere. They come from all over the Arab world. They love this man. I do not understand that for myself. They do not know him the way that I do. If they did perhaps they would not be so anxious to follow him. I do not know how they know of him or why exactly they love him, but they think he is a *god* of some kind. They bow down to him.”

Abramson: “Really, bow down?”

Boulos: “Oh yes, not on their knees, but stooping over like this.” (Boulos stands bows from the waist facing the floor and walks a few steps backward)

Abramson: “Do they seem to be afraid of him?”

Boulos: “No... well, wait a minute... maybe, yes. The followers are not, but the ones close to him, his soldiers and advisors... yes, I think it is true. I think that they are afraid of him. He can be harsh. Once I was in the camp, they had captured a man and tortured and killed him. *The Great One* wanted to watch and had the man brought in front of the entire camp for this to happen. I am a tough man, but I did not like to see this thing.”

Abramson: “Were you there when they brought in a small girl as a captive?”

Boulos frowning: “No, I had not heard they did that. I do not know of this thing.”

Abramson: “Do you know the names of any of his associates or advisors?”

Boulos: "I do not know his whole name, but there is a man, a Syrian man, who is called his Chief Advisor. That man has connections within his government and reports to them. I am not sure where are his loyalties lying. Perhaps he is not sure, as well. The first name of this man is Zuhair. I do not know his last name, but he is rather young, hefty and has lots of dark hair without any grey in it."

Abramson: "Can you tell us anything else about this man?"

Boulos: "Well, he has a mark, a strange mark like that Russian symbol. It is on his face. It is purple I think."

Abramson: "Russian symbol?" Picking up a pencil he sketched a hammer and sickle.

Boulos pleased: "Yes! That is it exactly. Like that part there." He points to the sickle.

Abramson: "Was this a tattoo or something he was born with?"

Boulos: "I am certain, born. It is not so perfect like a tattoo and then there is the color. Who would put the color purple on his face?"

Abramson: "Where on the face is this mark?"

Boulos pointing to his cheekbone near his eye. "It is there, right there."

Abramson: "And this man is from Syria. Are there many others from Syria?

Boulos: "There are some I cannot say how many. I say most every Arab country except Egypt and Yemen have sent people, official people to meet with this man. People do not say what country they are from, but I hear their voices and can make out many accents. Every country wants him to be their friend especially that is important if he becomes famous and has much power. He has the ear of the poor farmer. Many governments shall we say curry his favor. They fear him and want to make sure he doesn't grow too strong. But there are some governments who are seeking to make him famous. They give him money."

Abramson: "Do you think he started this group and is the designer of its ideas and beliefs?"

Boulos: "That is a definite yes. This is, how you say, his baby. That is a definite. No one knows the ideas like he does. When he reads to his followers from one of his books, it is a great occasion. Like a holiday. He reads and others sit and listen and they praise him many times over and there is food and music. He has many books. Some look like they are years old. In some, the paper is yellow and the pages are torn along the edges. He has been writing in these books for many years. These books contain all that he wrote about his group. They are like his Koran *Allah* forgive my saying so."

Abramson: "How about his defenders? Does he have an army? Do they have weapons?"

Boulos: "It is hard to tell about this question. They have many people around the camp walking with guns and acting like they are soldiers. I do not know these uniforms. They are not real ones like from any country's army I see. Sometimes more come in by truck and sometimes they leave and go somewhere. It seems there are many and they have much weapons but I do not know about this for sure."

Abramson: "Do you know the commanders of this army?"

Boulos: "There is one I know. He acts like the boss of all the army. He is called Rashid. He is tall and very thin with a scar across one eye, but he can see with this eye. I think a knife went like this," he mimes a movement across his eyebrow to his nose. "I believe he is Iraqi. He is another who I think serves two masters. I do not know this for sure, but it seems to me like that is so. I have seen *The Great One* being very angry at this man and when that happens, this man gets a certain look in his eye that tells me he is wanting to kill *The Great One*. It is more than his pride that is injured, I think. One time I see him talking to an official who came in from that country. The man wore a splendid black robe over a suit, like a Shite cleric with a black turban on his head. I think it was a secret meeting and that Rashid was giving reporting to that man."

Abramson: "Where do you think the organization gets their money?"

Boulos: "That I do not know. I do know that they get much money from somewhere because their camp is large with many people and it costs much to feed and clothe all these people and to have an army and buy all their guns. I do not know where all the money comes from, but they have much of it. They must for these ones do not work or produce any money on their own. It is from others that they get their monies. Wealthy oil rich Arabs give them money, but I do not know who those people are."

Abramson: "How long have you worked for them?"

Boulos: "For about a year now, but my friend, you are now straying into forbidden areas. Not to talk about me, was that not our agreement, no?"

Abramson: "You are right. I am just trying to figure out how long you've known them so we can get a sense of how current your information might be."

Boulos: "Oh yes, well about one year, maybe a bit longer. And I was there in his camp often."

Abramson: "What do you think the goals of this group are?"

Boulos: (Looking around the room he said expansively) "To destroy everyone in the world who is not an Arab."

Abramson: "Really? Everyone?"

Boulos: "Yes, really, it is definitely true. Israel, the US of A, England, yes everyone else who is not Arab. Shukri al-Sierawan swears that *Allah* will put some bubble made of plastic, maybe, around his people and save them."

Abramson: "How is he planning to destroy the world?"

Boulos: (Shrugging) "With bombs perhaps? Or gasses... something like that. I was asked to supply certain products for explosions...big ones. But remember we are not to discuss these personal things for my own safety, remember my friend?"

Abramson: "Boulos, you have been most helpful. Before we stop for today can you tell us where they are camped right now?"

Boulos: (Shrug) "Who knows? If they have left the place where I saw them before, then I think they are going to a more hidden place. *The Great One* gets in touch with me no matter where I am or where he is. It is like magic!" Boulos grinned. "I never am told where he is any time. If he needs me he finds me and I am brought to him at his camp."

Abramson: "Do you think you could look at a map with our experts and make some guesses as to where they might go? I know you visited two of their other camps so you have some idea about the things they are looking for in a campsite."

Boulos: "Of course I can do that for you, my friend." He smiled and reached over to pat Abramson's hand. "But for now I am tired. Perhaps some food and a good night's rest would help my memory be fresh."

Abramson: "That's fine. Let's stop for now, but one more thing. Have you ever known *The Great One* to meet people away from his campsite?"

Boulos: "No. It would take a lot for him to do this. The meeting would have to be very important, with a very important person for him to leave the safety of his camp. This is a very cautious man. Perhaps if he did something like this, it would be to meet with a high level government official of some sort." He shrugged. "I do not know of such a meeting you understand, it's just what I think."

Abramson: "These men," he nodded toward 2 guards, "will see to it that you have a good meal and show you to your room for the night. Have a pleasant evening Boulos, we'll meet again tomorrow."

Boulos: (Looking warily at his guards) "I am most certain that these men will take good care of me according to your instructions my friend."

Abramson: "Of course, my friend, according to my instructions. Rising they shook hands and Boulos left the room, accompanied by his two guards.

33 BEST MADE PLANS

His legs and back were killing him, scrunched up as he was. His greatest fear was that he would need to spring into action and would be unable to get up! Lots of help he would be then! The traffic in the ER miraculously had slowed. The waiting room now held just two injured people waiting to be seen. In the doorway, he saw an ambulance driver chatting up an ER nurse. In the hallway, he watched a woman leaning over a gurney brush her fingers gently across a man's forehead. He supposed the man was her husband. Gil texted Hadara saying he had to move around a bit but got no answer. Painfully, he pulled himself to a standing position and limped toward the blue curtain surrounding the child's bed. Looking in, he saw that they were both sleeping soundly. Hadara leaned forward, her cheek on the child's pillow; her Glock19 clutched in her hand. Gil moved his neck back and forth to loosen the tight muscles and shuffled downheartedly toward the waiting room. Far in the back near the rear exit, the two limping men watched him steadily. He stretched and scratched his head as if to wake himself up and ambled toward the coffee machine.

Yawning, he sipped his coffee and wandered outside. The night air felt good, a bit cooler than he expected, but pleasant. As he sipped his coffee and smoked a cigarette he scanned the area. Positioning himself to keep one eye on the limping men, he scrutinized the end of the parking lot where two jeeps sat; their motors off and their lights out. In the moonlight he could make out two figures watching the ER entrance. These men, he assumed completed the assault team assigned to kill Saroyah. He wondered what their plan was and what they were waiting for? Grinding out his cigarette stub, he returned inside.

She knew that before she could ask a single question she had to change the situation. Musnah could not be questioned in the kitchen with everyone standing there watching her, judging her. She had to be placed in a safe room with only Layla and herself present. Meeting with Jamila and her parents in the living area she explained who she was and why she was there. Jamila refused to allow Musnah to be unchained or removed from her guards. "Where will she run to?" Elisabeth asked Jamila. "Where? You and the house guards can be right outside the door. Please let me question her in a way that will get us the information we need."

"I have seen many investigations on the television, even American television," said Jamila. "I know they are not careful about how the person feels. They threaten and scare them. That is what you should do."

"I do not operate that way. I operate differently. I ask you to please cooperate. We don't have much time. We are working on big plans that have delicate timing and we can not afford to waste time this way."

"You are blackmailing me," Jamila shrieked, losing her battle with self control.

"Jamila," her father interupted. "This woman has come from a great distance to help us. Hadara asked her to come. You must let her do her work.

"I will not let Musnah be unchained," Jamila said again. "My child is missing and she is a criminal."

"My daughter," her father continued, "this is a horrible time, but you must keep your wits about you. This is not the time to lose your perspective."

"Lose my perspective! I have lost my child!" Jamila shouted at her father and weeping lept to her feet when her mother spoke, her quiet voice pulling Jamila to a stop.

"My dearest one," Hala Faysal said, "Come and sit here with me so we can speak in private for a moment."

Jamila returned to her mother's side. The older woman pulled her in close so they could whisper to one another.

Sensing that the mood had shifted Elisabeth spoke softly "Jamila, Hadara brought us here to help. You must leave this to me, we do not have much time." Elisabeth said firmly. Jamila looked up and gave her assent with a slight head nod.

Elisabeth and Layla walked toward the kitchen, "Do not hold this against my mother," Layla implored following her, "she is not usually like this, she is very upset."

"I completely understand," Elisabeth assured her, "but we need to get ready to talk with your cook. Push those thoughts from your mind, I need you to focus so I can brief you on our plan. Please listen carefully to everything I say and do exactly what I ask you to do."

Layla looked at her and solemnly nodded her head. "I will do my very best," she agreed as Elisabeth settled down in front of her and spread a paper out on the table between them explaining her strategy.

The first thing she did when they were settled in a small room near the kitchen, was introduce herself and explain that she not the police and had no authority over her and meant her no harm. She explained that she was talking to her on behalf of the Faysal family and was there to help. She said she knew that Musnah was a good person, that Hala had hired her to work for this family when she was just a teenager. She said she knew that Musnah loved this family, but she also loved her own family and had been placed in a difficult situation. Musnah remained silent and fearful.

Elisabeth leaned over to Layla and made a suggestion. Immediately the child left the room returning minutes later with her grandmother. Hala Faysal was amazing. She knew exactly what to do. As if trained and briefed for this mission, she leaned forward and spoke to her old cook in a familiar tone assuring her that she was in no danger, that the family needed her help and to please answer Elisabeth's questions truthfully. Layla translated carefully and Elisabeth could tell by the older woman's expressions that she understood what was being said. She smiled encouragingly at Layla and Musnah then said "I know you are worried about your grandson and about Saroyah. You feel either way you turn you may hurt one of them. But let me assure you nothing you say will be used to hurt your grandson. He is being held by the Israeli government. I give you my word that nothing you say can harm him but it could help us save Saroyah." Haltingly the story emerged.

The grandson was spending time with his uncle Muhammad who was not a very good person. Musnah heard rumors he sold guns and things to the wrong people. She had urged her grandson to stay away from this uncle. This uncle has no blood relationship to Musnah. He was married to her daughter's husband's sister, who died many years ago. Musnah's daughter's family had not seen or heard from this uncle for many years. He was traveling, she heard in Afganistan. He returned a few months ago and contacted people he used to know, among them her grandson Imad, who she called a *kharoof* (sheep). She said since he was a little boy, her grandson was easily led and influenced by others. She said when this uncle returned from Afghanistan, Imad began to spend time with him, lots of time. Then she received a note from that uncle Muhammad saying that Imad would be in great trouble unless she did one favor for them. The note instructed her to leave a small side gate unlocked on one specific day. It was the day that the child was taken. She said she had not known what to do. She had been frantic, but she said, tears rolling down her wrinkled cheeks, that she had not done it. She refused to open that gate even for her own grandson. She said a short time after that the child was taken and her grandson and the uncle were captured. She said she did not know who had opened that gate and repeated that she had not done so. Someone else did this terrible thing that led to the child's capture.

As Musnah wept, Elisabeth encouraged her to continue. Musnah said that was all that she knew. She didn't know who opened that gate or who came in through the gate and didn't know who sent the note. "Do you have that note?" Elisabeth asked. Musnah nodded, slipped her hand into her apron pocket and handed Elisabeth a wrinkled square of paper with some Arabic script scribbled across it. Elisabeth handed the note to Layla who studied it for a few moments and said, "It says *'your grandson will die unless you unlock the side gate in two mornings. Tell no one or he dies.'* There is no signature," Layla, her brown eyes wide, stared at the note dangling from her fingertips.

"That raises more questions than it answers," Elisabeth murmured almost to herself. Raising and walking to the window she gazed out toward the olive trees, it was then she noticed two workers watching her.

Asking Layla to accompany her she walked outside in their direction. The men turned away averting their eyes but seemed interested in her. "You have something to tell me?" Elisabeth asked the men as Layla translated. Hesitantly the men answered, "Yes, we were uncertain what to do about this when the little girl was taken, but we decided we have to tell you things we saw." They glanced worriedly at Layla. Elisabeth understood that they didn't want to speak in front of her but as she couldn't talk with them directly there was no other choice. So she said, "Layla is helping me now.

You can tell us what you saw without worry," she said, "and please speak freely."

One of the workers nodded sadly and said, "Several men met here the day the child was taken. One man looked familiar; he looked important, dressed in a Western suit. He arrived in a limousine." The worker paused and looked at his friend. "He had several guards. Another man was older, he wore a long garment; he had a long beard, he looked like a holy man, a soldier with a gun guarded that man. There were two other men who also came. One of those men was older and one younger, they stood close together. They carried a large box. It seemed they were going to show what was in that box." ... here the man hesitated.

Sensing there was more, Elisabeth asked, "was anyone else there?" Still the man hesitated, Elisabeth said, "please..." and the worker looked at Layla and sadly said,

"There was another man. He did not come into the meeting but stayed inside the limousine. We saw him through the fence. We could see his face. Layla, it was your father. We are sorry to tell you this. He did not come inside to the meeting, he waited outside the gate but he came with the fancy dressed man in the big black car." The other worker nodded and looked down at the ground. "We saw him, your father sitting in the back; the window was down because he was smoking a cigarette. He did not see us. We saw him. We are so sorry."

The other man said, "We do not wish to say bad news for you or your family. We are very sorry."

Layla had gone pale and looked about to cry. "Please go on," Elisabeth prompted reaching over and taking Layla's small hand in hers. "This is important. What happened next?"

"Well," said the first worker, "The fancy dressed man and the bearded man talked about something referring to the box. They opened the box and took out guns, different kinds of guns, not like the guns we have ever seen. The fancy man seemed to know the two men with the box but the bearded man did not and he was uninterested in the box. That bearded man was interested in the fancy man; he talked mostly to him. That man's guard was interested in the box and spoke with the bearded man about the box." said the second worker.

"We left then to return to work," the second worker continued. "We never saw them again. We don't think that they saw us. We did not see Saroyah and did not see them take her. If we had seen that we would have stopped them. I assure you we would not have let them take the child. Later when we heard that she, the child, was gone we worried that it had something to do with that meeting. But we also worried that if those men knew we had seen them they would return and kill us or our families. We grieved for Saroyah but also we feared for our own children. We hope she is still alive but fear that she is not. These were frightening men, Layla. They had hard eyes, very hard eyes."

Pulling out her cell phone, Elisabeth texted a summary of what she learned to Gil and Hadara. The text she received expressed her feelings exactly "It's getting harder and harder to put this puzzle together."

34 DECISIONS AND COLLISIONS

They whispered together in the back seat of the black SUV, trying to determine their next course of action. Zuhair Bayan, his most trusted advisor seemed unsure of himself and that made *The Great One* uneasy. Galed Rashid had texted details of what appeared to be an American Cowboy-style standoff in the parking lot of the Yitshak Ben Zvi Hospital in Beersheba. It was ludicrous. It was completely unacceptable! They were *The Sword of Justice*. They were meant to work in the shadows. They were meant to be hidden from the public eye except when they were able to carry out a grand act in the name of *Allah*! Then they would burst into the spotlight of the world. Clever, respected and feared. Declaring the greatness of *Allah*! Speaking against the impurity of Israel and the West, they would lead their faithful Muslim followers into the dawn of tomorrow. But now they looked like fools. Stuck in some parking lot waiting to kill or capture some little girl. It was beyond ridiculous and yet what choice did they have? The child had seen more than she should have. She had seen his face! She had seen him with a Lebanese official! They should have killed her when they caught her. Now they were stuck. Should they bomb the whole hospital? Should they breech the building and shoot everyone surrounding the child? NO, that would shame and invite criticism, not awe and respect. Their followers would not be pleased with such an action. All they could do was to wait until the child left the hospital and was in a more neutral area. Then they would capture her or shoot her, and only her.

Zuhair Bayan was worried. This was indeed a complex problem with no easy solution, but what worried him even more was *The Great One* himself, he seemed so hesitant and uncertain. He didn't look well. Bayan, *the Leader's* doctor not just advisor, felt his pulse and checked his heart but there were no drastic signs of distress. He had no medicine to prescribe. *The Leader* shrugged the doctor off. "This is not necessary," he said. "I am physically well, my friend. I am worried, that is all. I have the weight of the world on my shoulders; that is all to be said." Bayan considered the situation, *the Leader* was a thoughtful man given to introspection, but this was different, the man was changing; he was more distant but Bayan couldn't put his finger on exactly why. He thought it started when the boy called Rafi arrived at the camp. Zuhair Bayan had a strange feeling about that boy. He was too perfect and his connection with *The Great One* was too strong. A youngster, a complete stranger won *The Great One's* ear. Out of thousands of followers, this young man had been chosen. Just like that. It made no sense. There was something magnetic about the boy, something almost hypnotic. Bayan didn't understand it; he didn't like it.

He sighed and felt a deep worry settle into his chest. He had been trying to turn *The Great One* against the boy with suggestions and innuendos. He wanted to eliminate the boy to kill him like the traitor he believed he was. He worried this was backfiring and that every negative utterance was turning *The Great One* against HIM and not the fledgling. He felt *The Great One's* eyes on him when he was not looking, staring at him, watching him. One the one hand he wanted to kill the boy and be done with it. On the other hand he feared that *The Great One* would be infuriated if he took such drastic action against his protégé. He thought, *What if it is a mistake? It could never be undone. What if this turns The Great One against me? He believes that this young man is destined to be his voice to the world, that he is meant to lead The Sword of Justice.* Bayan made a final decision as he reached for his cell phone. *Better to be safe than sorry,* he thought as he began texting.

~~~~~~

Simon and Sammy disguised in caps and beards had been preparing the props and costumes needed for their grand production. Pockets full of shekels; they combed the area around the hotel introducing themselves as agents for Continent Film Producers hiring extras for a documentary on "How Israel's Transit Authority Handles the Handicapped." They had a whole spiel about the forthcoming film due to air on 60 Minutes in mid-September and coached people as they handed out money, maps, and instructions. People eagerly offered their time and talents for the venture. A dress rehearsal was scheduled to begin shortly using several entrances and exits in the hotel's garage. Everything had to be letter perfect, no exceptions.

~~~~~~

Elsewhere, Elisabeth and Layla were doing their best 'CSI' imitations in the compound, focusing on the area near the side gate. Walking through the compound they found a small area near the animal pens where several chairs and a small table were arranged and the ground was littered with cigarette butts and several discarded bottles of soda. Footprints in the soft, sandy earth showed different sized sandals and a few pairs of hard soled men's shoes. Elisabeth collected the bottles and several cigarette butts from the earth while Layla searched the broader area. Inside the feed shed, Assi approached her meowing for attention. "This is Saroyah's cat, Assi," Layla called to Elisabeth bending over to pet the cat's head, "She just had a litter of kittens. They must be around here somewhere."

"See if you can find them," Elisabeth suggested, "Maybe this is why your sister was out this way. I don't think those men came here looking for her. I think they were meeting here and she saw them. Find Assi's litter and we will have another piece of our puzzle."

Five minutes later, Layla called to Elisabeth from a nearby shed. Turning, Elisabeth saw Layla's eyes staring at her through a slit between two logs. Elisabeth was triumphant! Focusing her cell phone camera on the shed she declared, "This is where those men had their secret meeting. Your sister was captured because she saw them. She can identify them. Whoever they are they could not risk being seen together. I don't know why they were here to begin with but this much is clear. They didn't want to be seen and she saw them.

Maybe this stuff," she held up the evidence she'd collected, "will give us fingerprints that will identify those men and help us figure out what they were doing here in the first place."

Hadara and Gil took turns watching the jeeps in the parking lot and watching Saroyah sleep. The 'limping men' took turns pacing past the curtained ER rooms and talking with the men in the jeep. Everyone pretended to be unaware of each other, moving at a slow casual pace, avoiding eye contact and feigning disinterest. Gil concluded they did not intend to attack the child in the hospital, but were waiting for her to be discharged. That meshed with their plans perfectly.

During the night Mikhail Gendel, arrived to help. Moaning, with his head wrapped in bandages, he was assigned to the cubicle next to Saroyah's. From his vantage point, he could watch the child and the action in the hallway. Around 6AM, Yosef appeared wearing green surgical garb. Stethoscope around his neck, he busied himself checking patient charts and examining Mikhail and Saroyah. By mid-morning two more jeeps bearing reinforcements joined the two parked at the perimeter. The totals were four – for Mossad and ten – for *Sword of Justice*. Hadara would have been worried, but she knew reinforcements were en route.

~~~~~~

Jamila and her children arrived at the ER. Grim-faced and determined, they had packed their crucial belongings. Most would be shipped to Chevra Hatzollah Headquarters in Chicago and some they would carry. The hardest thing for Jamila had been the talk with her parents. This was the worst possible time for her to be leaving them, now that they were getting older. Jamila had devoted her life to the Olive Grove. The business and family responsibilities had been her main focus. Now, it had come down to one decision. She had to choose her children's safety. Her parents would be safe where they were. The servants would care for them, protect them if necessary. And it's not as if they were incapacitated.

Her parents sat silently hugging their grandchildren as they listened to their daughter. This was a lot of information to absorb and they were emotionally overloaded. Her father was the first to speak. His mind still strong and clear; he understood Saroyah's situation; he knew about *The Sword of Justice*. He and his wife had been apprised of the situation and were not surprised that Jamila was planning to flee with her children to another country. If they weren't safe here they agreed that Jamila and the children should go. Amal and Hala Faysal were not extremists, they were peace-loving Lebanese, strong believers in the Muslim faith, but not against or opposed to other faiths or other ways of life. Through the years they had traveled the world extensively. They appreciated many of the things that other countries had to offer. They especially loved America. New York City with its Broadway shows and gourmet restaurants was a favorite of theirs. Fifteen years ago, they purchased a condo on the Lower East Side so they could vacation in New York every year. "You must do what you must do," Hala said as she hugged her weeping daughter and kissed her grandchildren in turn. "We will be fine here; we will keep things going until you can return."

"Go in peace, my daughter." Her father added "Keep your children safe and return to us as soon as you are able." Amal hugged each of his grandchildren close, "We will keep you in our prayers," he said to them.

As they were getting in the car, Amal approached his daughter and asked, "Do you know where the men are?" He was, of course, referring to his two sons and his son- in-law, Jamila's errant husband Gamil.

Jamila shook her head, "No, Abii, I have not heard from any of them." Amal frowned and shook his head.

"I will try and find them," he said to her.

"Do be careful, Abii," she said, "Do not take any unnecessary risks."

"Do not worry about me, I am not unused to troubling times you know," her father said with a sly wink.

Saroyah was awake and overjoyed to see her family crowding into the small curtained cubicle. Hadara allowed a brief reunion and then sat them down for a briefing. It was of the utmost importance for each and every one of them to be clear and to know exactly what would be happening and when. Tension flooded the small curtained cubicle as the complex plan was outlined.

35 JIGSAW

Homeland Security agents locked the door behind them and draped the entrance of the Tudor with "Crime Scene" tape, after photographing every inch of the house and loading every scrap of evidence into three large blue vans. This had been a treasure trove and they had Mossad and some obscure undercover Jewish group to thank for it. And thank them they did, profusely. They met T-Max and Pablo at an Inter-State rest stop where they took custody of one indignant Herr Friedrich Müeller, who was demanding to see his lawyer. The weapons dealer was tucked away in back of a heavily guarded Police Department van that was headed for a remote airstrip in the Illinois countryside where an Air Force jet was waiting to fly them to Washington, D.C. Every law enforcement agency that had anything whatsoever to do with fighting terrorism or protecting the United States had been alerted. Cell and landlines rang, faxes buzzed, computer keyboards clattered and every satellite that could be tasked was busy with surveillance activities related to the capture of this former Rare Documents Specialist.

Since they had played a key role in unearthing this terrorist network, the Director of Mossad and six advisors were being flown into Washington, D.C. aboard a U.S. Air Force Jet accompanied by a squadron of 6 fighter jets. The Joint Chiefs of Staff, the heads of the CIA, FBI, Homeland Security, State Department, Defense Department, and the U.S. Secret Service had been in lengthy briefings with the President and the Vice President and were prepared to move to an international level with this process. The National Terrorism Advisory System had been cranked up to orange.

Duqaq Boulos stood at the window watching a pair of hummingbirds as they flitted around the red bougainvillea blossoms. It was fascinating to watch them hover aiming their tiny beaks at the flowers' nectar, the speed of their wings so fast he could scarcely see them as they moved. It amazed him that the birds never landed but zoomed from place to place like tiny helicopters with wing beats possibly as high as 200 times per second. Boulos had always liked birds, they interested him. He often wished that he could fly. How wonderful that would be, he thought, to be able to soar over the land, see things from a distance. Hearing the door knob click he saw that Sol Abramson had returned, "Well, my friend," he said to his interrogator turned benefactor, "Have you more questions for me?"

"Only a few," Sol replied, "What do you know about a German called Müeller?"

Boulos turned slowly from his window view suddenly wary. There was something different in the other man's attitude. Boulos didn't know what had caused the change, but he had learned to pick up signals that were almost imperceptible to others. To him it was as clear as the wing speed on the tiny hovering birds he had been watching. Something had changed and before he answered any more questions he resolved to find out what it was.

~~~~~~

Samira moved across the room toward her brother, "What is wrong, my brother, you are suddenly in a different space," she whispered sliding in next to him. Ari looked at her curiously, "You too are perhaps becoming telepathic, my sister?" he teased.

"Come on, Ari, give…" she demanded somewhat impatient, "what's going on?"

"It's Rafi," he responded. "He's in trouble. I contacted his back-up at Mossad and let them know what I know but I'm worried."

"Tell me what you know," Samira directed, "tell me everything and we will figure out what to do."

"Tell us too," Stella said coming over to sit near them. "We're all in this together and seven heads are better than two."

Ari hesitated for just a moment then he agreed. Everyone gathered around to listen to Ari speak. *The Reinhardt's had identical twins in their family too, Ari thought, so perhaps they will be familiar with some of these phenomena.* He started with, "My brother is in danger and you have proven yourselves worthy of my trust."

"Rafi and I can communicate with each other," he began. "It started when we were small and has grown more complicated and intense over time. We are what you call telepathic. We can contact each other and know what the other one is thinking and feeling. This morning I got an urgent message from Rafi. He was in a truck traveling through an unknown desert with members of the terrorist group *The Sword of Justice*. He has infiltrated their group and is presenting himself as a staunch devotee of a man named Shukri al-Sierawan who is called *The Great One*. Rafi has established a close relationship with him but feels that others are envious of that relationship and he fears they mean him harm. One who is most distrustful is the leader's Chief Advisor, Zuhair Bayan, a former Syrian official. This man has the power to authorize his arrest. He feels that might happen behind *The Leader's* back and without his knowledge. His handlers are putting an extraction plan in place but there is no assurance that it will happen in time or even that they can get to him at all. I am most concerned."

Reina turned to Ari and asked "When was the last time you were in contact with Rafi?"

"Nearly 5 hours ago," Ari said.

"Try and reach him now and see what the situation is," Reina urged. "Go into the other room if you need to be alone and get in touch with him. We will start planning an intervention from our end."

~~~~~~

Hakim Faysal received regular coded reports from his many contacts but he was out of action now, spirited away from a little café by guards and escorted to the Prime Minister's Palace. He'd been here for hours. He dared not use his cell phone for fear that his messages would be intercepted. Hakim sighed as he looked around the room. He did not think he was a prisoner, but the Prime Minister had asked that he remain here and await further orders. Hakim of course complied. He never argued with the Prime Minister; he was not a man who tolerated dissention. His position of leadership in Lebanon had come at great cost. He had fought for his power and he knew how to keep it. He trusted few people and dealt harshly with those who betrayed his trust.

Consulting text messages he'd received earlier he knew that Saroyah was safe and that Hadara was knee-deep in her protection detail. For the moment his wife and children were accounted for. He paused. But he was the missing piece! He didn't know what Hadara knew about him. He doubted she had any idea how much trouble he was in. Hakim had been functioning for the last 10 years as a special attaché and public policy advisor to the Lebanese Prime Minister. That was common knowledge, but there was much that people didn't know about him and that fact could put him in conflict with his wife. Hadara Eiliat was a purist. In her book regardless of its reason there should be no lies between husband and wife. Hakim Faysal could not get over the sense of foreboding that hovered around his heart. Something was wrong, but he couldn't put his finger on what it was. He reviewed his actions over the last several days but could not identity what went wrong. The last thing he remembered was racing through the desert as their compound exploded behind them. Somehow Abdullah's assignment in the Beqaa Valley, the importation of chemical bomb materials, even his niece's kidnapping was tied up with the reason he was being 'held' in the Prime Minister's Palace. He referred again to his cell phone and began texting but stopped mid-sentence and turned the phone off. If he was under suspicion everything he did on his phone could be tracked. Anxiously, he stared down at his black phone screen then looked around the room for signs that he was being watched. I better not be, he thought as he scanned the bookcases for hidden cameras.

~~~~~~

Gamil crouched near the Grove's oil loading dock watching his family depart. He was weeping so hard he could barely see through his binoculars. He wanted to race from his hiding place, to run to them, to hold and comfort them, but he could not. He could not go near them until his problem was resolved. This problem, as he thought of it, had to be resolved, but he could not for the life of him see how that could ever happen. He had made a mistake, a horrible mistake and for that he feared he would lose his family and perhaps his life. It was a horrible price to pay for a small mistake. But then, he asked himself, was this a small mistake? Perhaps it was a big one! A big, huge, horrible mistake! A mistake for which he would spend the rest of his miserable suffering.

Gamil worked as Financial Advisor to the country's Agricultural Minister. In his role as consultant he inadvertently stumbled across some mysterious figures in the Ministry budget. One mysterious line item kept cropping up over the past several months. Large payments, oddly labeled 'Seeding' were being funneled to an obscure import/export company located on the Syrian fringe of Lebanon's northern border. Further investigation showed that the money was ending up in the coffers of a small local Mosque translated from Arabic was 'Allah's Hand.' Further investigation revealed that Allah's Hand, made regular cash contributions to a fund managed by a man by the name of Zuhair Bayan, who it turned out was Chief Advisor to Shukri al-Sierawan aka *The Great One*, undisputed leader of *The Sword of Justice*.

Gamil hastened to report this discovery to his superior the Agriculture Minister Isma'il Marzuq. As he explained what he found, the man grew eerily quiet. His face darkened and his jaw tightened. "Sit down, Gamil," the man commanded. Uncertain, Gamil did as he was told. "I am not pleased that you have discovered this, shall we say, little investment. This new group offers great promise for all our people. They will grow stronger than Hezbollah which as you know opposes my re-election. I have been supporting this new group because of their opposition to Hezbollah. They promise to grow large and powerful and will take down the entire Western world and wipe Israel off the map." Gamil was horrified. For the first time he felt he did not know this man who always seemed reasonable though somewhat detached. Hearing these words he felt frightened. He thought he knew this man he'd been working for but apparently he had no idea who the man was. "Now Gamil," the man continued his tone hard, "You must tell no one of your findings. You must now prove your loyalty to me. To do that you must do me a little favor. It is essential that I meet with the leader of this group. If I'm going to continue to support them I need to meet with their leader, a man called Shukri al-Sierawan. You will arrange for me to do that. The meeting needs to take place in a quiet remote area as we must never be seen together. To be seen together would threaten our whole arrangement. You will set up such a meeting. If you do not do this you will be arrested, tried as an enemy of the state and executed. Do you understand me?"

In the days that followed, Gamil did as he was told. He told no one of his accounting discovery; he set up a meeting between Ishma'il Marzuq, *The Great One* and some illegal arms dealers. He set it up at the one place he thought was safe, remote and peaceful...the Olive Grove. Gamil now realized the mistake he had made. He had steered these terrorists, because he knew that's what they were directly to his home; he put his family in danger and had gotten his child kidnapped. In trying to appease the Minister of Agriculture he had destroyed his family and had become an enemy of the State.

~~~~~~

Sammy and Simon had all the film they needed. They were ecstatic. The guest actors had played their roles to perfection! They went off, happy and well paid for a few hours of work and if they searched the internet for the film they just shot they would be disappointed to find that the program had been cancelled due to lack of funding. Up in their hotel room the twins uploaded the videos to Manny's network so he could put the rest of their plan in motion. Simon and Sammy reviewed the specifics of the escape plan then they packed all their equipment and everyone's personal belongings into shipping crates, checked out of the hotel and headed toward the Airport. The Chicago branch of Chevra Hatzollah was leaving Tel Aviv.

Watching from his spot in the parking lot, Galed was surprised to see an empty school bus pull up to the ER entrance and a driver climb out. He sent two of his men to learn what was going on with this school bus. The men came back shrugging and reported he was told the bus was transporting sick and injured children to a rehabilitation facility.

Shaking his head, Galed got out of the jeep thinking "If I want something done I have to do it myself..." and walked across to the bus driver, who was leaning against a lamp post talking on his phone. "It is interesting, my friend, that there is a bus here in the parking lot of a hospital. Since when do sick children ride somewhere on a bus?"

"It is a puzzle to me, too," the driver shrugged, "I, myself only take orders and my boss, he tells me to come here and pick up some children."

Galed intent on getting more information said, "Well, we all have to work, do we not?" and then asked, "Where are you taking these sick children to ... schools?"

"No my friend, I think to a hospital that has a school in it."

From whom do your orders come, my friend?"

"From the local school district, my boss has his office there."

"Do you have the man's name, my friend?" Galed asked knowing he was going way out of a limb here.

The bus driver looked at Galed skeptically, "His name? Why do you want to know his name? Are you hoping to drive a bus full of children, yourself?"

Galed smiled and said, "No, it is for my brother, he is out of work and looking for a job."

"Oh," said the man, "your brother needs to apply with the office of schools in his district. I wish good luck to your brother. This is an easy job if you can stand the screaming children! But if it will help you the name of my boss is Jacobeen Harif."

Galed was annoyed when he returned to the jeep. He had wasted time, exposed himself in public and found out little. For curiosity, he looked up the number for the school district bus driver's boss. He found that indeed there was a Jacobeen Harif working there. Annoyed that his 'lead' amounted to nothing except for verifying the bus driver's information, he barked at his men and told them to get into the ER and make sure the kid was still there. He was growing impatient with this whole assignment. He wished he could go inside, shoot the child and whoever else was with her and be done with it, but he could not. Orders were orders and this one came directly from *The Great One* himself.

～～～～～～～～～～～～～～～～～～～～～～～～～～～～～～～～～～～～

They had arrived at the campsite a few hours before dusk. Everyone worked cooperatively and quickly to get the camp operational. *The Great One* had not yet arrived as he and his advisors were taking an alternate route to the site. Working in concert with Yosef, Manny had been able to access Bayan's cell phone data and retrieve the coded text message that ordered the truck drivers to stand down and take no action against the person in question. Yosef notified Moshe and Moshe told Rafi that for the moment it appeared he was safe. Rafi was temporarily relieved, but would not feel completely safe until *The Great One* arrived. He felt he could only one person could ensure his safety.

As soon as the new location was identified, Mossad agents set up a short distance west of Al Burayj and embedded themselves with a National Geographic camera crew photographing the migration of European white storks.

Rafi was surprised to note that his guards didn't seem to be watching him anymore. He assumed that was a good sign, but couldn't be sure exactly what it meant. He settled into a tent with several others who had traveled a distance to be here in the presence of *The Great One*. Rafi kept a low profile listening and learning as much as he could from those around him. Rafi spoke only when he was spoken to - as befitting a young man in the learner's role. Since he couldn't communicate with Moshe, or write anything down, he rehearsed everything in his mind, hoping Ari would pick up his thoughts and record them for him. He didn't know for sure if that would work given the distance, but he hoped it would. Ari was his best bet.

In the parking lot of the Beersheba Hospital ER, the bus was being loaded with children of all ages and in all conditions. It was a slow process. The school bus, it turned out, was handicap equipped; wheelchairs were secured to automatic platforms that carried the children up and into the bus. Stretchers were carried up ramps and locked into floor bars. Each child was accompanied by at least one attendant clothed in hospital garb and carrying bags or medical equipment. Staring at the mass through his binoculars, Galed could not tell one child from the next. All were wrapped and swaddled in cloth; they all wore light blue head scarves with pink flowers on them. He could not imagine where these children were being taken, but he needed to find out if his quarry was among those being loaded onto that bus. In a fury, he rushed to the ER, but the entrance was blocked off because their bi-annual window washing was in process; Galed was obliged to race around the building in search of an open door. By the time he found his way to the Emergency Department, Saroyah and the loaded school bus were gone.

Traffic at the Ben Gurion Airport was a tangle. It was the middle of the day, busiest for tourist travel. The temperature soared past 101, scorching the earth and the people on it. Bumping along in the yellow school bus, the four children remained quiet and still. Two lay bundled on stretchers and two were slumped in their wheelchairs. The children had papers indicating they had been selected to participate in the Starnet Program in Chicago. Established by the State of Illinois the program provides coordinated health and social services programs for children with special needs. The children, with their attendants, and paraphernalia would be off loaded at the United Airlines terminal. Simon and Sammy would meet the bus dressed identically right down to the number of pens in their nursing uniform pockets.

Galed was in such a state as he raced to catch the bus that he never noticed the beat up looking car trailing after him. He and his troops arrived at the terminal time to see the empty bus driving away. They spotted two girls in wheelchairs; they looked alike and both could have been Saroyah. They were being pushed by male nursing attendants, middle-aged men who looked surprisingly alike. Confused Galed leaped out; he divided his men, assigning one group to follow one wheelchair and the other group to follow the other one, they rushed toward the airport. Galed never saw a man in jeans and a baseball cap approach the jeeps and slide underneath them.

Dressed in a United Nations Uniform, Galed showed his fake credentials to the security department staff, as he presented pictures of Saroyah and related a story about her being kidnapped from an important Iraqi family. He asked to review the security tapes and see if he could find her. Since his paperwork appeared official, the security officer allowed him to enter. On the tapes, he saw several pictures of the same man, balding and grey haired, wearing glasses and a white nursing attendant's uniform pushing a wheelchair. The child in the wheelchair appeared roughly the same size as Saroyah. She was swaddled in cloth she had her head covered in a pale blue headscarf with pink flowers. She held a tissue up to her face blocking out her features. As he stared at the monitors watching the male nurse, he became confused.

First he saw the wheelchair man walking toward the east side of the airport and then toward the west. He seemed to be everywhere. Galed could not understand what was happening. Perhaps the man could not read the signs, although they were displayed in many languages. Then he wondered how this same man could be in so many places at once. Over and over again he saw the wheelchair man push from one departure gate to another. It made no sense but the time stamps seemed accurate. Impatiently he called his men to see if they were having any better luck, sadly they were not. The followers kept bumping into one another at various points in the airport. Wheelchair man would suddenly appear then disappear only to appear again in another location.

In a rage, Galed told his men to capture the man the next time they saw him. "Capture him!" Galed screamed. But by then the nursing attendant was nowhere to be found. Galed searched the tapes in the security office again and concluded they were of no use. "I know what I saw," he claimed. He ran from the security department toward the International gates. At the Alitalia gate, which he had seen the man enter, the gate agent denied having any disabled children board any of their planes. He got the same answer from the British Airways gate agent. How can that be? Your security tapes are ridiculous. I saw these men pushing wheelchairs. I know I saw them!" he cried. For three hours Galed checked with every airline and every gate agent but each time he was told no sick or handicapped children had boarded all day. Enraged Galed stomped out of Ben Gurion Airport.

Four hours later, Elisabeth ushered her party through customs. On their way out of the airport, Hadara and Yosef passed Simon and Sammy, wearing business suits and carrying briefcases, rushing to board the plane. In the parking lot Gil turned to Hadara and said, "Okay, now that that's over let's go catch us some bad guys!"

36 ARRIVALS AND DEPARTURES

There was great rejoicing in the baggage claim area at O'Hare Airport. Amidst the horde of weary passengers anxiously texting, lugging fussy toddlers and searching for pieces of luggage, Elisabeth embraced her sisters while Samira and Ari hugged Jamila and her children. Stella and Manny drove Jamila and her children to a safe house in Highland Park, where Saroyah would receive medical treatment and the family would have the chance to relax and regroup.

Following their brief reunion, Ari and Samira navigated through O'Hare to the El Al counter where they purchased tickets for the next flight out of Chicago. They had accomplished their mission. The Chicago connection to the terrorist nuclear pipeline had been dismantled. Müeller was in custody; the other Mossad teams on this mission had some new leads for completing their missions. No one had been killed or discovered, so all in all, it had been a successful mission. Ari and Samira now focused on other matters.

On the plane, they whispered back and forth. "I'm worried about Rafi," Ari said.

"Me too!" said Samira "When we get back he is our priority."

"I can think of nothing else," Ari replied, "Its first and last on my agenda."

"Well, we'll have to check in with our bosses at Mossad and get some direction on this." Samira told him.

Ari gave her a hard look, "I'll do what I have to do for Rafi; our bosses can go to hell!"

She looked at her brother in shock, he never spoke that way, "Wow, look at you getting all combative, I didn't mean you would ignore Rafi. I won't either. If it comes to that, we'll both do what we have to do. You're not his only sibling, you know," Samira snipped.

"Right, but I'm his only twin!" Ari retorted.

They were silent for a while then Samira asked, "What do you think is going on with *Abba*? That was really weird of *Eema* not to say anything to us about him and to avoid telling us where he is. Do you think she doesn't really know?"

"That is just what I do think. Eema has no clue and that is why she is being evasive. She would not worry us unnecessarily."

"I guess you are right, but it's weird that she doesn't know where he is. After all, they are in touch nearly 24/7. Do you think they're in a fight?" Samira asked.

"Not at a time like this. Even if they were in a fight, they would stop in order to deal with all of what is going on. NO! Something is really wrong with *Abba* and we will need to find out what it is and where he is."

"Put that on our list," Samira replied grimly. "And where is *Am* Gamil? It's shocking that he's not around to help with Saroyah! Where is the world has he gone? His kid is kidnapped and nearly killed and his family leaves the country and he's nowhere in sight? What the hell is that all about?" Samira shook her head in disgust. "That's just weird and unacceptable."

"Now, Samira, do not start judging everyone. There is something wrong. Our family does not act in this manner. We know them. This is not them! Something is most surely wrong. They are mixed up in something, being held against their will or they are compromised in some way. It is not logical to think otherwise."

"Okay," Samira sighed, "but logic doesn't explain everything. You are too logical! None of this is typical behavior for any of them." She paused and then said "and what about *Am* Abdullah? He's missing too! What in the name of *G-d* is happening to the men in our family," Samira exclaimed.

"Last time I heard of him," Ari said in his reasonable tone, "he was on a secret mission in the Beqaa Valley capturing important materials. After that it seems he disappeared. I assume he went to report to his commanding officer but after that who knows…"

They slept and whispered and slept some more knowing that upon arrival they would need to hit the ground running. They needed to report to their commanding officers at Mossad and they needed to see their mother and help find their father, but most of all they needed to help their brother. Hadara met her children at Ben Gurion Baggage claim. She was ready with big hugs and several minutes of blessings in which she held them and praised G-d for their safe return. When their bags arrived, they rushed out of the airport into a waiting car. Yosef grinned at them and off they sped toward the darkness of the desert. The plan was to rendezvous with Gil and Elias who had affixed tracking devices to the Jeeps Rashid and his men were driving. He and Elias had been following them for the last several hours. The soldiers for *The Sword of Justice* had crossed into Jordan and were traveling north at a high rate of speed.

Holding his cell phone to his ear, Yosef drove and reviewed strategy options with Gil while Hadara briefed her children about family matters. Then they called their commanding officers at Mossad. Their commanders praised their work in America and told them to take a few weeks off. "You need some time to rest," their commanders said. Samira grinned at her mother and asked, "You have anything to do with our 'vacation' *Eema*?"

Hadara smiled and patted her daughter's cheek, "Of course, *Tatala*," she said, "We need a family reunion, right? Now all we have to do is find our family so we can have that reunion."

"Ari, are you up for this?" Hadara asked him.

"What do you think, *Eema*? I need to go sunbathing on a Mediterranean island? I need to connect with Rafi and I need to find my father and missing uncles. What do you think?"

"That's just what I think, dear," Hadara said putting her arm around his shoulders. "That's just what I think."

Hakim was getting nervous. He paced the room again, this time checking the doorknobs to see if they would turn. They did. He slowly opened the door a crack and peeped out into the hallway. Two men in army uniforms stood at opposite ends of the elegant carpeted corridor. They did not notice him. They stood at attention, guns at their sides staring toward the main lobby. He carefully leaned his ear toward the doorway; he caught a few snippets of whispered conversation.

"...in the holding cell...?"

"No he's to remain here for now..."

"Keep an eye on him..."

"It won't be long now..."

"...orders are for us to stay here..."

The Prime Minister's official conference room was at the other side of the building, but the office where he usually worked was the one in which he'd been sitting for the last six hours, just three doors away from Hakim's own office. It was not lost on Hakim that he had not been sequestered in his own office but in the Prime Minister's. Straightening to a full and confident stride he approached the soldier closest to him. "I've been waiting for the Prime Minister for several hours now, I suppose he is extremely busy and I unfortunately have the need to use the bathroom facilities. Can you let the Prime Minister know that I'll return shortly?"

The soldier looked at him impassively and said, "I'll take you there, Sir."

It was then that Hakim knew with certainty that an ill-wind had shifted in his direction. For years he walked these halls without interference. He had no idea what or why, but he was certain as he traced the perfect strides of the young officer that he was headed toward imminent doom. "Thank you," he nodded to the soldier, "I am most appreciative for your help."

As they turned down a long corridor, Hakim mentally reviewed the blue-print plans for the building. He participated in its re-design several years ago and recalled vividly where the exits and entrances were located. Knowing his escort would be waiting outside for him, he entered the large, attractively appointed Gentleman's Rest Room and began his escape. Beside the last stall was a locked janitor's closet. Inside that closet, he remembered, there was a window. Outside was a ten foot drop to a courtyard with a large, formal garden with many carved marble statues and at the far end of that garden stood a hinged wooden gate locked from the inside, leading to the street.

Abdullah pulled Shamir aside and asked "What has the prisoner said?"

"Not much," Shamir shrugged. "I have been questioning him for hours now, but he says nothing. Either he knows little or he is a very stupid man. I am not sure which."

"I will talk to him myself," said Abdullah, annoyed that he had to sully himself with such menial work, "Shamir, you get in touch with those who are following that pilot and find out what he has said to them."

"Yes Sir," Shamir said as he left the room.

Abdullah had been waiting at Army headquarters for days now; waiting for information about the pilot; waiting for information about the explosion at the compound. He was angry that he was being detained this way, like he was a prisoner! They had taken away his cell phone and were not permitting him to make phone calls. They told him they contacted his wife and told her he was alright. He didn't know whether to believe them or not.

Opening the door to the interrogation room, Abdullah was shocked to see the prisoner's condition. He had changed drastically from when they pulled him into their SUV in the Beqaa Valley. He seemed exhausted, injured and sickly. Immediately, Abdullah ordered that the prisoner be released from his chains and given food and water. He sat calmly next to the miserable man and spoke softly to him. "I am sorry for your suffering," he said. "I am the one responsible for you being here, but I did not mean for you to suffer. I will help you and you will help me. Do you understand?"

The man nodded. After he had water and some food, he was allowed to clean himself and say his evening prayers. All the while, Abdullah sat in the room and waited quietly for the man to come and sit near him. It took the man one hour. Then, he sat near Abdullah and asked, "Can you get me out of here?"

"That depends on what you have to tell me. Remaining silent is not in your best interest. You were caught in the desert retrieving nuclear materials to be used in the making of huge destructive bombs. Did you know that?"

"No," said the man, "I was told to go to the desert with my friend and pick up packages that would be dropped from a plane. I was not told what was in those packages."

"Okay," said Abdullah, "who was it that told you to go get the packages?"

"A man called Muhammad Chehab. I am told he is from Riyadh, but was living in Lebanon. He goes around with his nephew, named Imed Massoud. I know little of them. They approached me outside a café where I was looking for work, my friend and I both. We were sitting at this café and a man came up to us and asked if we wanted work. We both said yes and he told us what he wanted us to do."

"Where were you to take what you got from the desert?" Abdullah wanted to know.

"We were to carry the packages to a small compound outside Nabaa el Kbir. About 3 kilometers north," he said. The prisoner swallowed some water and again asked Abdullah if he could get him out.

"We'll need to check out your story. If it turns out that you were a mere courier and that's all, then we can let you go. One more question, before I leave," Abdullah added, "Do you know the name of the group this man Muhammad Chehab worked for or who he was reporting to?"

The prisoner thought for a few moments then added, "He did not say this to me, but I heard the two of them talking, the uncle and the nephew, they talked about someone called 'Great'. I thought he was an Iman or something like that. But they also called him by the name Arman. I thought that was odd, because leaders like Iman's are called by their titles, not their given names, it seemed disrespectful to me."

"Thank you for your help," Abdullah said and got up to leave. Then he turned to the man and said, "I will return, do not be afraid."

"Thank you, Sayyd, the man said bowing low.

~~~~~~

The pilot was a simple man. Hired it seemed for a simple job. He knew nothing else only what he had been instructed to do, by whom and for how much. Nevertheless, Lebanese Intelligence would hold him and question him for days, maybe months. He was an unfortunate casualty of the continual crisis in the Middle East. The information he gave however simple was important. The man said he had been hired by the Russian mob. He was a freelance pilot. He was a Syrian national and had no idea how the Russians came to contact him. He was, he said, just a simple man who asked no questions. In Syria, jobs for pilots were hard to come by. This was a big job and money was scarce. He had a family to feed. The man said he was grabbed on a street near to his home and was driven into the country blindfolded. He said he was taken to a small house where he met with three men. The house, he said was well guarded by men with guns. One man, who was very reverent toward the Russian man, spoke Arabic with a Lebanese accent. That man said very little but was called Gamil. The pilot described that man as good looking and nicely dressed.

A man named Borisovich Kliemkov had given the pilot $100,000 US dollars to fly items of some sort to this spot in the Beqaa Valley and toss them from the plane. That was the sum total of his knowledge. He seemed to knew nothing else.

The pilot was being held in the same cell block as the prisoner Abdullah and Shamir had been questioning but they were not told that the pilot, whose information was so vital to their investigation, was confined just a few feet away. Only their superior officer had received reports about both of the prisoners and he intended to keep that information very private indeed.

~~~~~~

The caravan carrying *The Great One* finally arrived. They were met by those assembled in the camp; they cheered and bowed as the man appeared from the car. "I am most grateful that you are all here to greet me," he said to the assembled crowd and offered some brief prayers to the gathering arms outstretched. "I need some time to refresh myself and then we will gather for prayers and a meal. You have done much work serving *Allah*. You are pleasing *Allah* by being here on this Holy mission. *Allah* will most assuredly praise our work."

Rafi stood a bit back from the crowd watching the proceedings. He was aware of the plot against him and was keenly aware that one person at this campsite would protect him. That one person was *The Great One*. He knew that *The Great One* supported him at the moment, but was uncertain about how long that might last. He didn't know the range of influences that abounded, but assumed that there were many of them. Rafi assumed the pose of a devout follower, making the appropriate sounds and movements, but his anxiety mounted as he watched the chief advisor watching him from afar. The man didn't take his eyes off of him. Rafi wondered if he was looking for something in particular.

He became suddenly self-conscious. Was his ear piece showing? Had his contact lenses slipped? Under the cover of the crowd, he noticed his enemy watching him and wondered how long it would be before the man made a move against him. He then wondered what he could do to get the man to change his mind about him. Perhaps I just need more time. As he stood with the listening crowd Rafi reflected on the message he got earlier from Ari and began to devise a plan. He knew Zuhair Bayan was his enemy and he had to win him over. In order to do that he needed more information about Bayan's history and goals. He either needed to align himself with him or he needed to get something over on him. While everyone was busy in the main tent, he slipped away hoping his absence would not be noticed.

37 GRATEFUL CONNECTIONS

Ari leaned back against the slats in the wooden bench and stared at the sky. The sun was just going down leaving the sky a radiant pink and orange. But Ari was not aware of the beauty around him, he thought only of his brother's plight. Rafi was up against a determined enemy who had the power to crush him like a bug. Ari knew that he was Rafi's best chance of survival. He had left his mother, sister and Yosef pursuing jeeps full of soldiers and made his way back to the family home in Menara. He quickly checked the perimeter and made sure that no one had tampered with the locks and alarms. Once inside, he devoted himself to helping his twin. Tapping into his technical knowledge, he hacked into the Syrian Embassy's database to review Zuhair Bayan's personnel file. From there, he hacked into the man's bank accounts and reviewed his personal financial information. Then he located Bayan's personal computer files stored on the Embassy's main server. They were password protected and the data was encrypted but Ari thought he could infiltrate the account given enough time. He didn't know what he was looking for, but thought he'd know when he found it.

Tucked inside a folder labeled favorite games he found his first clue. Several items had been scanned and stored there including a yellowed photograph and a scrap of paper with several scribbled names in Hebrew. One name was Zeryka Ben Harav. Immediately he set about searching the data base for that name. It would, he was certain, lead to an important clue.

Zuhair Bayan, regarded as a purist by his Syrian Brethren, was intelligent, capable and completely devoted to Islam. Although he was married, he and his wife had borne no children and seemed on the verge of a break-up. Ari decided that one of the easiest things to do was hack into the Bayans' email accounts. In reviewing his wife's emails, Ari found that Bayan was a womanizer and there was another suggestion that he had become addicted to drugs when he was in medical school and still used occasionally. It was clear that his wife was discontented with her husband and looking for some way to get even with him, but these facts, even if proven true, would have little positive impact on Rafi's situation. No, Ari needed to find out what made Bayan tick; he needed to give his twin some tools to better manage his relationship with the man. Research into his life could provide them with the key. Sipping dark, syrupy coffee he worked through the night. It was early dawn before he found something that seemed worth pursuing. It was a single entry in his bank statement. It indicated a payment of 100,000.00 Syrian pounds to a small synagogue in Israel called Bet Kehilat Shalom. That was odd, to say the least, an impassioned Jew-hater giving money to a synagogue?

It could be that the synagogue was a front for a terrorist group, it could be a payment for confidential information or perhaps Zuhair Bayan had a secret connection with Israel. Ari thought about these options as he poured another cup of coffee and opened an online connection to Bet Kehilat Shalom's website which turned out to be tiny and located near the Jordanian border. Upon closer examination of their historical records, Ari found a few early photographs, including clergy and founding members. Among the old and worn pictures he found one tattered and faded showing a group of men and boys gathered on the steps of a nearly completed building. Nestled between two bearded men was a small child. Mouth agape, Ari grabbed his cell phone.

～～～～～～～～～～～～～～～～～～～～～～～～～～～～～～～～

Hakim moved stealthily through the crowd blending in as best he could. Using the reflection from windows he passed he checked behind him to make sure he wasn't being followed. He crossed the street several times, always with a crowd doubling back to see if he was being followed. So far so good, he thought. He boarded a city bus and sat in the back, peering out the rear window, studying the crowd as the bus lumbered forward. He needed a plan and he needed one fast. He couldn't use his cell phone, but he had his wallet and fortunately he remembered the important numbers by heart. A half hour later, he exited the bus and found a small store that sold miscellaneous items. Browsing, he found sunglasses and a black turban along with a disposable cell phone, a newspaper and a lady's compact. Opening the paper he held the compact open with his thumb so he could keep an eye on the street behind him. Thus disguised, he wandered to the back of an open air café, ordered mint tea and began making phone calls.

～～～～～～～～～～～～～～～～～～～～～～～～～～～～～～～～

Shamir was waiting for him when he left the prisoner. Abdullah had gotten the information they needed but was filled with uncertainty. Abdullah was focused on the answer to his last question. "Why didn't you tell the other interrogator these things? It would have gone much easier for you." The answer startled Abdullah.

"I did tell him these things. For what would I not tell them?" the man had asked. Abdullah believed him. Indeed why would he lie about such a thing? Where is the benefit in that? So if the prisoner was telling the truth why had Shamir not given him that information? In fact why had Shamir insisted that the man had been uncooperative? With downcast eyes, he approached his long-time friend and helper and said. "Explain why you were unable to get information from this man? He was cooperative and offered no resistance to me." Shamir appeared offended.

"My friend," he said, "I did my very best to get him to talk. I used all the usual tactics, but he said nothing. Perhaps you have a special gift for getting people to talk," he smiled.

Abdullah was in no mood for flattery. "So that's your story?" he spat. He frowned, wondering if there some reason Shamir wanted him to talk to that man. Perhaps he needed to get me out of the way for a while, he thought.

Shamir backed up a few steps and looked at his boss. "*Sayyd*, I would have no reason to do such a thing. I have done nothing to justify your suspicions."

"Perhaps you are right," Abdullah said sullenly, "I am not sure what is going on here and why I am being treated me this way. I am being excluded and have been barred from leaving and they have taken my cell phone."

"They are treating us both that way, *Sayyd*, I do not know why, but I too have been barred from leaving and they also took away my cell phone."

Abdullah faced Shamir and asked, "Have they asked you any questions or talked with you at any time when I was not present?"

"Yes, yesterday they asked me to tell them the story of our travels and I did so. It was perfectly straightforward. I told them what we did and how everything happened. There are no lies, I said what occurred and that was all. They asked no other questions and said nothing else to me."

"Well," Abdullah said appearing to soften, "I will see if I can find out what is happening" and he walked off. Shamir leaned against the building's basalt blocks and watched him go. Then he slipped his hand in his pocket, pulled out his cell phone and entered a number.

~~~~~~

He was walking back from his tent when the man called Jalal, the book carrier, approached and softly said, "*The Great One* wishes to have a word with you. I will take you to him." He was an elderly man; stoop shouldered wearing a loose fitting didashah. Rafi followed him through the camp thinking if the book carrier had been sent for him *The Great One* must be settled down somewhere with his books. Jalal led him to a small tent. It was draped with several carpets and set apart from the others. The tent was guarded in the front and the rear by armed soldiers wearing uniforms of the Iraqi army. Feeling anxious, Rafi entered the tent bowing low. Inside the space was covered with carpets. Candles sat on a small table topped with a brass tray along with a brass carafe and two cups. Shukri Al-Sierawan sat in a meditation pose at the back of the tent. His eyes were closed and he rocked slightly in keeping with the rhythm of his chants. Rafi approached the man silently, slid down to the carpet slightly in front of and facing him and picking up with the tone and rhythm of his chants joined him, miming every movement and word. This went on for a while without a word being spoken. Rafi was not completely sure that *The Leader* even knew he was there, but when he opened his eyes, their eyes met.

Smiling slightly he said. "It brings me joy that you have joined me in this manner. It is the correct way for an apprentice to join the master."

Rafi bowed his head reverently and said, "I am honored to be permitted to serve *Allah* at the feet of one who is so wise."

Their conversation continued in this poetic worshipful vein for several more minutes. At length *The Leader* said, "There is someone in this camp who does not trust you. He had plans to destroy you, my young one. I put a stop to the last plan, but may not always be able to do that. I am not sure how to keep you safe."

Rafi looked at the man uncertain about how to respond. At length he said, "I am honored that my leader thinks so well of me that he put a stop to the plot against me. If it is *Allah*'s plan that I should depart this earth before many years have passed, then I will bow to his greater wisdom."

The Great One looked at the younger man for a long time before saying,

"You are wise beyond your years. That is why *Allah* has sent you to me. You are a gift to me from our Lord and I will do everything in my power to keep you safe, but do remember that although I decreed you safe passage to this man who wants you dead, there are many ways to die. I cannot prevent them all." With that, *The Leader* raised his hands and placed them on Rafi's shoulders, "Let us pray together," he said.

With his hands on Rafi's shoulders, Shukri al-Sierawan traveled in time to his own memories of childhood. There had been a boy, a boy named Roshan whose father worked in his family's textile mills. Roshan came often to work with his father and became Arman's friend. It was this boy in whom Arman confided his greatest secrets. When Arman told his friend of his visions, of his idea that he was born to become a great leader, a holy man and that he wanted to change the world, Roshan had been awe-struck. "You will be exactly that which you wish to be," he told Arman. "You will be a great leader and I will come and join you and we will serve *Allah* together." These memories emerged now as Arman Shaloub aka Shukri al-Sierawan aka *The Great One* looked at Rafi's bowed head and knew with certainty that this young man was the reincarnation of his lost friend. It had been less than a week after sharing this with his friend that Roshan had been killed, crushed by some machinery in his father's factory. Arman wondered if his friend's death was a punishment for telling him his secrets. He felt so guilty about that this he never shared his secrets with another person and he never again formed a new friendship. He had never gotten over that loss. It had made him more reclusive and introverted than ever. He carried a deep resentment toward his father, his textile mills, his brothers and their businesses, even his mother for her pride in her husband's success. He associated them all with the loss of his friend. To Arman, their financial success had come at the price of his only friend Roshan's life!

No, Arman Shaloub never forgot his friend and today, as he looked at Rafi Tahan praying at his side, he felt a joy he had not felt since he was a child, playing in the factory with his friend. He thanked *Allah* over and over again for this second chance. He knew he would do anything to keep this young man by his side. Rafi was Roshan returned to him from the dead and this time he would never let him go.

38 IN GOD WE TRUST

Galed and his men had stopped for the night. They had pulled off the road and laid out their sleeping bags near an outcropping of rock. They had no idea that two cars had been tracking them from afar. Watching from their GPS tracking screen, Gil saw the jeeps pull over and followed suite. Hadara, Yosef, and Samira, following behind decided to join them. That's when the call came in. Hadara grabbed the phone and stared at the screen. Not recognizing the number, she hesitated, but it kept ringing so she answered.

In a cautious voice she said, *"Cain?"*

"My darling, Praise *Allah* I found you," Hakim gushed. "I have been so worried. Are you alright? Are the children alright?" He was in tears now, desperation in his voice.

"Hakim? Hakim is it you?" Hadara whispered anxiously. "Are you alright? What happened to you? Where are you?"

"I cannot talk much. I was held captive. I will explain later. It is not safe. Just tell me you are alright."

"I am fine. The two who were away together have returned. The other one is still away. Can you come to me?"

"I will try. If you can meet me it would be pure heaven. If you cannot, tell me where you are and I'll come to you."

"I cannot tell you that; it is not safe. We are," she hesitated, "away. I will meet you at the usual place when I can... be safe. I love you."

"I love and adore you, my precious one. I will see you soon."

Hakim hung up and looked around the café, now packed with the late night crowd. No one seemed to be paying him any attention, but of course if they were good at their jobs, they would not appear to be listening, would they? He figured he could get to the Olive Grove and from there he could cross the border. He would wait for a while and then move. He ordered Lamb Shawarma and more tea as he plotted his escape route. Once he was safely away, he would try to figure out what had gone wrong and why he had been held captive by the government he had served for so many years.

Amal and Hala Faysal whispered together in their bedroom. They had heard from Jamila that she and her children were safe in the United States. They had received a message from Hakim that he was safe and would be arriving soon. He asked them to leave the door by the back stairs open for him. He promised to come to their room as soon as he arrived.

They had not heard from Abdullah or Gamil; where they were seemed to be anyone's guess. All the servants had been asked to remain at the Olive Grove so that they would not be alone in their palatial residence. Fawz had carried up some tea and cakes a short while ago and told them that Musnah was still under guard, confined to her room in the servants' quarters. Fawz was worried about her because she was still refusing to eat or drink and would not stop crying. She asked that Hala come and talk with her. She agreed.

Hala walked slowly down the back stairs toward Musnah's room. Softly, she knocked and entered the room to see Musnah sitting on the edge of her bed, head in her hands, rocking back and forth. "We do not think this is your fault, Musnah," she said, "We think they were here to see someone of importance. We do not think your nephew was at the center of the problem. We are not sure who did what exactly but we believe you did not betray us. Please do not blame yourself. Please calm down and have something to eat. You are not in trouble here. We have always cared for you and think of you as a member of our family. Please, Musnah, calm down." Hala reached out her hand and patted the old servant's hands.

Musnah sighed spoke quietly. "There are things you do not know, my honored mistress, things I know that you do not know. Very bad things," she said softly.

Hala felt a jolt of alarm run through her body. "What things?" she asked.

"Things that will change everything," the servant said.

~~~~~~

The room was opulent. The men perfectly attired. The atmosphere was solemn. Each man thumbed through a thick report describing momentous political developments in neighboring countries and possible problematic activities by some of their own, respected citizens. "Situations here in the Middle East," said the Prime Minister, "are often complex and fraught with critical decisions. In this instance several of our own are being accused of engaging in questionable activities regarding this group that calls itself *The Sword of Justice*. There have been questions raised about my own trusted emissary, whom you all know well, Hakim Faysal. He was being held for questioning but it appears he left the premise of his own accord and cannot now be located. It pains me to say that warrants have been issued for his arrest. Now of course this does not mean he has committed any crimes but questions have been raised and they must be explored. Our guards are under orders to detain him without bloodshed so that we may question him about these issues. We do not wish harm to come to him but we need some answers."

The Prime Minister paused before saying, "Hakim's brother, Major Abdullah Faysal, a highly decorated officer in our military assigned to the Northern Command has also come under some scrutiny. As you all know, he is a highly respected officer holding many medals for bravery. To arrest him would create chaos among those who know him. We have decided not to detain him against his will but rather to engage him in a matter of some importance so that he will need to remain in the command headquarters where he can be monitored. Also their brother- in-law, Gamil Ajram, who has been a financial advisor to our Finance Minister, is also missing. There is no word as to his whereabouts. We have no idea if the fact that he is missing is related to these other two matters or if all these issues are independent of one another. We have to be clear about our facts and make responsible decisions. We cannot accuse an entire family of men without solid proof. The Faysal family is held in high regard by this government and by the citizens of this country, so we must proceed with extreme caution.

Surreptitiously an aide entered the room and slipped a note into the Finance Minister's hand. "If I may speak, Your Excellency," a man wearing a General's uniform and chest full of medals stood at attention, "Our information about Abdullah Fayal is that he has conducted himself with outstanding bravery according to his orders." Opening the note, Schma'il Marzug read *"Gamil Ajram in custody. Awaiting your instructions."* The General continued his remarks "...recently intercepted an illegal shipment of nuclear materials and captured one of the couriers. It is my understanding that this man, the captive, has revealed important information to Major Faysal. We tried to turn his long-time aide against him, but it seems that Major Faysal has done nothing against the best interest of our country. We recommend he be released immediately before word of this issue leaks out."

"Prime Minister, sir, if I may speak," the Minister of Agriculture interrupted. "There are serious accusations here, ones that involve the illegal transfer of government funds and espionage at the highest levels. It seems this whole family may be involved in some questionable activities. I suggest they all be arrested immediately and brought before this body for questioning." Arguments went on in this vein until well after midnight with no resolution. There were accusations and questions about suspicious activities. There were responses and explanations. The critical issue beyond these three men was the question of the government's relationship with a new radical Islamic group. From what they knew, popular support was coming from Syria, Iraq, Saudi Arabia, Jordan and even Lebanon. But not all these governments had stated public support for the group. Interest in the group seemed to be spreading like wildfire, but its ideas were highly explosive and many governments were leery of it.

In the end, they decided to table the question of their relationship with *The Sword of Justice*, to release Abdullah Faysal, but to have him followed and to continue to search for Hakim Faysal and Gamil Ajram. They all hoped for that good outcome as they bid one another good night.

~~~~~~

Jamila and Elisabeth sat up until late talking over cups of hot tea. There were many worries to discuss, chief among them Saroyah's emotional state. Since her rescue, she had been displaying acute trauma reactions, over-reacting to sounds or sudden movement, crying and having trouble sleeping. She had gotten very clingy and refused to do anything without a family member by her side. Elisabeth gave Jamila some practical suggestions and said she'd to refer the child to a colleague who specialized in these issues.

Jamila was relieved to hear all of this and the conversation moved to her missing husband. Not a word had been heard from Gamil and Jamila was terrified. She knew that Hakim had contacted Hadara, but had no details about that conversation. Her brother, Abdullah, was still missing and no one knew where he was either. His wife had phoned the Faysals and said she received a call saying he was alright, but had no further information. Now that her children were safe, Jamila was considering returning to her homeland to look for her husband. Elizabeth counseled against that and urged her to be patient.

After Jamila went off to bed, Elisabeth spent some time thinking about Gamil's situation. She had some ideas based on her findings at the Olive Grove and they weren't good. She texted her concerns to Manny and T-Max and went to bed, knowing that more news would be coming soon.

~~~~~~

They had found that the purest form of communication occurred when there were no other distractions, when it was dark and quiet. Ari went into his bedroom and lay silently on the bed. Closing his eyes he breathed deeply and focused on opening the channel of communication to his brother. Within minutes Rafi was there. He, too, was alone in his tent. They exchanged information – information about Zuhair Bayan and Rafi's emerging relationship with *The Great One*. No matter how many warnings Bayan received accidents happened and evidence could be manufactured. They both knew that the situation was a powder keg and Rafi needed a good plan. The options boiled down to threats or persuasion. Neither seemed really good. Based on the picture Ari found they assumed that the man had Jewish roots and that heritage alone could be the death of him in his current circumstances. What they didn't know was whether or not he had truly converted to Islam or whether he remained loyal to his birth heritage and may be working undercover for the Israeli cause.

In the event that he was a convert and loyal to Islam, Rafi could threaten to 'out' him and his Jewish roots to *The Great One*. In the event that he was in reality a Jew working for Israel, Rafi could reveal himself to be a Jew also and align with him. The problem was they didn't really know how Bayan felt about being Jewish. He might really be a convert to Islam and hate the Jews like he proclaimed. They didn't know his reasons for sending money to that little synagogue or if, in fact, that was what was really happening. It could be a front for some other organization, it could be a back channel to his family or even blackmail of some kind. No, as of now the information that Ari had gotten, while interesting and potentially crucial, was not yet useful. Ari needed to find out more about this man, this Zuhair Bayan or Zeryka Ben Harav, whatever his name was and where his true loyalties were. The brothers signed off in their usual way, using their shared language. It made them smile, a tiny bright light in a sea of gloom.

~~~~~~

Sol Abramson was silent as he read through the report that had come in from the Chicago agents. In it, the chemical weapons found at Herr Müeller's home were detailed. Illegal sales information obtained from his computer was also detailed. Abramson shook his head in disappointment. He had made a deal with Boulos, a good and fair deal and now he knew the man was holding out on him. His name and other identifying information had been found on the German's computer in Chicago and never once had Boulos mentioned those transactions. Now Abramson was a fair man. He was a man of G-d, a deep believer in the system of justice, spiritual and secular. He thought he and Boulos had a clear understanding but now he felt deceived. Throughout their negotiations Boulos had spoken only of nuclear weapons but now there was the issue of chemical warfare. Boulos had been withholding key information about chemical weapons such as sarin gas and anthrax that he was planning to sell to *The Sword of Justice*. Their deal was off.

As was his practice in times of trouble, Abramson turned to G-d. He was always his last salvation and his greatest guide. In the words of his *father and his father's father,* Abramson returned to ancient Hebrew. He began to pray. Until his head was clear he would not speak again with his prisoner/informant. Time ceased to have temporal meaning as he turned inward and upward waiting for guidance.

39 SIDEWINDER

It was pitch black. He walked like a blind man, feeling with his feet and holding his hands in front of him. He knew the area but it was still risky. There were rocks and gullies, walls and trees; he moved slowly and hoped that his memory would serve him well. He dared not turn on his flashlight for fear of alerting others to his location. He lost track of the time, but knew from his aching muscles and growling stomach it had been many hours since he began this journey. Inch by inch he moved forward until his feet bumped into a hard flat surface. Slowly, step by step hardly breathing he crept forward. His fingers crawled around the door frame then edged toward the knob. He maneuvered the lock inch by fraction of an inch, as he turned the key he felt the door swing open. Scarcely breathing, he stepped inside. A metallic click stopped him dead in his tracks. "Don't shoot, I come in peace," he said to the gun barrel pressed into his cheek.

"*Abba?*" said the voice holding the gun, "*Abba* is it you?"

"*Ari? Ari*, my son," Hakim said in relief wrapping him in his strong arms.

"I heard you coming. I could not see that it was you," Ari explained, "I am sorry to frighten you, *Abba*."

"My son, you did what was right, I am so glad to see you and to finally be home," Hakim said choking back a sob.

"It is safe here, *Abba*, it is safe," Ari said turning on a dim light and walking with his father toward the kitchen. "You must be hungry and tired. Let me fix you something to eat and we will talk." It was 3AM. They updated each other about family first, progress on their various situations, who was found and who was still missing. They talked and ate until dawn.

~~~~~~

T-Max and Manny got the text in the morning. They had spent the night at their headquarters and were up and ready before the sun rose. The message was specific: Gamil is the key! Find him!

They each started typing. They searched databases for terrorist groups in and around where he was last seen. They searched police databases for recent arrests. They piggybacked onto the CIA's satellite and viewed camps throughout the Middle East to see if they could detect pattern changes. They contacted Chevra Hatzollah agencies around the world for help in locating the missing man. It was mid-day before they got a glimmer of hope. It came from intercepted text messages between a low level staffer working for the Lebanese Minister of Finance and the chief of police in Beirut. In it Gamil was described as a traitor with a coded message to shoot on site. This message contradicted a previous message from the Prime Minister that specified no harm should come to Gamil whom he referred to as a person of interest needed for questioning. The Prime Minister's message further stated that the man may have information important to the safety of their country and needed to be kept safe. Alarmed Manny notified Elisabeth and Hadara by coded instant messenger. Mossad issued an order to get Gamil before anyone else did.

~~~~~~

Galed and his men were up at the crack of dawn driving into the desert toward the *The Sword of Justice's* new campsite. Galed drove with reluctance of a doomed man, knowing that death awaited him. He had failed to kill the child. Failed *The Great One* and failed his government. He would meet the fate of those who fail, and he had to be ready for it. He would go to *Allah* and pray for HIS forgiveness. In the jeep beside him, his subordinates knew what he was thinking. They remained respectfully silent and obedient to his every wish. Collectively, however, they were thinking of their own futures. One of them would most likely be chosen to succeed Galed. One of them would become the new commander of *The Sword of Justice's* armed forces. This was a job with great prestige and importance. While they liked and respected Galed they all knew that his time of leadership was rapidly dwindling. These things were sad and they would miss him, but this was the way of the world. One didn't question such things; it was the word of *Allah* and *The Great One*. One simply obeyed.

~~~~~~

Gil, Elias, Yosef, Hadara and Samira spent some time planning their moves once they reached the campsite. There certainly were not enough of them to attack the whole camp. Even with Rafi's back-up team a frontal assault would not be successful. They might be able to eliminate the leader but could not take down the whole group. The group would dissipate once its leader was gone. Charismatic groups depended on their leader for continued survival. They needed to formulate a plan that could accomplish that goal.

The tracker placed on Galed's jeep beeped loudly alerting them to movement. They piled into their vehicles and trailed after him. They were bumping along the uncharted desert floor when Ari's text came in. *Abba is home* was all it said, but that was enough. There was rejoicing in the Jeep! Yosef, Hadara and Samira burst into cheers, they hugged one another in relief and chattered together joyously. Suppressing their urges to call home and talk with the men, the women immersed themselves in planning until another text arrived, then they texted their coordinates.

～～～～～～～～～～～～～～～～～～～～～～～～～～～～～～～～～～～～～～～

The child lay curled in a fetal position. She was silent, kept her eyes tightly closed and her arms crossed defensively across her chest. Her breathing was hardly apparent. She could have been in a coma except that she wasn't. Elisabeth sat next to her, breathing in tandem. After a few moments, Elisabeth increased the sound of her breathing including audible deep breaths as used in Yoga. The child's breathing became more audible. This process continued with Elisabeth first joining the child then modeling some type of increase, including sighing, audible exhaling, then she verbalized body movements "I can straighten my fingers," "I can wiggle my toes." After 20 minutes the child opened her eyes, after 40 minutes she was sitting up and moving easily, after 50 minutes she was talking.

Earlier that morning, Elisabeth had been woken by a terrified Jamila who was unable to wake her daughter. Elisabeth had gone into the child's room and tried to get her up and functioning. Now that the child was sitting up, she offered her an array of art supplies and sat with her as she drew, talking while she worked. There was no coaching. There were no probing questions asked. The approach was to follow the child, reflect her self-expression and repeat her words as closely as possible. Slowly, Saroyah unraveled her experience highlighting spontaneously the horror of being blindfolded and helpless, of not knowing where she was or why she had been taken, hearing the terrifying sounds of the prisoner they had killed. Being able to put these memories into words while being grounded in the present was an important first step for the child who had been through so much. Their session ended with Elisabeth looking into the child's eyes and assuring her that she was safe in this place, that she had many personal strengths, and that she had survived this ordeal because of the inner strengths that were part of her.

~~~~~~

The plan was slow to crystallize, but form it did. It was Ari's last message that made the difference. Rafi decided that if Bayan was indeed still loyal to the faith of his childhood it could be put to the test. Like Solomon in the Bible, he would design a test. Bayan playing the role of the two mothers would have to choose between the life of his family and his role as chief advisor. To do this, Rafi needed more information. He had been sitting in the circle of advisors listening to *The Great One* speaking about the importance of recruiting more supporters. Supporters meant more workers, more pressure on Middle East governments and more money. Money was the key. They needed money to buy weapons, to buy information and to finance their Holy War against the godless westerners and in this effort Shukri al-Sierawan felt they were in competition with other radical Islamic organizations. He thought those groups, such as Fatah al Islam and Hamas needed to be destroyed if his group were to succeed.

He decided to preach this idea to his assembled followers, send it up as a trial balloon, so to speak. He wanted to see if his trusting followers would turn against their brethren. If the idea seemed acceptable to his gathered masses he would then incorporate the idea of destroying other similar groups into his overall plan. If they seemed disinclined he would eliminate it from his current rhetoric. His voice rose crescendo-like to a fever pitch as he proclaimed death to his rivals. It was as if a bolt of electricity ran through the stifling tent. As with one voice the crowd responded, shocking even *The Great One* with its fury!

40 WHAT GOES AROUND

Husain Hatolla paced back and forth across the concrete floor. He wanted to get out of here already. He was impatient to return home and not just a little anxious. He had not heard from the UN committee that they accepted his report. The report was bogus, of course, but he thought it would pass muster, his reports usually did. He had a good reputation with the committee. Morocco was not seen as a hotbed of radical activity, so the UN was not greatly concerned about his veracity. The delay in response time, however, was worrisome. Now, he awaited instructions from his connection. That was the one he was most worried about. That was the tricky one. Husain Hatolla had been working with this connection for many years and he hated himself for it. They were abhorrent to him; they represented all he had fought against during his professional life.

He had to admit though he'd been well paid for his efforts and that money had made the difference between life and death. Not for him, but for his wife. His beloved Neima had been suffering from Lou Gehrig's disease for years and the best treatments were available only at the Mayo Clinic in the United States. She was at the end of her life now and he had to help her. Theirs had been a marriage of love, not just of convenience. Yes, it had been an arranged marriage, but within a year he had fallen deeply in love with her. She was his moral compass, his center and soon she would be leaving him. He could not bear to think of it. He was grateful that he had been able to get enough money to help her during her last days. He prayed she would never find out where all that money had come from. That he thought surely would kill her.

At first, the side work had been easy: a little text message here, a little listening device planted there. It progressed, photocopying, breaking and entering. Soon, he was in over his head. A full-fledged spy, con artist, cheater, liar! Husain Hatolla looked back at his life and he could not believe all this had happened to him. He was an educated man from a good family, one of the best that Morocco had to offer. And he was a good Muslim. He could not reconcile the man he used to be with the man he had become. He must be an innocent victim of circumstance; he rationalized and told himself he had done what any loving husband would do. He had not really betrayed his country. He had just helped someone out. The fact that who he had helped was a criminal, whom neither his government nor the United Nations defined as an ally, well that was a troublesome fact he mostly ignored.

Husain looked down at the man on the floor, the trussed and injured man and he could not believe that he was responsible for this man's condition. He had received a text asking him to report to the Lebanese Prime Minister's palace. There he met with the head of the Palace Guards and accompanied them on a ride into the desert. They were transporting this man, the one who now lay at his feet. They brought the man into the building, it was an abandoned bunker really, and left them there, just the two of them.

He wanted to blame the man himself for his situation and tried to do that, but in his mind he knew better. He knew what he had done. He had beaten and starved and interrogated this man. He asked the questions he'd been told to ask. "What do you know about the Russian pipeline? Where is your brother-in-law Hakim Faysal? What does Hakim know of the pipeline?" The man answered what he could, but it wasn't much. He told what he knew of the Russian connection, that the Finance Minister Schma'il Marzug was diverting funds to sponsor *The Sword of Justice*. He seemed to tell all that he knew. His Russian bosses wanted to know if Marzug had betrayed them. They wanted to know what Gamil knew about his boss so they could decide whether or not to eliminate Marzug from their list of associates. Their associates list was an ever dwindling one. Marzug himself had claimed loyalty and innocence but they needed a corroborating source. That source was Gamil Ajram.

Gamil resisted at first but soon gave up all the information he had about the Russian connection and Marzug's involvement with the new radical group. What he wouldn't talk about was his family. He claimed no information at all about his brothers-in-law or their locations. Husain Hatolla felt guilty as he looked down at the wounded man. He had done the unthinkable to a man who had been manipulated into keeping a secret and setting up a meeting. That was it, really. Not good, but not the worst thing a person could do. He had beaten a man for doing far less than he himself had done for an even worse master, a monster really. Husain could no longer justify his own actions. He could not rationalize this behavior. This thought turned his stomach. Nauseated by his own actions, he raced to the bathroom.

~~~~~~

Shamir had been with him for years and Abdullah thought of him as a friend, however once broken trust is hard to regain. There is often a lingering worry, a prick of doubt; he had to make a hard decision. As the car drove through the mountains of Jezzine, he struggled with his dilemma. There had never been a sign of disloyalty. But since their 'detainment' at the Army Headquarters, Abdullah had been increasingly uncomfortable. It was only a hunch, a feeling, really, with no hard proof. And, he reasoned, they had been released so if Shamir had really turned against him perhaps that would not have occurred. And yet, there was this nagging suspicion, something base and instinctive. There was something different about the man. He was trying too hard, he was uneasy, he was nervous. Perhaps, he rationalized it was because they had been detained. Abdullah had been treated poorly by his superiors; he had lost face so perhaps Shamir had less respect for him. Abdullah thought about that for a while then he thought perhaps ... Shamir had something to be guilty about.

Abdullah reviewed his options. *I can simply send the man home, on the excuse that we have been gone a long time and Shamir needs to see his family. That would be the most humane thing to do. But if Shamir is under orders to watch me, then he would have to refuse leave me.* He thought for a while. *That just isn't solid enough proof. I can pull over and torture him until he tells me the truth, but there would be no coming back from that. If I do that our relationship and all that it has meant would be over. But then, perhaps it's over now anyway. Then,* he thought, *I can just kill him. I can pull out my gun and shoot him. We could have an accident driving over these treacherous mountains; I could lose control of the car and Shamir would be crushed as we tumbled over the edge of the cliff. A tragic accident! The loss of my closest friend!*

Drastic choices, thought Abdullah. The decision was made for him when Shamir broke through the silence. "I have a confession to make, Sayyd," Shamir began. "They asked me to spy on you, they let me keep my cell phone so I could text them messages about you. They told me to stay with you and report your whereabouts so that they could re-capture you if they wanted to. They threatened to kill my family if I did not. I don't want them to kill my family, Sayyd, but I cannot spy on the best friend I have ever had. What shall we do?"

Abdullah's breath caught in his throat. It was like Shamir was reading his mind. Quickly he pulled off the road and turned off the car. Facing Shamir, who was sweating profusely, he said, "I appreciate your honesty, my friend. We will drive now to the town where your family lives and drive them to where your wife's family lives. Then we will go to the Olive Grove and you will send our commanding officer a text letting them know where we are. We will find a way to use your status as a spy to our advantage. We will ponder the situation and figure out a way out for both of us." He reached over and placed his hand on his aide's shoulder. "Thank you for your trust, my friend. I hope you will never again give me cause to doubt you. For the next time, he said sadly, I am afraid there will be no discussion."

~~~~~~

They thought long and hard about the plan and concluded it made the best sense. Samira was primed and ready. She would go undercover with her brother. A cadre of servants was arriving that afternoon, according to their sources at Mossad. They were coming from several locations and were strangers to one another. It was the best opportunity for Samira to slip into the camp. She had a duel agenda. The first was to support her brothers in their mission, the second was to assess Zuhair Bayan and determine whether he posed an independent threat of terrorism. He had the reputation as a womanizer and though that was not confirmed the possibility of it offered Samira opportunities. Dressed in a loose, floral gandora with a matching hijab artfully draped around her shoulders, she assumed the bearing of a servant, knowing if a connection with Bayan was possible her captivating eyes and seductive smile would be all she needed.

From his position in the circle of advisors, Rafi heard Moshe's voice reporting that Samira had arrived and would be assuming the role of food server. Moments later, he saw her standing with a tray near the tent flap listening ardently as honeyed words of hatred surged from *The Leader's* mouth. The response of the assembled was immediate. They agreed! Yes, they shouted, we will destroy our enemies! We will destroy the other groups who compete with us! We will be the one and only martyrs for *Allah!* We will be under the bubble and when they are converted to our way of thinking all other Arab brothers and sisters will join us! Shouts of victory and shouts of death to vile enemies of *Allah* were loud and spontaneous.

The Great One smiled his shy, quiet smile and leaned back on his pillows. He was done speaking now. He had his answer. His message to his followers would include 'death to the fake reformers'. His followers would unite against the other Islamic extremist groups occupying the vast desert. He would take down Al Queda, Hezbollah, Hamas and all the rest. His group would grow to be the largest in the Arab world. He would subsume his competitors and take over the entire world. Quietly, he looked around the circle at his small trusted group of advisors and his gaze fell on his newest protégée. Rafi aka Roshan, who had returned to him from the grave! His lost friend was found again. *The Great One* was a happy man.

~~~~~~

The clicking woke him mid-morning. The sound of rapid clicking snuck into his consciousness and woke him with a start. Wandering into the computer room Hakim saw his son sitting in near total darkness intently staring at a dozen monitors taping on a keyboard. "What are you working on my son," he asked putting his hand on Ari's shoulder. "Ah you're awake Abba, good morning to you. Would you like some coffee?" "You seem hard at work, let me get it for us and then you can tell me what you are working on," Hakim answered.

Forty minutes later, crowded in front of monitors overrun with moving data, Hakim pointed to a number. They had been tracking properties owned or leased by the government. "Let me see what that one looks like," he said as Ari clicked and a small sketch appeared on the end monitor. "Where is that one located?" Hakim asked as they studied the map and the small sketch. "That's got to be it," Ari said "it meets all the requirements we outlined. That's got to be it."

"Okay," Hakim responded, "Let's do this!"

~~~~~~

Hala Faysal was frozen with fear. Whatever could this woman be talking about? What could she know that was so terrible? She wanted to go up and get her husband, but was afraid to stop the woman from talking and also she thought that Musnah would not be so free to talk in front of a man. Leaning forward with the calmest voice she could muster, she encouraged her servant to speak. "Tell me what you know," she said, "Please, tell me."

Sighing, the woman remained flat on her back across the bed. Closing her eyes she spoke as if to herself. "I have seen and I have heard many things," she said. "My grandson Imad came under the influence of his uncle on the other side of the family. That man is a bad man. He does many things that are not right. For money, he does many things. First my grandson comes to me and asks me to help him rob the Olive Grove. I say to him 'NO! Never in my life would I do such a thing!' He goes away. Then he comes back another time. Then he asks me to leave open the gate. He says many important men have to meet. They need to meet here. I ask why they need to meet here. He says he cannot say. Again I say to him 'NO'. I will not open gates that have to be locked. I will not help him do wrong things. Not to my special family...I mean this family...," she adds in a whisper. "He goes away. Then, another time he comes back again and says he does not need me to help with these things but I must never tell that he has asked this. This time, I see that his uncle is with him and also another man. They do not look at me; they are talking to each other. My grandson says that he has others who will help. I am alarmed. Who is your other help I ask? Who helps you do bad things? He smiles and says do not worry *Situ* for him it is not breaking the law. No one who lives here would do bad things. He laughs at me and says I am naïve. He says if the price is right people will do anything.

"Then one day, I am taking food out to the men who are gathering olives. I take them food and drink and I see your son-in-law Gamil. He is arguing with that bad uncle. He is upset. Yelling and maybe also he is weeping. I am not sure. The bad uncle takes out a knife, a long one and puts it to Gamil's throat. My grandson is smiling and talking to the bad uncle. I think they are making fun of Gamil. I am hiding, so they cannot see me. I am afraid they will find me and kill me.

Later Gamil comes to me and says, 'Did you see what happened?' I say, 'Yes, I saw.' And then he says to me never to tell that I saw these things. He is taking care of it. He says things are not always what they seem. Then my grandson is taken then Saroyah is taken. Then all the men disappear. Then Jamila and the children go away and now it is just us here alone.

I feel I am to blame for all of this. I should have told you, but Gamil say not to tell and he too is my boss, is that not right? I do not know what to do. I do not know what is right to do." The woman stopped talking as abruptly as she had started and lay back as if asleep. She was done. Just done...

41 A CERTAIN JUSTICE

He was kneeling on the cold tile floor in front of the porcelain commode puking his guts out. He could not believe how terrible he felt. It was as if someone had been beating HIM instead of the other way around. He felt sick to his stomach every time he thought about it. How could he, a man of faith, a respected appointee from the Moroccan government to the United Nations stoop to such low acts? He had to get out of this mess he was in. Perhaps he should kill the man and get it over with rather than waiting for instructions. He was bending over the sink washing his face, when he heard a creak in the floorboards. Whipping around he found himself staring into the barrel of a Glock17.

The man holding the gun motioned for him to go into the other room. Husain Hatolla did as he was told. He saw an older man kneeling down tending to his prisoner. The first man put handcuffs on Husain; he blindfolded and gagged him and tied him to a chair. Across the room the men talked to each other, but so softly he couldn't make out their words. Inside he was frightened not just for himself, but for his wife. He had left a detailed will and was confident that his children would carry out his wishes so if this was the end of his life, at least he would die knowing that his wife would be well cared for until her time came. He only hoped that his death would be swift, which he acknowledged was more mercy than he had shown his prisoner. He wasn't sure that *Allah* had mercy in store for him. He could only pray that this would be the case.

The brilliant Greek sunshine poured in the window as Boulos waited for Abramson's next words. He wasn't sure what had happened to change the man's mood, but for sure something had. He hoped it wasn't what he worried it was. He remained standing and assumed a look of complete innocence as he waited. "Please, sit," Abramson directed pulling out a chair for himself. "It has come to my attention that there may have been other types of weapons involved in your negotiations with *The Sword of Justice*. These have not been discussed. I need you to address these issues now."

Boulos held his gaze for a moment or two while he decided what to do next. He knew that this was a game changer. "My friend," he began "your information is of course correct. I spoke with a man called Müeller one time only. I had taken a trip to Chicago in the United States and talked with him about many matters. I was not sure about all the things he had or did not have. He was my only contact in the United States. I found him to be an evasive and unpleasant person and did not trust the things he said. We talked only of nuclear materials nothing else."

Sol Abramson gave the man a hard stare. He had received a lengthy report and an encrypted transcript a few hours ago from his staff at Mossad. "I have it on tape from that evasive, unpleasant person himself that he spoke with you about chemical weapons. Why would you deny having such information? Why would you withhold it from me?"

"But, my friend" said Boulos, "it was only a passing comment or two. It was nothing really. I was not being paid to deal with these materials so I did not listen to him speaking of this."

"Really" Sol scoffed, "that's your story?"

"Why would you take this manner with me, my friend I have done nothing to suggest I would transport such ugliness. These things are despicable to me," Boulos continued.

"Shall I play you the tape I have from our unpleasant arms-dealing Nazi?" Sol asked.

Boulos, ever vigilant, could tell by the tone of the conversation that he was running out of wiggle room. His mind raced ahead working through scenario after scenario that might get him out of trouble with his new would be benefactor. He honestly didn't know why he had withheld this information; he guessed it was just a habit to hold something back from negotiations. Putting up his hands as a gesture of surrender he said "Let me tell you the whole story, my friend. You are right, I have been holding out on you, but only because I did not want to add to your worries. If you thought that chemical weapons were at play you would have been more worried, is that not so? I assumed that the man was captured and therefore the authorities would seize the chemicals and all would be well," he added with an ingratiating smile.

"I'm not at all certain 'all is going to be well,'" Abramson replied with a somber expression.

~~~~~~

Galed Rashid bowed low before *The Great One*. He had explained all that transpired since they last spoke and claimed that he had done his best and that the Israeli Airport Security tapes were to blame. They were ridiculous, he said, the same man in different places at the same time. Who could be so foolish as to believe such a thing? Were it not for those tapes, he claimed they would have captured and killed the child easily. He then turned to his men to back him up, but they were strangely silent. Frowning, he called them out one by one. They grudgingly nodded assent, but did not elaborate and failed to match his enthusiasm for the blame game. Galed had known from the outset that he was doomed and was determined to face it like the soldier and devout Muslim that he was, but when it came right down to it, he didn't want to die. He wanted to live. As the minutes passed, he found himself more and more willing to fight for his life and less willing to simply submit to death. So as his men became less willing to support his story, he became more accusatory toward his men and more inclined to blame them for the mission's dismal failure. Perhaps, he offered, he could track the child down in the United States. Perhaps, he should be dispatched immediately to travel there and locate her. Perhaps, *The Great One* thought, he should be dispatched immediately. He nodded at his 2nd in command.

~~~~~~

Ari and his father decided Gamil needed a hospital, but were not sure where to take him. A man with these severe injuries would be reported to the authorities. They could not take that risk. They didn't know what Gamil had or had not done but he was family and deserved the chance to explain himself. In his current state, he could not speak or think coherently. Then there was the problem of their prisoner. They couldn't leave him and they didn't want to drive around with him while they looked for medical care. In the end, they decided to put their dignified prisoner in the trunk. It was risky because of the heat, but they felt they had little options. They couldn't very well be driving through Israel with a wounded man and a handcuffed diplomat and not attract the authorities.

They drenched Hatolla with water to keep him from burning up in the heat of the trunk, punched a few breathing holes through the hood and stuffed him in. They then wrapped Gamil in whatever materials they could find and carried him out to the car. Ari wanted to contact Mossad, but Hakim was wanted by the Lebanese authorities and if the Israeli authorities were alerted to this fact, they might arrest and question him. This operation had to be covert. Texting Yosef, Ari learned about a doctor who would help and within twenty minutes Gamil was delivered to the back door of a local clinic; his fate unknown.

A ripple of energy flowed through the men of the inner circle as soon as she walked in. She bowed low, her tray laden with food, her face strikingly beautiful. She moved with the grace of a gazelle, her eyes shone like emeralds and her smile was dazzling. Never before had they seen a woman so lovely. Zuhair Bayan was immediately attracted to her; when she sensed him watching her, she lowered her eyelids in the way of chaste Muslim women. Inside she was cheering! Her demeanor composed, she moved back and forth with trays of food and drink, polite and modest as the Koran directed. Rafi took in all the interactions with a straight face, grinning on the inside as his sister caused the assembled to fall all over themselves politely thanking her for serving them, unusual in itself as servants, male or female, were rarely noticed and never thanked.

Once she knew that Bayan had noticed her, she knew it was only a matter of time before he came for her. She noted too the attention that *The Great One* was bestowing on her brother. Clearly he seemed as infatuated with Rafi as Bayan was with her. When she noticed Bayan looking at Rafi, she understood the dynamics that were forming. A fixed triangle had formed with Rafi as the object for both of them. One hated him and the other loved him. She wondered about the strong emotions Rafi had stirred up. She felt this bubbling pot heating up and grew more concerned for her brother. The emotions brewing here had to be shifted before Rafi got hurt. *Leave it to me, little brother*, Samira thought as she approached the men with a tray of pastries filled with honey and nuts, *just leave it to me*.

Sadly, Abdullah gazed at the body of his long-time friend, now twisted and tangled in scrub brush in the valley below. It had almost worked, he thought as he looked at the small screen in his hand, almost but not quite... The man had made a fatal error. He had not just told their commanding officer of their whereabouts, he had told him that Abdullah was planning to pass them inaccurate information. Shamir had been turned; his confession in the car had been a ruse. This is what Abdullah had feared. Knowing

Shamir had betrayed him he had no choice. Abdullah gave the man a chance to prove himself and Shamir had failed. The mountainous winding road provided the perfect solution. As Shamir stared out the window, Abdullah shot him in the head and pushed his old friend out of the car, watching as his body crashed onto the rocks below. It was most likely that his body would never be found. It would probably be eaten by buzzards and roving red wolves before dawn.

He slipped Shamir's cell phone into his pocket and put the car in gear. Now, he had another problem on his hands. His superiors had released him conditionally. They did not trust him or they would not have turned Shamir against him. If they didn't trust him, after all these years of loyal service, he assuredly could not trust them either. Until this situation was resolved, if it ever could be, he would not be safe. He could not return to his home and endanger his wife and children. He could not return to the Olive Grove and endanger his parents. There was only one place he thought he could go. He prayed that he could find a way to get there.

42 IF WISHES HAD WINGS

Realizing his fragile denials weren't going to help at this point, Boulos said "Okay, Okay, my friend just ask me questions and I will reveal to you all that I know, this is our agreement, it is not? Our gentleman's agreement... Have I not been cooperative and open with you? Am I not honoring our arrangement my friend as a just and honorable man would do, is that not so?"

Sol gave him a hard eyed stare and said "Cut the crap, Boulos, I need names. You and the Nazi are middle-men connecting several points in a long chain of transactions, taking your cut of the riches and moving death from one point to another. So give me the name of the person who sold this stuff to the Nazi and give me the name of the person you were delivering the stuff to, I want delivery information and I want it now."

Rubbing his hands together, Boulos said, "I do not know the name of the person who sold these things to this German but I will tell you where I took a package once before. It was a package of similar contents and I took it the time I met this Müeller person. I traveled to the city of Chicago in the summer of last year and picked up a package at a museum. It was in a sealed briefcase. Since I would not be able to get it through airport security, I traveled by car through the United States and entered Canada by some back woods route. From there I traveled east to Newfoundland and flew out of the Paradise River Airport on a small plane to the Keflavik Airport in Iceland. There I rented a car and drove to Landatangi, a small port in East Iceland and boarded a fishing vessel there to BrØnØysund, Norway. From there I went by car through Finland to Moscow. There I meet a representative of a Russian-Azerbaijani organization and they take the things from there." Boulos spread his hands in a simple 'there you have it' gesture and smiled at Abramson.

"Thanks for the travelogue," Sol said dryly "if this deal falls through you can get a job at AAA."

Boulos looked at him questioningly, "Is this not what you wanted? The information about transport of those poisonous substances?"

"People, Boulos. I want names. Who did you contact in those places? Who helped you? Who did you meet in Moscow?"

"Ohhh," Boulos said reassuringly, "please to remain calm my friend, I was getting to that. The people I met in Moscow had no names. I was to meet a man who was to guide me to another location. Actually I was met by three men, large men with guns. They looked like American gangsters to me, but of course they were not Americans, they were Russians. They did not speak to me or to each other. Everything was done in silence and by gesture. You know, a head movement means go that way and a push on the back means keep walking. Well these men drove me to a place called Penza where we stopped. There was a small open market where people sold their wares. Beside this marketplace there were some concrete houses with tin roofs. They were not in good condition and many poor people lived in each building. The windows had bars on them and some of the windows were boarded up with thin wood. It was here that we met; the second house down from the market on a little street. The house had a little shack built on the edge of it and was overgrown with weeds." He looked at Sol as if to ask 'how am I doing?'

Sol nodded and said "Go on."

"In this house was a group of men waiting for me. They right away inspected the briefcase I carried. They nodded the okay and we sat to talk. The main man to talk was called Borisovich Kliemkov. He is a Lieutenant in the Noukhayev Crime Family, which operates from Moscow and sells weapons and does a lot of finance. The head of that family, Khozh Noukhayev, he is very smart guy," at this Boulos tapped his forehead, "he went to university and studied about law and learned much about money, then he left for Baku, Azerbaijan and worked with the Chechen underground before he got connected with weapons in the Middle East. So at this meeting beside this Boris fella was man from government of Lebanon. He was called Marzuq. He looked very official and very uncomfortable. He kept touching his hair and looking at his watch. He had many guards with him. They too looked very nervous. He wanted the chemicals I carried. The Russians were getting paid to arrange for my travel and have the meeting but the goods were going to this Marzuq person. Then during that meeting there was a disturbance. A group of men they thought were spying on them was there. The meeting broke up and all the guards and mob men ran out of the building. They looked for hours to find those who were spying on them but never did. They were very angry and searched the room for bugs. They found four of them. That's when things got very tense. The Middle East people thought that the Russian mob people had betrayed them and they threatened to shoot one another. There was much shouting and threatening. I ducked down underneath the table and prayed to *Allah* that I would not be shot too."

Sol frowning asked "When exactly did this meeting take place?"

Boulos scratched his head and thought for a minute. "I have lost track of time, my friend, what day is it now?"

Sol made no response, since the current date had nothing to do with the date in question.

After a few moments, Boulos said, "it was in the summer of last year, I was in Chicago in July, I remember because that holiday of fireworks was about to happen. I think it took me over a month to make my travels. I did not rush, it was more important not to be tracked than to be fast. So this meeting in Penza would have been in August or early September."

Sol summarized "so you picked up the stuff in Chicago and traveled across the world with it and handed it over to this Middle Eastern official at a meeting hosted by the Russian mob. Right?"

Boulos nodded.

"How much were you paid for your service?"

"$500,000 American dollars," Boulos said quietly, "It was quite a lot of work."

Sol looked at the man then slowly nodded, rose, and left the room.

~~~~~~

After a careful check of the perimeter they pulled into the garage and lowered the steel reinforced door. Silently they entered the house, checking the doors and alarm boxes for sign of intruders. It was a simple task they performed every time they returned to their empty house. On the porch they noticed that the paper they left stuck in the lock was missing. Pulling their guns they glided the sliding glass door open and stepped into the living room back to back. Abdullah greeted them with a laugh, "Don't Shoot!" he mocked putting his hands high up in the air "I give up!" The three embraced relieved to see each other. To ensure his safety the prisoner was brought in and tied in a back bedroom, blindfolded and gagged. Ear-buds connected to an I-pod loaded with popular Israeli tunes, were stuck in his ears to ensure their privacy and the three men retired to the kitchen.

Over coffee and Challah they told their tales. The main focus for everyone was what was happening at *The Sword of Justice* campsite. They reviewed various options and agreed that they would split up their tasks. The Faysal brothers would remain in Menara and interrogate their prisoner. It was unclear how he fit into the larger scheme but if he had information they needed to be successful at the campsite, they intended to find out what that was and to do so before Ari launched his plan at the enemy campsite.

~~~~~~

The meal had ended. *The Great One* had retired to his tent and the advisors had wandered off in different directions. Samira sat on a stool in the servants' tent sorting dried lentil beans when she felt a tap on her shoulder. Bayan keeping his face averted, motioned to her to follow him. "You are very beautiful," he said to her when they had walked a distance from the others. "Would you do me the honor of sharing some mint tea with me?" Samira smiled a shy little smile and flicked her lovely green eyes in his direction. "Your eyes are amazing," Bayan said to her, "never have I seen such a color. You must be of another heritage." It was a leading question she knew, there were right answers and there were wrong answers. Wrong ones could get you killed. Samira sighed and gazed at her shoes.

"I do not know, Sayyd, I am an orphan. Never have I known my heritage. I was cared for in a home for lost children after the war happened between Kuwait and Iraq and Saudi Arabia. I do not know where I came from, but that was when I was found."

Bayan looked at her with kindness in his eyes. His own childhood memories came flooding back to him. The home of his childhood, how it was bombed by Arab terrorists, how he saw his parents die. He remembered the kindness of those who cared for him and the other children who survived the attacks. He felt a kinship with this lovely woman, an attraction yes of course, but even more than that a kinship. She was shy as was appropriate for a woman of her status but she had a confidence about her that was unusual. She spoke with an intelligence that sparked something in him, something beyond the usual. To say he wanted her was true but more than that he wanted to learn about her, talk with her.

Bayan had had many women. They were just passing fancies, something with which to entertain himself. This was different. He worried because he was not sure this was the time for such a thing. He had too many things to deal with, there was too much at stake. Silently he gazed at the woman. She stood her ground, looking down but not moving away. He caught her scent, a faint floral scent, perhaps from her hair. He caught just a glimpse of her long black hair a few curls had slipped from under her hijab. It was lovely. It stirred a memory of someone, someone from long ago.

Samira was grateful for Ari's research. He told her Bayan's mother was named Sarah and his sisters were named Shayna and Shira. He sent a few pictures of Bayan as a child. In one of them he was sitting on a woman's lap leaning against her. She wore a head scarf like the one Samira wore now, pale blue with swirls of yellow. In the picture the woman's hair had slipped out and lay curled against her shoulder as Samira's did now. She sighed deeply and waited for the memory to take hold.

"What are you called, my lovely?" he asked.

"Soshana," she answered. He paused for a moment absorbing the name.

"Come with me my little rose," he said, translating easily from Hebrew as he reached for her hand.

~~~~~~

Elisabeth found her weeping silently in the living room. She was clutching her cell phone kissing the top of it. She was muttering prayers in Arabic as she kissed the phone. Elisabeth sat down beside her. She too had received the text. She reached out her hand and Jamila placed her small slender hand into it smiling a tearful smile she said, *Subhan-Allah* over and over again. They had just learned that Gamil was responding to treatment and would survive. He was to be released within a few hours with a dozen medications and Hakim was to pick him up and take him back to Menara. "They're running a rogue operation out of your house!" Elisabeth had texted Hadara. "Prisoners, patients, wanted fugitives! You better get back there before Hakim starts running his own spy network!"

~~~~~~

The mirror was small and clouded with age so it was hard to see exactly what he was doing. Holding it at various angles he caught a ray of light seeping through the clothes thrown over the jeep and was able to get them in. He blinked with the discomfort. *However did people wear these things every single day?* he wondered, blinking to get the contact lenses in place. Glancing back at the mirror he was surprised to see how different he looked. Placing the ear-bud in his ear he adjusted his clothing and his equipment. His body was a veritable fortress. Guns, knives, listening devices, cameras and other assorted weapons were dispersed across his body, sewn into his clothing, perched under his turban. I won't be in there too long, Ari reminded himself as he inched forward through the drowsy dromedaries lazily chewing their cuds.

A few feet away, Rafi strolled past him walking in the opposite direction. He knew that his twin could do what he was unable to do. He had regrets about it but knew that it had to be done. Part of him wanted to turn and stop it, to rescue and protect him. But he could not. The man was not all bad. Not all evil. Rafi was one of the only people who knew that Shukri al-Sierawan had a gentle side. A side that made Rafi feel loved and cared about. True it was a thin line of rationalizations, but it was how he felt. Ari could do what had to be done, he would do what Rafi had laid the groundwork for and Rafi could not do. *The Great One* would not know. He would never know the difference. He would feel crushed and betrayed all the same regardless of the ostensible technicality of it not really being HIM who did the thing. Rafi felt tormented and could not wait for the mission to be over.

43 LOOSENING KNOTS

Husain Hatolla cringed when he felt the man's hands on his ropes. He knew that he was in trouble and no amount of lying would get him out of it. He had been thinking about this for hours. Granted they had not harmed him. They had let him use the facilities and given him food and water. They had been kind, well as kind as captors could be. He had lots of time to think about his options and was ready to die if death is what lay before him. He had little future to go back to, he reasoned. His wife would be dying soon, his children were grown and self-sufficient and with the money he left them they would be comfortable for the rest of their lives. He was ready to meet *Allah;* it was alright with him. He just hoped that his death would be a speedy one and that he would not suffer in the process.

He was ready when the men took off his blindfold and sat opposite him. "Tell me why you captured and beat that man," Hakim Faysal demanded.

Husain Hatolla bowed his head and said, "I am truly sorry for what I did. Is the man alright?"

"Answer my question," Hakim commanded.

"I was ordered to obtain information from him," Hatolla replied, "there had been a meeting during the summer, it happened somewhere in Russia they told me. The meeting was a big secret. No one was to know about it. Important people were there; men who were not to be seen together. This man," he referred to Gamil, "works for one of them. They are worried, the important men I mean, that this man, your friend," again referring to Gamil, "knew about that meeting. They thought he had been there spying on them. They worried that their secrets would be revealed."

230

"What is the name of the man who ordered you to do this, who wanted that information?" Hakim asked.

Without hesitation, Hatolla told them, "He is named Borisovich Kliemkov. He works for the Russian mob, the Noukhayev family."

"So this Kliemkov met with others in a secret meeting, is that right?" Hakim pressed. "Who else was there?"

"There was also another man, of lesser status. He traveled a long way with a briefcase containing something important. They were very interested in that briefcase."

"Do you know the name of the man with the briefcase?" Hakim asked

"No, the Russians did not seem to want any information about him. He was not their concern. They wanted me to ask questions of your friend called Gamil about the other 'important man'." Hatolla explained.

"What do you know about this 'important man'?" Hakim asked.

"I am not certain of this, but the man is an official in the Lebanese government," Hatolla answered.

"Do you know his rank or title?" Hakim asked.

"It is in the Cabinet, I believe. I believe the man called Gamil works for him," Hatolla said. "I was instructed to get information from your friend by any means possible. They, the Russians, told me just enough to know what questions to ask. I know only what they told me to ask. I myself know nothing about this meeting or its purpose. The Russians wanted information from your friend so they could decide if the 'important man' had been telling them the truth. I think if they believed your friend's story they would kill this government man."

"So there were three men at this meeting, the Russian, the one with the briefcase and the important man from Lebanon? Right?" Abdullah asked.

"Yes that is what I was told; remember I was not there at that meeting." Hatolla stressed.

"What is your relationship with these people, these Russian mob people?"

231

Abdullah queried.

"I have worked for them over the years. At first it was innocent. At that time I didn't know who was behind the requests. They were small favors that had big rewards. It started with small pieces of information, memos, meeting dates things like that. They were simple things that seemed to have no real meaning. They were most generous in their payments for these small favors and before I knew it things had become more complicated. I was trapped. My wife she is very sick. I worried these people might harm her and my children. They didn't exactly threaten to do these things but somehow the threat was there, hanging in the air like a whisper. I did what any man would do. I played along and hoped for the best. I tried to quit but they would have none of it. There was no solution." Hatolla looked miserably into the faces of his captors hoping for understanding. He got nothing.

"What do you know about an organization called *The Sword of Justice?*" Hakim asked.

Hatolla grew silent, "They are new and growing. They have very bad ideas about the world. I try to avoid them."

The men talked for 2 hours before Abdullah asked, "Do you know of a man called Zuhair Bayan?"

"Bayan…" Hatolla repeated drawing the man's name out like a string.

Abdullah nodded.

"I am not certain, there are several with names like that one," Hatolla hesitated, "do you think he was involved with this meeting?"

Curtly Hakim said "You tell us."

"I cannot be certain. I have heard his name somewhere in my travels. Can you tell me something about this man? Perhaps you could describe him to me?" Hatolla suggested.

Hakim smiled inwardly. He knew then that Hatolla knew Zuhair Bayan. "Describe him? This man has a mark on him. Does that sound familiar to you?"

Hatolla nodded. "A mark," he repeated. He could not avoid this truth any longer. "I have met this man. He has a mark just here," Hatolla pointed to a spot on his face, "it is like a Russian mark, a sickle," he drew a little mark on his face in the shape he was describing. "I saw him when he was a little boy. I was on a fact finding mission for the United Nations. It was the early 70's, a time of much unrest; there were many Palestinian attacks against Israel. Bayan's father was with the resistance. He brought the boy, maybe 7 years old along with him to our meetings. There was a small Jewish synagogue in the south," Hatolla jerked his head toward the south, "it was a front for those resistance fighters. The boy's father was a Rabbi for that temple. It was part of his cover, I have heard."

"What became of the boy?" Abdullah asked.

"Well I had no contact for many years. I heard rumors that their little village was bombed and most everyone was killed. There are several stories about this child. One story goes that the child was taken to a home and raised as a Muslim and became a devote Muslim. The other story says that he remained hidden in Israel and did not give up his Jewish roots. There are many stories. I hear he returns to visit relatives. He has two married sisters who live in that area. They say he is devoted to them," Hatolla shifted in his chair feeling more confident now. He thought that his captors were pleased with him.

"I saw him only one time when he was a grown man. I was attending an International meeting of the Arab Coalition and he was there representing Syria. I heard him speak before a large audience. I knew him instantly by that mark on his face. It made my blood run cold to see him there, a Jewish child grown up to become a leader in an Arab nation. It was at that meeting that I heard him called by his other name, the name Zuhair Bayan. As a child he was called Zeryka Ben Harav.

Abdullah and Hakim exchanged looks and Hakim left the room. They were getting closer to the truth.

~~~~~~

The aroma of freshly brewed mint tea permeated the space. Leaning against a brightly patterned pillow he absorbed her beauty. Never had he seen such symmetry, such coloring, such astounding perfection. Never before had he felt so intrigued, so besotted. Gazing at her he felt no need for words; they were superfluous. He only needed to see her, to listen to her voice, to be with her. And her name, it felt so right. *Shoshana... Shoshana...* The sound of it echoed in his mind. Those few strands of hair that escaped her hijab stirred feelings deep within him. "Shall I make music for you, Sayyd?" she asked. It was the custom for women to entertain their men by song or dance. Bayan nodded as he poured them each a cup of tea. "Call me Zery..." he stopped, cleared his throat and corrected himself, "Call me Zuhair, my sweet." He was alarmed by his mistake. Never before had he misspoken this way. Samira smiled coyly, tucked his 'error' away in the back of her mind and began by humming some ancient tunes. She put no words to the sounds. Primal melodious sounds filled the space as Bayan gazed at her he slipped into a trance.

His memories transported him back to his childhood, back to the home of his family, back to his mother Sarah and his sisters Shayna and Shira; back to his roots before he converted to Islam. As she slowly hummed tunes vaguely Chasidic, stirring his ethnic origins he watched her through a romantic haze. She had become a blend of images, a convergence of loved ones; with her it was harder to remain in his assumed identity. She took him back to a time before he became Zuhair Bayan. He looked at her through misty eyes and knew that he would do anything for her, for this woman he just met, this stranger, his love.

~~~~~~

Hadara, Yosef and Gil McCray sat hunched over the laptop transmitting coded data. The mission was underway, everyone awaiting orders. Information was coming in fast. Sol Abramson reported that according to his informant, Duqaq Boulos, Bayan remained loyal to his Jewish roots so his intentions regarding *The Sword of Justice* were unclear. It was decided that Samira would work to determine his true intentions and would use her position to ensure that her brothers remained safe. Theories were bounced back and forth but none made much sense. If Bayan saw *The Great One* as a threat why hadn't he taken the opportunity to eliminate him? If Bayan was loyal to Israel he had to see the man and his organization as a threat. On the other hand, if he had converted to Islam and had turned against Israel, why was he sending money to the little synagogue and continuing to visit his family there? Bayan's duplicity was a problem and could derail their plan. They decided to leave the Bayan mystery to Samira.

~~~~~~

From Husain Hatolla, Hakim learned that his brother-in-law had been undermined by Ishma'il Marzuq, the Agricultural Minister, who was threatened when Gamil discovered government money was being funneled out to fund a terrorist group. When Marzuq, a man of vast political ambitions feared that Gamil would reveal his discoveries, he developed a two-pronged plan to destroy him. In the Middle East, as in most places, a well-placed rumor went a long way to destroying a man's reputation. First

Marzuq devised a rumor that Gamil had terrorist connections and hinted that his brothers in law were also involved in a plot to undermine the Lebanese government. This was spread throughout the higher echelons of the government. Then he informed the Noukhayev Crime family that Gamil planned to reveal their involvement in the nuclear weapons deal thereby engendering their destructive efforts. A warrant for Gamil's arrest was issued by his government and he marked for execution by one of the world's most vicious criminal networks.

Within a matter of hours Gamil went from being a well-respected consultant to a wanted fugitive. Marzuq pleased with his scheme waited for word that Gamil had been eliminated.

Gil speculated that Gamil's predicament had led to Hakim and Abdullah's fall from grace. Suspicion proliferates in a climate of distrust and since the three men are family, all three tumbled under a cloud of suspicion. That put everyone in this extended family in danger. Political instability throughout the region increased the likelihood that rumors spreading rapidly would be treated as truths. A few well-placed lies and a few reckless rumors would go a long way toward creating an avalanche of mistrust.

As luck would have it, an Interpol operative had been tracking the Russian mobster and followed him to the secret meeting in Penza. Photos were taken on that meeting and all those present including Marzug, Boulos and Kliemkov along with the contents of the briefcase and a shot of the money changing hands. When an international alert was posted, the photos were made accessible to Mossad and passed on to Hadara and Yosef. These photos were embedded in email attachments sent to the Prime Minister and all members of the cabinet, except Marzug, subject heading "Traitor in your Cabinet."

At the same time, fingerprint and DNA evidence mysteriously appeared that helped indict the Cabinet Minister. That evidence proved without a shadow of a doubt that Schma'il Marzug and Shukri al Sierawan had at some point been in the same place at the same time. Marzuq was brought in for questioning and the results of the investigation into his conduct established that he was guilty of misuse of government funds and had been working to undermine the security of the country, therefore he was guilty of treason.

Arrest orders for Gamil, Hakim and Abdullah were revoked. Apologies from a grateful country were forthcoming; the men were reinstated with full compensation to their previous positions and the Prime Minister awarded them medals for bravery in the line of duty. Whether or not they would agree to return to work for their grateful government was another issue. For the moment the choice was theirs.

~~~~~~

Manny read aloud from the CNN headline marching across the screen, "*BREAKING NEWS... A highly placed official in the Lebanese government accused of treason. Ishma'il Marzuq, Director of the Finance Ministry- removed from office - accused of diverting government funds to fuel illegal arms trade.*" News reports coming in from Beirut, Lebanon and Baku, Azerbaijan indicate a Russian-Azerbaijani connection in the arms trade deal linked to Marzuq. Interpol, Mossad, and several other governmental organizations are investigating these world-wide links to terrorist networks." The members of the Chicago branch of Chevra Hatzollah relaxing around the room cheered in unison.

44 LAY DOWN THE SWORD

The Great One was sleeping when he crept into the tent and knelt down before him assuming a meditative pose. His eyes moved across the space observing everything. The multicolored carpet spread across the hard-packed sand, the large colorful pillows that surrounded the man, the green glass shisha pipe its three arms hanging limply, the bronze etched samovar. The tent flap blew slightly in the breeze. The air was warm. Slowly he pulled a tiny brass vial from his pocket. He paused for a moment before extending his hand toward the top of the samovar surrounded by small etched cups. As he began to unscrew the top he felt the older man's eyes watching him. "And so, Rafi, you wish to betray me?" his voice cracked with sadness. "You have turned from devotion to *The Sword of Justice?*"

Remaining bowed the younger man said "Sayyd, your plan for destruction of the world is cruel and without mercy."

"My son," he asked, "Do you think the lovers of western civilization have been just? Have they not spread moral decay across the world? Have they not taken lands which were not their own? Because of their multitude of sins against *Allah*, do they not deserve to die?"

"But not all of them are guilty," the younger man stressed, "what about the children, the women, the innocent animals who would be destroyed. Surely there are other ways."

"Rafi, my son, you are innocent, pure and innocent and wrong. My plan is the only way. The world has become corrupted and it must be destroyed. All of it!" *The Great One* sat forward eyes intent and worried.

238

"Sayyd, have we not committed crimes ourselves? Are we not guilty of being selfish, caring more about money than about *Allah*? Have we not taken lands from one another? Killed one another? These things are true of the human race, not just of the Westerners. We are not innocent by-standers. Look what those who own many oil wells have done. Have they given their money to the poor? No! They have lived selfishly with great wealth while others live in poverty outside their gates."

The air inside the tent had grown warmer; the noises from the camp around them seemed to fade so that all the mattered was the two of them.

"My son, sadly there are many truths. One Truth is that *Allah* is our *G-d.* It is he who we follow and this is his plan."

"How do you know that this is *Allah's* plan? Did he tell you? Did he write it down? No it's your plan and you created it not *Allah*," the young man tried urgently to convince his mentor.

"It came to me in a dream. A clear dream in which *Allah* outlined to me the plan we speak of... a dream as in the *Quran*...as in the Hebrew's bible. Do you not think people have dreams? Sleeping dreams in which truths are revealed? Have you never dreamed, my son?"

"Of course, Sayyd, but I have not assumed my dreams to be the truth."

"Maybe they haven't been, you are very young and *Allah* may be waiting to give you his truth."

"But, what makes *Allah's* truth more true than that of the Christian *G-d* or the *G-d* of the Hebrews? There are many *G-ds* worshipped by many people throughout the world. The followers of those *G-d's* believe in them as we believe in *Allah*. Why do we assume that we are more right than those others? That our *G-d* is more right than those other *G-ds*?"

Tears filled the older man's eyes and his voice grew soft. The impending loss struck him as a mighty blow. He had counted on Rafi and now he was losing him. Had he misjudged him so? "I am bewildered, my son," he said reaching out his hand. "What has happened that you suddenly turn against me? You who held my hope for the future; you who I raised above all others to serve me; you who I have come to love as my own flesh and blood?" His warm soft hand reached toward his apprentice.

"I have not changed, Sayyd," the young man replied, his tone grave "it is not I who you have loved. It is another. The one you love did not turn against you. The one you see now has never before been seen."

These words did not make sense to the older man and he frowned and squinted as he tried to determine their meaning. "You do not make sense, my son, you are speaking nonsense. You are the one I have chosen are you not?"

"No Sayyd, I am not. I am not your chosen one. I appear to be him but I am not."

"My eyes see you sitting before me just as you have done so many times," *The Great One* asserted. Leaning forward for a better look he said, "Come closer for my eyes deceive me." He reached for his apprentice's arm to pull him in for a closer look; it was then that Ari poked a tiny needle into *The Great One's* hand.

On behalf of his brother he said, "He, who you loved, loved you in return. He saw in you a good I do not see. He could not deal with you harshly as I have done. So out of love for him I have come to do what he could not do. Rest assured he loved you well, but sadly for you, I do not."

Ari watched in silence as the leader of *The Sword of Justice* collapsed sideways onto his pillows.

~~~~~~

Saroyah was distraught. Her mother was going to leave and return home without her and she did not think she could manage here without her. Her three siblings tried to comfort her but their words fell on deaf ears. She cared only for her mother and was inconsolable. "I want to go home, she cried. I want to be with Umm. This is not right that we should be punished for the things others have done. What did we do that we should be sent from our home? What did I do that I should have been taken? I was held prisoner," she screamed as if they were deaf she screamed it over and over again. "I WAS A PRISONER! Do you not understand how that hurt me? I was hurt and scared and now I am being left again! I cannot stand it! I will run away from here. I will jump from a high window! I cannot be left again…" Layla tried to calm and comfort her but her efforts were rebuffed. Lutfi ran for help. Several others came and tried to work their magic on her with words of love and caring but in the end Saroyah cried until she was hoarse and nauseous and fell asleep on the floor.

When Elisabeth arrived the child was sleeping. She sat on the floor next to her and rubbed her back gently. She was going to have a bigger problem caring for these children than she had thought. She considered what resources might be needed and began to make plans for relocating them to another setting. If Saroyah should decide to run away from this place it would be hard to find her, calling the police or the FBI could attract unwanted attention to their situation. Chevra Hatzollah's last mission in Israel had to remain under wraps. They had acted without authority in a foreign country; they had engaged in covert activities involving a terrorist organization; they were housing the children of a wanted fugitive without legal authorization. The list goes on. In the end Elisabeth decided changes had to be made and the team would have to figure out its options fast.

Jamila had gone leaving her four under-legal-age children in her care. Saroyah was becoming a management problem because her mother's priorities had changed. Gamil had moved to the top of Jamila's list. They would have to manage, she thought. Jamila was doing what she felt she had to do and Elisabeth would have to do the same.

~~~~~~

They heard him say "I'll tell them not to disturb you until evening prayer, Sayyd," as he bowed and backed out of the tent closing the flap behind him. Three of the advisors had been on their way to speak with *him* when they saw the young man called Rafi leaving his tent. "Tell us," one said, "what does *The Great One* wish us to do about the threat from Hamas? I've been in touch with my colleagues in Beirut and they are asking for direction." Bowing low in the manner of respect, Ari replied "You will have to get that information from *The Great One* himself, I have no knowledge of his wishes in this regard."

"I was interested," said another, "in what you said yesterday, about the role of the follower. It seems you have a different view on this point. You were saying that the follower should assume that a direction has been implied and take actions without specific permission, is that correct?"

"Why yes, I…" the conversation was interrupted when the new servant girl approached. "Forgive my intrusion, Sayyds" she said, hijab covering much of her face, head bowed "I have been asked to deliver this message," she handed a folded note to her brother.

"Many apologies for my rudeness;" said the new apprentice scanning the note, "My presence has been requested elsewhere. Many apologies, I must leave you and attend to this with great speed." Turning with a low bow he followed the servant girl as she led the way to Bayan's tent. Slipping between two tents she motioned him to keep walking.

~~~~~~

Both of them heard Moshe's voice speaking rapid Hebrew and each hurried to the specified location. Inside a ragged lean-to were two sacks of chickpeas and buried within were costumes, wigs and makeup along with passports, airline tickets and a receipt for the limo rental. For the first time since the start of this mission the twins were acting in concert; one dawning the outfit of a limousine driver, a loose fitting thobe and taqiyah and the other more outfitted to look like a Sudanese diplomat. After applying face paint in dark base tones and facial hair with spirit gum they examined each other carefully and agreed that they would pass muster. Yosef joined them dressed as the diplomat's servant who would ride in the farthest limo seat. Armed and scripted they drove east with Yosef filling them in on the details of their cover story.

They had to cross the Syrian-Lebanese border, exactly where would depend on a number of issues. The arrest of a key Cabinet minister caused problems throughout the country. Riots and rebel groups both for and against Marzuq took their propaganda to the streets. There was a heightened level of alarm and when news of *The Great One's* assassination hit the airways, groups would turn against each other looking for the one responsible. Israel would heighten its threat level and prepare for the worst. Violence at the borders seemed inevitable. They could always hope that al Sierawan's death would not be seen as an assassination since there were no obvious wounds. *That would be too good to hope for*, Ari thought.

~~~~~~

Panic and chaos radiated in the cries of anguish that could be heard for miles. Their leader was dead and there was no one to take charge. People rushed back and forth talking in a jumble of words. Bayan was called to *The Great One's* tent. He was *The Great One's* doctor. He spent two hours with the man's body unsure of what to do. He could find no external marks save for a tiny prick on the man's hand that probably came from one of the many insects roaming the desert. No bullet wounds, no knife wounds, no evidence of poisoning. There was nothing. In the end Bayan determined that the man died of natural causes, most likely a heart attack. Ironic he thought, given his love for this young man who recently arrived at the camp, that it was his heart that would in the end be his demise. And where he wondered was that young man? The one who had caused so much trouble? So devoted was he to *The Great One*, he wasn't even in the crowd of mourners gathered outside the tent! That was an outrage after all *The Great One* did for him! Where was the boy?

He pushed the thought away as there was much work to be done. He needed to get advice from his superiors. Would they want him to continue with the group, ascend to a leadership role, become *The Great One*? Or would they want the group to disband and want him to return home and resume his duties there? He needed to talk with them. He walked to his tent thinking of Shoshana and her beauty, thinking of the missing boy, thinking of his wasted year with *The Sword of Justice*, and for what? Truly it was nonsense anyway. He knew that it had been a horrible plan – the destruction of the world, an invisible tent over the Arab people? Where did he get that idea that the earth could revolve at the speed of light and blow everything from its surface? Really? What nonsense! In his heart of hearts Bayan had never been on board with all of this. In his heart of hearts he had never been on board with anything in this life he had been living.

It fell to Samira to do the tidying up. That meant collecting all the relevant writings and removing them from the scene so that resurrecting *The Sword of Justice* would be impossible. To do this she had to make contact with Abdul Jalil, the carrier of the books. She found the man prostrate with grief outside The Great One's tent. He lay face down on the ground his precious basket of writings beside him in a heap. Softly she approached calling his name with a lilting voice. "Loyal servant," she said, "our beloved master has left us. We alone are left to do his bidding. We have been appointed to protect and preserve his wondrous words, to hide his manifesto from those who would destroy it. Abdul, you and I have to carry out his mission. Come quickly before unworthy ones surge forward to grab his precious writings and destroy them. Come we must act immediately."

The old man raised his tear streaked face and nodded, "*The Great One*, praised be he, instructed me to do just that."

"Of course he did," Samira said encouragingly, "he was so wise. What were his instructions to you, Abdul? Tell me and I will help you carry them out."

Pulling himself to his feet the old man sighed, gathered together the books and papers and said "We are to walk to the furthest point visible from this place and bury them deep in the desert sand. I will go and get a digging tool," he said. Silently Samira followed the man and did as he requested until every bit of *Cataclysmic Regeneration Plan* had been wrapped in prayer rugs and buried five feet under the burning sand. As the carrier of the books turned toward the camp, Samira knelt as if in prayer and wedged a small egg-shaped gadget under her knee.

~~~~~~

Every TV network across the world from the BBC, to Al Jazeera to CNN to the Korean Central News Agency blasted these headlines:

"LEADER OF *THE SWORD OF JUSTICE* FOUND DEAD IN TENT!- Shukri al-Sierawan, known as 'The Great One' was found dead in his tent located in Western Syria at approximately 4PM Syrian time. *The Leader* was the founder of a new movement calling itself *The Sword of Justice* which was growing in membership every day. The popularity of the message was thought to be due to its extreme ethnocentric message which called for the destruction of the entire world except for the Arab nations. Al-Sierawan was declared dead of unknown, probably natural causes, by his long-time physician and advisor, Zuhair Bayan, a consultant on loan to *The Sword of Justice* from the Syrian government. Al-Sierawan who was 58 years of age was a native of the Al Qubayyat region of Lebanon. Born Arman Shaloub, he was the youngest member of a family of five. The family is well known in the textile industry and owns businesses across the globe. Al-Sierawan who studied in England is known for his treatise entitled the Cataclysmic Regeneration Plan which he claimed was handed down to him from *Allah*. He believed that the only people on the earth who would survive his end of the world scenario would be the Arab people and devout followers of *Allah*. He claimed his plan was the answer to the problems in the Middle East.

"Supporters and opponents of the group rioted in the streets of Beirut, Damascus, Tehran, Baghdad, Riyadh, and Abu Dhabi. Israel raised its threat alert level to high in anticipation of accusations of involvement in Al-Sierawan's death. A request for riot troops was submitted to the United Nations' Security Council. Reportedly both Russia and China are preparing to submit sanction requests against Israel, Britain and the United States on grounds that they were behind the death of the group's leader.

"Shukri al Sierawan's was not married and had no known children. His body will be returned to the Shaloub family in Lebanon where funeral services are being arranged."

Rafi sat on the porch at his Menara home and stared into space. The morning copy of *Haaretz* hung loosely from his fingers. Ari sat beside his brother watching him read and re-read the article, feeling a flood of unfamiliar emotions wash over him. Rafi had been unreachable since they arrived home. The Border Patrol Guards were so preoccupied with the riots they easily slipped by in their limo and disguises. The exhilaration of their clean escape faded as evening approached and Rafi withdrew into a shell of silence. Both Hakim and Hadara approached him but his responses were lethargic and monosyllabic. Ari, sensing his twin's despair remained at his side, even though he understood at some non-verbal level he had become part of Rafi's problem. He stuck by him. They were always together and Rafi's self-imposed mutism did little to change that for Ari. No matter what happened their twin-shop prevailed.

~~~~~~

She had just returned her cell phone to the pocket inside her robes when she heard him outside speaking to the crowds. It was amazing; she thought that he had carried this off so well. It was their good fortune that the man had been *The Great One's* doctor. It was her good fortune that her subtle comments had plied their way into his mind so seamlessly.

"*The Great One* has the weight of the world on his shoulders," she had said at one point. Another time she had commented on how exhausted he looked, pale and thin. "When I take away his plate," she said sadly, "so much food remains. The man eats less than the desert lark. "

She was glad, as the man's doctor, he had not come under suspicion. She liked this man and would not have wanted to harm him. As the chief advisor there was a chance he would ascend to the role of leader, but it did not seem to be going in that direction. She was grateful for. Bayan entered his tent and took her in his arms. "Come with me Shoshana. Wherever I go and whatever I do, I want you to be with me," he said as he held her. She smiled at him with her beautiful smile and said. "There is much to be done here, Zuhair, this is not the time for us to speak of such things," this was the first time she had spoken his given name and he looked at her with an amused expression on his face. A servant girl with nerve! *Chutzpa*!

"You are wise, my lovely, I have many things I must attend to and you must get back to your duties. Let us speak later, after the evening meal perhaps?" Again he hugged her and she left for the kitchen tent. Bayan unfolded his prayer rug and took out his laptop. He needed to let his handler know what was going on and get his orders updated. Alone in his tent, he typed in a long series of passwords and identification codes so he could skype with his handler. "Shalom, my friend," said a smiling Sol Abramson, "how goes it with *The Sword of Justice*?"

~~~~~~

They could not be in a public setting, Elisabeth told herself. There was too much publicity about this situation. There were news articles about the Finance Minister's removal from power, speculation that there was a connection between this and the death of the leader of *The Sword of Justice* and there were riots throughout the Middle East. In practically every major city bombs were going off, people were being shot and the police were being out-gunned at every juncture. This was certainly not the time to introduce an entire family of Lebanese children to a Chicago school system. It was too suggestive and all they needed was another situation which would make these children feel unsafe and unwanted. They had nearly lost their little sister, had been ostensibly abandoned by their father, and had fled their native country, the only home they had even known, and now their mother left them here in this strange place with strangers. The last thing these children needed was another shock.

She's been observing them closely and knew that even though the older children were acting well and adjusted there were signs that things were not really going so well. Their appetites were off, even though they were being served familiar foods, they were very quiet and overly compliant; they stayed to themselves, spoke only when spoken to, and showed no interest in things that would otherwise have interested them.

Picking up the phone Elisabeth located some in-home teaching resources and made arrangements for the children to begin some structured education the following week. Meanwhile, it was time to sightsee. She and her sisters and brothers gathered up their grandchildren, rented a few vans and took off to visit the zoo.

∼∼

In the kitchen tent, Samira listened and smiled to herself. It had been a little test, she knew she could not have feelings for an evil man and was relieved to find that was true. As her ear-bud vibrated from bug she planted, she listened and thought beyond her little game of the heart. She was initially surprised Sol was Bayan's handler but the thought of it pleased her more than she thought it should. Bayan was a Mossad agent just like she was. That made him kind of family, she thought. She wondered what Sol had in mind for Bayan. This could play out in many ways she knew. He might be asked to assume a leadership role with The *Sword of Justice*, to step in and take over for *The Great One;* he could be asked to return to his former role as a consultant in the Syrian government or he could be recalled from both missions and returned to his homeland. She had no role to play in the decision-making process but she did have a preference or two.

As Samira performed her duties she listened to her earbud and heard Sol say "Let's play these options out for a moment." He did not want to impose a mission on someone if they were deeply opposed to it so he outlined the options as he saw them.

Bayan was silent for a moment considering. "Let me say what my impressions are as to the possible success or failure of each option," Bayan said thoughtfully. "I do not believe that I can remain with *The Sword of Justice*. My role here has been behind the scenes. I am not and have never been the charismatic leader or am the one to whom others turned for leadership. Shukri relied on me but the others barely tolerated me. They saw me as their enemy, always watching and guarding Shukri from them.

"His death has everyone running in every direction trying to find a way out of camp and back to their homes. The camp will break up and the people will disperse to their various homelands. There is no stopping them. Half of them are already gone and the other half are looking for ways out. *The Sword of Justice* fell when *The Great One* died. There is no role for me here. It's too late for that."

"Okay," Sol agreed, "Let's move on to option two. What about returning to Syria and resuming your role as consultant to the leaders of that government? You're undercover work for them has established quite a bit of credibility. You provided them with important information and you have proven your loyalty. You would have a hero's welcome."

"Yes, those are valid points," Bayan acknowledged, "however in my absence certain enemies have also gained strength. There are many who are envious of the esteem I have attained and there are many who have moved into the power vacuum my absence created." Bayan sighed. On a personal note, it is rumored that my wife of many years has taken up with a younger man and they are nowhere to be found. Then again it is possible that my enemies started these rumors, or worse," he added thoughtfully. "I have not been able to reach her. Not that I've tried awfully hard."

"Do you know who these enemies are and can you subdue them?" Sol wanted to know.

"Perhaps," Bayan answered. "That is not a certainty but also it is not impossible. Option two remains a possibility, what about Option three?"

"Well that is an open question. I could offer that you return to Israel and join me in Kidon's Emergency Readiness Division. There are many important roles you can fulfill here. So the questions are: Where are you most needed? And where do you most want to be?" Sol offered.

"If you were going to leave the world of covert operations, my friend, this would be a good time to do it. There is so much chaos and confusion, so much random violence that anything could happen and no one would be the wiser," Sol said. "Syria could spend weeks searching for me with no results," Bayan sighed and then said "but I do not think my friend, it is time for Zuhair Bayan to retire from the field. I think there are greater tasks ahead for me."

31 THE WINDMILLS OF YOUR MIND

The twins stood shoulder to shoulder, hands on the thin railing watching the sunset over the fish farms near Menara, gazing toward Syria. Bright pink and yellow rays peeped around the edges of the strata clouds spreading across the sky, glistening beauty to end the passing day. They were silent as the stood and watched, absorbing every minute as fully as any person could. They had much on their minds. Chief among their thoughts were the final words Elisabeth Reinhardt had spoken before she left. "Let your feelings inform every step you take." The phrase seemed significant. They would leave here in the morning to begin their journey toward healing, at least that's what they hoped would happen. They trusted she would be a wise and patient guide and help them resolve their conflicts. A few weeks had passed since the death of *The Great One* and the dissolution of *The Sword of Justice*. Ishma'il Marzuq had been removed from office and was being tried in the High Court and things seemed a bit less hazardous in their part of the Middle East. Elisabeth Reinhardt seemed like the twins' best option. Removed from the chain of command she was the essence of confidentiality. The twins had stabilized and they all agreed a break was indicated. Living in Chicago for several months would be good for them. After what had happened at the camp, they had not returned to their normal activities.

Rafi carried the burden of guilt as great as if he had done the actual deed. None of it, he reasoned, could have happened without *him*. Without the trust *The Great One* had in him, Ari would not have gotten close enough to do it. Rafi knew he had betrayed *The Great One*, as truly as if he had stuck that needle in himself. That weighed heavily on his spirit, creasing his handsome young face with lines of sadness. As he sat in her office he spoke of these things. The anger he felt anger toward his twin was something he had never experienced. His mind and heart were detached. He knew what happened was for the good of the world, for the good of humanity. There was no choice. The man, *The Great One*, was poison to the world. His message lethal. His goal was the end of civilization. How could such a person be allowed to carry out his mission of hate and destruction? Clearly that could not happen. Yet the guilt and anger persisted. Rafi was tormented by what had happened. He hated feeling anger toward his twin who had done what he did for him, to shield him from endless torment. And still Rafi was scarred by what had occurred.

He could admit that to her in that room so far from his home, so removed from those who would be hurt by his words. He could tell it to her. He could tell her things he could not tell his mother or his twin, although he feared that Ari already knew these things. That was one reason he remained so distant from him. He didn't want Ari to know what he thought, yet assumed he already did. The intrapsychic connection between them had always been beyond words so he assumed Ari knew and he didn't like his twin knowing that he felt such anger and disdain for him. Ari had only been acting out of love when he stepped in and completed Rafi's assignment.

Looking across the room at Elisabeth Reinhardt, as she sat calmly in an over-stuffed chair, he felt safe. She had a way of listening that went beyond hearing; it was more like absorbing. "I cannot get beyond this," he had said. "I hate myself for feeling this way. It is wrong. It is sick and crazy."

"Rafi," she had answered. "It is none of those things. You are none of those things. You will get beyond this, it will take some time but you will sort it out. You feel what you feel because of the circumstances you were placed in. You are not wrong or crazy. In carrying out your assignment, you essentially became a prisoner in that camp. You weren't in chains but you were nonetheless held captive by the role you had to play. You were placed in a position where you had to bond with the man you were assigned to kill. You had to gain his trust in order to carry out your assignment but then you became dependent on him for your survival when you were threatened by Bayan. And in addition you were dependent on him to protect you from others in that camp who would destroy you. He was your protector and you became both his lost childhood friend but also his hope for the future of his mission. His feelings mushroomed and you absorbed them. He was 'the great and powerful leader' and he worshipped you. That's got to evoke some powerful emotions in even the best trained agent. His admiration and love amplified the conflict between your mission and your relationship with the target of your mission. That is the very essence of a double bind. Does that make sense to you?"

"Not exactly," said Rafi. "If I know it had to happen to save civilization why am I angry with Ari? Why do I see the act as repugnant when I know it had to happen?"

"Rafi, it's your mind's way of coping with your conflict. You focus those conflicting emotions on your brother because no matter how you rationally understand that the man had to die you still cared for him. You saw good things in him. He protected you and he idealized you and he loved you. All of that carries a high energy charge."

"I suppose that makes sense. It felt like he truly loved me, the way he looked at me and talked to me. It was so intense and private. It was scary. What's the matter with me? Why would I have been so vulnerable, so susceptible to something like that? I am not an orphan. I have many people who love me. I …. It feels like … I think it's crazy. It makes me worry that… well it makes me worry …," his empty words hung in the air.

"Worry that…?" Elisabeth prompted.

"It's nothing, I mean… I just… worry."

"No Rafi, it isn't nothing. It's something. Something you are worried about. That makes it important." She paused giving him time to think about it.

"I…it…do you think…I …" he stopped and looked out the window at the building across the street.

"You are having worries you never had before, is that right?" She asked.

"Yes…" he nodded.

"And these worries and conflicts are not specifically related to the assignment or the man's role as leader of a terrorist organization is that right?" She asked.

"Yes, this has nothing to do with any of that." Rafi said

Elisabeth nodded and said, "Are you wondering how you could feel so close to another man? Is that part of your worries?"

Rafi locked eyes with her but remained silent.

She waited holding his gaze. After a few minutes she asked, "Is that part of your worry, Rafi?"

He nodded.

She waited.

"I have not felt such things before. Not really felt... I mean... it's not exactly... It makes me worry about myself. Do you understand what I mean?"

"I think I do," she said. "I think I understand what you mean and it makes sense to me that these feelings would come up for you because we human beings are a tangle of interconnected emotions and physical responses and cultural assumptions."

Rafi stared at her in silence.

"Shall I go on?" she asked

He nodded.

"When people are in vulnerable situations, prolonged life threatening situations they form attachments to whom-ever offers safety, kindness and hope. You were in that situation and over the weeks of your assignment you spent a lot of time with Shukri al-Sierawan. You entered and lived in the world of your assumed identity, you *became* your role. And in that process this attachment developed. You not only sensed that he would rescue you from harm but he actually said it. He told you of the danger directly and you knew he was your only hope there in that camp where anything could happen at a moment's notice. It is natural that he would become important to you, a lifeline if you will and because we humans cannot maintain a high level of anxiety forever your mind found a way to reduce your fear. Your attachment to him was that way. It was how you managed to cope with your terror and fear of death."

Rafi nodded, somberly absorbing her words.

"From his end you became his lost childhood friend, whom he loved as a young boy and lost in a traumatic way. He never resolved that loss and you became the answer to his guilt and grief. Through you, he resurrected his dead friend Roshan. You became that boy as well as his new protégé, his hope for the future. You were his answer to a traumatic loss and his dream for the future those are two powerful transferences. What is powerfully transferred is powerfully evocative. In effect it was a role reversal, he worshipped you! You became *his Great One*! When you became a powerful figure in his emotional life, your attachment to him was also strengthened. He was not just your savior he was your worshipper as well. From your end, being the recipient of that intoxicating combination was impossible to resist. Do you see it?" She stopped talking and waited.

Rafi nodded. "I do see it. I see all of that. It explains a lot. I couldn't understand how and why I had suddenly become the center of this man's life. Suddenly I was so important. I couldn't understand it. It was like I was more important to him than anyone else. That made no sense, he just met me. My assignment was to be a member of this larger group, to blend in but suddenly I was in the center of it. And I was alone there. I was so alone." Rafi bent over and rested his face in his hands. He sighed. He rubbed his hands through his hair and looked at Elisabeth with red- rimmed eyes. "Yes I heard Moshe's voice in my ear periodically, but that was it. So much had happened! Saroyah was held captive in a tent that was just a few feet away and I had no way to save her. It was horrible knowing she was a few feet away, frightened and vulnerable, and I her big cousin could not help her. I could not even let her know I was there. And I had no one to share any of this with. I should have been stronger. This should never have happened. I am well trained. I have been doing ops like this forever. What's wrong with me that I let this get the better of me?" He balled up his fists as if to punch someone.

"Okay, now wait a minute." Elisabeth held up a hand to stop him. "Look how easily you slipped into self-blame. You seemed to understand the complexity of you situation until you brought up Saroyah and then snap." She snapped her fingers to underscore the point. Just like that you slipped back into blaming yourself for another situation that was beyond your control to begin with. Resolving your dilemmas requires that you empathize with yourself. Rafi, do you understand why?" She asked leaning forward.

"Not really," Rafi replied.

"Blaming yourself takes you out of your own place in the experience and puts you in an opposing role; the role of judge and jury. In order to heal you need to stay with your own experience not step out of your place and look in, as if from another person's point of view. Does that make sense to you?" she asked.

"I'm not sure," Rafi said slowly, frowning, unconvinced.

"Go back a few steps. Stay in your own feelings. You were alone with only Moshe's voice in your ear. You were surrounded by people who thought you were a fellow follower, just like them, then suddenly you had this special place, you were elevated and the people disliked, resented or even hated you for that. You were a newcomer, unproven, an outsider. They had been followers of extremist regimes for whole lifetimes. They believed in Jihad. They were proven followers of this movement and then their leader the *Great One* seeks YOU out. Chooses you over them! In a culture where death and violence are everyday occurrences they could have killed you as easily as look at you.

"As time passes, you became more special to him, he loves you; perhaps he is even in love with you. You don't know how to handle it. You were not prepared to have this huge emotional charge directed toward you. Not only is it confusing but it escalates your risk because just like with Joseph and his brothers, favoritism created resentment and jealousy. Is that right?" she asked.

"I can see that. It was a double edged or quadruple edged sword," Rafi said. "His attachment to me made me feel safer, but it also put me at greater risk, yet I could not back off from him. I had to maintain that connection for the sake of the mission and for my own sake. And then there are these feelings..." he stopped, thinking.

She waited. "Then there are these feelings..." she prompted.

He paused then began haltingly "If a person feels love and connected with another person...does that mean.... well I'm not sure... I mean... what if.... Do you think I'm gay?"

"If this is your only indication of that then, no, if there are other reasons why you might think that then we should talk about those reasons," she replied.

"That's what I'm confused about," he interrupted, "there are no other reasons why I'd think that. I never ever thought those things before but I'm looking for answers and trying to understand what happened. The word *love* is tripping me up. This whole thing is crazy. I hate that man. I hate everything he stood for, everything he believed in. Before I started this mission I had nothing but contempt in my heart for him. He wanted to destroy everything I hold dear. He wanted to destroy the entire world! He's crazy," Rafi corrected himself, "I mean... was crazy. Real looney tunes. But somehow, and here's *the disconnect,* he was also nice and he loved me. I mean

I think he really loved me."

Elisabeth smiled and corrected him, "Here's the thing to remember Rafi. He loved the *you* he thought you were. He didn't know YOU. He didn't know the real you. He loved the role you were playing, he loved the character you had created. He loved the 'you' that reminded him of his lost childhood friend. He loved the you he thought he was creating to lead his group. It was all smoke and mirrors."

Rafi was calm, pondering those words for a few minutes. "I think you're right. I never thought about it that way before. He didn't know me as I really am, the real me. He didn't know anything about the real me. He couldn't have loved me. Even though it was *me* he looked at, *me* he talked to, it was *me* he trusted."

Rafi stopped, frustrated. "I'm having trouble," he said, "It's hard to take ME out of the equation." Rafi struggled with his emotions; he sipped some water to calm his nerves. He had a lump in his throat that he could not wash away.

Elisabeth waited then said, "There's a thin line between the actor you and the real life you. The two you's have very different perspectives. We need to understand that the core of this struggle remains the conflict between those two you's. It's like the song lyrics 'like a circle in a spiral like a wheel within a wheel,' do you know that song?"

Rafi shook his head and said, "I think it fits though, that's what it feels like, endless spinning from one me to the other."

"It sounds that way," Elisabeth affirmed.

"So, let's just merge them and we'll be done, right?"

Elisabeth smiled and said, "I'm afraid it's not quite that easy, Rafi. It's a process not a simple two step fix. What we need to do first is look at the whole picture and that involves Ari and the feelings of anger you have toward him for killing Shukri al-Sierawan. Your anger at him is your way of coping with your anger at yourself."

"Ari has always felt like my other self. We're so close. This is the only time in my life that I've ever felt this way about him and I feel horrible about it. He came in to rescue me. He came to do what I could not do and how do I thank him? I get mad at him! Now that's.... well that's horrible!

Unforgivable! I know I hurt him and he's confused about it. Poor Ari! I have to help him out of this mess I created for him."

"Wait just a second Rafi. You didn't create this situation and your feelings are not unforgiveable. They are absolutely forgivable and changeable. Let's let Ari deal with Ari's feelings for now." Elisabeth suggested. "You have enough to deal with just with yourself. Okay? We'll pick up with this next time. Tonight I suggest you do something to get your mind off these troubles. Okay?"

Elizabeth Reinhardt, PhD

Great Lakes Bank Building

Suite 315

Chicago, Ill 60601

CLINICAL PROGRESS REPORT

Patient's name: Rafi E   Date of Contact: ___6/10/2013_____

Nature of Contact: Office Visit _X___ Phone Call _____Email _____Other
_____

1. Reason For Contact: Scheduled ___X__ Practical _____Update
    _____Emergency _____ Other _____

2. Presentation: Normal __ Depressed/Low Energy _X____ Upset/Agitated
    _____ Frustrated/Angry _____ Dissociated/Detached ___ Anxious/Panicky
    _____ Obsessive/Worried/Guilty __X__ Overwhelmed _____
    Desperate/Dependent _____ Confused/Conflicted __X____
    Guarded/Defended _____ Moral/Spiritual _X_____

3. Urgency: Suicidal _____ Self-Destructive _____ Homicidal _____
    Other _____

4. Requires hospitalization: a) Yes_____ specify plan_____
                              b) No ___X_____

5. Appearance: Neat __X_____ Disheveled _____ Inappropriate _____

6. Substance Use/Abuse: Yes _____ No ___X____ Specify _____

7. Orientation: Oriented: X   Disoriented: Time _____ Place _____
    Person _____

8. Areas of Concern: Self/Symptoms ___X__ Personal Relationships
    __X_____ Work __X____ Finances _____ Health _____ Safety _____
    Functioning _____ Moral/Spiritual ___X_____

9. Session Narrative: Trauma secondary to work-related role and conflict about actions that had to be taken. Twin brother's role in the action taken causing conflict between them. Confused re: feelings between self and another person in situation causing identity crisis. Larger moral dilemma about pervasive sense of right and wrong and larger geo-political and religious viewpoints. History: capable well developed, hi functioning and intelligent. Good family support

10. Diagnosis: Axis I: PTSD, Depression (situational)_____
                     Axis II: none

11. Recommendations: fully examine and understand current conflicts, use cognitive and insight oriented techniques to help guide resolution. Self-acceptance re: feelings essential. Family/twin sessions needed.

12. Referrals if necessary: _____None_____

13. Clinical Impression: Rafi is an intelligent, capable young man dealing with a situational crisis involving trauma and feelings of helplessness. Patient is in conflict with twin over confusing work situation. Evaluate real world safety. Good prognosis.

14. Treatment Plan: Begin assessment. Encourage him to talk about feelings and experiences which led to problem.

15. Appointment Scheduled: Yes __X____ No _____

Elisabeth Reinhardt, PhD: *Elisabeth Reinhardt, PhD*

Date: 6/10/2013

46 WHAT LIES AHEAD

She decided the best way to learn about the city was on foot, stepping around piles of rubble from a recent bombing she passed into an open air market, crowded with narrow booths displaying hanging ropes of figs, baskets of spices and lentils, and woven bags of every shape and size. Colorful rugs, fabric and clothing cluttered the narrow doorways while people pushed past one another in pursuit of their daily needs. An apricot lace hijab draped gracefully around her head and shoulders; she modestly averted her eyes as she walked purposefully toward the exquisite, ornately appointed Great Mosque, their designated meeting place. Their meetings were always accompanied by sparks of excitement at being reunited. Greetings were polite but remote, as custom demanded. They were determined to remain unobtrusive. They walked together until they came to a small park, benches were scattered among the well-tended gardens. They selected one and sat quietly together.

"Did you do it?" she asked her face tilted in the opposite direction.

"I did, my beloved," he whispered. "Do you think you were followed?"

"No, I do not think so," she answered still looking away from him, "I checked many times with my compact." It was agreed that their agents would not be following on the ground. Instead tiny GPS devices were woven into their clothing which allowed their handlers to track their every movement. "Are we set for tonight?" she asked.

"Absolutely, dearest one, I await that time with anticipation," he extracted a small square object about the size of a nickel from his pocket and placed it on the bench between them. As Samira slipped her hand over the object

260

her emerald green eyes slid up to meet his eyes in a mutually symbolic kiss.

~~~~~~

It was dark when she unlocked the rear gate. Entering through the kitchen door she made her way to the back stairway, feeling her way with her hands she crept up the stairs to the master suite. The house was silent. She preferred it that way. It was critical that no one know she had returned. She found the knob, turned it and glided into the room. "Habeeby?" (my love) she whispered.

"Alby" (my heart) came the weak response from across the room. She inched her way in the direction of his voice and lay down beside him. Their reunion was full of relief and desperation; of love and worry. There were no words until hours later when there were explanations, when the anger spilled out and prayers for forgiveness poured forth. Gamil did not himself know all that had occurred. As they talked he realized that he was not directly responsible for his daughter's kidnapping, but of course was responsible for arranging the meeting and bringing those men to his home in the first place. Jamila found, as she lay in the dark with her husband that her greatest anger toward him was his secrecy. In that moment, she found herself forgiving him for what he had done. He was not a bad or a careless man, he loved his family and had suffered greatly for his mistakes. "If you had only told me we could have worked this out together," she had said.

Given the state of unrest throughout the region they felt that they should remain in seclusion at the Olive Grove, upstairs in their room, unseen by all but the most trusted servants and of course her parents until Gamil was well. They decided that the children would remain in Chicago until Gamil was well enough to travel. Then they would join their children until it was safe for the whole family to return home. As they lay whispering, listening for the slightest sound in the silent house, they agreed they would slowly rebuild their life together.

47 RIPPLES FROM A PEBBLE

He leaned forward on the edge of his chair. Elbows digging into his knees, he scrubbed his head hard with both hands as if washing his hair. He sighed audibly but said nothing. She wondered if he was weeping. She said nothing. The clock ticked. She sighed deeply letting her body relax into the chair waiting patiently.

After a while she said, "Ari, talk to me. Tell me what you're feeling."

Face down he said, "I cannot."

"You cannot what? Tell me? ...Talk?"

He said "I cannot speak in a way that makes sense. I am a logical person. I have many university degrees. I am an independent thinker. I ... I...I think... I am..." then his voice dropped to a bare whisper "...lost..."

"You feel lost...is that right, Ari? You feel lost? You cannot make sense of things you feel? Is that right?" she asked gently.

With quivering lips and a low voice, Ari said "No, I mean yes you are right. No, I cannot make sense. I am a failure. Never before have I felt like failure but I am a failure now." Ari said, head bowed toward the floor.

"You feel like a failure because...." She nudged him with her words.

"I have let everyone down. Rafi depended on me and somehow I deserted him. I took over and did something he felt unable to do and still he's upset, distant. Somehow I failed him but I don't know what I could have done differently." He sighed looked down at his hands.

"None of this makes sense to you, right? You are a logical person and logically this doesn't make sense. But for your brother, it's an emotional thing. Not a logical one," she said.

Ari was depressed. He had done the world a favor, saved it from a madman. That does not make sense to you, I get that. Let me ask you something. Until you knew Rafi was upset, were you?" Elisabeth asked.

Ari considered for a moment. "No, I was not upset then. I felt good and clear when I walked away from his tent that day. I did what was expected of me. I rid the world of a tyrant intent on world destruction. When I felt Rafi's confusion I became confused. It seemed Rafi blamed me for what happened. Instead of positive feelings, he was withdrawn and sullen. I could not reason with him. Objectively I did a good job but that is not how it feels. I feel I abandoned my twin, but think maybe he abandoned me too. For the first time in our lives we are at odds.

Ari was silent, twisting his ring around and around on his finger he added, "I worry that perhaps he is right, that I did the wrong thing, that this man should not have been killed but arrested perhaps and made to stand trial. This thought puts me in conflict with my family, my job, everything I hold dear. It puts me in conflict with my own logic." Ari stopped and twisted his ring some more, staring at the floor he muttered, "If I hadn't killed him the world could stand in judgment of him and his ideas yes but the risk of that was too great. His supporters would rally around their martyred leader; there would be cries for revenge, bombings across the globe, blood in the streets. But Rafi wouldn't be mad at me." His voice cracked and he stopped talking.

"This must be so hard for you Ari. You did the right thing for the whole civilized world but Rafi being mad at you is just tearing you apart."

Ari looked at her and tears filled his eyes. "It has never happened before. We are not just twins, we are more than that. We are more like... well it is more like...we complete each other. We count on each other. I just cannot explain it."

"You explained it very well, actually I do understand what you are saying."

Ari nodded. Then reverted to a fact-based approach... "A trial, you see anywhere in the world would be impossible. He would have become the center of the international stage for years to come and it would be the start of the next world war. So in the end Shukri al Sierawan would have had his way."

"So," Elisabeth clarified, "you are saying you were not conflicted about what you did until you encountered Rafi's feelings and they overran your own?"

Ari nodded and she continued, "You absorbed his conflict about the killing even though you didn't feel attached to the man yourself. You saw al Sierawan clearly from one point of view. Your conflict is not about what you did or how you feel about what you did it's about how Rafi feels about it. Those are not your conflicts they are Rafi's. The conflict you can own is the lack of congruence between you and your twin and the lack of congruence between the logic of your actions and the resulting feelings." Ari watched her in silence.

"Because you are a scientist you expect the world to make sense."

"Yes, what you say is true. I was without conflict until I sensed my brother's feelings. We operate as one. It is not usual," Ari said, "that we would be in conflict over an action such as this."

"Well," Elisabeth countered, "what about your brother hearing from *"The Great One,* that he was expected to act as one with *him*? Your brother was being pulled into a different and opposing sort of twin-ship."

Ari stared at her anger gathering, "How can this be? He is *my* twin!" he was shouting now, "We are *The Chameleon*! How could he abandon our twin-ship and form a bond with that stranger, that killer, that madman? It is outrageous!"

"It is infuriating," Elisabeth added, "You are infuriated! But let us remember that Rafi had no true freedom of choice. This did not happen with the Rafi you know this happened with an imprisoned, traumatized Rafi even a Rafi in a drug-induced state. Over and over again during those days undercover, he was captive, smoking hookahs laced with hashish. His induction into the group and into the intimate relationship with al Sierawan was intensified because of those two factors.

Ari was completely silent as he looked at the woman sitting calmly in her chair, knees crossed, beige silk shawl draped casually around her shoulders. He had not before considered what his brother's attachment to this man, this enemy meant to him. Was he jealous of it? Did he hate this man so much because he had been a threat to his relationship with Rafi? The thoughts shot through his mind like jolts of electricity. These were things he definitely needed to consider. He had never felt such hatred toward anyone and now he had to consider whether jealousy could be a part of it.

Elizabeth Reinhardt, PhD

Great Lakes Bank Building

Suite 315

Chicago, Ill 60601

CLINICAL PROGRESS REPORT

Patient's name: Ari E   Date of Contact: 6/10/2013

Nature of contact: Office Visit __X__ Phone Call _____Email _____Other _____

1. Reason For Contact: Scheduled __X___ Practical _____Update
    _____Emergency _____ Other _____

2. Presentation: Normal _____Depressed/Low Energy _____ Upset/Agitated
    _____ Frustrated/Angry _____ Dissociated/Detached _____
    Anxious/Panicky _____ Obsessive/Worried __X___ Overwhelmed _____
    Desperate/Dependent _____ Confused _____ Guarded/Defended ___X___
    Aloof/Distant _____

3. Urgency: Suicidal _____ Self-Destructive _____ Homicidal _____Other
    _____

4. Requires hospitalization: a) Yes_____ specify plan b) No __X_____ if no
    specify reason_____

5. Appearance: Neat ___X____ Disheveled _____ Inappropriate
    _____

6. Substance Use/Abuse: Yes _____ No __X_____ Specify
    _____

7. Orientation: Oriented: _X_____ Disoriented: Time _____ Place
    _____Person _____

8. Areas of Concern: Self/Symptoms _____ Personal Relationships __X_____
    Work __X____ Finances _____
    Health _____ Safety _____ Functioning _____ Moral/Spiritual
    __X_____

9. Session Narrative: Concerned about twin and conflict between them related to work situation. The twin bond historically very strong with ESP and special language/communication skills. Since work problem feels walled off and unable to communicate w twin. Worried and anxious re: twin's depression/distance. Feels responsible for problem. Moral/religious/political issues of right and wrong strongly presented as areas of conflict. Strong intelligent healthy young man, good family support

10. Diagnosis: Axis I: Generalized Anxiety Disorder with Obsessive features
                  Axis II: None

11. Recommendations: articulate concerns, identify personal/versus assumed issues, work on areas of conflict and separation/individuation w twin

12. Referrals if necessary:

    _____

13. Clinical Impression: Patient is a capable, intelligent young man in treatment to work on concerns about twin, anxiety about their relationship and help twin heal from work-related trauma, deal with larger life dilemmas

14. Treatment Plan: Meet 2x week; b. Begin full diagnostic assessment.

15. Appointment Scheduled: Yes ___X___ No _____

Elisabeth Reinhardt, PhD   *Elisabeth Reinhardt, PhD*
Date: 6/310/2012

48 IMPLANTED AND EMBEDDED

Across the Mediteranean on a beautiful Greek Island Boulos met with Sol Abramson one final time. Seated comfortably on the floral sofa he eyed Sol as he entered the room.

"Good morning, my friend," he saluted cheerfully.

"Good morning Boulos," Sol answered brusquely.

"You seem dismayed, my friend. What could be spoiling your mood on this fine sunny day? I hope it is not me who has disappointed you." he exclaimed.

"Indeed I believe that finally you have told us everything that you know. However you did try to hold out on us, which violated our agreement," Sol said "so there are now a few slight modifications to our contract."

Boulos' face fell and he grew still, watching warily from his seat on the sofa.

"You are to wear this." Sol said holding up a tiny device no bigger than a housefly. "Well, wear may be a slight misnomer. What I mean is that in order for us to let you leave and in order for us to be sure that you will not again engage in illegal activities, we will need to keep an eye on you."

"How is it that you plan to do this? With that little thing in your hand?" Boulos asked with a frown. "You wish for me to keep that, say in my pocket?"

"'Fraid not, Boulos, it's a bit more complicated than that. We will implant it in you. The implantation will be relatively painless. The tracker will be located in an area of your body not easily reached, so it will be impossible for you to simply cut it out of yourself. Oh and by the way, the device is programmed to explode if attempts are made to remove it. Otherwise it is perfectly safe and will not endanger you in any way. Data regarding your location will be immediately transmitted to us so that we will be able to locate you without hesitation. Do you understand my meaning?"

Boulos stared at him carefully. "This was not our agreement, Sol, my friend. You promised me freedom and money and an ongoing contract for more future work."

"You will have your money. A lot of it by the way. And you will have your freedom. You can go wherever you like and do whatever you like. As long as what you do is not criminal you can do it. As to our working together in the future if you have more information for us, you will be able to reach me at this number," Sol handed Boulos a business card sealed in plastic. The card read:

Aegan Information Ventures
800-777-932-4111
We are never far away!

The remains of a feast was scattered across the kitchen table a demonstration of Hadara's continued interest in the culinary arts. Hadara, Hakim, Yosef and Abdullah, four of the five childhood friends shared their successes. Jamila and Gamil were still in seclusion at the Olive Grove, Gil had returned to the United States with Ari and Rafi who would be working with Elisabeth. Samira had gone undercover in Damascus with Bayan.

Yosef, reaching for another falafel joshed "Hadara, you can always take up catering if you get tired of spy games." Hakim grinned and blew his wife kiss in appreciation of the food she prepared. "

"So," he said, "also not bad for a few weeks work! We took down "The Leader" and eradicated *The Sword of Justice*; and with a little help from our American friends caught a Nazi nuclear arms trafficker and his pipeline of coherts. We rescued Saroyah; captured and turned Duquq Boulos into an informer and we sent Bayan back in Syria as an agent in place with Samira as his handler. Not so bad for a couple of old fogies!

Abdullah groaned, "I do not know how you do this all the time, it's

269

exhausting all this cat and mouse stuff. I'm ready to let you guys handle the spy stuff and go back to my nice ordinary job in military intelligence."

"Yea like you have a boring desk job," Hakim quipped. "Are you in good standing now?" he asked.

"Not yet, it's in the works but I am told that it will be soon. Then I will return to my carefree life," Abdullah replied.

"We all lead such carefree lives," Hadara commented turning serious.

"What do you hear from the twins?" Yosef asked.

"Oh they are working on their issues," was the non-commital response. The men looked at her questioningly. "They are not doing well; this thing is very complicated. Rafi went too far underground this time and it's hard for him to shed that identify and return to his own. I am frightened for them. Ari is distressed. He doesn't understand these emotional entanglements he's a fact-based thinker. This is way out of his league."

"Well," said Hakim "I think they are in good hands. Look how much Elisabeth helped Saroyah, she's doing very well now, going to school, making friends. It's a miracle that she's recovering so quickly. Thank G-d they didn't do her more harm."

"*Baruch HaShem!*" (praise G-d) Yosef said.

"Exactly," Abdullah replied, "*Allahu Akbar* (Glorified is Allah)!"

Hadara took her husband's hand and smiled around the table, "No matter how we say it, we are all deeply grateful for our good fortune."

~~~~~~

His rigid body exuded tension. His handsome young face etched with distress. He sat motionless in an armchair opposite her staring at the floor. The ticking of the clock and the dim backdrop of passing traffic were the only sounds to be heard.

"Rafi," she prompted softly. "Did you heard what I asked you?"

There was no response.

"Do you miss him, Rafi? Do you miss al Sierawan?"

There was no response.

"How about Ari? Do you miss Ari?" she asked quietly.

Nothing.

"I can't get a sense of what's going on with you Rafi unless you talk to me."

Nothing.

"Okay," she said, "let's try something else. I'll just make some statements and if you feel something, anything at all, about that statement glance up at me. Okay?"

Slight shrug. Rafi was about as far away as he could get. He was frightenly close to a break down and she needed to act fast.

She began with "I feel blank…"

Slight eye movement

"I feel confused…"

More eye movement

"I'll take that as a response, okay" she said.

Tension mounted in the room as Rafi remained mute and Elisabeth's questions became more intense.

Ten minutes later she said, "Sometimes I think about being dead so I could be with him…"

Rafi raised his frightened eyes and looked at her.

She said, "Okay, you have some feelings about that statement, right?"

Nod.

"I miss him and wish I could talk to him about what happened…is that right?" she asked.

Head shake.

"You aren't thinking that, right?

Nod.

"Still you feel you can't get the words out. Repeat it if it's right, correct it if it's wrong," she said.

Nod. "I can't get the words out, there is so much chaos in my head…" he said.

Rafi's eyes bore into hers, they seemed haunted.

"Let's try 'I feel crazy. I can't understand why I am feeling the things I feel.' If that's right repeat it, if it's wrong correct it." she prompted.

Nod and eye contact. Tentatively he said, "I feel crazy…"

"I think I'll be judged if I say what I think and feel," she continued, "if it's right repeat it, if it's wrong correct it."

"You are right," Rafi said in a low pained voice. "I cannot possibly say what is in my mind or my heart. I cannot possibly do that. I would betray everyone in my life if I said these things. It would betray Ari, my twin. Even more than that he's a part of me. Together we created a unique 'character' in the world of espionage. We were astounding. We were unstoppable. But something has happened to me. I am not who I used to be."

The room was still as Elisabeth leaned forward, "Many things happened to you Rafi. We must identify what happened. Are you ready to do that with me now?"

"I think so," Rafi said hesitantly. "I'm…I'm…"

"Afraid?" she offered

"Yes…" Rafi answered slowly. "I am afraid…"

Elizabeth Reinhardt, PhD

Great Lakes Bank Building

Suite 315

Chicago, Ill 60601

CLINICAL PROGRESS REPORT

Patient's name: Rafi E   Date of Contact: ___7/1/2013_____

Nature of Contact: Office Visit _X___ Phone Call _____Email _____Other _____

1. Reason For Contact: Scheduled ___X__ Practical _____Update
   _____Emergency _____ Other _____

2. Presentation: Normal _____Depressed/Low Energy _X____ Upset/Agitated
   _____ Frustrated/Angry _____ Dissociated/Detached _____
   Anxious/Panicky _____ Obsessive/Worried/Guilty __X____ Overwhelmed
   _____ Desperate/Dependent _____ Confused/Conflicted __X____
   Guarded/Defended _____ Moral/Spiritual _X_____

3. Urgency: Suicidal ___x?____ Self-Destructive _____ Homicidal
   _____ Other _____

4. Requires hospitalization: a) Yes_____ specify
   plan_____
   b) No ___thoughts and feelings w/o plan _____

5. Appearance: Neat _____ Disheveled _____ Inappropriate
   __X__(slouched/mute)_____

6. Substance Use/Abuse: Yes _____ No ___X_?___ Specify __possible
   residual from use undercover_____

7. Orientation: Oriented: Disoriented: X Time _____ Place
   _____Person _____
      a. Appears dissociated or 'out of touch'

8. Areas of Concern: Self/Symptoms ___X__ Personal Relationships
   __X_____ Work __X____ Finances _____ Health _____ Safety _____
   Functioning _____ Moral/Spiritual ___X_____

9. Session Narrative: Today pt. seems dissociated/depressed/remote/mute. After much effort have been able to determine he is not in the midst of a psychotic episode but dissociated and traumatized by his own feeling and thought processes. Feels cannot speak about feelings for fear of judgment or rejection by others. Confused by his reaction having pervasive self-doubt.

10. History: capable well developed, hi functioning and intelligent. Good family support

11. Diagnosis: Axis I: PTSD, Depression (situational)_____
                          Axis II: none

12. Recommendations: Aid self-expression and encourage resumption of 'normal' activities with twin.

13. Referrals if necessary: _____None_____

14. Clinical Impression: Rafi is in a depression, has existential issues of far reaching nature, feels conflicted about self and his relationship w another person/R/O catatonia/dissociation NOS

15. Treatment Plan: Begin assessment. Encourage him to talk about feelings and experiences which led to problem.

16. Appointment Scheduled: Yes __X____ No _____

Elisabeth Reinhardt, PhD: *Elisabeth Reinhardt, PhD*

Date: 7/1/2013

Samira sat at the French Louis XV roll top desk marked by exquisite marquetry inlay and read from the small screen before her as she listened carefully to the dialogue in her headset. Bayan was doing well, she thought. He'd been accepted back into the fold by his higher ups and he was given a hero's welcome. That fact offered no comfort though in this country, you could be a hero one day and dead in the street the next. The uncertainty of their situation was terrifying and Samira needed all her confidence and training just to get through every day. Things could flip at a moment's notice. It was her job to ferret out the dangers and get him out the moment his safety was compromised. An orange dot flickered in the corner of her gold Movado indicating the building's outer door had opened. She turned to the tablet open on her desk and watched as Bayan entered the outer door to the 10 story brick apartment building. Quickly she logged off and tucked the tablet away in the intricate desk.

Turning she rose and greeted him in the fashion that had become theirs. He folded her into his arms and they kissed tenderly. "Have you checked the street and set the alarm?" she asked, as was her habit. "Yes my lovely," his usual response but there was a touch of worry in his voice. She picked it up instantly. "What happened?" she asked studying his face.

He guided her to the window and looked down into the street. A bearded man wearing traditional Syrian clothing was standing across the street smoking steadily and looking at nothing in particular. A cluster of men gathered in front of a small market chatting and casting glances at their apartment building. The solo man and the group of men exchanged covert glances. Bayan lived in an upscale section of the city and often vagrants wandered by looking for opportunity. These were desparate times and people were not predictable. "Watch them," Samira told him and returned to her desk where she opened a channel to her handler. Quickly coding an urgent message she awaited a response. Her mother answered within seconds, "V*acate immediately. Rendevous with watch unit. Await instructions.*"

Boulos awoke to find himself face down on a table covered with a white sheet. His head ached and he was disoriented. The last thing he remembered was a conversation about a chip that would track his movements. An area just above the base of his back throbbed slightly. He tried to rub it but could barely reach it with his fingertips. This must be the spot, he thought. This is where they put that device. But then there was another spot that bothered him, it was at the top and back of his right leg.

Puzzled he focused on his body and the various spots where he felt something different. Another spot at the rim of his left shoulder blade also felt sore and then there was another on the far side of his left buttocks. What in the world had they done to him, he wondered. He felt like a pin cushion! How many devices had they planted in him anyway? Then he thought perhaps they cut several incisions just to throw him off base, so he would be less likely to start cutting himself up looking for the implants.

He sighed. This last piece of action had him stumped. He thought he could trust Abramson and now this. He thought he had a good deal going and now for all he knew they would end up sending him to Guantanamo Bay and that would be the end of him. He lay on the table and thought about his options. If they sent him to Gitmo what could he trade to get out of there. Did people ever get out of there? He wasn't really the type for that place, he reasoned, *I'm not a terrorist after all. I am not committed to Jihad. I'm just a simple business man doing a days work. It is all about supply and demand,* he thought. *I'm just a supplier.*

~~~~~~

Hatolla slumped in his chair in the basement room of the Menara home. He felt like a tired old man. Exhausted and ready to end it all. He expected the worst and was prepared to face what he expected. He hoped only that his family would be spared and that his beloved wife would live out her years with as little pain as possible. He felt he had done all he had done, risked all he had risked for her. Just for her. He hoped that she would never find out what he had done and that she would never feel anger or disappointment because of him.

He had been here for many hours now. How many he didn't know. He had been fed and treated humanely so he waited patiently for whatever would happen next. He was not looking forward to his captor's next visit. The longer they stayed away the better, he reasoned. He was dozing off when he heard the door knob turning and a young man walked in. He held up a video camera and proceeded to film Hatolla from many angles. Then he asked him some questions and recorded both the questions and the answers. Then he asked Hatolla to hold up two newspapers one in Hebrew and the other in Arabic and photographed him with the newspapers. Then he left the room and Abdullah entered.

Sitting opposite him he said. "Husain Hatolla you are free to go. You are free to return to your life just as it was before on one condition. You agree to work for us. You will be our source about the Russian mob and anyone else who asks you to spy for them. You will be in constant contact with us."

He handed Hatolla a small compact cell phone and said "You are to keep this with you at all times. It has all the numbers and information you will need to keep in touch with us. It automatically encodes all messages and deletes everything you send us within 2 minutes of the time that it is sent. You are to send us detailed reports three times every week. We are also interested in anything related to the weapons trade and terrorist activities. Is all of that clear to you?"

Hatolla nodded tapped some buttons on the phone and said, "Yes all of this is clear to me."

Abdullah then left the room saying, "Memorize your instructions. Take all the time you need to do that. We will quiz you before you leave to make sure you have everything straight. You will not be harmed. You do not need to be afraid as long as you work with us. Now familiarize yourself with the phone and memorize the instructions and you will be home with your family before dawn."

49 RESPECT THE PROCESS

He arrived the following day pallid and downcast. Sitting down he began immediately. "I did Rafi a favor, I saved him from having to complete an abhorrent task that would have marred his soul but Rafi's soul had been marred anyway."

As always Ari knew Rafi's feelings. He felt them. Now he felt he had harmed his twin when he was trying to help him. He could not understand how helping his twin ended up causing such a wedge to come between them.

"There is something I am not seeing," he said to her.

"Right, there is something missing. We are not taking Rafi's feelings about al Sierawan into consideration," she agreed. Objectively you did a good thing and it had turned out bad. You worry that the damage to your twin-ship is irreparable."

"I cannot imagine living this way. I cannot imagine feeling this conflict with Rafi. This level of anxiety and turmoil is intolerable," Ari said.

"I went to help him, to fulfill his mission. He called out to me. In our way he told me. I knew. I understood. And now he is upset, angry. I ... I don't know what I did wrong. I must have harmed him somehow. I mean ... it doesn't make sense it's not logical. Give me a formula, an equation and I can understand that. This is just crazy. It makes no sense," Ari said.

"It may not be logical," Elisabeth said softly, "but it does make sense. You are seeing only part of the picture. Look at all of it. Open your eyes Ari see what your brother sees."

"He...no, that is not right. He does not see me as the villain. He feels he himself is the villain. He feels he betrayed a trust, the trust of that man Shukri al-Sierawan. That man cared for Rafi, cared deeply for him. I think Rafi cared also for him. It was somehow mutual. Rafi was seduced into that relationship. It went beyond an undercover assignment. It is like Rafi was brainwashed. He developed an attachment; felt sympathy toward his captor, like those kidnapped in Stockholm so many years ago. But it is not logical. He knew he'd be able to leave there. He knew we would rescue him." Ari said.

Elisabeth shook her head, "Logic is not the answer here. This is not a math problem. This is about feelings, feelings that grew in a potentially lethal situation. There are many variables to be considered and they are abstract, not quantifiable variables. We are dealing with things like fear and trust and seeing your reflection in someone else's eyes.

"Al Sierawan idolized your brother. He saw Rafi's wonderful qualities and saw his future and the future of *The Sword of Justice* wrapped up in Rafi. Rafi became the answer to many of his needs. And Rafi responded to those views or reflections. He responded to al Sierawan's idealization of him."

Ari was silent for a long time then looked up and met her eyes. "Are you saying Rafi was in love with that man? That they were in love with each other?"

"Not in love in the usual sense but there are many kinds of love; The Leader saw Rafi as a miracle, his miracle! In his mind, Rafi was his answer to the problems of the world. Rafi was the answer to his personal problems. His problem of guilt over the loss of his childhood friend, of emotional isolation, perhaps even to the problem of being childless. It's more than not having someone to carry on his name, his mission or his message, Rafi became the answer to his existential aloneness. Through Rafi he would have life after death. He would carry his torch throughout eternity. Their relationship became a role reversal of sorts for as Rafi worshipped al Sierawan, he in turn worshipped Rafi."

Ari sat stricken, processing these words and their implications. When his eyes met hers he said nothing. They sat in this way for a few minutes when Elisabeth added, "Everyone has vulnerabilities, Ari. This was a powerfully traumatic time for Rafi. Unable to leave, living an alternate identity, constantly exposed to hashish and al Sierawan's doctrine, having to repeat those doctrines and extemporize about them while living in constant fear of death would have had a powerful impact on his mind and identity. He would have been particularly vulnerable to this type of connection with an older man who idealized him, praised him, valued him and protected him.

Ari silently absorbed her words. "It was a wrong assignment for him. It should have been me instead. I would have been less vulnerable to those pressures. I am less people-oriented than my brother. I would not have connected to that man. It should have been me undercover in that camp!"

"You seem determined to make this fiasco your fault. The assignment was not your choice and while I understand your characterizations regarding interpersonal vulnerabilities, you actually have no way of predicting how exactly you would have behaved under the same circumstances. You just don't know. You may not have done what Rafi did but you would have done something, reacted some way that you cannot honestly know. It is entirely possible that if you had been chosen and had played things out differently the plan would not have worked at all. It is entirely possible that the only reason this mission was successful is because Rafi connected with that terrorist and that allowed al Sierawan to connect with him."

Ari nodded. "I see your point," he said. "I just feel so helpless. I wish to make it different if only in my mind."

"I understand," Elisabeth said.

Elizabeth Reinhardt, PhD

Great Lakes Bank Building

Suite 315

Chicago, Ill 60601

CLINICAL PROGRESS REPORT

Patient's name: Ari E   Date of Contact: 7/2/2013

Nature of contact: Office Visit __X__ Phone Call _____Email _____Other _____

1. Reason For Contact: Scheduled __X__ Practical _____Update _____Emergency _____ Other _____

2. Presentation: Normal _____Depressed/Low Energy _____ Upset/Agitated _____ Frustrated/Angry _____ Dissociated/Detached _____ Anxious/Panicky _____ Obsessive/Worried __X_____ Overwhelmed _____ Desperate/Dependent _____ Confused _____ Guarded/Defended ___X___ Aloof/Distant _____

3. Urgency: Suicidal _____ Self-Destructive _____ Homicidal _____Other _____

4. Requires hospitalization: a) Yes_____ specify plan b) No __X_____ if no specify reason_____

5. Appearance: Neat ___X____ Disheveled _____ Inappropriate _____

6. Substance Use/Abuse: Yes _____ No __X_____ Specify _____

7. Orientation: Oriented: _X_____ Disoriented: Time _____ Place _____Person _____

8. Areas of Concern: Self/Symptoms _____ Personal Relationships __X_____ Work __X____ Finances _____ Health _____ Safety _____ Functioning _____ Moral/Spiritual __X__

9. Session Narrative: Distressed about relationship with twin, feels guilty about role in the episode. Feels should have done something differently though knows that he did what had to be done. Twin bond has not returned to normal both are distant from each other. Sorting out the nuances of their situation having difficulty with the lack of logic in R's responses and his relationship with the party in question.

10. Diagnosis: Axis I: Generalized Anxiety Disorder with Obsessive features
                  Axis II: None

11. Recommendations: help him to understand twin's dilemma from the twin's point of view – role reverse without judgment of twin or self.

12. Referrals if necessary:
_____

13. Clinical Impression: Patient is a capable, intelligent young man in treatment to work on concerns about twin, anxiety about their relationship and help twin heal from work-related trauma, deal with larger life dilemmas

14. Treatment Plan: Meet 2x week; b. Begin full diagnostic assessment.

15. Appointment Scheduled: Yes ___X___ No _____

Elisabeth Reinhardt, PhD   *Elisabeth Reinhardt, PhD*

Date: 7/2/2013

They walked down the back stairs single file. Having tossed the laptop in a safe behind the headboard, they changed into nondescript clothing and fled. They did not see the small group of men who had been watching their windows break up and move stealthily across the street. They made their way through the war-torn streets as quickly as possible, he striding several feet ahead, as was the custom, she following head down hands wrapped around a small basket. It took them fifteen minutes to get there. Walking to the back of a bombed out building they ducked behind a ragged wall and waited to see if they had been followed. Then they climbed up a few wooden steps and slipped through a broken window.

They found themselves in a space without walls. The concrete floor was covered with bits of glass and debris. Two bare electric light bulbs pale and bleak cast drab shadows. Guns clasped at their sides, they moved at once toward the back where a steel door hung on rusty hinges. After a coded knock, the door squeaked opened. A grubby man greeted Samira and Zuhair muttering "we've got action" he moved toward a bank of computer screens displaying their condo building from every angle and all rooms inside of their condo. On the screen three men split up and crossed the street. One walked to the front of a the building where a small restaurant was housed on the ground floor. The man wound his way through the crowded tables and exited through the kitchen. In the hallway behind the kitchen he entered an old freight elevator and pushed a button. Another man walked in the front door and meandered through the lobby. Stopping to examine a newspaper on a side table before approaching the elevator in the lobby. The third man strolled to the back to the fire escape and slowly climbed up the side of the building.

Feeling a chill, they saw the three assassins enter their home. They moved with deliberation, guns drawn, knives at the ready. Puzzled to finding it empty, they began to search the place. Rummage through drawers and closets, searching behind framed art and under their counters. They had been in the space for ten minutes when two closets opened and black clothed figures emerged. The intruders were captured, bound, gagged, stuffed into a large grey waste bin and wheeled down the hallway toward the freight elevator.

He sensed his life had changed the minute he saw her. The woman had a powerful presence about her that went beyond her conspicuous good looks. She approached him casually, handed him a stack of fresh clothing, said "get dressed" and left the room. Minutes later he sat across from her in a small empty room with only two straight backed chairs. He was wary and tense as he watched her.

"Where is my friend Sol Abramson?" he asked.

"Gone," she said "I'm here now. You can call me Mother."

"Oh, such a homey name," he crooned, "it is so warm and loving. So, Mother, to what do I owe the honor.."

"Cut the crap, Boulos," she snapped, "this isn't a social call. I'm here to offer you a deal and if you take it good for us and if not bad for you."

"I see you prefer a blunt conversation so I will respond as you wish," Boulos said flatly. "Tell me what you want."

The woman nodded, pleased that he was cooperating. "You might say I want the opposite of what Sol wanted. I want you to remain our informant, however instead of avoiding criminal activity, I want you to immerse yourself in it. I want you up to your neck in every mess you can find and I want to know everything you know. I want reports on everything you see or hear or smell. I want details. It will be like I'm riding on your back. You will be my donkey, my mule, my ... well I shall avoid using impolite terms but you get my point I am sure."

"I get your point," Boulos said coldly "and in exchange for being your ... um mule what exactly do I get in return?"

"Besides your freedom and your money?" she snapped.

"Yes, I was already getting that from my friend Mr. Sol Abramson." Boulos spat. "What will I get from you?"

The woman's cold grey-green eyes glared, "Your life. If you do not cooperate you will see the inside of Gitmo and nothing else for the remainder of your sorry life."

Boulos his jaw set tightly muttered, "How do I get in touch with you?"

"We'll reach you," she said rising to leave. "You'll be freed this afternoon and taken to the location of your choice. We'll give you a pocketfull of cash to last you until your next installment. Whatever monies you obtain via illegal activities are yours to keep, tax free. You will have enough money to live well and will not need to do your usual work. You will work just enough to maintain your contacts. That is what we care about. We want your contacts and we want to know what each of them are up to."

"I understand what you want," he said with a sneer. "I do not like you, M o t h e r. I do not like the way that you treat me. I resent it very much. However I will cooperate because you are, as they say, holding all the cards."

"I am indeed," Hadara sneered derisively, "And Boulos," she said turning at the threshold, "you can hate me all you like but do not make the mistake of thinking you can escape me or outsmart me. That will never happen."

50 CUTS AND SCARS

Ari had just returned from a 4 month assignment in Turkey where he was investigating weapons trafficking with the Armenian mob. Rafi was to have joined him but there had been a last minute change in the assignment. His handler told him Rafi was working undercover elsewhere. Ari had not been able to contact him. Their psychic connection, requiring no wires, batteries or devices had been severed. Ari was devastated and confused. Hadara had been shut down by her Mossad contacts every time she tried to find out what was going on with her son. Standing side by side on the balcony, she and Ari stared toward Damacus wishing they knew where Rafi was. They were silent standing there locked in their own worlds. So much time had passed without a word, so many questions flooded their minds. Finally Ari said, "I should go look for him."

"I'm not sure that's a good idea," his mother answered. "Either he doesn't want to be found or he's deep undercover and finding him could put him in danger."

"I cannot take this," Ari said. "I need to find him. I know there is something that is very wrong. He needs me. He is lost."

Hadara looked at her son's perfect profile. The precise image of his brother. Two perfect images, two perfect boys, now two perfect men. She could not put into words the depth of love she felt for her sons, her twins. Amazing as individuals, as a duo they were unstoppable. It had been a joy to raise them. To watch as they negotiated their world. She knew their super-human connection meant the world to them and could only imagine what a loss it must be without it. She was deeply concerned about Rafi. Her happy, loving, outgoing, social son. Never depressed or confused by anything until now. That last assignment had changed him. Made him unreachable. Somehow Shukri al Sierawan had brainwashed him. Even in death the man had a hold on Rafi; he somehow managed to take a part of Rafi with him to the grave.

"Ema," Ari said turning to her, "We have to find him."

"Let me think about this, Ari, I am not sure what we should do. If he's in his right mind and just working something through, we should let him do it. If he is not thinking clearly, for whatever reason, we should immediately mobilize our resources to find him." Ari turned to her his grey-green eyes were dark with anguish, "If we do not locate him we can not determine his state of mind."

~~~~~~

The beige feathered comforter folded around her naked body as she rolled over watching him dress in the pale pre-dawn light; his muscular outline filled her with pleasure. A smile graced her lips as she recalled the night before as their love flourished with each embrace. Samira was a woman in love. This man who had entered her life as an assignment had transformed into the centerpiece of her life. His brilliance and sensitivity were astounding. His passion for her unending. She trusted this man like no other even though she was his handler. Her superiors had cautioned her against becoming too comfortable with him; they were less certain of his loyalty than she was. Pushing those conflicts aside she gazed at him. Soon he would leave; *Fajr* began at dawn. She would follow him to the mosque as she did 5 times every day. She would wait at a nearby bazaar while he prayed, monitoring him through the trusty earbuds tucked safely inside her hijab.

There had been rumors, just rumors that *The Sword of Justice* was re-emerging. There were rumors that a replacement for *The Great One* had come forward. The thought was horrifying. Mossad had tracked several leads to this particular mosque. Her job was to observe and report. Observe everything and everyone, record and unobtrusively photograph as much as possible. Her camera hidden in the small basket she carried was programmed to snap every few seconds. This afternoon a *Tahajjud* was scheduled at the mosque. It was a special prayer and could last up to 2 hours. Longer prayers were most beneficial, providing more opportunity to do their job but for Samira is presented a challenge in case she was being watched. Syrian women did not remain idle on the streets of Damascus, so she needed to move to different places and alter her appearance frequently to avoid detection.

Zuhair would cover the Mosque from the inside, she from the outside. They were a good team. In sync on and off the job. Samira shrugged off her lingering doubts about the man she loved deciding her handlers were being overly cautious and comforted her restless mind with a handful of passionate memories as she strolled through a booth fingering the beautiful fabrics swinging softly in the wind.

The building was huge and overwhelmingly beautiful with its sculpted minarets and intricately tiled walls depicting biblical scenes in diminutive detail. These mosaics were reportedly among the best in the world. Surrounded by beautiful grounds and gardens, with carved brass doors stretching toward arched painted ceilings, this mosque welcomed hundreds of worshippers into its hallways. The central space carpeted in shades of red surrounded by etched golden walls surrounded the worshippers who knelt on their prayer rugs for mid-day prayer. The Imam's voice could be heard high and loud chanting above the din leading the assembled in worship. Bayan wearing a long, brown Didashah glimpsed up from his prayers, scanning the room to see if he had been followed. He had been feeling more suspicious of late, noting changes in the crowd around him, surreptitious glances, forced smiles. He knew he needed to be careful. Here in the great mosque surrounded by knelling strangers it was hard to determine exactly what was happening. Samira had assured him that he had friends watching his back but he couldn't tell them from the dozens of others milling about or crouching on the mats around him. He drew comfort from the fact that Samira was nearby, listening to every sound, coordinating the operation, scanning everything, missing nothing. She was the one thing he could count on. She was his comfort, his love.

In an archway leading to the side of the mosque he noticed several men who were not engaged in prayer. In the small gathering he could make out a younger man talking with a shrouded older man, dressed like a Muezzan. Amid the rustling knot of worshippers, the two stood closly together in a manner suggesting collusion. Looking furtively around, they retreated into the shadows. Around him Bayan heard the chanters praying in unison:

Allahu Akbar. Allahu Akbar.
Allahu Akbar. Allahu Akbar.
Ash-hadu an la ilaha ill-Allah.
Ash-hadu an la ilaha ill-Allah.
Ash-hadu anna Muhammad-ar-Rasoolullah.
Ash-hadu anna Muhammad-ar-Rasoolullah.

Hayya 'alas-Salah. Hayya 'alas-Salah.
Hayya 'alal-falah. Hayya 'alal-falah.
Allahu Akbar. Allahu Akbar.
La ilaha ill-Allah.

As he prayed he watched the two figures wearing djellabas huddled in the shadows. A memory had been triggered. He felt had seen them before. The younger man seemed familiar but he could not place him. Unable to see their faces he was left with a fleeting impression. There was something about the man's posture, his movements. Before he could identify it the prayers ended and the assembled rose around him, gathering up their prayer rugs, speaking casually to each other. While Bayan did the same, he noticed the two had moved down another hallway; for a split second he caught sight of them, two men disappearing inside a distant room. The door closed behind them. Positioning himself so he could watch the door, Bayan spoke softly into his folded sleeve and remained in a prayful pose.

Thirty minutes after the mid-day prayers had ended a man bearing an uncanny resemblance to Shukri al Sierawan opened the door to the room, turned down a corridor and slipped through an archway out of the mosque. Bayan crept toward the heavy wooden door; he put his ear to its surface but heard nothing. He eased the bronze lever downward. The door was unlocked. Glancing over his shoulder he eased the door open a crack and peered inside. The room was empty. Puzzled he opened the door and slipped in.

The room was large and shady. It was a library with long broad tables piled high with prayer books. An ornate Koran was open on a stand in the middle of one table and a massive carved desk was angled into the corner. A few padded arm chairs and heaps of pillows were scattered about. Set into the carved wooden panels of one wall were three large windows with a perfect view of the courtyard. Aside from the windows and the single door leading to the room no other exits were visible. Being a man of conviction and courage, Bayan proceeded to search the room, determined to find the exit through which the young man must have left. He checked behind the handmade wall hangings and ran his fingers along the sides of bookshelves but he found nothing. Bayan photographed the room from every angle then troubled and disappointed, he left the room.

Through a tiny hole carved into the desk's delicate inlaid front panel, Rafi Eliat watched him leave.

ABOUT THE AUTHOR

Love of the mystery/thriller genre combines with psychotherapy training and experience to produce emotionally supercharged dramatic novels. Nancy Alexander has devoted much of her professional life to helping survivors of trauma. Their distress has made a lasting impression and its ever-present influence allows her to create characters who give voice to their plight. Her tales of intrigue, complex psychology, and triumph over adversity are a natural interlacing of professional, literary and creative interests.

Connect with Nancy online at www.nancyjalexander.com.

Proof

42009142R00182

Made in the USA
Charleston, SC
13 May 2015